IS MOSCO'

An Alternative History of the Second World War

Book 2

Vincent Dugan

Douglas Clouatre

Cast of Characters

Natasha Merkulkov   The beautiful Russian translator caught in the storm of chaos generated by the Nazi Blitzkreig, desperate to reach Moscow.

Johann Franks   A Luftwaffe pilot who gained experience in the Spanish Civil War and is an early member of the Fallschirmjäger, the new German parachute forces.

Hans Oswald   Also a Luftwaffe pilot, he flies the Stuka, the effective dive bomber developed for the Blitzkreig style of modern warfare.

James J. Reilly   After helping the Soviets develop their tank fleet, this American engineer is trapped in a collapsing Russia by love and war.

Rudi Kleime   Leading his Panzer platoon through the Russian countryside, Rudi is in the front lines of the German war machine, the very tip of the Nazi spear.

Etienne Descoteaux The French diplomat juggles a new wife and a long time mistress as he struggles to keep France out of the war.

Albert Reichenau Captain in an Einsatzgruppen squad, this Great War veteran is haunted by a shameful family secret.

Ianu Cohnescu A Rumanian Jew, he watches his adopted country descend into a Nazi inspired charnel house.

Westbrook Pegler The American reporter views the upcoming presidential election and the war with the same cynical eye.

Alexander Grotnov Better known by his nickname Sasha, this Russian peasant conscripted into the Red Army as a laborer is overwhelmed by the Blitzkreig.

Alexei Protopopov Cursed with a name dating to Russia's czarist past, he rises to the heights of influence in the Kremlin and witnesses the paranoia and incompetence of the Stalin regime.

Waltraud Shriver A Mischling with one quarter Jewish blood in his veins, he flies missions for a Nazi regime dedicated to the eradication of his people.

1

June 7, 1940   **Berchtesgaden, Germany**

Colonel Gunther Blumentritt turned his face upwards to the morning Bavarian sun. The breeze generated by the modest speed of the open top Mercedes staff car was refreshing. He was rested and ready for the upcoming conference, having spent three days of leave recuperating at his home in Munich. Since the war against Russia had begun in May, he had traveled repeatedly to the front and back to general staff headquarters. The Bolsheviks were losing but they had millions of men and many more tanks than expected. While Goebbels' news reels suggested an imminent Russian collapse, Blumentritt knew there was much hard fighting left between their current positions and a Soviet surrender. Smolensk was not Moscow.

The constant travel had worn him down and he had contracted a serious cold. The summer Bavarian weather was exactly what he needed to regain his health. He enjoyed spending time with his wife Mathilde and their two children.

An hour later, the Berchtesgaden Alps rose skyward partially obscured by scattered low clouds. He confirmed his overcoat was beneath his luggage. It would be cold at Kehlsteinhaus or the Eagle's Nest, the setting for the luncheon before the two day meeting with the Italian general staff. He doubted the sessions would produce anything of value to the Germans but it had been made clear, the Fuhrer wanted the Italians engaged and an enthusiastic supporter of the Wehrmacht's drive to crush the Soviets.

At noon he stood with Colonel Giovanni Genovasi, his assigned companion for the next few days. The Italian wore a smartly tailored uniform, complete with rows of gleaming medals. Blumentritt guessed they were of similar age and responsibility. The two staff officers watched together with the other attendees as the Italian dictator Benito Mussolini laughed with the German Fuhrer Adolf Hitler in front of the red marble fireplace in the Diplomatic Reception Haus. Clearly the fascist leaders were in a jovial mood. The volume of their voices indicated that it was not a private conversation but was intended to be heard by the 40 assembled staff officers.

"Il Duce, once again I thank you and the Italian people for this wonderful marble fireplace. It truly displays the fine craftsmanship of your people," remarked Hitler.

"It is a mere token of the respect our people have for the Fuhrer and our German allies. Respect that has been heightened even further by the Wehrmacht's victories against the Poles and now the Bolsheviks," replied Mussolini in Italian accented German.

Hitler grasped Mussolini's elbow. The Fuhrer was delighted. He used his arm to turn the pair to face the assembled generals and colonels.

"Gentlemen, during the next two days we direct you to exchange ideas and work together to discuss strategies to defeat our common enemies. Our recent success in Russia must be but a starting point in our battle to rid the European continent of Bolsheviks and the impure, weak minded democracies. The reports from the Russian front have exceeded even our own expectations. The Soviet Union and their criminal leader Stalin will soon be defeated. Your days will be filled with discusions relating to strategy and tactics. They are important for the future of our two countries and our destiny."

Hitler's words were met with an approving chorus of "Sieg Heil" from the German officers while the Italians raised their right arms in a fascist salute.

Mussolini clapped and after the accolades and offered his own impression.

"Italy has been honored to assist our German allies in favorably settling the Sudetenland problem at the Munich Conference. We were proud to participate in the Fuhrer's historic diplomatic initiative enabling the French to see the criminal nature of the Polish treatment of ethnic Germans and adjust their loyalties. Every day the German army marches towards Moscow vindicates France's decision."

The Fuhrer nodded as Mussolini spoke. Normally he preferred to launch lengthy tirades but on this day he allowed Il Duce to continue.

"The Bolsheviks will be defeated." Mussolini jutted his jaw outward. "Our two countries will continue to cooperate to achieve a Europe and Mediterranean where our strength is recognized and accepted."

Mussolini glanced at Hitler and finished his comments. "Thank you Mein Fuhrer for this wonderful setting for our meeting. The Italian people, in the tradition of our Roman heritage, shall provide whatever assistance the Reich requests-including our planes, ships and men."

Hitler nodded his head in approval. He waited for the applause to subside. He began his conclusionary remarks with a firm voice. "The Bolsheviks are the greatest threat civilization has ever known. I accept Il Duce's grand offer of assistance on behalf of the German Reich and its people. You will work out the details over the next two days and beyond. We will not rest until the communist scourge is cleansed from Europe."

Hitler paused for effect. Blumentritt knew what was coming next, the rallying cry. Hitler began with a low voice, building to a crescendo. "Each and every day when I speak to my generals, I will not start with situation reports or troop deployments. I will ask one simple question. The only information our people crave and need to prosper for many years in the future."

Hitler stopped and looked around the room. He thrust his fist skywards and shouted his final three words.

"Is Moscow burning?"

The Fuhrer's closing declaration was met with thunderous applause and shouts of enthusiasm. The introductory comments concluded, the attendees broke ranks and headed into the main hall for the luncheon. To the chagrin of the Italians, alcohol was not served-not even wine.

Blumentritt was rather surprised by Mussolini's comments. The Wehrmacht general staff had never discussed assistance in the Russian campaign from anyone other than the Rumanians. The conference promised to have more meat on the bone then expected.

After lunch, the officers clustered in small groups on the veranda, lighting cigarettes en masse. Blumentritt motioned for

Colonel Genovasi to join him. They puffed and gazed at the mountains and the valley below. The temperature was barely over 10 degrees Celsius. Blumentritt was damn glad he had his overcoat.

Blumentritt smiled and began the conversation. "So you are offering troops and planes?"

Genovasi shrugged. "Il Duce feels Italian territorial needs are not being considered. He wants to move against the English in North Africa. The Fuhrer wants him to wait."

"So how would a brigade of Italian infantry in Russia change that equation?" asked Blumentritt.

"He says a few thousand Italian dead gets him a seat at the negotiating table," replied Genovasi. "He is becoming impatient."

Blumentritt stubbed out his cigarette with his boot. He turned to face Genovasi. "I do not understand this logic."

"It is fairly predictable. The Italians started the Fascist movement and have supported the German version quite reliably. We fought together in Spain. While we act as if the Italian leadership was aware of your negotiations with the French, we were almost as surprised as the rest of the world. Who could have predicted the French would betray the Poles and refuse to join the British in declaring war on Germany?"

Blumentritt smiled and commented, "Ah, the French betrayal. Without a doubt the Fuhrer's greatest diplomatic achievement and there have been many." He motioned for the Italian colonel to continue.

"Now the Wehrmacht is blitzing its way through Russia and Italy is sitting on its hands. The English are doing very little beyond dropping leaflets and losing a few ships to U boats. With the French and Italians neutral there is no effective blockade. Everything

Germany needs comes though France and to a lesser extent Italy. The whole world is standing by like movie goers, waiting to see if the Fuhrer really can topple Stalin."

"The success of our panzer forces has been even greater than expected," replied Blumentritt.

"I am not sure how any military strategist could have planned such victories," agreed Genovasi. "I understand your men fight non-stop around the clock, forgoing sleep by taking little pills?"

Blumentritt responded, "Many of the men have been issued Pervitin, which is certainly not a new product. Housewives and industrialists have used it for years in the Reich to enhance alertness."

Genovasi was generally familiar with the methamphetamine based drug. "I have heard of this Pervitin but was unaware of its potential military application," declared Genovasi. "Perhaps we Italians should test its suitability for our forces."

Blumentritt directed the conversation back to Mussolini's offer of troops for the Russian campaign. "Does the Italian general staff wish to send men to Russia?"

Genovasi pointed to the town of Berchtesgaden in the valley below. "It is really beautiful here. But very cold for summer."

"Ja, it is. I grew up in Bavaria, in Munich. It is fortunate we have this area within our boundaries."

Colonel Genovasi pointed to the hall. "We should go in. And does Italian assistance really matter? Your panzers sliced through the Bolshevik frontier defenses like a hot knife goes through butter. Smolensk is done. Moscow will fall before your Oktoberfest festival. We believe the Bolsheviks are finished. As you said, a brigade of Italian infantry will not make a difference."

Blumentritt found that he liked Genovasi. They walked around the side of the exterior to the side entrance. They passed a group of naval officers deep in conversation.

Once inside, Genovasi leaned in to Blumentritt and gestured towards the navy men. "There have been some discussions with the French regarding a joint naval exercise with the Italian navy in the Mediterranean. The French appear to be impressed with the speed of the German victory in Poland and now Russia. I am not saying they are ready to join our countries in the Pact of Steel-at least not yet. However, it does appear they want to send the English a clear message. The French will not fight our countries."

Blumentritt spotted empty seats at a table near with other infantry officers. He led Genovasi to the table. He sat and waited for his meal to be served, looking out the massive windows, watching mist envelope the mountaintop retreat.

2

June 8, 1940   East of Smolensk, Russia

The guttural drone of aircraft engines jolted Natasha. She raised her head and surveyed a sloppy room in a peasant hut. Sitting up, she realized it was not a room but an entire pathetic dwelling. Her nose twitched at the overwhelming scent of urine. She shivered, a chill penetrating the early June day as bits of weak sunlight wiggled through the cracks in the decrepit walls. The room lacked windows, but she sensed the sunrise had begun a new day. Natasha was uncertain whether to dread or welcome its arrival.

Natasha waited for bomb blasts that did not come. Satisfied she was not in danger she stood and wrestled with her brown uniform, fabric rough to the touch. "What a disgusting costume."

"What?" The voice came from the corner, behind a wooden table that lay on its side on the dirt floor. A kitchen table, thought Natasha, and the only useful furniture in the dwelling.

Natasha swung toward the voice, squinting at the shoes poking from behind the table. She relaxed. They were civilian, not military, shoes. "Show yourself. Who are you?"

"It's Dmitry."

Natasha saw a pale, almost feminine hand grasp the edge of the wooden table. A grunt as the intruder struggled to stand. He crept from behind his shelter, face streaked with blood. His thin blonde hair was matted and clumped.

"Dmitry, the engineer who traveled with you along with the American from Moscow to Smolensk," he said. "We were to test the three new KV-1 tanks against the Germans."

Natasha said nothing as Dmitry pushed against the table. It skidded in her direction as he nearly tumbled then fell backward into the dirt. Natasha laughed.

Dmitry lay arms and legs prostrate until he could summon the strength to roll first to his side then his knees then his feet. His struggle tired her nearly as much as it tired Dimitry.

"What did you mean by costume?"

"It is not your concern, little man."

"You do not remember me? I was the lead engineer that accompanied the KV-1s," said Dmitry. The KV-1's were serious business to men like Dimitry, the latest in Russian heavy tanks, only a handful having been completed. The Red Army was eager to test it against the Wehrmacht's lighter panzers. "You are the interpreter for the American named James Reilly."

"Of course I know who you are, you fool," spat Natasha. "I saw you run away when the Fascists threatened with their baby tanks."

Dmitry raised his hand. "You do not speak to me like that." His lip curled. "A mere woman, a whore for the American capitalist."

Natasha's eyes widened as Dmitry hurtled at her. When his clenched fist swung forward, Natasha's soft brown eyes hardened, rage darkened her skin. Her hand grabbed Dmitry's wrist, pulled his body past her and slammed her knee between his legs. Dmitry collapsed to the floor, moaning. For good measure, Natasha drove her boot into Dmitry's ribs.

Dmitry remained motionless in the dirt, straw clung to the muck on his cheeks. Natasha eyed the hovel for something, anything of value. She found little of use, the room stripped beyond the table and a few scraps of wood and metal. With the prostrate Dmitry unlikely to help soon, she stood at the door considering the world outside, hesitating to enter the wasteland she knew lay beyond.

Outside the peasant hut was a world Natasha could barely fathom. The Soviet Union, the country she had served her entire adult life, was in dire trouble. A native of Moscow, she had lost her husband Boris years ago in an accident at the tractor factory. Natasha shed few tears for him. Usually drunk and willing to beat her, he always focused on her inability to produce a son. Her uncle, Mikhail Koshkin was a senior Party official, who offered escape to Moscow University and then to the city of Kharkov where she was assigned to the American tank engineer, James Reilly. She accompanied Reilly on his travels as he advised her countrymen on the adaption of the Christie tank design. The Russians had purchased early models of the Christie tank despite the American embargo prohibiting the sale of weapons to the Soviet Union. Reilly was the technical assistant who came with the deal.

The German destruction of Poland in less than a month had barely registered when it happened. She and Reilly spent much time together at the tank factory known as Kharkov Locomotive Factory nr. 183. They became intimate. Instead of watching Reilly and reporting on his movements and contacts, she listened to his every word for her own enjoyment.

Reilly convinced her that the Soviet Union's tanks were the best in the world. He assured her not only did her beloved country have more tanks than all other nations combined, they were also superior in quality. "Let the Fascists come!" was the confident cry of the workers at the tank factory. Natasha had joined those cries on more than one occasion. Now she knew that better technology did not always mean victory.

Natasha sighed and returned her attention to Dmitry. Since May 10, 1940, the day the Nazis crossed the border into Belorussia, the world she knew had changed forever. The vaunted Stalin Line, the fortresses protecting the border, had been swept away with little effort. The Germans had captured Minsk and swept past Smolensk. Natasha realized the Russian people had been lied to since the start of the war. The government's radio and street loudspeakers proclaimed heroic victories over the Fascist criminals. It was nothing but propaganda used to make people fight and die in a hopeless struggle.

Dmitry stirred, delaying her from leaving the relative serenity of the hut. She strode to his writhing body, preparing for another kick with her black boot.

"No, please no, no more."

Natasha considered the curled body, the drool leeching from the side of his mouth and she took pity. "I will spare you for now, Dmitry."

"Why are you acting this way? I thought you were an interpreter. A babysitter for the American, James Reilly," croaked Dmitry. "Did he force you -."

"Don't be stupid. Reilly did not assault me," snapped Natasha. She paused and ran her fingers through her auburn hair, stopping to press on a gash above her right ear and feel the dried blood.

Dmitry sat up and pulled straw off his face. He waited for Natasha to speak, but she offered nothing.

"Why did you assault me?" He asked.

"Because you were going to hit me in the head."

"You were not like this before. You were pleasant. Where is the American? Are you rude because he is dead?"

"I don't know if he is alive or dead. We were separated during the battle. He does not matter now."

"But you loved him, no?"

"Dmitry, are you stupid again? Of course I did not love him."

"I saw you kissing him before the air raid in Smolensk. You loved him."

Natasha ignored the question and returned to the entrance of the hut. She straightened her uniform again and reached for the door handle.

"Where are you going? It is dangerous out there," said Dmitry, eyes wide, pleading. "Do not leave."

Natasha stopped and turned, "Because I am a soldier, Dmitry. A soldier committed to our socialist way of life. I must kill Fascists."

Dmitry laughed, "You are no soldier. You are not Red Army. You are or were an interpreter for the American tank engineer James Reilly. I think maybe more."

Natasha slammed her boot into Dmitry's side as he finished his taunt. He rolled to his back, clutched his ribs and whimpered. "Enough Dmitry. I may keep you alive because you may have some value to the Motherland, though not as a soldier. Perhaps somewhere in our tank production." Natasha paused. "But maybe I will kill you because you are a coward."

"What kind of interpreter are you?"

Natasha stepped toward him and he cringed, hands protecting his face. "I am only asking, not mocking. I don't understand. Who are you?"

"Who do you think I am?"

Dmitry stared, sizing up her petite frame covered with a plain uniform of the Communist Party. She appeared to be old by Russian standards, past normal child bearing age. Her skin was pale, hair auburn. She possessed an aristocratic attitude. Natasha was likely of Central European descent. Dmitry thought she was over 30. Something happened to her husband, for she had to have had a husband along the line. Women with Natasha's beauty were not spinsters in Russia.

"I guess that you were the secretary of an important Party member. You are educated, and speak foreign languages. You may have been outside the Soviet Union. Something bad happened and you were punished with the assignment to interpret for the American. Maybe you were overhead criticizing Comrade Stalin."

Dmitry stopped, waiting for another kick, but Natasha eased onto one of the straw beds supported by a homemade frame. It creaked as she motioned for him to continue.

"You didn't mind the assignment to Reilly. His work with us on tank design was unusual and technically complex. He was handsome and alone. He had been in our country on and off for many years, ever since we imported the American Christie tank. He was Christie's engineer, the technical advisor we were promised. You became interested in him."

Dmitry halted again, waiting for Natasha's reaction.

"Continue Dmitry, a handful of extra minutes here will not hurt the Motherland's efforts to stop the Nazis."

"You were separated from Reilly during the bombing of the tank training center in Smolensk a little more than a week ago. Now you are heartbroken, having fallen for this American." Certain he was right, Dmitry delivered the final blow. "Natasha, you know that it is likely James Reilly is dead. There were dead everywhere. You saw the bodies of the Red Army conscripts, peasants and children. It was horrible."

Natasha nodded, lips locked, eyes looked past him.

"I stumbled upon you last night out there," said Dmitry, pointing to the wood plank door. "I recognized you immediately. I suspected you fell and hit your head on the wrecked lorry on the road in front. It didn't appear serious. You were muttering something about James and Chicago, the American city." Dmitry stood and puffed his modest chest out, ready to receive accolades. "I carried you into this hut. The German Army has passed us, far gone. You are safe here."

Natasha rose and approached Dmitry. He sensed that her attitude toward him was changed but he was mistaken. He smiled and revealed a sizable gap in his yellow teeth.

"Thank you Dmitry, but you are still a coward," spat Natasha. "I am not as you believe. I am Major Natasha Anatolievna Merkulkov of the NKVD. It is simple to understand why I was assigned to James Reilly the American. Now that he is dead or captured or drunk, any of which are likely, it is my duty to return to Moscow."

Shocked, Dmitry plumped down on the straw bed Natasha had been occupying. He frowned and looked at his feet.

"Don't worry, Dmitry. Help me find a way to Moscow and you may be spared," stated Major Merkulkov as she shoved open the door and stepped into the sunlight.

3

June 14, 1940   Northeast of Barysaw, Belorussia

The summer mid-day heat and humidity bore down on Sasha, robbing him of energy. He crept through the thick forest, searching for game. Sasha was not a trained soldier, although he wore the semblance of a uniform. He had been conscripted into the Red Army straight from his collective near Barysaw, Belorussia. When the Nazis invaded he was in a labor battalion working on the Stalin Line. The Germans sliced through the much vaunted fortifications in a day, leaving Sasha and comrades stranded in the dust.

Sasha survived the initial onslaught, walking at night and avoiding death mostly by chance. He used all of his strength to return to his kolkhov or collective, only to find death and destruction. His family and friends were gone but he discovered his beloved Marina, the girl he wanted to be his wife. Marina was alive, beaten and assaulted by a German soldier old enough to be her father. Sasha tended to Marina for days. They hid and survived on morsels he scrounged from burned out huts and the forest floor.

Eventually, Sasha found others separated from their units or men simply unwilling to surrender to the Nazis. They had formed a partisan unit of sorts. Their small band was more a collection of starving Red Army soldiers and camp followers than a military organization. Now, they were camped deep in the woods, somewhere in the northeast part of Belorussia.

Empty handed, Sasha made his way to the camp. He heard voices and could smell potato stew. A pain clutched in his stomach, Sasha rattled to a stop and sagged against a tree. He thought of his last meal, captured German field rations consisting of some type of canned meat mixture and hard bread. Since none of their group could read German, the ingredients were a mystery, but they had attacked the meat with gusto. With his stomach and intestines threatening his sanity, he worried the bounty had been tainted.

Sasha knew of only one cure, emptying his bowels and eliminating the foul sludge that was wriggling inside of him. He squatted in the bushes and prepared to answer nature's call. Having grown up working the fields on the kolkhov, he was accustomed to taking care of such matters outdoors. However, ordinarily there were not 15 other people but 30 meters away.

While he was in the middle of the process, he sensed movement to his left. With considerable difficulty, Sasha halted all movement and noise. He silently reached for his captured German Mauser rifle, propped carefully against a tree, ready to claim a rabbit for the evening meal.

Big Misha and Marina appeared. It was not the first time the Red Army staff sergeant had been with her. As the days passed, Sasha could not ignore Misha's obvious interest in Marina. Fear sparked within him that the attraction was not one sided. Sasha was uncertain that he could blame Marina. Big Misha was an imposing figure with a scraggly blond beard and enormous shoulders. He appeared to a Viking more than a Russian. Everyone was in awe of Misha, especially Sasha.

Sasha was simply not equipped to handle Marina's apparent affection for their leader. He alternated between dismissing Marina's actions as innocent and convincing himself that he had lost her forever. He lay awake at night replaying each encounter between Marina and Misha, searching for the answer. He simply did not know what to think or do. Sasha concluded that there was not much he could do. Big Misha was in charge and Sasha was but a boy on the fringes of the group. The others would send Sasha packing instantly if Misha so directed.

Misha took Marina in his arms and Sasha watched her reaction. He hoped she would pull away or perhaps beat her tiny fists on his chest. She did the opposite. "Big Misha, why would you want anything to do with a girl from the Barysaw beet collective?"

"You are the most beautiful creature I have laid eyes upon," replied Misha.

"But the Fascist pigs hurt me." Marina's eyes fluttered at Misha, tears rolling down her cheeks.

"It is of no matter. There is war and horrible things happen."

"I feel so empty," said Marina, pointing to her chest. "In here, in my heart."

"Marina, it will dull as time passes. You must live for you. If you are dead, what you feel in your heart is of no consequence."

"I will survive, Big Misha," exclaimed Marina, reaching for his neck, pulling his face to her lips. Sasha was surprised to see Misha retreat.

"I know you will Marina, look what you have done already. We must not go further now, we must wait."

"Why must we wait Misha? It is only our business"

"My mother and sister are in the camp. You are younger than you claim," reasoned Misha. "And there is Sasha."

"Sasha? What about Sasha? He is my friend from the collective, not my husband."

Sasha's heart sank further, stomach pain forgotten.

"Marina, he saved your life and cared for you since you were attacked. He loves you."

"Da, I see. I know. But I want to live through this awful war. Sasha is not strong. He could never be a leader like you."

"If there was no war, would you have married him?"

Marina looked down at her feet, covered with ragged ill-fitting boots heisted from a dead Fascist soldier. She did not reply.

Big Misha grabbed her arm.

Marina jerked, eyes hard. "Yes, I would have married Sasha. It was planned since my 13th birthday. But I did not know men like you existed. I have never even been to Minsk."

"Marina, the first step is to not die. The rest will fall in place," advised Misha. "I will look out for you and Sasha while you are with us. But that is all."

"Never more than that?" whined Marina.

Big Misha shrugged his massive shoulders, "Who knows. I cannot see the future. Let us get back to camp."

Sasha watched Misha and Marina turn and walk in the direction of their camp. He wearily finished his original mission and tried to understand what he had heard. Face wet, he wanted to blame Big Misha but could not. Misha was attracted to Marina but had pushed her away.

Sasha shook his head. He had expected the undisputed leader of their little unit of outlaws to take what he wanted. They were in the wilderness. No one would know and if they did, no one would blame Misha. He had not forced himself upon her. Marina clearly wanted to submit to whatever he wanted.

Big Misha was not the problem. He cursed under his breath and slung the Mauser over his shoulder. It pained him, but he knew. Marina was the problem.

0

"Well there you are," exclaimed Marina, taking Sasha by the arm. "Where have you been?"

"I was scouting for fresh meat."

"We have plenty of food from the raid on our kolkhov," exclaimed Marina.

"It will run out Marina," warned Big Misha. He strode over to Sasha and put his arm around him. "I approve of your enthusiasm."

"Thank you Comrade Sergeant," replied Sasha. "I was unable to find anything."

"No matter, you tried," smiled Misha. "Everyone gather around and we will discuss the raid on Sasha and Marina's kolkhov."

The group assembled around the fire, standing in expectation.

"Comrades, this will take some time, so please sit," directed Misha, pointing to the stumps and logs that they had been using as makeshift chairs.

"First, let us review our objectives," started Misha. "Number one was food. Two was weapons and ammunition. Three was a radio transmitter. Four was to slay any Fascist at the kolkhov. Let us take each in turn."

"We certainly were successful on the first objective, Misha," stated Tanya, his raven haired sister. "The canned food was right where Marina said it would be. We also took the supplies and rations from the Germans we killed. So much we could barely carry it all"

"Yes Tanya, you are correct. The first objective was completed," agreed Misha. "And as for weapons and ammunition?"

"Not much, two Mausers, a couple hundred rounds of ammo and a Luger," replied Volodya.

"Correct. Clearly these were supply troops and their truck broke down," affirmed Misha. "They were probably lost or looking for plunder. They were not well armed and unprepared to remain in the field overnight. They paid with their lives."

"No radio transmitter, Misha," offered Tanya. "And we did kill all the Fascists that were there."

"Da, four Nazis that will no longer give the Motherland trouble," agreed Misha. "Comrades, here is how I see our situation."

Big Misha paused and looked at each of the assembled group. Oddly, Sasha was not angry with Misha. Marina was the betrayer.

"We are 15 in number. We have ten Red Army soldiers, with only five with any real training. And then we have three women, my mother, sister and Marina. Two farm workers from the collective south of Barysaw," Misha stopped and looked at the laborers from the fields. They were unarmed.

"We have a handful of rifles and one pistol. There is food for a few more days," continued Misha. "The Fascist airplanes fly high above. There are none of our airplanes in the air. I believe the war has passed us."

"What shall we do brother?" interrupted Tanya.

"That is for each of you to choose. The Germans own the sky. If we are spotted from above, we will die from their bombs or the soldiers they send after us. We must not move in the open at day, only in the forest."

"Comrade Sergeant, where are we going?" asked Volodya. Sasha saw him glance at Marina. Misha was not the only one to notice her.

"I am going to Rogachev. Any of you are welcome to join me," advised Misha.

"Why Rogachev, it is so far?" wondered Tanya.

"The way it looks to me is that the Germans are driving towards Smolensk and then maybe even Moscow. It is not like the last war. They move much faster with their tanks. There are no trenches. They are many kilometers to the east. They are not bothering with the flanks. Rogachev is well south of the Minsk-Moscow highway. Perhaps it has been untouched," explained Misha.

"But won't the Fascists come looking for us when they find their dead friends at the kolkhov?" observed Tanya.

"I don't think so, sister. The Nazis moved too fast to control anything but the highway and the towns along the way," said Misha. "They may patrol during the day but at night they will hide in the cities."

"Why? When they are so powerful?" continued Tanya.

"Because at night out here in the woods their bombers and tanks are of no use," reasoned Misha. "It's a man against man struggle, where the strongest and most vicious will prevail. We own the darkness."

Marina stepped forward. To Sasha's horror, she looked at Misha and whispered, "I will walk with you, Misha."

Sasha watched all of the Red Army soldiers stand and accept Misha's plan. Unsurprisingly, the farm laborers' shook their heads and pointed in the direction of Barysaw. They trudged out of camp towards their collective and the Germans.

Big Misha stood in front of Sasha, "Come with us."

Sasha looked at Misha's smiling face. He paused and cast a glance at Marina. He turned and watched the laborers slowly disappear.

Sasha knew he was at a crossroads in his life. The laborers were heading to death. He did not want to die. He stood and nodded, "I will go with you."

4

June 25, 1940   Philadelphia, U.S.A.

The opening of the Republican convention had columnist Westbrook Pegler scrambling for a story. Many of his colleagues had already composed their leads, the buzz across the press was of a Willkie surge. Throughout the first day meandering speeches poured from overheated politicians while delegates maneuvered over platform language. None of it was any interest to readers – who could not understand the tedium of policy – or reporters – who did not trust those who wrote the platform.

On assignment from the publisher Scripps Howard, Pegler looked every inch the hard bitten political reporter. It had not always been that way his writing career included a stint as a sports reporter. Instead of following the speeches and debates, Pegler and others scoured the city for sources, waiting in hotel lobbies and the Philadelphia Coliseum entrance to see who was speaking and whether it constituted a story. Unfortunately for Pegler he had neither seen nor heard enough to make a passable column, forcing him to return to the press gallery as the convention approached the first ballot. Bennet was directly in front of him, and a host of younger reporters were scattered about him. Their eyes were bright, much like those of the Willkie supporters who tried to drown out the speakers below with their demands of "We Want Willkie."

"Did you see the polls?" asked one of the eager Hearst writers, a fervent Willkie follower.

Pegler grunted. "Little better than sorcery."

"Willkie's gaining."

Another snort. "Willkie is Ogden Reid's boy."

"Ogden Reid?" The young reporter's eyes widened. Reid was publisher of the New York Herald Tribune, the most powerful Republican paper in the country.

"Reid's got a bug up his ass about the war, he and Luce. They will fight until the last American boy is dead." Pegler had never liked Henry Luce or his magazines, Time and Life.

"If it ain't Dewey," Bennet cut in. "Then it will be Willkie."

Pegler had heard otherwise but was in no mood to argue, instead he settled in, wondering if the Republicans could pick a candidate to beat Roosevelt.

The nomination speeches ended, having fulfilled their role of announcing the candidates for the nomination while extolling their many achievements. Pegler settled in for the first ballot, which was the first real test of candidate strength. Keeping score was easy with one thousand Republican delegates and 501 delegate votes needed for the nomination. As states were called alphabetically, a delegate would rise and announce the number of votes for each candidate. Several reporters had printed scorecards, states at the side, candidates penciled in at the top. Pegler was less systematic, unconcerned about the state counts and tallying only the candidate's totals. He understood, unlike some of his younger colleagues, that delegates were pliable and their votes could be rented if not purchased when guaranteed a government job of their choice.

As the first ballot proceeded, Taft jumped out to an early lead. He had purchased the votes of southern Republicans in states like Arkansas and Alabama, places where the Republican Party was limited to postmasters and federal officials. As the count wound toward the end of the alphabet, it was clear Taft and Thomas Dewey were the frontrunners. The New Yorker Dewey swept his home state and states such as Pennsylvania and New Jersey along with the west coast. Taft's support was strongest in the Midwest where isolationist farmers agreed with him in keeping the United States out of war. Dewey had claimed over 300 votes while Taft was more than a 100 behind and Willkie was third.

"We Want Willkie, We Want Willkie." The cry from the galleries echoed through the convention hall, occasionally drowning out the various state chairmen as they called out their state's delegate counts. Pegler was initially amused - he doubted screaming college kids would influence hard bitten political professionals on the floor – but his amusement quickly turned to annoyance as the frantic shouts throttled his arithmetic skills. Ears ringing, Pegler's only choice was leaving the press gallery for the floor. From there he could gauge support, vote switches and strategy outside the roar of the Willkie crowd.

"I'm heading down," Pegler growled to Bennet, propelling his stolid frame from the gallery. The convention "floor" was the very model of political chaos and lacked the excitement assigned it by reporters. Instead Pegler found that wandering hallways, buttonholing state leaders and loosening tongues with whiskey ensured a publishable story. The strategy was not much different when covering sports, but Pegler hoped to fill his next column with gossip or leaders talking in a corner, the surest signal of a potential deal.

Reaching the convention floor, Pegler caught the eye of James Eli Watson, the senior member of the Indiana delegation. Watson was a dyed in the wool Taft supporter who held enough votes to decide whether Willkie or Dewey would challenge Roosevelt in November.

"Pegler," Watson sported a voice that would rise or fall an octave based on his excitement level.

"You still got Taft?"

"Until the end. He is guaranteed 150 votes no matter what."

"You need 500."

In his mid-seventies, Watson had been out of office for eight years but remained respected in Washington. Known for dispensing with extraneous outerwear during the excitement of his Indiana stump speeches, the former senator was always good for a quote. "Our delegates and Dewey's, Vandenberg's and Hoover's delegates are over five hundred. Willkie can't win."

Pegler pulled a cigarette from his jacket pocket, lit it, puffed and blew smoke in the air. "A deadlocked convention."

The senator remained mum. The last thing he wanted was a Westbrook Pegler column reporting the Taft camp wasn't trying to win, but rather was only preventing another candidate from winning. Such a strategy, true as it was, did not mark the attitude of a president.

"What about Willkie?" Pegler pressed. "Taft will never support Willkie?" He studied the senator's face and immediately knew his answer. What he got though, was the quote of a lifetime.

"Willkie," he sputtered. "If the town whore came to church one Sunday I would be the first to lead her to the front pew, but I wouldn't let her lead the choir."

Pegler scribbled furiously, using his peculiar brand of shorthand that oddly enough included a symbol for "whore."

"There is a gathering tonight," Watson revealed. "To stop Willkie."

"Where?"

"John McKay's suite." McKay was Vandenberg's campaign manager. "We can't have it in Taft's because it would attract attention."

"The Bellevue-Stratford?"

"Eighth floor."

"The suite?"

Watson nodded.

Pegler thought of his days covering Connie Mack's Philadelphia A's. The old man had used the Bellevue-Stratford, had a few talks with Pegler, sometime as manager, other times as general manager and at least once as owner. "Lots of connecting doors in these suites. Someone could sit in one suite, crack the connecting door and listen."

Watson managed a weak smile. "Eighth floor," he repeated. "An hour after adjournment."

It was an invitation Pegler could not refuse. He tipped his hat at the senator and continued onto the floor. The "whore" quote would be in the morning edition, he would see to that. If anything could derail Willkie, a flash in the pan, it was a smart ass quip. Entering the floor Pegler was greeted by another round of "We Want Willkie" reverberating from the Coliseum's roof. The low murmur of hundreds of voices talking, chairs scraping the floor, shoes squeaking, members begging for the attention of the convention chair tended to dilute the gallery's effect. Pegler paid none of it much mind, instead searching for Willkie leaders. After a few moments he spotted the Massachusetts congressman, Henry Cabot Lodge Jr.

Something less than a chip off the old block, the younger Lodge bore little resemblance to his grandfather. The original Henry Cabot Lodge had turned aside Woodrow Wilson's internationalist pretensions and defeated the Treaty of Versailles with the flaccid League of Nations attached. His grandson, though, was a fervent internationalist and on the ground floor of the Willkie surge.

"Where's your boy headed?" Pegler didn't have to waste time on introductions.

"He'll be in second place by the third ballot and win by the fifth." Confidence rather than braggadocio marking his tone.

Pegler eyed the board with the first ballot results. "Who is he going to take from?"

"Dewey."

"Dewey?"

"He is closest to Dewey on the world position. Once it is apparent Dewey can't win, where will his votes go?"

"Dewey can't win?" Pegler tried to sound surprised even as he agreed.

Lodge smiled. "We have at least a hundred Dewey delegates lined up on later ballots. We have some Taft and can peel away Vandenberg's and some loose delegates for three hundred, three hundred seventy."

"You need five hundred."

"Once it starts moving in our direction, it will happen. Remember 1920?"

Pegler vaguely did, his focus at the time on the unfolding Black Sox scandal. He recalled reading that Harding had broken a stalemate after one of those hotel meetings where everything was decided. "What about Republicans nominating a Democrat?"

"Former Democrat."

"Barely rehabilitated," Pegler smirked. He dropped his cigarette and ground it into the concrete floor.

"It will happen." The Massachusetts' senator raised his arms toward a still shrieking gallery. "Wendell Willkie is the man of the people prepared to lead Republicans out of the valley of darkness."

"Wendell Willkie is a utilities lawyer who lost his job when the TVA was created and is looking for a promotion."

Lodge did not stop smiling. "That's why I like you Pegler, you tell it as you see it." He hooked the reporter's arm and pulled him close. "This is between us," he hissed. "The big money's on Willkie, the Brits are funneling it through Reid. They want a pro war candidate, someone who won't challenge Roosevelt on the war. It's taking over the party. Taft and his bunch are finished. Willkie or Dewey are the future and if you want to survive you better jump on board."

Pegler shrugged. Conspiracy theories were not his thing and the British government interfering in an American election sounded like another tall tale from the isolationist right. Lodge was anything but an isolationist and for a moment Pegler gauged whether the congressman's words held a kernel of truth.

Lodge left the reporter without another word. Pegler remained in place, lost in his thoughts for several moments until jolted by a member of the nearby Maryland delegation who was babbling about the wonders of Wendell Willkie.

As the second ballot proceeded, the heads of each state delegation marched to one of the few microphones and through a barrier of feedback offered their states' – usually divided – votes. Watson was wrong. Willkie swept into second place on the second ballot while Taft slipped into third and Dewey stagnated. The "We Want Willkie" chants became louder and raspier. Pegler doubted the young voices could last beyond the fourth ballot.

He would not test his hypothesis. The chair recognized Charles Taft, the leader of Taft's Ohio delegation, who asked for adjournment for the night. It was a momentum break for Willkie, whose delegates screamed in favor of their candidate, but were much softer on the adjournment question which was pushed through on a voice vote. Pegler checked his watch as the delegates began filing out of the convention hall. It was ten thirty eight. He had an hour to reach his listening post on the eighth floor of the Bellevue-Stratford.

5

June 25, 1940   **East of Smolensk, Russia**

"Be nimble as a greyhound, tough as leather, hard as Krupp steel. You shall be the German warrior incarnate," recited the young men of Hauptmann Johanns Franks' company. He stood on the rear deck of a demolished Soviet T-26 tank and reviewed the company with his one good eye. They stared back waiting for Franks to continue his address. Finally he bellowed, "Brave men of the Second Company remember that is the most important of the Ten Commandments of the Fallschirmjager!"

As members of Luftwaffe's 7th Flieger Division, Germany's sole true airborne division, the paratroopers bristled with eagerness to battle the Bolsheviks before the war ended. As the Wehrmacht moved east, they feared the Communists would be defeated before their skill and courage could be put on display.

Franks knew their apprehension, having experienced it in Spain before the war. He recalled his desperate need to prove himself, mixed with the fear of failure. Only then he was a Condor Legion pilot flying an early model Messerchmidt Bf 109 against the very same foe his unit now faced, the despised Communists.

"The Poles were too weak for the slaughter to last long enough for our services to be needed," exclaimed Franks. "The Russians are no better."

The men nodded and grumbled, disappointed their only involvement in the Polish campaign resembled crowd control at a Nazi party rally. The Second Company of the First Regiment had not entered battle from the air, but was driven to its assignment in trucks. Their mission was to stop fleeing Polish officers from reaching the Rumanian border.

"The Wehrmacht has driven the Red Army toward Moscow, but the war is not yet won," Franks admonished. "There are more victories to come."

The paratroopers clapped, howls and shouts reserved for victories. Franks understood their malaise. The lack of action after months of constant training was taking its toll on their morale. Each man in the unit wore the gold diving eagle badge on their uniform, signifying completion of rigorous training including six jumps from an aircraft. They were all volunteers and very young, the average enlisted man in the company was barely over 18 years of age. Since entering the Soviet Union two weeks earlier they had yet to meet the enemy.

Franks paused and made an effort to look at each man. Their helmets were markedly different from the standard Wehrmacht issue, rounder and with less pronounced ear protection. They wore camouflage smocks over their uniforms. Franks continued, "You trained hard today, as you must. Tomorrow, we will train even harder."

Franks spotted General Kurt Student approaching the assembled company. The muscles in his neck twitched. Student was the 7th Flieger Division's commander and the founder of the German airborne force. A shot of adrenaline raised Franks' voice to a crescendo, "Men of the Second Company, we will deploy against the Bolsheviks! We will fight in the final battle! Heil Hitler!"

The company erupted, returning Franks' stiff Nazi salute in unison. Franks concluded, "Company dismissed and get some rest. Tomorrow we start again."

He dropped from his perch on the back deck of the T-26 and rushed to greet General Student. "Welcome to the Second Company, Herr General."

"An impressive speech, Hauptmann Franks," grinned Student. "Perhaps you missed your calling."

"The men needed encouragement."

"A knife that is repeatedly sharpened must be used to be of value," Student agreed. "Of course, you know of no such plans to use the 7th Flieger."

"No, I do not," admitted Franks. "After Poland and now this - it is becoming difficult to maintain the company's morale.'

Student motioned Franks to walk with him to his staff car.

"I understand your men are spoiling to enter the fight. I have witnessed the same throughout the division."

Franks remained silent.

"I will say your men appear the most eager in the First Regiment. You have done well."

"Thank you, Herr General."

"I know how disappointed you were when your accident in Spain ended your flying days," stated Student. Franks absently touched his black eye patch. Student raised his hand, halting Franks before he could protest.

"There is no need to say anything, Johanns. I have known you since the early days of the Fallschirmjager. You have picked yourself up from the dirt and thrown yourself into your duties, and have become one of the division's finest officers."

Franks' chest nearly burst from his uniform.

Student halted 10 meters from the waiting Mercedes. "We built an airborne division from the Luftwaffe, not the army and we did it from nothing in less than two years."

"You constructed the 7th Flieger, Herr General."

"It was Luftwaffe officers such as you who volunteered and made it a reality," observed the General. "Now we shall have a test."

"A test, Herr General?"

"Franks, it is not yet official." cautioned Student. "The OKW has directed our staff to plan an operation against the Soviets in the upcoming battle."

Franks opened his mouth, curiosity nearly overwhelming him, but held his tongue.

"There can only be one destination," Student coughed and spit. "It is Moscow."

"Moscow."

"As our mobile forces approach, the 7th Flieger and possibly the 22nd Luftlande Division will land on the approaches west of the city, cutting the rail lines and preventing reinforcements from entering the battle. We will be supplied from the air until our relief by panzers."

"We are ready for this mission."

"It will be a difficult fight. It is expected Stalin and the rest of the Communists may attempt to flee, if they are still there," warned Student. "Our objective will be simple: no one in and no one out."

Franks turned and pointed to the tents of his company. "When can I advise the men?"

"Not for some time, Hauptmann. We are beginning the planning stage and the panzer divisions must first achieve a breakthrough." General Student resumed walking to his staff car. "It is worthwhile for my officers to know that our 'sharpened knife' will be used shortly."

Student saluted as he climbed into the Mercedes. "Continue training your men hard, Johanns."

6

June 25, 1940   Philadelphia

Westbrook Pegler's memory of the eighth floor of the Bellevue-Stratford Hotel was pristine. Senator Vandenberg had positioned his campaign headquarters in a large suite that included two bedrooms, a sitting room and a conference room with circular table that could be used for anything from high stakes poker to choosing a presidential nominee. He staked out the Bellevue-Stratford lobby in search of Senator Watson, originator of the whore at church comment. The former senator arrived, appearing as inconspicuous as possible, only to find himself alone with Pegler in the elevator.

"Get me into McKay's room. I know where to be to hear everything." A pair of whiskeys at the hotel bar had energized the red faced Pegler.

The old man shuddered at the thought. McKay was chair of the Republican national committee and Senator Vandenberg's campaign manager, a man who could make a Republican politician's life hell, even a retired one. "I shouldn't have told you, I can't get involved."

Pegler was in no mood to be denied. "If this works and Willkie is stopped it will be the biggest political story of the year. I can write it and you can be my source."

Watson reached to punch a floor button but Pegler caught his hand. "I already have my cover story, asking the managers their next move. You get me in to talk to McKay and I do the rest. Your name won't be mentioned."

The old senator studied the columnist's expression, Pegler offering his best bulldog impression. The senator sighed. "I'll get you in and then it's your ass. If McKay throws you out," he wagged his finger.

Satisfied Pegler stepped aside and allowed the old man to punch the eighth floor button. Sliding off the elevator, they headed toward the Vandenberg suite, Pegler with determination and Watson with rising trepidation. The columnist knocked on the suite door.

McKay, tall enough to see eye to eye with the columnist and broad enough to block his path into the suite, eyed Pegler. "You want a story," he barked.

"Just a comment."

McKay turned and waved him inside. "Comment on what?"

"Willkie."

Vandenberg's manager strode to the window and looked out, an old tactic to hide his expression. "He has no chance of winning. Can't get to five hundred because there aren't five hundred delegates available."

"You made sure of that."

A low laugh. "Willkie wasn't in the trenches fighting the New Deal day and night. He even voted for Roosevelt."

"Puts him in pretty good company," Pegler murmured. He had also voted for Roosevelt in 1932. A mistake not to be repeated.

"He won't win, the votes aren't there."

"And the senator?"

"He has as good a chance as anyone."

"With seventy five delegates?"

Pegler's tone caused McKay to spin around, glaring. "The convention has tried out Dewey and Willkie and found them lacking. The senator has as good a chance as any of the remaining men."

"What about rumors that Willkie is being funded by the British?"

McKay eyed Watson who was standing behind Pegler. "Mouthing off again about that are you?"

The old senator reddened and shifted from foot to foot.

"It's nonsense," Vandenberg's manager said.

Pegler shrugged. He was interested in what was ahead of Willkie rather than who was behind him. "So you have a plan?"

McKay would not bite. "We don't need a plan. Willkie never had a chance."

Pegler did not press the subject, he wanted to remain and witness the planning. "Willkie is in for a surprise," he said. "I have talked to his people and they are convinced they can swing the Dewey delegates and some of the Taft delegates by the fourth ballot."

Another knock on the door and McKay opened it to reveal Taft's southern leader. The Colonel, R. B. Creager, was not a man to be trifled with. He often reminded his northern brethren they didn't vote for Republicans in Texas, they shot them. Having wrestled control of the Texas state organization from his dead hand predecessors, Creager was determined to make the party a force in his home state. Anger at New Deal limits on oil production, mistreatment of Texas native and vice president Cactus Jack Garner by the New Dealers and Eleanor Roosevelt canoodling with the Negroes heated the blood of more than one Texas Democrat. They may not vote Republican but they were, at last, willing to listen.

"What the hell is he doing here?" The gray haired colonel was not intimidating until he opened his mouth. Eyes glittering behind his wire rimmed glasses, he focused hard on Pegler.

"A mistake," McKay grunted, eying Watson. "He is leaving."

The colonel frowned. "Can't trust these reporters. He'll be out there chin wagging with his buddies."

Pegler, not one to be trifled with, raised his head, gaze meeting the Texan's. "I stay," he murmured. "Everything I hear stays." Creager growled at the promise but Pegler raised his hand. "Until you got your man, Willkie, Taft, Dewey or," he nodded at his host. "Vandenberg."

"He ain't staying." Creager jabbed a finger at McKay. "He's here, I leave."

McKay, having slogged his way to the top of the Republican National Committee, knew a bluff when he heard one. "I will call Charlie Taft," he murmured, glancing about for the room phone. "He will stand in for you." McKay wandered over to the phone near the bedroom door.

The colonel's eyes opened and for the first time in his dozen sightings of the Texan, Pegler saw fear. Charles Taft, the candidate's brother, was a Democrat with New Deal leanings. Loyal to his brother, there was strong doubt he felt the same toward his brother's party. For a moment a range of silence spread – anger from the colonel, determination by McKay, bemusement from Pegler – then the Texan tossed in his hand. "Where's the bar." He motioned toward the columnist. "I gotta sit with that son of a bitch I gotta get a snort."

McKay released the phone, another knock at the door was Tom Dewey's man Ed Jaeckle, who stepped inside, nodding at Pegler. McKay motioned for all to sit, with Pegler finding a straight chair behind his host's high backed one.

Creager grasped the glass of bourbon and branch while positioning to watch Pegler while complaining about his presence. None of the other three Republicans in the room paid much attention.

Jaeckle opened the conversation. "I thought we had Illinois and Massachusetts coming?"

McKay nodded. "I talked to Joe Martin. He can't be seen at a meeting like this because he is convention chairman, but he agreed to hold the Massachusetts delegation until he can put them over the top." He motioned to the former senator. "Watson knows Everett Dirksen, he will hold the Illinois delegation to do the same.

Creager sputtered. "You trust Joe Martin? That son of a bitch hates the South."

McKay pursed his lips. "We are here to stop Willkie," he murmured. He turned to Jaeckle. "They are saying Ed that your people are looking to jump to Willkie on the next ballot."

Pegler smiled that his information would be passed around so freely.

Jaeckle was not one to panic, but the columnist saw him squirm. "Who told you that?"

"My sources are my sources."

"If you people fuck this up," Creager growled.

"They are going after yours too," McKay warned.

Taft's manager laughed. "Willkie ain't gettin' Taft votes."

"The senator is going nowhere without us." Jaeckle snapped.

Pegler covered his mouth. It was worse than he imagined. If this group could not agree on dividing their votes, they could never prevent a Willkie sprint to the nomination. If the lawyer won, Pegler would be left to write how the Republicans bungled the 1940 election.

"Fellas," McKay was the calm voice of reason. "Let's focus on how to stop Willkie."

"I want those kids booted from the gallery," Creager growled. "The press is eating up that story."

"Ed?"

"We are printing duplicate tickets. Our people will get to the hall an hour early and scream as directed."

"Little Democrat bastards," Taft's manager growled. "It's bad enough we got that crippled son of a bitch running for a third term, he wants to run against a Democrat."

Pegler closed his eyes. Ranting about the last eight years was not going to elect a Republican.

Ed Jaeckle returned to the subject of Willkie. "Dewey is leading, he deserves the first run at Willkie and the support of the other candidates."

Creager shook his head. Vandenberg's manager was more supportive. "I can swing most of my people on two ballots, but after that-."

Dewey's manager tried to do the math. "We need at least a hundred and fifty to get within thirty and pick off Hoover's and other loose delegates."

"What about Willkie's delegates?" McKay asked.

"Fully committed." Jaeckle grumbled.

"Damn Democrats," Creager growled

Vandenberg's manager ignored him. "You have our support for two ballots."

Jaeckle was direct. "It depends on Taft."

"You want our people to nominate your candidate?"

"It is better than Willkie."

This drew a grunt.

McKay tried to soothe feelings. "I believe once Willkie knows he can't win he will release his delegates to the frontrunner."

Jaeckle shook his head. "They are absolutely committed. They think they are going to save the party from extinction with Willkie."

"Nominate that bastard Willkie and the party will be extinct."

McKay asked. "If they don't break what is our back up plan?"

"Taft."

Jaeckle shifted. "You won't support Dewey but expect our people to support the senator?"

"Ask Republicans who they want."

"The Gallup poll says Dewey," Jaeckle shot back. "The senator has fewer delegates than Willkie."

McKay interceded. "We can promise our votes for Dewey on two ballots then Taft for two more ballots but if you guys cannot work out an agreement we will be back here." He waited for the Taft-Dewey response but the two camps did not protest. Jaeckle and Creager stood, eyeing each other then left with Watson. McKay motioned for the columnist to remain.

"You witnessed it," he said. "They are never going to get together. I will keep my promise but unless Taft votes for Dewey or vice versa we will remain deadlocked. The longer it lasts the better Willkie will look."

It was a frightening possibility, but Pegler had little advice to offer.

McKay held up his hand. "Senator Vandenberg allowed me to offer the Michigan and Pennsylvania delegations to Willkie. The senator wanted the State Department." He shook his head. "That son of a bitch Willkie said no deals."

Pegler headed for the bar. A Republican deadlock, a Willkie victory and four more years of Roosevelt was enough to make him thirsty.

McKay followed him, standing at his side. "Dewey or Taft can't win," he declared. "You saw it."

Pegler sniffed the whiskey decanter. "Then it's Willkie."

McKay snatched a glass and held it out for Pegler to fill. "I have a plan, involving the seventh ballot, Illinois and Massachusetts -."

Pegler listened, impressed by McKay's strategy but wondering if he and all the other Republicans were simply whistling past the graveyard.

7

June 26, 1940   **East of Smolensk, Russia**

Stabfeldwebel (Staff Sergeant) Rudi Kleime climbed down from the bed of the Mercedes truck and reached for his gear with his left hand. During the battle for Smolensk a month earlier his right hand had been scorched with burning petrol. While his wounds had healed enough to allow him to return to duty, the pain in his hand was too severe for much use. He did not need it, having little to carry. There was nothing left from Helga, the destroyed Panzer PzKpfw III that took much of his crew with her.

The driver pointed to a collection of tents, halftracks and armored cars, "25th Panzer Regiment's headquarters is over there."

"Thanks for the lift." Rudi slung the pack over his shoulder. His orders were simple, catch up with the 25th Panzer Regiment's HQ to join with remnants of the 3rd Panzer Regiment that were forming a special task force to be attached to the 7th Panzer Division. Rudi paused and took a deep breath. Anxious to greet his brothers in arms, he dreaded learning the names of the fallen.

"Sergeant Kleime?" called out a familiar voice. Rudi spun in the direction of the voice to receive the shock of his life. Bounding toward him was Corporal Adolf Brauch.

"Brauch?" stuttered Rudi. "You are alive!"

"God only knows how," grinned Brauch, nearly crushing Rudi in a hug. "When we were hit, I got out of Helga in a hurry."

"What about Werner, Braun and Kroening?" asked Rudi.

Brauch looked down and pushed dirt with his foot, "They didn't make it. The turret was a mess. Kroening escaped, but the Russian machine guns." He shook his head.

Rudi slumped to the ground. Brauch was the only other survivor. Rudi watched him kick gravel aimlessly.

Several moments later, Rudi rose. "The rest of the battalion?"

"Not good. We were already below half strength. That damn Russian monster tank really fucked us," answered Brauch. "What is that thing called?"

"The Bolsheviks call it a KV-1."

"And you killed it. Ran right up to it from behind, poured petrol on its back deck and lit it on fire," said Brauch, slapping Rudi on the back.

Rudi was quiet, not wanting to relive the horrific day, even with his driver and oldest friend in the regiment.

Brauch could not help himself, "I heard the other 'Corporal Adolf' pinned that Iron Cross, First Class on your uniform. That must have been something."

"I don't want the Goddamn medal, Adolf," Rudi spat. He fixed his gaze on the horizon. "I must write the families of our brave crew."

"They would appreciate it. I know Lieutenant Schmidt has already sent them letters," Brauch said.

Rudi stared at Brauch, "Schmidt is alive?"

"He is in that tent discussing our mission," Brauch said. "He will be damn pleased to see the most famous man to wear the uniform of the 3rd Panzer Regiment."

Rudi followed Brauch to the command post, a tent adjacent to a hovel with a straw roof. They stopped 40 meters from its side, out of earshot of the officers. The heat generated by the baking sun made it necessary to roll up the tent's sides. Rudi peered at the figures inside and spotted Lieutenant Schmidt among the unknown figures.

"So what's he like?" asked Brauch.

Rudi glanced away from the command tent, "What's who like?"

Brauch playfully punched Rudi in the arm, "The Fuhrer?"

"Well, the whole thing was fast. He has incredibly powerful eyes, as if he can detect the doubts in your soul," replied Rudi. "Other than that, I'd say he was shorter than I thought he would be."

"About my height?"

Rudi laughed, "No, he's not a midget."

The meeting concluded, the officers saluting and shaking hands. Schmidt emerged, fumbling with a sheaf of papers. Rudi waited until the Lieutenant was less than ten meters from colliding with them before greeting him.

"Lieutenant Schmidt, Staff Sergeant Kleime reporting as ordered."

Schmidt stopped in his tracks and smiled. German officers were generally discouraged from running, maintaining such haste suggested a lack of discipline. Schmidt covered the remaining distance in violation of this tradition.

"Rudi, I am pleased to see you." Schmidt exclaimed as his hands squeezed Rudi's shoulders. "Have you recovered from the burns?"

"Ja, Herr Lieutenant. I am as good as new."

"I am sure you could have used a rest in the Fatherland, but we can use you here," said Schmidt, leading Rudi over to a bench by the command tent. "Corporal Brauch, allow me to brief Sergeant Kleime regarding our mission."

Brauch saluted and departed as the men sat.

"We have a key role in the next assault. I need you to lead a platoon of panzers in my company," advised Schmidt. "You will have five units, but they are unlike what you are familiar with."

"I am aware the 7th Panzer is equipped with the Czech PzKpfw 38s."

Schmidt shook his head. "Sergeant, it is an ad hoc company of the remaining crews from our 3rd Regiment and it will have a mixed compliment of equipment," he said. "One platoon will utilize the Czech 38s. However, the two lead platoons, including your platoon, will deploy captured Soviet BT-5s."

"I do not understand."

"Do you remember the battle at Shklov? When the some of the Bolsheviks abandoned their tanks and ran away?"

Rudi nodded.

"We have recovered a number of the BT-5s almost intact or slightly damaged. They have been repaired by our recovery crews and are ready to be used against Stalin."

Rudi pondered the idea, finally offering, "Would not engaging in battle in the enemy's tank, which is his uniform, make me a spy?"

"Not at all Rudi," replied Schmidt. "German crosses have been painted on the front and sides and the rear deck will have a bright red Nazi flag to protect from inadvertent attack from the Luftwaffe. There is nothing unusual or inappropriate about using captured equipment."

"Do I have a choice?"

"Absolutely. We seek only volunteers for this mission," Schmidt said. "However, you should know General Rommel specifically requested your participation in the lead platoon of the whole plan."

"Rommel?" The name held a mystique second only to the Fuhrer for Rudi.

A nod.

Rudi, though, could not shake his concerns. "Why do we use inferior Russian tanks?"

"We have suffered many losses of panzers, although mostly to breakdowns. Selective use of captured equipment alleviates problems caused by the losses," explained Schmidt. "But more importantly, General Rommel believes that if used at the right moment, the surprise generated by the use of the enemy's own equipment may tip the balance of a local engagement."

Rudi again listened but added nothing.

"General Rommel's plan is not to use the captured BT-5s at the main point of attack, but to wait until we have a breakthrough. Then as the Soviets retreat and the battlefield becomes chaotic, the BT-5s rush ahead potentially seizing a key objective such as a bridge," concluded Schmidt.

"But the Russians will easily spot the German markings."

"We believe the confusion of a collapsing battlefield makes any identification difficult. Secondly, General Rommel intends to launch you at dusk, when visibility is poor."

Rudi pondered for a moment, stood and saluted. "I would be honored to lead a platoon in your company and volunteer for the mission."

Lieutenant Schmidt waved for Rudi to relax, motioning for him to retake his seat.

"There's something else I would like to discuss, Rudi. I know that crossing the border and at Smolensk some of your men didn't take the Pervitin pills that were issued."

Rudi nodded, looking Schmidt in the eyes. "I don't deny that Lieutenant. That shit is bad. I told them they didn't have to unless they wanted to."

"Sergeant, Iron Cross or not, don't you think the Wehrmacht's doctors would know a little more about what is good for the Fatherland's men?"

"We all know people that have taken those pills and then couldn't stop taking them," replied Rudi. Word had spread that the methamphetamine contained in Pervitin was addictive, causing unpleasant side effects. It had been initially banned by the Nazi Party but was now being issued to German troops to keep them alert and awake.

"I don't entirely disagree but remember, orders are orders and it is not for us to question," countered Lieutenant Schmidt. "Think of it like this. If our men take Pervitin and it gives them the strength and stamina to succeed in battle and survive, isn't that worth the risk of the side effects?"

Rudi looked at his boots and waited. Lieutenant Schmidt rose, indicating an end to the meeting.

"I will do as ordered, Herr Lieutenant," announced Rudi.

"Very good, Sergeant Kleime," said Schmidt. "You will be pleased to know Corporal Brauch has also volunteered and I have assigned him to your platoon. He has spent the last week familiarizing himself with the BT-5s."

Rudi watched as Schmidt left for the command tent. He turned to find a smiling Brauch motioning him over past the thatched dwelling. Rudi strode over to Brauch, who offered his unsolicited view of their new equipment.

"These Russian tanks are shit, we'll be lucky to make it 20 kilometers down the road."

8

June 26, 1940   Philadelphia

The third day of the convention was of two worlds. The first world was that of the chattering classes, reporters and hangers predicting a nomination. Their stories had the strutting Willkie men spewing confident predictions of imminent victory, which in turn fed the reporters as the radio reports quoted Willkie supporters.

The second world, the smaller one that included Pegler, was part of the conversation on how to make sense of the growing chaos on the convention floor. The third day of the convention was theater, good theater, manufactured by the Vandenberg campaign. If it succeeded, the Willkie's men's confident predictions were little more than sifting sand.

The day began with the morning papers predicting a Willkie victory with more attention on Pegler's "whore" quote. That afternoon the columnist received a visit from a Willkie associate who demanded to know his source. Pegler smiled, shrugged and told him to worry about the delegate count.

By early afternoon the delegates had settled into their seats. The third ballot would be a battle between Dewey and Willkie. Pegler's colleagues were confident of a Willkie victory, composing stories bursting with quotes from the Willkie camp which had been predicting a fifth ballot win trimmed back to the fourth ballot with the overly optimistic believing the convention ended on the third ballot. Pegler had other ideas. His eyes trained on the Ohio delegation. If there was a break in Willkie or Dewey's favor it would come from Taft delegates.

"Who have you got in the pool for Willkie's vice president?" The comment came from one of the Pulitzer men sitting two rows behind Pegler in the press gallery.

"Only lay money on a sure thing."

The Pulitzer man grinned. "Westee's got something." He leaned over and tapped Pegler on the shoulder with a rolled up newspaper. "What you got? They going to do another smoky room like Harding?"

Pegler flinched, cheek raising to one side, a sure sign at the poker table he was holding a big hand. "Willkie and Dewey right now." He snatched the paper and pointed it at the Pulitzer man, "Willkie's got to beat Dewey then he's got to beat the rest of the Republicans."

The paper was snatched back by its owner. "You know something."

Before Pegler could deny the knowledge he had, the roll call began. Alabama and Arkansas were bellwethers, the Republican delegates auctioning their votes to the highest bidders, though only for a single ballot. As they had in the first two ballots, their delegates remained loyal to the Ohioan. Pegler eased back in his chair. For all of the talk about foreign money backing Willkie, none of it had seeped into the pockets of Southern Republicans.

The roll call continued and there was little change in the votes. Dewey maintained his lead, Willkie had picked up a couple of Illinois votes but his surge had slowed. The shocker for the convention came from Vandenberg's manager, John McKay, who arrived unexpectedly among his delegates. It was unusual for a state leader and campaign manager to participate in the floor vote unless he had something dramatic to offer.

"Mr. Speaker. Michigan pledges its delegates to the toughest prosecutor in the country and the next president of the United States, Thomas Dewey."

The roar of approval from Michigan was drowned out by a roar of victory from the New York delegation, which sensed their candidate was about to be nominated. To everyone but Pegler in the press gallery, Michigan's change of heart meant Vandenberg was out of the race. His seventy votes would place greater distance between the New Yorker and Willkie but Dewey remained over a hundred delegates short of the nomination. Willkie and Taft's totals combined were some five hundred thirty. After talking with Willkie's overconfident managers Pegler knew Willkie was not bowing out while Taft's people seemed to hate Dewey and Willkie equally. It was going to be a long convention.

The "We want Willkie" cries had become a memory as the duplicate tickets served their purpose and filled the gallery with a more neutral audience. When the third ballot showed Dewey at 417, Willkie at 302 and Taft at 242 even the worst mathematicians recognized Dewey could not reach 501 without Taft or Willkie votes.

In the press gallery the focus was on the Michigan delegation switch to Dewey.

"How'd he do it?" Bennet asked. Pegler's friend was just as clueless as his colleagues.

"Must have promised Vandenberg the State Department," this comment from a younger reporter who featured a conspiratorial element in his stories.

The Pulitzer man had his theory. "Willkie and Taft will join together to defeat Dewey."

Pegler could not remain silent at this bizarre possibility. "Taft would never give Willkie the nomination. The winner will be the one who can steal the southern delegates."

"That bunch will sell out to anybody," a Washington based AP reporter said.

Pegler did not disagree. He guessed Willkie had enough financial backing but not enough experience to know how to buy delegates while Dewey either lacked the money or the Machiavellian spirit to bribe them.

The fourth ballot began but as with the previous Taft's southern support held as did thirty stubborn Hoover delegates who believed a rematch was in the party's best interest. At the end of the ballot Dewey had gained eight moving to 425, Willkie had gained a single delegate while Taft had lost three. It left the New Yorker seventy six from victory, but Pegler knew it might as well have been seven hundred and sixty. The meeting in Vandenberg's suite had wrung a promise of Michigan voting for Dewey on two ballots then switching them to Taft if the New Yorker did not hit 501. The question on the fifth ballot would be whether Dewey delegates would accept their defeat and move toward Taft or stay with the New Yorker to the end.

The fifth ballot began the same, southern delegations sticking with Senator Taft with no new votes for Dewey, but with Michigan came the switch which stunned the press gallery other than Pegler.

McKay's voice rang out from the convention floor. "Mr. Chairman, the state of Michigan now casts its votes for our neighbor to the south, Senator Robert Taft."

This time the Michigan announcement was greeted by an Ohio roar while the press in the gallery began muttering. Taft was the least popular of the candidates, Democrat or Republican, a man of the past, known mostly for his sour disposition. However the Michigan switch suddenly made it a Taft-Willkie battle. Dewey's campaign manager, Ed Jaeckle, was left scrambling to hold the Dewey coalition together.

Pegler watched, the switch expected even as it was unclear whether Taft or Willkie would benefit. Vandenberg's supporters moved to Taft as did some of the Illinois and Massachusetts delegates. Others shifted to Willkie, preferring the more liberal candidate to the Republican loyalist. The floor quickly descended into chaos, men taking off their ties and swinging them in the air, hats thrown up, yelling, and fists shaking. Among the New York delegation there was an abundance of red faces, with spittle directed at the Michigan delegation along with the type of language usually reserved for dockworkers. Up in the gallery Pegler waited for the fist fights to begin, frustration usually spilling over once the realization hit that their candidate was not going to win.

A quick back of the envelope calculation on the convention floor, in the visitors' gallery and the press section revealed a stalemate. Pegler did not need a written count, he saw immediately that the Taft tidal wave was more of a ripple and nodded when the convention chair called out the totals. Willkie remained in the lead with 346, Taft jumped into second with 321 and Dewey tumbled to a close third with 309. With each candidate boasting a third of the vote only a coalition could win. In a three-way race, Pegler figured Taft was the third wheel, neither Willkie nor Dewey willing to surrender their ambitions to the grouchy old senator.

"Willkie's ahead," cried one of Pegler's less perceptive press colleagues.

"Sixth ballot," exclaimed another who'd plunked down a week's pay on Willkie on the sixth ballot in the press pool.

"Taft's finished," chortled another. "The Republicans know they can't beat Roosevelt with some conservative son of a bitch."

"Don't overestimate Republicans," Pegler growled.

Bennet perked up. "You know something Peg?"

Pegler remained discreet. "They aren't going to nominate Willkie, they don't know him and don't like him. Dewey and Taft can't win without the other."

"Vice president," shouted the Pulitzer man.

Pegler shook his head, more exhausted than irritated by his colleagues' ignorance. "Or with the other, it won't be a Dewey or Taft but another."

"Hoover," came the cry of a Roosevelt fan.

Pegler laughed. "We'll see."

9

June 26, 1940   Berlin

James Reilly sensed he was in a metropolitan area, away from the war. The unmistakable bustle of civilian life rushed through an open window not more than ten feet from where he was seated. A horn honked impatiently, announcing the presence of commercial traffic. The normal sounds of a functioning city convinced Reilly that he was no longer in Warsaw. If he could only look out he would be able to see signs and advertisements, revealing at least what country he was in.

Reilly was alone, his hands and legs cuffed and firmly secured with an additional length of chain to a hook on the wall. He was not in a cell but a space more akin to a law office conference room. There were no bars on the window. Reilly shifted in the chair. It was upholstered and comfortable. He concluded that he was definitely not in prison.

He reflected on his journey since his capture by the Germans near Smolensk, Russia. Captain Karl Scheller announced their destination as Warsaw. As the big Junkers Ju-51 tri-motor approached its airfield, he saw the smoldering city. The Polish capitol was simply flattened. After landing he was led by Scheller to a medical tent and injected with an unknown drug. For several days he drifted in and out of consciousness.

Reilly leaned back on his chair and tried to yank the extended chain from the wall hook without favorable result. He snickered at the futility of his effort to gain liberty. On the lam in an unknown foreign country with shackles attached to his limbs was something to be avoided anyway.

Suddenly the door opened and Captain Scheller entered the room carrying a thick file. He took a seat across from Reilly and smiled.

"Good morning Mr. Reilly."

"Where the hell am I?" croaked Reilly. "You said we were going to Warsaw."

"We did go to Warsaw. It just wasn't our final destination," explained Scheller.

"I was drugged when we landed," complained Reilly.

"Just something to help you relax for the remainder of the trip," said Scheller.

"Where are we?" repeated Reilly.

"The headquarters of Abwehr, 76 Tirpitzufer, Berlin, Germany," replied Scheller. "Welcome to the Third Reich!"

"Why the Abwehr?" asked Reilly. "I thought you were Army Intelligence."

Scheller snorted, "I am but I've been assigned to the Abwehr. I specialize in English speaking intelligence assets."

Reilly stared into Scheller's pale blue eyes, "Then what were you doing in the Soviet Union?"

"Looking for you," laughed Scheller.

"Why look for me?" demanded Reilly. "What do you want with me, I am not a spy?"

"James, I agree that you are probably not a spy," admitted Scheller. "Others are not sure where your loyalties lie."

Scheller opened his green folder and turned it so Reilly could view the first page. It was a grainy photo of Reilly standing on the rear deck of a Soviet BT-5. The tank displayed the markings of the Spanish Republican forces.

Reilly reached for the folder but the shackles prevented access. Scheller spoke softly, "We have known about you for a long time, James."

"Then you know that I have been a technical representative for John Christie assigned to the Soviets in connection with his sale of early model tanks and nothing more," countered Reilly.

"James you have spent many years in Russia," reasoned Scheller. "Are you suggesting that you are not a Communist."

Reilly immediately protested, "No I am not a Communist! Their country is pathetic. I am an American doing a job for money."

Scheller stood and walked to the open window and observed the street below.

"Karl, didn't you say you lived in Milwaukee in the twenties?" asked Reilly. "That didn't change you or your beliefs."

Scheller turned and grinned, "Well I do like the Chicago Cubs. I went to a World Series game in 1929."

"That's exactly what I am talking about. You went to American baseball games and now you are a Germany Army officer attached to its intelligence agency," said Reilly.

Scheller returned to the long conference table and reached into his pocket. He retrieved a pack of Lucky Strikes and passed it to Reilly. "Cigarette?"

Reilly was stunned. "Where did you get American cigarettes?"

Scheller chuckled, "Germany is not at war with America. I obtained these especially for you."

"I thought there is an embargo," replied Reilly. "Aren't the British blockading your ports?"

"The American embargo only applies to arms and there is no restriction of any kind on shipments to our French and Italian friends," answered Scheller. "The British will not risk expanding the conflict. Anybody may sail to a French or Italian port, with any cargo."

Reilly struggled to free a cigarette from its green pack, eventually succeeding. Scheller leaned across the table with a light. Reilly took a long drag and smiled.

"Thank you Karl. I haven't had a Lucky in years."

Scheller smiled back, "Oh, I don't think that's quite true, is it James?"

Reilly frowned, "I've been in the Soviet Union."

Scheller sat and flipped through Reilly's file. He paused and placed a report in front of Reilly. Reilly attempted to read the document but he was not sufficiently fluent in German.

"We have information that you returned to the United States not long ago," stated Scheller.

Reilly continued to peer at the report, noticing the words "Philly" and "Joseph Edwards."

"Come to think of it, I was in Philadelphia a few months back," admitted Reilly. "So what?"

"James, let's make this easy. You are either a dedicated Bolshevik or an American spy. If you are a Red, I am not able to help you. If you are an American spy, that's another story," advised Scheller.

"I am neither. I am just a guy trying to make a buck," countered Reilly. "There's nothing wrong with that."

Scheller shook his head in disapproval. He leafed deeper through Reilly's file.

"James, despite what the war monger Roosevelt says, many in America want the Third Reich to eliminate Stalin. It looks like their wish will come true before the summer is over."

"So what do you want with me?" asked Reilly.

"The Wehrmacht has encountered small numbers of Soviet tanks that are much larger and more capable than what was expected from intelligence advisories. The war will be over soon. We will capture many examples of these new tanks and their factories." Scheller stopped and pulled the meeting summary from Reilly's hands. He re-assembled the file on Reilly, set it aside and continued.

"The Abwehr is forming a special assignment section to evaluate Soviet armor. We believe you should be a part of this effort."

Reilly was confused, events were moving too fast. He needed to apply the brakes. "I would like to speak to someone at the American Embassy."

"You will not be a prisoner and we will pay you," added Scheller. "Much more handsomely than the Bolsheviks I am certain."

"If I agree, will my people know what I am doing?" asked Reilly.

Scheller laughed, "James, the American spy Joseph Edwards gave me the Luckies."

Captain Scheller stood and straightened his uniform. "I will have some good German beer brought up for you to celebrate. Perhaps you would like to enjoy your country's independence from its oppressive British master a few days early."

" July 4th ?"

"Ja, enjoy tonight and I will return in the morning for further discussions," replied Scheller. He paused at the door. "Your Independence Day was always my favorite American holiday."

Reilly merely nodded and watched Scheller exit. His mind was racing, running down the confusing scenarios. If Joseph Edwards knew Reilly was inside Abwehr headquarters, he would surely arrange for Reilly's release. Reilly turned to the window and considered another option. Perhaps Edwards wanted Reilly to examine Soviet tanks with the Abwehr.

10

June 27, 1940   **Philadelphia**

Day four of the Republican convention promised to be decisive or just another day in an interminable deadlock. Pegler had slept late, a long night of questioning and wheedling information from sources yielding little.

The evening began slowly. His source from the Taft camp was nowhere to be found, Pegler suspected he was crying in his cranberry juice over the senator's certain defeat. The Vandenberg suite had been closed, the Bellevue-Stratford yielded nothing suggesting a deal had been reached out of Pegler's earshot. The confident Willkie men no longer caroused the bars, buying drinks for newspapermen while bending ears over their man's exploits. The only ones who were talking on the third night were those who knew even less than the scribes whom they were talking to.

Pegler had taken up his position at the corner of the Peddler's Tavern, able to hear conversations down both sides while fending off Bennet.

"You know something," Bennet said.

"I knew something," Pegler corrected him. "But that's gone now."

His friend blinked at the confession. "You knew Willkie wasn't going to win."

"Anybody with brains knew that Willkie wasn't going to win. The Republicans aren't so desperate this year that they would nominate a Democrat." Pegler shook his head. "I knew they would push Dewey for a couple of ballots then they would push Taft for a couple of ballots and that neither would likely win."

"Today," Bennet said. "What about tomorrow. Do you know what is planned for tomorrow?"

Pegler's lips were pressed tight. "Nothing," he lied.

"It if ain't Willkie, Dewcy or Taft who's it going to be?"

Pegler wet his lips. "The one who made it possible."

This set Bennet to thinking. Pegler guessed what was about to happen but not who would start it. The chattering at the bar revealed little, though the solons of the printed page remained heavily for Willkie. Few of them had ever been to a convention, particularly a contentious one such as the Democrats in 1924 or the Republicans in 1920 and generally picked the frontrunner. Pegler relied on his baseball knowledge, recalling how hundred game winners in the regular season were swept by a lesser opponent such as the A's in '31 and the Tigers in '34. Dewey had been the convention frontrunner followed by Willkie, but winning required good convention leaders and timely action, something both men lacked.

"Willkie's picking up in the Midwest," came one prediction, the certainty in his tone revealing how little he knew. "He's from Indiana and once Ohio switches from Taft he'll wrap it up by the ninth or even the eighth ballot."

Pegler glanced down at the red faced talker, stringer from
Colonel McCormick's Chicago Tribune and a man with the
reputation for talking the loudest when at his drunkest. Pegler joined
in the contests – when nights were dull – to imbibe the stringer then
let him chatter, writing down his most ludicrous predictions,
everything from Roosevelt not running for a second term to his
reappointing Oliver Wendell Holmes to the Supreme Court two
years after the old man had died. Besides providing humorous
entertainment for the reporters he also offered an avenue for getting
back at McCormick, much despised by the New Dealers for his
isolationism and dislike of Washington spending.

The McCormick man awakened memories and the possibility
of another source. Excusing himself from Bennet, still puzzling over
the convention's next move, Pegler hailed a cab and directed the
driver to the Colonial Hotel, each floor occupied by a different state
delegation. His taxi driver fortunately knew a rear entrance as
Pegler was too well known to enter without being noticed. A three
dollar tip later the reporter was at the service entrance and the
elevator linked to the kitchen.

Pegler greeted an old colored waiter pushing a cart covered
with a white tablecloth with the Colonial Hotel label on it to deter
thieves, including the waiting staff. The waiter looked up, puzzled
by the appearance of the jut jawed and solidly built white man.
"Sir?"

"Where you headed?"

The waiter stared, white coat and black pants well starched,
red carnation in his breast pocket just above the gilded stitching
identifying him as Pheebus. "Sir?"

Pegler pointed to the nearby elevator. "Where are you
headed?"

"Third floor, sir."

Pegler pulled out five dollars. "Third floor then."

The waiter eyed the bill. Tips had fluctuated during the convention depending upon the guest's alcohol intake and how close the convention had come to choosing the "right" candidate, but five dollars was five dollars and not bad for an elevator ride. He snatched it, pressed the up button on the elevator and waited with Pegler. When the doors openned, the waiter pushed in the cart followed by the white man and the doors closed behind them.

The elevator inched up, offering Pegler the opportunity to pump the waiter. "You been to the Mr. Dirksen's room?"

The waiter blinked. "Mr. Dirksen?" He would not forget Mr. Dirksen after the ten dollar tip he gave for the waiter.

"Yes. What floor is he on?"

"Fifth floor, sir."

This was all Pegler needed to know. He folded another five dollar bill and slipped in into the waiter's pocket just above the carnation. "I'll need the elevator after you are done."

The waiter shrugged. Ten bucks for riding an elevator, he wondered how white people had any money left. They reached the third floor, waiter and his cart exiting, Pegler tugging down the door and punching the fifth floor button.

As the elevator struggled upward Pegler considered Everett McKinley Dirksen. The blowhard Tribune reporter at the bar had been partly right that the Midwest would break the deadlock. If its delegations moved away from Taft or Dewey it would create a flood of votes. Dirksen had the Illinois delegation in his pocket, twice voting for Dewey then doing the same for Taft as McKay promised. Dirksen's next choice might be the next president.

The service elevator shuddered to a halt. Pegler lifted the door and moved his stocky frame as stealthily as physics allowed. The service corridor fed into the main corridor at its middle, allowing Pegler to peer down both ends. He stood back, foot keeping the door cracked, listening for the familiar ding of an elevator alighting on a floor. Of course, if the Illinois delegation was making a deal with the Vandenberg campaign he might not take the regular elevator. Instead he might follow Pegler's route, the waiter picking up more folding money.

More worrisome for Pegler were his instincts going awry and the Illinois delegation sticking with Taft until the end. Pegler shifted his foot, propping open the door. Politicians had the reputation for jumping onto popular issues, but most of them were stubborn men who clung to outdated notions because change was more frightening to them than potential defeat. It wasn't much different than baseball fans sticking with their hometown team no matter win or lose. White Sox fans immediately came to mind, their team's perfidy not dimming Chicagoans desire for another World Series humiliation.

The elevator sounded. Pegler squinted through the crack in the open door to see an attractive female exiting, diverting Pegler from his mission for a moment. The woman disappeared into one of the rooms at the end of the hallway and Pegler's mind was set at ease.

Grumbling as his foot grew numb, the columnist lit a cigarette to calm his nerves, knowing how ridiculous he would look if discovered spying in a service elevator corridor. He resembled a Dick Tracy cartoon, though Pegler knew a reporter could never measure up to the hard bitten detective. Dick Tracy would squeeze information out of a suspect using a blackjack, while Pegler was left with liquid refreshment and a promise of a glowing profile in the newspaper. His methods worked, though he heard just as many self-serving lies as the truth.

The elevator bell rang. This time Pegler hit pay dirt as McKay swept onto the fifth floor. Pegler waited for a companion but the congressman was alone. Pegler bit down hard on his lip, his hunch not having played out, yet. McKay knocked at the suite, Pegler craning his neck to see down the corridor, ear cocked. He heard nothing but saw Dirksen's face flash by as he and the campaign manager slipped into the fifth floor suite.

Pegler's heart thumped. There was no better feeling than being right. He left his viewing spot and strode down to the suite McKay entered. He leaned against the door, straining to hear the conversation behind the thick door. Stifled he considered peering into the keyhole, but in the middle of a long hallway he was asking to be discovered.

A solution came in the form of a chambermaid. The elevator bell sounded and a few moments later a youngish woman made her way into the hallway. Pegler adopted his best imbibed form – not a stretch for a man who ended many evenings feeling quite good about himself – bent over, head close to the numbers on each door, hand reaching out to steady him, feet crossing each other to produce a heavy stumble. He bumped into the wall, cursing and muttering while glancing surreptitiously at the maid who sped to his side.

"Sir?" She was in her early twenties, a naïf who would be embarrassed by a drunk and willing to do what he said to get him off her hands. "Do you need help?"

"Lost my bley."

"Excuse me?"

"Lost my bley, my bley, can't get in the room."

"Your key."

Pegler lurched, shoulder smacking the door jamb a little hard than he intended and flinched. He turned to her. "You're pretty," he mumbled, reaching for her. The chambermaid's expression told him he had won, she would get him into the room.

The maid ducked away then tugged at the master key attached to her belt. She slipped it into the lock, turned and pushed open the door. "Here," she said, stepping aside and allowing Pegler to tumble into the room. He separated from her then closed the door hurriedly, locking it behind her.

The room was occupied, a suitcase sat open on a table, cigarettes, a half filled gin bottle and several freshly pressed shirts marked the presence of a 1940's politician. Pegler, though, was unconcerned with the occupant as long as he did not return. Spotting a glass beside the bed he pressed against the wall, ear against the bottom, voices from the next room hollow but audible. He listened and within twenty minutes knew how the fourth day of the convention would end.

Eighteen hours after his successful delving into political espionage, Pegler sat in the press gallery, tired but pleased. He listened to the chattering among reporters who speculated about the next Republican presidential nominee.

"It's got to be Willkie," said one of many. The gallery was packed with the lawyer's supporters, some because they approved of the man, others believing Roosevelt would crush him in November and a smaller group because they had Willkie in the reporter's pool.

Pegler held his tongue through the various discussions, careful to keep his scoop of the year from the ears of reporters who spent the night at bars loosening tongues of men who knew nothing. His column was already written, the inside story of how Dewey, Taft and Willkie had all been outmaneuvered by the eventual winner. His words would become part of the history of the 1940 Republican convention and very possibly American history.

The convention was called to order and the roll call began with Pegler most interested in Alabama and Arkansas. There was no change in the early voting beyond the odd independent delegate switching and a groan sounded through the press gallery as another deadlock beckoned, another long hot day. Pegler did not groan and while his colleagues settled in for the long count, Pegler ran down his state delegate list, stopping on the state that could start a political avalanche.

"What are you looking at?" Bennet asked. He squinted at the list in Pegler's hand. "Illinois? They are firm for Taft."

Pegler held up his hand. He didn't need any of the press gallery to hear about Illinois. The two reporters waited as Georgia again voted for Taft then Dirksen stepped forward in front of the Illinois delegation and caught the chairman's eye.

"Mr. Chairman," he called, voice reverberating through the hall. "The great state of Illinois, home of the first and greatest Republican president, casts its votes for its neighbor to the east, the senator from Michigan, Arthur Vandenberg."

A great cheer erupted from the Michigan delegation while the sound of boots scuffing the floor echoed from the press gallery. "Vandenberg," exclaimed one of the Willkie boosters. "He's out of it."

A few minutes later Joe Martin, head of the Massachusetts delegation and permanent chair of the convention went to the floor and switched his state's votes from Taft to Vandenberg. Close on the heels of this Michigan recast its vote for the senator though New York remained tied to Dewey, slowing the momentum. Pegler's finger dipped on his alphabetical list, a short wait for Ohio. Taft's manager, filled with fury at Willkie and Dewey for denying the senator the nomination, bellowed out his state's switch, nearly all going for their northern neighbor Vandenberg.

The Ohio switch sent the southern delegations scrambling, as the leaders of Arkansas, Alabama, Georgia, Mississippi and North Carolina tried to catch the attention of the chair and be the first to switch their votes to Vandenberg. The seventh ballot ended with Vandenberg at 370 delegates, most of his votes coming from former Taft states and a few from Dewey as the prosecutor dropped from 309 to 287. Willkie had also lost some though he remained in second place at 331 while a few stubborn Taft holdouts remained true to the senator.

"Shit." The cry was repeated in the press gallery as reporters faced the possibility of rewriting their stories.

"You knew," Bennet said. "You knew Illinois was switching to Vandenberg."

Pegler grunted. Several attempts by Willkie and Dewey supporters on the convention floor to get an adjournment were rejected by the newest Vandenberg supporter, Joe Martin.

The eighth ballot opened, Southern delegations were whipped into shape by Texas' Colonel Creager, almost all of the delegates switching from Taft to Vandenberg. The Michigan senator had gained fifty votes when the count reached New York. Pegler and the press gallery searched the floor for Ed Jaeckle, a messenger penetrating the New York delegation, paper flapping in his hand.

"They are going for Willkie," cried one of the less perceptive stringers.

Pegler did not waste time with correcting the deluded soul.

Quiet descended on the convention, Jaeckle suddenly the most important man in the universe. He required only a moment to glance at the telegram then begin pushing through the delegates, catching Joe Martin's eye then sucking in air to project his voice.

"Mr. Chairman," he bellowed. "The Empire State of New York casts all of its votes for the senator from Michigan -," the rest of his words were drowned out by an explosion of noise from the nearby Michigan delegation.

"Shit." General disdain swept through the press gallery. In the visitor's gallery, the few remaining hoarse Willkie supporters were silenced for all time. Pegler sat back, realizing he had the scoop of his career and began figuring how much money to put into the Election Day reporters' pool.

11

June 29, 1940   Letcani, Rumania

Ianu Cohnescu would not forget the day of exile. The Carpathian air had receded into the mountains as summer dawned. From eastern Rumania he watched troops march past his family store in the direction of Russia. There were rumors of the Russians halting the Rumanian and German armies then driving across the border toward the Prut and Iasi, the Red Army scheduled to be outside the city within days.

None of it was true and a month into the war the Red Army remained a distant threat. The only sign of a war were the growing casualty lists, families receiving the news that a son or sons had been killed or wounded far from home and without reason. For the first time Ianu was rewarded for his Jewish heritage, ignored by the Rumanian army as it drafted hundreds of thousands of young men for service on the eastern front.

His joy receded as the army trundled through Letcani, his hometown. First came the soldiers, uniforms once fresh but dirty now as the soldiers marched. The journey to the east began on foot, then rail and ended digging trenches somewhere in Russia. Then supply trucks, struggling over the ruts in Letcani and creating their share of new ones. Ianu had stood at the window of their shop, watching the unending line of machines until pulled away by his father, Saloman.

"The floor, the floor," Saloman pointed to the wooden planks that seemed to sprout dirt.

Ianu grabbed a broom and glared at his brother, who was stocking goods on the far side, Manu also focused on the road, a fact not ignored by Saloman when several cans tumbled to the floor. He berated his youngest son, noting that every dented can would be noticed by sharp eyed women who would demand a discount to buy damaged goods. Ianu worked quickly, careful to keep his back to the windows as he collected a sizable pile of dirt in a corner. Only a knock on the door drew him from his task. Saloman stepped to the front of the store and was confronted by a hulking figure blocking the sunlight.

The store was swept by an overwhelming scent of diesel as a soldier stepped inside. Ianu blinked, the brown uniform unfamiliar. It took him only a few moments to realize they were not talking to a Rumanian. "Jude, was ha du auf die strasse zu tun?"

Saloman stepped away from the German - a Nazi in Letcani, the worst fears of the Cohnescus and their neighbors. He glanced toward Ianu, who shrugged. Rumanian with a mix of Russian was the only languages spoken at home with Russian banned outside its walls. German was beyond Ianu though the German's hard expression and "Jude" demonstrated what he thought of the Cohnescus in particular and Jews in general.

The German worked his mouth, eyes narrowed, face wrinkling from the impudence of Jews. His hand slid to his sidearm, Ianu stiffened knowing well what the Germans did to the Juden who did not follow orders. Relief came in the person of Horvath, his green shirt marking him as a member of the feared Rumanian Iron Guard. He marched into the shop and eyed his surroundings as if seeing it for the first time, which he was. He nodded at the German who eyed the Cohnescus then left the store.

"Sabotage," Harvath muttered. "The Jews have conspired with the Bolsheviks to slow the Rumanian war effort."

Ianu glanced at his father, who remained still, expressionless, sensing danger in the form of the Iron Guard. Harvath marched to the elder Cohnescu. "The army requires this road." He snatched at Saloman's arm, fingers digging into the older man's flesh and causing Manu to make a sudden move toward Harvath. A quick glance from his father halted him in time as three guardsmen entered the store.

"These Jews outside," Harvath shoved Saloman, who was followed by his two sons into the chaos that was Letcani's main street.

The three Cohnescu men stumbled and dodged the bouncing, struggling wagons carrying Rumanian soldiers to the front. Harvath kicked at the ruts deepened by the over weight machines, a puff of dirt rising in the air. "There Jews, fill the holes."

Saloman steadied himself. "Where?" He rubbed his face, suddenly darkened by the dust that hung over them.

"There." Harvath heaved Saloman toward the western end of the street. "The dirt over there."

The father and two sons began the trek to the open fields clogged with weeds and the remains of discarded machines. Ianu knelt, fingernails clawing at the dirt, tugging at the weeds, sharp edges cutting at his fingers, some sticking to his skin. He scooped a handful of dirt from the field, pushing to his feet only to have one of the green shirted guards smack at his forearm, scattering his effort over the weeds.

Harvath laughed, shoving Ianu back to his knees. "Dig," he kicked at the weeds, entangling his foot and nearly tumbling.

Ianu ripped at the soil. His father rose, dirt cupped in his hands only to have it smacked free. Saloman returned to his duty without comment. Manu was stronger. The Iron Guardsman unable to smack the dirt from his hands. Instead Harvath was forced to allow the youngest of the Cohnescus to walk to the road and spill dirt into the rut. Ianu scooped dirt from the field, cupping it between his hands to protect it from another attack. Forttunately, the Iron Guard had lost interest in harassing them, heading off in search for water as the afternoon sun broiled them.

The "road construction" continued for several hours, Ianu's legs aching as he dropped and rose to carry handfulls of dirt to the roadside across from their store. Back and forth, sweat sticking his clothes to his body then slowly evaporating, a cold clamminess threatening him. Ianu swayed, Saloman slowed, Manu the only one unaffected by the heat.

The Iron Guard had melted away, their search for water keeping them a distance from the Jewish "saboteurs." The single guard, wiping his brow, mouth open, tongue hanging out was relieved when the local constable appeared. Ianu relaxed. Bubrick the constable was a frequent customer of the store. As the Iron

Guardsman disappeared he halted the Cohnescus one by one as they dumped the dirt into the ruts.

"This is Harvath's work."

Saloman, face reddened by the sun, nodded mutely as he he collapsed on the wooden plank sidewalk, hand clutching his throat, lungs struggling to suck warm air into his body. Ianu followed then Manu, the three Cohnescu men sagging near the uniformed constable. Bubrick nodded to a pail, one of the leaky ones that Saloman kept in the store.

"Water," he offered. "Quickly before Harvath returns."

Ianu dove his palms into the pail and gulped at the water, hands dirty and shaking from his road work. Manu had fallen asleep on the crushed grass outside of the store. Only Saloman seemed to have a spark of energy, eyes bright even as he was distracted by the continued procession.

"Why?" He murmured. Ianu cocked his head, barely able to hear over the clatter. His father continued. "Why so many? Why do they keep coming?"

Ianu did not know, did not care. The Iron Guard was his only worry. They had come to Letcani as his uncle had predicted. He had also said the Cohnescus could survive as the Rumanians needed them too much.

"It is the war," said Bubrick. A medal was pinned to his uniform, the one he had been given personally by the first King Carol after knocking out a Bulgarian artillery piece during the second Balkan War. He wore the medal everywhere, allowing all to admire it but never to touch in case they wiped off the thirty year old monarchical fingerprints he could not see but knew were there.

Bubrik handled his medal with gloves, placing it in a warped wooden box also handed him by the king.

Ianu swallowed the water and flexed his fingers to retrieve the feeling in them. Saloman blinked, mind returning to the present and Bubrik's words. "The war?"

The old man nodded. "They are coming from the Hungarian border, Transylvania. They believe the Hussars might seize more land with the Rumanian Army in Russia."

The Hussars. The very name stirred patriotic fervor in Ianu. The Hungarians had taken Transylvania from Rumania with the Nazi's help. It was another reason to hate the Germans.

"They are headed to Russia."

Saloman eyed the extended convoys. "But the trains, why are they walking?"

Bubrik had relatives in Bucharest and knew more about the war than the entire village. "The Germans used the trains for supplies and for the oil."

Ianu knew the Ploesti oil fields, the main reason the Germans allied with Rumania. The oil and the thousands of men like Milosh sent to the Russian front. Ianu perked up. Perhaps Milosh was among these men, a stop in Letcani would be necessary for one of its former residents.

Saloman swallowed his water. "Your uncle said the Iron Guard was in the cities, not here."

Bubrik's forehead crinkled, ancient eyebrows giving him the appearance of a mythical creature. "The Iron Guard is in control," he murmured. "The army is too far away and most of them -." He hesitated at the sound of fast approaching horses. "I can no longer talk," he snatched his baton and deserted his neighbors to the tender mercies of the Iron Guard.

"What are you doing?" Harvath's voice made Ianu jump. The Iron Guard, over a dozen in number approached on foot. "Fix the road." Harvath grabbed Saloman by the scruff of his neck and pushed him into the ruts. "Your store," he pointed across the street. "It is open for business. You will have customers."

Saloman eyed the green shirted men, suspecting a trick but a shove from one of the bulkier guards sent him stumbling into the rutted road. Ianu and Manu followed, the three Cohnescus separated upon reaching the store. Saloman was behind the counter, Manu on one side, Ianu close to the window. From there he saw the people of Letcani being herded into town, some peeling off for other stores, a smaller group halting outside the Cohnescu's. Harvath greeted them, most were older, longtime customers who traded at the store since the Cohnescu's arrived from Russia. They were led into the store singly and Ianu watched as Harvath and one of the guards ordered the Cohnescu men to gather goods and assemble them on the counter before Saloman.

The total was calculated then Harvath stepped to the counter. "You purchase this from the Jewish store?"

The first customer, a woman in her fifties and forced to care for her grandchildren after their parents deserted all, nodded, eyes watery with exhaustion.

Harvath jabbed his finger at the goods. "Take those goods." He leaned over at Saloman. "Pay her."

Saloman stared. "Pay her?"

Harvath's hand flashed, a blow across the cheek silenced the old man. "Do it." Ianu jerked forward but found one of the guards blocking his path. Saloman was left to pile the goods into a well-worn box.

"Pay her." Harvath's order bounced around the store. "Pay the money cheated from the widow woman."

The woman opened her mouth as if to protest, but a glance from Harvath silenced her. Saloman counted out the money, Harvath snatched it from his hand and led the woman from the store. Two hours of the same followed, the Cohnescu's running out of currency before their shelves were emptied. Without money, more goods were taken as payment with Ianu, Manu and Saloman forced to watch their stock disappear. Most of the men and women were eager to take, poverty and ignorance convincing them the prosperous deserved to lose what they had. Others understood what looting the Cohnescu's meant, no more store in which to trade, supplies disappearing with the Jewish shopkeeper.

Ianu noted the different expressions. Some were gloating, sneering, grasping people who felt entitled, standing with arms against their hips. Others hugged their bodies, hopping when Harvath yelped an order then leaving, heads down as the goods were carried with them from the store.

Harvath stood in the middle of the store, legs spread. "Where is the gold now?" He barked. "The Jews have tried to buy their freedom, but when the gold disappears." He bared his teeth.

Ianu swallowed, thinking of his uncle who believed he could bribe his way free of the Iron Guard's clutches. Harvath was not one to be swayed by mere gold to release "his" Jews.

"Work to be done." He pointed to the road. "Jews must be busy or they will steal from decent people." He nodded and the Iron Guard pushed each of the Cohnescus from the store, door left open as there was little to steal if thieves were nearby. They were shoved down Letcani's main street, followed by their laughing tormentors.

Ianu shielded his eyes from the late afternoon sun. He knew the path well, the Cohnescu farm north and west of Letcani. Relief rushed through Ianu as he realized it was not their destination. Joni and their mother were at the farm, safe from the Iron Guard.

The walk became a trudge, the heat and a day without food slowing them. Saloman struggled, even after they left the uneven road and crossed the fields. Wheat snapped at their knees then corn stalks sliced at their arms. The same punishment came to the Iron Guard, Harvath and the others cursing, swatting the back of their head. Ianu took his punishment quietly but cringed when Manu was struck though his younger brother's temper did not show.

The sun had reached the tallest tree tops when they reached their destination, a field, recently picked clean but filled with people. As they stumbled toward them, Ianu guessed there were hundreds, most sitting, all of them kept in order by armed men. Ianu guessed more Iron Guards, their "uniforms" mismatched, some in modern dress, some in traditional clothing favored by Horia Sima, leader of the organization. Their weaponry was just as diverse, everything from army rifles to hunting guns to worn pistols dating to the previous century.

"There." Harvath pushed Saloman to the edge of the crowd. "Sit." The three Cohnescus did as ordered.

Ianu looked about, recognizing few faces, gliding over the unfamiliar ones. The men he knew, though, told the story. The Iron Guard had collected all the Jewish men from the area. Relief washed over him again as he saw no women. He touched his father on the arm.

"I do not see mother and Joni."

Saloman shook his head, a warning to never mention the Cohnescu women. Harvath, of course, would know them and while an absence of women offered hope it was also worrisome. The concentration of male Jews made it likely they did the same with the women and children.

"Why are we here?" Manu groaned, looking at the scratches and bruises on his arm the result of his tussle with the army officer. "They can't keep us here, Harvath is *nemernic*."

Ianu smiled, Harvath was the very definition of an "asshole," but Saloman was not amused. He smacked his youngest. "Enough," he hissed. "We must remain silent." He nodded in the direction of the armed men. "They will do what they will do. We will live if we remain calm and silent."

Manu frowned, mouth opening but his father's warning had the desired effect and he slumped onto the field. Ianu required no warning. Recalling the night in Iasi when his father and uncle watched the Iron Guard destroy the house of Jews who would not pay, Ianu knew the danger of drawing their attention.

Ianu rolled, prickly pain tearing at his back. He reached, fingers touching something half buried in the soil. He slid it free and stared. A turnip. They had stopped at a turnip patch. He touched his father and nodded at their first food since the morning. The Cohnescu men began digging, unearthing several peaked looking vegetables. Hiding it in their clothes they ate quietly but quickly, ensuring no one noticed their treasure. Ianu chewed and swallowed without tasting, stomach rumbling with gratitude. It would be their last meal for the foreseeable future.

12

June 30, 1940   **East of Smolensk**

Corporal Adolf Brauch removed the stencil and stepped back to join Schmidt and Kleime. "I'm done."

Brauch was shirtless and sweating in the stifling midday heat. He wiped his brow with a tattered cloth.

"That's our *Balkenkreuz?*" asked Rudi. "Is that a joke?"

"Nein, Stabsfeldwebel Kleime or I mean Leutnant Kleime," replied Brauch. He held out the stencil and the paint jar. "This is what they gave us."

Rudi shook his head, bewildered as much by his battlefield promotion the previous day as by the barely visible national markings on the captured Russian BT-5 tank. "I hope our own guys know we are out there. Otherwise we will be lit up from the rear."

Captain Schmidt waved Brauch away and put his arm on Rudi's shoulder. He considered the newly painted black cross outlined in white on the side of the light tank. "Well it certainly qualifies as the markings of the Third Reich. Lieutenant Kleime, I don't think we want to highlight your true identity."

"I understand Herr Hauptmann, but what about our own forces? They certainly will not be able to see this emblem…its tiny and barely visible," observed Rudi.

"This is part of the plan Lieutenant. There have been numerous instances where our advance forces have driven undetected along columns of retreating Russians *in our own panzers!*" recounted Schmidt. "If we are in their crappy tanks they will never take notice and we can seize vital bridges and crossroads."

"It seems dishonest, like we are lowering ourselves to the level of the Slavs," replied Rudi.

Schmidt stepped back and examined the BT-5. He shook his head in disgust. "This BT-5 is crude, but they have many of them."

"I'm worried all of these the bolts will be like arrows inside the crew compartment if anything hits us," agreed Rudi, pointing to the tank's armor.

"Yes, it will be a dangerous mission. You will be followed by two platoons of Czech PzKpfw 38(t)s and a company of infantry mounted in halftracks. It is called *Kampfgruppe Schmidt*," smiled the Captain. "I will be in the lead of the first platoon of Czech panzers."

Rudi nodded as if their unit's temporary name meant something vital. "When do we go?"

Schmidt answered, "Very soon, the 7th Panzer has begun probing attacks near Sychevka yesterday…I'm sure you heard the artillery and saw the Stukas." He paused and looked Rudi in the eyes. "How do you like your new status…Lieutenant?"

Rudi shrugged, "I'd rather have Werner, Braun and Koening back. Not to mention Helga. This BT-5 is garbage, the seals suck and it leaks oil everywhere."

"Well your Iron Cross-First Class and battlefield promotion to Lieutenant are accomplishments, Rudi," stated Schmidt. "You have made your family and the Fatherland proud."

"And you are now a Captain, only Brauch remains the same," laughed Rudi.

Schmidt removed his hand from Rudi's shoulder and slapped him on the back. He walked off towards the Czech 38s further down the sandy road. He called back, "We shall see what can be done for our Corporal Adolf."

Brauch ambled over and leaned against the side of BT-5. "What's with him?"

Rudi ignored the insubordination. He had been through too much with Corporal Brauch to discipline him. "It seems Captain Schmidt has a sore throat."

Brauch smiled at the Wehrmacht slang referring to men that sought medals to wear around their neck. "I sure don't want him to get an Iron Cross sacrificing my skin."

Rudi smiled and patted the BT-5. "This is a piece of shit. How are we going to fight in this?"

"I don't know…surprise," offered Brauch. "I say we get through this and afterwards we find a better ride…maybe something even made in Germany."

Rudi watched Schmidt make his way to his Czech made panzer. "The Fatherland needs bigger and better panzers, Adolf. Captain Schmidt is no better off in a PzKpfw 38(t) than we are against one of those KV-1s."

"They are monsters, Herr Lieutenant," agreed Brauch.

"What do you think about the replacements?" asked Kleime.

"They are green but we have enough of our guys from the Third Panzer Regiment to make it work," replied Brauch. "Of course we only need 3 men per tank."

"Are the BT-5s ready?" continued Kleime.

"As ready as we can make them without manuals we can read and no spare parts," warned Brauch. "We have about half the ammunition we should. We do have plenty of petrol and oil. And we are definitely going to need extra oil."

Kleime nodded and climbed atop the green BT-5, standing on its rear deck. Their mount was a BT-5(v), the commander's version. It employed a cumbersome frame antenna that surrounded the turret and sides. It was an ungainly installation.

"We have four tanks and only one radio," remarked Rudi.

"The Wehrmacht radio has been installed and it works," said Brauch. He wryly added, "at least we can communicate with *Kampfgruppe Schmidt.*"

Rudi nodded, "the antenna contraption makes us look like the Red Army."

"Only we are better trained and more motivated," grinned Brauch. "How could soldiers of any army leave a functioning tank for the enemy to capture?"

"God only knows, Adolf," agreed Rudi. "We will make them pay for their foolishness."

A teen appeared from the woods adjacent to the BT-5 and saluted Kleime. He was slight and pimpled. Kleime returned the salute, suddenly feeling rather old.

"Panzerschutze Reiner, there's only three of us in this tank. You think you're ready to assist me with this 45mm gun?"

"Jawohl Mein Leutnant!" called out Reiner. "I have familiarized myself with the gun, the co-axial 7.62mm machine gun and the traversing system."

"What's our ammunition status?"

"We have 50 rounds of 45mm and about a thousand rounds for the machine gun," reported Reiner.

Rudi decided to take a moment to learn something about young Reiner. "How old are you?"

"I'm 18, almost 19," admitted Reiner.

"Where are you from? Tell me about your family."

"I'm from Dresden. My father is a school teacher. I have a younger sister," offered Reiner. "My mother is a volunteer at the hospital."

"Karl May is from Dresden," exclaimed Rudi. "I read all of his books when I was a boy."

Reiner smiled. "Everybody from Dresden has read his books."

"Your name is Gunther, but what do your school mates call you?" asked Rudi.

"They call me Gunther," said Reiner.

Rudi laughed and continued, "How long have you been in das Heer?"

"Almost 11 months Herr Lieutenant. I signed up the day our comrades crossed the border into Poland," advised Reiner.

Brauch interrupted Rudi's interview of the teenage warrior, "Lieutenant, Captain Schmidt is coming back."

Rudi climbed off the BT-5 and walked to meet Schmidt half way. Schmidt appeared agitated. Rudi saluted and waited for orders.

Schmidt acknowledged Rudi's salute. "The 7th Panzer has broken through the Bolshevik lines at Sychevka. The Red Army appears to be melting before our eyes!"

Rudi listened but did not speak. Schmidt slowed down and lowered his voice.

"Tomorrow morning at 0700, *Kampfgruppe Schmidt* will move up to Sychevka. At dusk, we will lead an assault towards Gzhatsk. The plan is to close the ring around Vyazma as quickly as possible. Our mission is to capture the town and an intact bridge over the Gzhat River."

"What type of forces can we expect against us?" queried Rudi.

Schmidt continued, "Aerial observations report groups of fleeing Russians, but nothing organized. It appears that the Soviet defense was not in depth."

"Chaos can be dangerous for us, especially when we are in the enemy's own tanks," remarked Rudi.

"We recognize the risks but if we can capture Gzhatsk quickly we may be able to meet elements of the IV Panzer Group advancing from the south," explained Schmidt. "There are at least six Bolshevik Armies that will be trapped in the pocket."

"How will units in the IV Panzer Group know not to fire on us? They are not going to see our markings and we have only one radio."

"Ideally, we will be alongside you with the PzKpfw 38(t)s and the motorized infantry," said Schmidt. "We have plenty of radios. We will also work out a flare system when we get to Sychevka."

Schmidt abruptly stopped and peered at his watch. "Have your men ready Rudi. It's 30 kilometers to Sychevka."

July 1, 1940   **Letcani, Rumania**

Dawn was peeking through the early morning mist when Ianu woke. In sudden and nearly unbearable pain he struggled to make sense of his surroundings. Curling his body in defense, Ianu's leg struck something. It was Manu. He swung his arm drawing a groan from the opposite direction. His father was nearby, grumbling at being awakened by Ianu. He would have much to grumble about that day.

"Up Jew." The voice from above was familiar. Horvath had returned – if he had ever left – and memories of the previous day rushed back to Ianu. He was granted little time to recover, Horvath delivering more pain to his shin. "Jews move today."

Ianu clawed to his knees, legs throbbing from Horvath's assaults. Satisfied he had roused his onetime neighbor, Horvath moved onto the next sprawled body in the field. The Jews of Letcani remained on the real estate where they had collapsed. Ianu's clothes were damp, skin clammy, the nearby Carpathians making even July nights chilly with an abundance of dew. In happier times Joni had tried to explain without effect about radiational cooling, warm air dispelling in the open fields into the open skies.

Ianu scooted to a sitting position, gaze sweeping over the darkened bodies in the field. Horvath was kicking and cursing, huddled figures stirring. As each rose Ianu realized he was surrounded by men. He reached around and shook Saloman. "Joni and mother are not here," he hissed, fearful any loud talk would bring Horvath.

Accustomed to a softer bed, his father groaned trying to stretch the kinks in his back. "What?" He snatched at the dirt, fingers slipping through the dewy grass.

"Mother and Joni, they are not here." The pain in Ianu's legs had subsided, replaced by fear for the two women in his family.

Saloman pulled himself up until sitting directly beside his son. "That is good news, perhaps they escaped." Ianu hoped when the men did not return the women had taken to hiding. Joni would have sensed the danger.

"Where is the food?" Manu groaned, his pain more internal, youthful body able to handle sleeping in the field.

Ianu doubted the Rumanian Iron Guard worried about feeding the Jews. Death by starvation or exhaustion offered the same result as a bullet in the head. Ianu kicked his brother, fearful Manu's loud complaining might draw Horvath to them. Manu rubbed his arm, grumbling reduced to a few shallow groans.

"What should we do?" Ianu faced Saloman. The few shriveled turnips they had found in the field had been delicious after a day of nothing but there would be no more turnips, the fields picked clean.

Hunger was replaced by fear, gun shots followed by machine gun bursts raising the figures in the field. Ianu helped Saloman, his father bent at the back. The others in the field crowded together, those who moved too slowly greeted with rifle butts. Ianu heard the crack of wood against bone, pushing him to move faster as the Jews of Letcani were herded, the rising sun to their right. The plodding, old and young bodies weakened from exposure and the previous day's long walk infuriated the guards. Ianu counted over a dozen armed men, most of them armed with old Mannlicher M1895 rifles, still in use by the Rumanian Army.

Shoved into the mass of men for one brief insane moment Ianu considered a mass charge at the guards, their rickety guns able to fire a few shots before being overrun by the massive numbers.

The first would surely die and Ianu waited for those on the fringe of the mob to charge the guard but none did, the guns too intimidating. He stumbled, the press of bodies making it hard to walk, his aching legs not helping him as a night on the hard earth had its effect. Ianu spotted the youngest looking guard, swaying under the weight of his rifle. He was yelling, face red, body jerking as he struggled to herd the prisoners. His uniform, a mismatch of Iron Guard green shirt and the battle gray of the Rumanian army, made him the least impressive of the guards. A bulge had formed in his section of the mob his Jews not keeping pace with the others.

Ianu jostled along, following the herd, feet trod upon, nose quivering from the scores of unwashed flesh pressed at him. Saloman and Manu were closer to the middle of the mob, safer from abuse but also further from freedom if they made a dash. Ianu slid from his father and brother, focusing on the young guard. He was Ianu's age, uniform hanging around his neck and wrist, slacks darkening at the cuffs as they dragged in the dewy grass.

"Faster, faster." His voice rose to a level of shrillness marking desperation rather than control. His troubles drew the attention of an older guard who approached. The lines stretching down the length of his face revealed age and dangerous experience.

Ianu edged closer, ten meters, eight, six, the two guards not noticing as they gesticulated. He flinched as the younger guard was sent skidding on his back, the older guard tired of his excuses. He did not rise, corporal punishment common in the Rumanian military. Ianu drew within five meters, a single body between him and the guards though the milling bodies around him masked his progress toward escape. Ianu stumbled, a root, a wayward foot or exhaustion. It was a lifesaving trip, the older guard unleashing his gun on the bodies close to him. Anguished cries followed as bullets ripped flesh. Others were luckier, the bullets finding a deadly spot and ending their suffering before their body hit the ground.

Ianu's hugged the dirt. A few bullets scraped the ground near his head, but within moments he was covered, the bullets clearing the bulge while others rushed toward the center of the mob. A volley of shots followed, the other guards using their guns to maintain control. Ianu heard the old guard screaming as he stepped on the pile, "That way, that way." More shots sounded above him, the old and young guards taking turns at shooting Jews.

He shifted, struggling to breathe. He tasted blood, praying it was not his. Legs heavy, he wriggled free as the shooting passed him. For a moment he was tempted to remain hidden and escape when the guards were out of sight but he would have to desert Saloman and Manu even as there was little he could do for them when at their side.

Ianu strained to see the Letcani Jews as they pushed in one direction then the other, finally heading directly toward him. Pushing aside cooling limbs, his hands slippery from the blood, he stopped as there was more shooting. The older guard was teaching another lesson with more bodies falling though these remained among the living. In their panic they trod on his every part - legs, back, hands and head - Ianu struggling to avoid the mob as it rushed from the angry guards. The shooting stopped, the mob stilled, people rising from the dewy dirt, Ianu one of the last, helped to his feet by an unexpected source.

"Where have you been?" Instead of his usual anger at Ianu's antics, Saloman was on edge, wrinkles making him look older, dirt smudging his face. "They are shooting, we must stay together."

Ianu lacked energy to disagree and was soon engulfed by the mob, running in one direction then the other until exhaustion overcame guards and prisoners alike. The ragged mob was finally tilted in the right direction, stumbling across the plowed fields which held mostly hay, fodder more valuable to horse heavy Rumania than corn.

The sun was in its full glory, the morning heat drenching prisoner and guard alike. Ianu shook off the heat and the cloying hunger as his stomach revolted. He focused instead on the ragged figures before him, recognizing a neighbor, Lev the wagon driver who transported goods from the Iasi rail terminal to the towns around it. He sported the best hands with reins and the best voice with a team of horses. His hard work meant a semblance of prosperity, four wagons, four teams, four drivers. Not yet fifty he was would have been the perfect husband except for the boils, innumerable, inescapable and unpleasant. No woman would massage those boils, catching flakes of skin in her fingernails, fearful of pricking one and drawing Lev's considerable ire. This day, trudging in the heat and dust, grain crunching beneath his feet, stalks whipping at his legs, Ianu found the boils relaxing, familiar.

Three were lined up on the back of Lev's neck, a fourth poking from the encroaching bald spot at the crown of his head. The boils drew Ianu's mind back to Joni during happier times after Uncle Viniu rewarded her with a medical book. The subject of Lev's boils had been raised after he had made a delivery to the store. Joni had went to work, trading her fascination with veins and circulation for skin conditions. Later at the dinner table she tried to explain, drawing a sharp comment from Saloman that such unpleasant subjects should be separate from eating. Though Joni stripped the mystery from Lev's boils, it did not make him any more attractive.

Ianu recalled enough of Joni's talk to distract him from the trek, Lev's uneven step revealing then hiding boils beneath his work shirt, sweat lining up on his neck, skin reddening from the unrelenting sun. It was all a connection to Letcani, and his once normal life.

"Where are we going?" Manu trudged between his brother and his father, shoulders and head sagging.

"Hush," Saloman hissed. He jerked his head to see the direction they were headed. "Roman is this way."

"Roman," Manu yelped. The town was thirty kilometers from Letcani. He choked, struggling to clear his throat, moisture slowly drying from his body. "That is two days walk."

"Move." Saloman cuffed his ear, his son's lagging producing a burst of energy in the father. "We cannot stop."

Ianu did not grumble. Lev's boils barely a meter distance, seemingly within reach, the old wagon driver displayed more stamina than men half his age. If Lev could walk to Roman then Ianu could follow him.

The traipse continued, hay fields replaced by forest, the trees and undergrowth slowing the pace. The guards prodded "faster, faster" but did not shoot. The absence of gunfire bolstered Ianu's belief the Letcani Jews retained value for the Iron Guard. The guards would not walk them through the summer heat just to kill them a kilometer away from where they began. Suddenly Roman seemed a possibility, hope of work, food, water. He shook his head, a few bits of sweat spraying, one dangling on his upper lip. He sucked it into his mouth, the salt drawing no reaction much like Lev's boils no longer made him queasy.

The forest offered its own troubles, sunlight was reflected away while the heat remained, caught in a war that only Joni could explain. Vines tugged at his legs, branches ripped from their trunks as he grabbed ahold to them to remain upright. It was not enough, Ianu going down while behind him a more surefooted trekker stopped firmly on his leg, grinding it into the moldy leaves that layered the forest floor.

"Damn you," Ianu cursed, reaching up with a burst of unexpected strength. He plunged the other man into a clutch of bushes.

"What?" the man rolled onto Ianu, who blinked, the face unfamiliar, the figure large and dangerous. Ianu tried to scramble free but an arm grasped his foot, pulling him back even as the trek around him continued.

Ianu kicked, it was deflected, Ianu's shoe split nearly in two. Saloman grabbed his son around the arms, a brief tug of war ensued, his father losing and tumbling, shoulder hitting hard against a tree and he slumped onto the forest floor.

"You tripped me." The man reared up, fist cocked, arm pointed at Ianu. "I get-."

He never finished his thought, a crack, his head jerked, eyes crossed then rolling back into his head, a red patch, black in the middle, spread as blood flowed from him. He tumbled, the mark of Cain felling him.

"Up, Jew." It was the younger guard. He kicked at Ianu, who climbed to his feet. Two kicks were required to raise Saloman, grimacing as he rose, arm stiff at his side. His sons guided him, each bump producing a low moan from the father.

"My shoulder." He tried to move his arm and howled. "I can't." Every step led to a moment of paralysis, body growing rigid then relaxing. It produced a pace certain to draw the attention of the guards who were eager to eliminate those unable to remain hidden among the mob.

"Carry, carry." Ianu glanced back at the young guard, done admiring his most recent kill and motioning for them to join the few stragglers plodding through the trees. Ianu snatched at Manu's arm, entangling them. "Carry, carry."

Saloman hooked his one good arm around his older son's neck as Manu, stockier than Ianu, struggled under the load, the three managing a lurching gallop through the woods. Respite came only after leaving the forest and they were allowed to sit in the sun. Their numbers diminished after some sought shelter in the forest haze. The guards split, those forced to return to the forest growling at their task, gunshots marking their trek to find the wayward prisoners.

"My shirt." Wobbling on his feet, pain receding as he was still, Saloman extended his uninjured arm. Ianu slid off his father's shirt, a yelp sounding as he pulled it over the injured shoulder, the pain cut short by the sound of gunfire from the trees. There was something worse than a dislocated shoulder.

Tearing the shirt into strips, Ianu constructed a sling, stabilizing Saloman's shoulder and allowing him to walk, settling his pain, muscles unfrozen.

"Where are we going?" Manu sagged into the dusty grass. "We walk and walk."

"Russia." The answer came from Lev, boils offering a bit of shade to parts of his cheeks and forehead. "They are shipping the Jews to Russia."

Ianu protested. "That is 200 kilometers. We cannot walk 200 kilometers, there will be no one."

Lev's round face, red and peeling, grew darker at Ianu's tone. "The train, the train. We are walking toward the train, it is a few kilometers from Letcani."

"The train." Manu sounded wistful as if the machine offered some type of escape. "We can leave Rumania."

"I heard they did it in Iasi," Lev said. They collected all of the Jews and shipped them east." Lev had relatives in the city. Leaders in their neighborhood, they had somehow offended Uncle Viniu who disliked their fundamentalism and hectoring of those who were weak believers.

"They will kill us all." An unfamiliar voice and face entered the conversation. He was much older than Ianu but younger than Lev or Saloman. He was not a customer, his narrow features were otherwise swallowed up by his nose and mouth. "The Nazi's are in Russia, they invaded and Rumania joined them. The Nazi's do not want Jews in their territory."

Ianu eyed the dissenter. "Why would they walk us here to kill us later?"

"To torture the Jews, to raise our hope, that is what they do."

Ianu slid away from the dissenter. It was too hot to listen to prophecies of doom. Saloman followed him, less dismissive of the possibility. He grabbed his son's shoulder. "He could be right. Your uncle predicted something like this, that is why he wanted you in Iasi, to protect you. He has money and contacts."

"They will not kill us, that is the Nazi's. Rumanians are not Nazi's. Milosh-."

Saloman cut him off, waving his hand then grimacing as his shoulder revolted at the sudden movement. "Milosh does not matter. If we reach Iasi, if they are moving us we may survive." He pinched Ianu's arm with his good hand. "You and Manu must escape."

Gunshots from the forest warned them about the danger of seizing opportunities.

"Find your mother and Joni." The last name was heartfelt.

"We will find them," Ianu promised. "The Cohnescu men."

Saloman smiled wanly, releasing Ianu. Several more minutes later the search ended, the guards emerging , scowling, dirty and sweaty from their search. A few shots in the air started the Jews toward the destination.

They reached the rail line a few hours late, barren, untraveled. Ianu recalled the rickety train that traveled from Iasi to the edge of the Carpathians and Transylvania. For the Cohnescus the rails were only for business, providing access to supplies they could not grow on the land. Ianu had seen trains, never mounted one.

They laid their father on the ground and waited, surrounded by familiar men from Letcani and unfamiliar men from other local towns. A cloudburst offered relief from the heat and offered the opportunity to calm their hunger and thirst. With the first drop they opened their mouth to the heavens, shirts extended to collect moisture, the first taste burning the throat, driving the thirst never to be quenched. After the skies closed puddles offered later relief while provoking squabbles, even muddy water a delicacy not be surrendered.

Then came the search for food in the deserted fields. Ianu and his brother dug their into clods of mud, collecting sunflower seeds, chewing and swallowing, husks cutting at dehydrated throats and settling uneasily into shrinking stomachs. Amidst this, the guards came with whips, displayed like a fresh toy. Ianu's limbs rebelled, mud coating him from the field, the slashing of leather ripping flesh drove adrenaline through his veins. He watched Manu, his skin coated to a dark brown and drawing a snicker until Ianu realized the same clung to him. Manu snarled, a sudden change in his temperament. No longer the whining straggler, Manu had learned to keep his temper in check, but it would not last forever.

Saloman had receded, shoulder worsening, bags growing under his eyes from the pain. He tottered on his knees, requiring both sons to raise him to his full height. Father holding sons' shoulders with a death grip.

Lev, boils shrunken – Joni could have explained – munched on sunflower seeds he had hidden through the night. "The train from Iasi," he sputtered, husks squirting from his mouth. "It will take us east." He offered a seed to Ianu who snatched and nibbled at it, trying to extend the meal for longer than any seed had been enjoyed.

Unfortunately Lev had his own chorus accompanying him. The bearded dissenter, gray hairs flecked with mud, was certain the train brought death rather than escape. Scraping the mud from his arms, flesh browned by days in the sun, lips cracked, scalp red and peeling, he offered the image of a forsaken old testament prophet.

"That is where the Germans sent the Polish Jews."

Ianu's eyes bulged. "To Iasi? Poles in Iasi?"

The question drew a grunt. "To the ghettos, to the cities where they would be easy to find and kill."

"They could kill us here." A husk from Lev's sunflowers found its way to the other man's beard, clinging unnoticed. Ianu eyed it hungrily.

More shouts, whips unfurled, driving the mass of men into a thicker, more manageable mass. Ianu held onto Saloman's good arm, steadying his father. He maintained contact as bodies milled about and mixed into an indistinguishable mob. Lev and the dissenter disappeared. The whips and shouts continued, bodies pressed until air became a luxury. Ianu pointed his face skyward, gasping in the heat, the odor and pressure of crushed bodies threatening his brother and father. He grasped the shoulders of other and propelled high among the others. He sucked in the air, hot but breathable. Below Saloman tugged and called for his son, mouth raised, but blocked by the crush of bodies. Ianu's hand slipped free but he could not drop to the ground, hips tight against the chests of men and unable to move.

There they remained, occasional shouts and unfurled whips keeping them pressed tight. Ianu struggled to move, glancing down at the mass but able to see only the top of heads, mouth sucking for air as he searched for his father and Manu. Wriggling, legs dangling several feet in the air, lips aching, body becoming clammy as it was unable to cool. Ianu spotted the train, the smoke, open cars, buckets of water sloshing, cool air, room to stretch, a ride to Iasi, a holiday.

A shot rang out, ending the joyous journey. A head lolled to one side, face stricken, peering at Ianu. Another shot rang out, another head sliding to one side. Ianu glanced about for the source, a third shot directed him to a platform used for the train while providing a bird's eye view for three Rumanians practicing their marksmanship. Ianu could see their faces. The proximity saved him for the moment, shooting a Jew from close range was not sporting, that would come later when they were drunk.

The shots set off a stampede, Ianu's body slipping, forcing him to grab shoulders for support. His head sticking above the crowd was dangerous, but falling among the legs and feet, unfeeling and uncontrolled meant certain death.

Whips and shouts corralled the mob, the sudden rush pushed the bodies tight against him, ribs threatening to buckle, feet growing numb as they dangled. More shots, a bit of blood spray landing on Ianu's lip, two more heads off to the side, the targets becoming fewer, death rather than competition the guards' obsession.

A rifle was aimed, a crack, no movement from the target, cursing from the guard, laughter from his companions. A new target was found, more jockeying, a shot, the bullet striking the target, a low moaning emanating from the area, all of it producing celebration on the platform. Ianu guessed a family member hit, another senseless death. He struggled to withdraw his neck into his body but it resisted. The rifle was swung around, barrel pointed in Ianu's general direction. He tried to duck, a sharp flash, the bullet rushing past his head, a low moan behind him evidence it hit its mark.

A new rifle, a different marksman, an unsettling target, Ianu bobbed and jerked his head, drawing laughter from the trio on the platform. His neck stiffened, head struggling to dodge, the rifle was set into place, body stiff.

A yell interrupted the shot, rails protesting as the locomotive pulled the enclosed boxcars toward the clearing. Lev had been correct. It was just in time as two of the guards climbed from the platform, leaving a single frustrated soldier, rifle stiff in his arms. He renewed his aim, arms grasping the weapon, eyes focused, finger caressing the trigger.

He proved the worst of the three, a jerk of a body and a spray of blood ten metres before Ianu unlikely to be his target. He recocked, preparing a second shot but the train had arrived and below him his comrades shook the platform, preventing another attempt. He slid down, defeated.

Ianu did not witness his descent or much of anything else, the train's arrival moving the mob toward the tracks. Suddenly he was on his feet, being dragged, stumbling as they were headed toward the halted cars. A sudden stop sent Ianu chin first into a figure below him. It was worse in the front, yelling, the slash of a whip and a single shot meant all was not well. Ianu strained to understand the yelling but it was muffled, worse were his other senses his eyes inches from the matted hair, flies alighting on it, nose poked at it by dried sweat, body probed by hands, fat double chins, noses, all of them pressed tight. His legs ached, feeling slowly returning to his feet, body otherwise leaden, only the momentum of the group keeping him upright.

More sounds of struggle, shouting and whipping. Instead of moving forward the crowd was stumbling back, the uncertainty of retreat better than the screaming guards herding them to the rail cars. Shots rang out, too many to count, the retreat became a charge for the first twenty to thirty metres then slid into chaos. The train stretched in front of them, two of the cars opened, Ianu squinting at the rags spilled onto the ground. Shuffling closer he saw the rags were occupied.

"Ianu." A heavy figure launched into him. It was Saloman. "We must stay together." He gripped his son's arm and tugged him toward the front car.

The mob was split, ordered to climb onto the front or second car. Whips, rifle butts and an occasional shot in the air cured indecision. Ianu followed his father, who yelled at Manu.

"No, no." The young guard blocked their path. He shook Ianu free from Saloman's grip and shoved him toward the second train car. His father drove his good shoulder into the guard, turning him slightly and was shoved to the ground for his effort. Manu stepped toward him and received a blow from the back of the guard's hand.

The brief struggle slowed the pace, drawing the ire of the older guard. He growled at the younger guard, jerking at his collar while jabbing a finger in his face before turning on Ianu. "You assault a member of the Iron Guard." The older guard removed his side arm, whirling and firing at the figure on the ground. Saloman jerked, hand going to his neck, blood spurting. Ianu lurched in his father's direction only to face the pistol at eye level.

"Death," he sneered. "For you." He cocked the pistol only to have his leg kicked from below. It was a diversion, Saloman kicking granting Ianu time to melt into the crowd as it trundled onto the railcars.

Ianu was thrust into a fight for survival, hands grasping, feet stomping as he followed the mass to the car. Choking with the memory of Saloman, tears unavailable, Ianu hit the mass of ragged clothing. A hand grasped him below the knee, fingers sliding down his leg. Ianu shook free before being catapulted forward. The heavy scent of death tugged at him as he fell face first into the heap. Flesh cushioned the fall, a low groan greeted him, another body pushed him deep into the sweating, dying mass, the smell of urine and decayed flesh defiled his senses.

Ianu rolled onto his side for a normal breath. Another body fell on him, this one from the rail car. He tasted blood, shifted again and was able to escape before another body tumbled. He pushed up and saw what was producing the trail of bodies. The rail car was three meters above the prisoners, and clambering aboard meant grasping the floor of the car. Those who dared touch the rail car had their fingers smashed by rifle butts, the guards enjoying the sport of hurling Jews to the rail cars then smashing them once they arrived. Some scrambled aboard, avoiding the heavy wooden rifle stocks by climbing on the occupied clothing, their owners too weak to move. The cars were packed, only the falling of bodies onto the ground outside creating space for the new arrivals.

Ianu scrambled, dodging leather against his flesh and the occasional gunshot. Jews plunged forward while beneath him hands clawed for help or warned him of the horrors he faced. Ianu knew remaining outside meant death while climbing inside was the great unknown. Saloman, though, had wanted him to live, his last desperate act was a signal to go forward.

Another body flopped at his feet, head cut by a rifle butt. The additional rise offered him a clear path to the rail car, he placed his foot on the back of the latest castoff, pushed forward, and flopped onto the train. By Providence he avoided the vengeful guards and wriggled into the mass inside. He did not look back, Saloman was gone. Ianu squeezed through the standing figures and instantly knew they were not going to Russia, the train was there to kill them.

14

July 1 1940   **Paris**

"Sir." Francois was smoothing his hair, a recent salon visit having gone awry.

His superior, the French Deputy Foreign Minister, did not look up. Etienne Descoteaux refused to be diverted from his reports, a lengthy typewritten analysis from the embassy in Moscow consuming his morning. "Yes."

"The ambassador has arrived."

"Two minutes, return." Etienne turned a page and Francois scurried off to deliver the unwanted news. Ambassadors were unaccustomed to being treated like an errant schoolboy forced to wait outside the schoolmaster's office. Etienne paid no attention. A request for a meeting from the Soviet embassy had stirred the foreign ministry. Laval had departed on one of his tours of his home to "reacquaint himself with the French citizenry," leaving Etienne to handle the Russians' curious request.

A member of the ruling party led by Pierre Laval, Etienne had been in his position for more than a year. Long on confidence, he believed he was a key reason the French had avoided the second European war in a generation. Unfortuantely, his efforts resulted in the French betrayal of her obligations to Poland. A veteran of the Great War, Etienne was prone to exaggerate his role in the diplomacy preceeding the present conflict. To the dismay of the British, France stood idle while Germany devoured Poland.

Etienne's personal life proved even more complicated. His Italian wife, Fiorenza, had announced their engagement without informing him of its existence. In true French style, his mistress Lisle was more amused than distressed to find herself in a relationship with a married government leader. Torn between the demands of two aggressive women, Etienne found his office at Quai d'Orsai, the French Foreign Ministry, his sanctuary.

The war had been going very badly for the Red Army, the announced capture of Smolensk put the Germans less than 300 kilometers from Moscow. News reports had the Russians fleeing in panic from German tanks and the Wehrmacht spreading across the countryside without opposition. News reports, though, could not always be trusted and delaying the meeting for two days offered Etienne sufficient time to scan official reports from Moscow.

The French military attache in Moscow estimated over a million Red Army soldiers killed and captured in about six weeks of war. Preparations were in motion to move the embassy east with a growing panic infecting the Soviet government. According to the embassy another purge was in the works with the general staff the main target, the politburo and the central committee also to suffer. Cutting off the top levels of government in the midst of war was a dangerous proposition, but Stalin was a dangerous man.

Etienne had spent two days plowing through thirty eights pages of facts, statistics, speculation and predictions with the conclusion the Red Army and Soviet regime was poised on the edge of collapse. If the French embassy in Moscow had heard the rumblings it was likely the same had been heard by the Soviet embassy in Paris, prompting the meeting request. With two minutes to spare Etienne girded for the expected request he had discussed with Laval, the Soviets asking for an armistice between the Red Army and Wehrmacht, the details to be negotiated through the French Foreign Ministry.

Up and out of his office, Etienne paused at a mirror, Francois a reminder that appearance was important. He found his assistant hovering outside the room which held the Russian ambassador. "He is with the other man," Francois whispered.

"The same one?"

A nod, Francois swaying from foot to foot, a sign the ambassador had rejected his offers of refreshment starting with water continuing to coffee and finishing with Cognac. If he was nothing, Francois was a gracious and persistent host.

The ambassador leapt to his feet at Etienne's entrance, scurrying over, clamping the Frenchman's hands between his. "Mr. Descoteaux" he butchered the name and at the sound of a throat clearing from the opposite side of the room backed from Etienne. "I have little time."

"That is good," Etienne said. "I have little time to give." Lisle expected him for an afternoon meal. Fiorenza expected him for an early return home a long evening out, the Paris night life appealing to her more and more as the summer days lengthened.

"The fighting must end," the ambassador blurted. He glanced at the spectator near the window. No reaction from that direction seemed to calm him.

"We do not entirely disagree," Etienne said.

"We seek the French government's aid." A throat clearing shut him down, the ambassador reorganizing his thoughts. "We seek use of the French government's friendly offices to enquire about the possibility of a ceasefire."

A louder throat clearing had the ambassador hopping. "Uh, uh, an armistice." A pause for a dissent. When none came he continued. "An armistice and negotiations using your good offices."

Etienne hesitated, the puppet show entertaining, disconcerting and irritating. "An interesting proposal," he said. "I would need to discuss it with Minister Laval. He is in the provinces for a few days but when he returns."

"How soon?" The question leapt from the ambassador.

"Three to four days." Laval was especially dilatory when difficult problems arose. Negotiating a Soviet-German peace went beyond difficult.

"Three to four-." An explosion was averted by a cough, summons and a hushed conference at the window between the two Soviets. Orders were given, received and the ambassador returned. "Is it possible for the minister to contact the German embassy and seek a conference?" He raised on his toes.

Etienne concealed a sigh. He was to host a gathering of newly appointed French consular officials the next day. He also had to endure a meeting with Ciano, the long winded Italian foreign minister who sought a Mediterranean alliance. There was also a reception for new ambassadors, the Yugoslavia crack up creating four countries from one and all demanding diplomatic relations with the most powerful country in Europe. Squeezing a meeting with the German ambassador amidst this to help the Bolsheviks escape the fate they deserved seemed a waste of time. He released the sigh. "In the next two days."

"Tomorrow."

Etienne felt his face grow warm. "Two days. The embassy will be contacted with the response."

The ambassador bit his lip, draining it of color, the two day wait one day longer than demanded by an anxious Moscow. A cough reoriented him. "Of course, two days. I eagerly-." Another cough interrupted him. "We await your answer and will consider it expeditiously," a growl made him jump "In due course." The door was opened and the pair departed, allowing Etienne to breath normally again. Francois was just as quick, dashing inside to announce. "They are gone."

"They are," Etienne agreed. "They seek an armistice."

Francois raised up. "Peace. Is it possible?"

Etienne allowed Francois to answer whether the Germans on the cusp of victory would halt their drive and allow the Russians to recover. "I have an afternoon meeting." Francois had cleared his afternoon, Lisle demanding his attention and possibly his affections. Her dalliances with the German military attache had earned Etienne his American subsidy and she demanded a form of payment from him in return.

His driver took him to the Hotel Maastricht, the café an extravagance that proved worth the expense as the cream of Paris society occupied a table or wandered by his. Being seen with Lisle sparked conversation, impressed conversation. Her table was waiting, Lisle not there but nearby. He was to be waiting for her even if she arrived first.

Ten minutes elapsed before her voice bounced through the trees and tables fronting the Champs Elysees. She floated by him, barely noticing Etienne, an old trick, their public relationship as mere acquaintances part of their charm. Everyone who knew them understood the truth, but maintaining the fiction was nearly as important as the relationship. After making the rounds she slid into the chair opposite him, dress white and magnificent, speckled bodice drawing the eye then redirecting it to her face. The waiter, familiar with them, was startled by a switch, her usual champagne replaced by a Perrier, Etienne continued his tradition of white wine. Lisle, granted the first word, always mentioned her companion's appearance. "Tired?"

Etienne agreed.

"Francois?"

His stories of the earnest but wayward assistant entertained Lisle who soothed his concerns about the future of France if Francois ever gained authority. "No." He twirled the wine glass in his hand "The Russians."

Lisle paused as her Perrier was opened and poured. The waiter discreet, understanding Etienne's position and conversations might be dangerous to his future and France's.

"They are trouble."

"The Russians," Etienne hissed. "They seek our aid with the Germans."

Lisle touched her crisp blond hair, the color highlighting the lips and eyes that drew men the moment they came within their sight. "Germans. What are you to do with the Germans?"

Etienne mouthed "peace" drawing a ladylike squeak from Lisle. He drew closer "Your friend in the embassy."

Lisle shook her head. "He speaks about nothing but the Russians. He hates them." The color ran from her face "He talks about killing them, the unt-" she paused, tongue working across her lips. "Unter," Lisle's forehead creased.

"Untermenschen," Etienne helped her.

She nodded, despair darkening her face. "He speaks of them as if they are animals."

It was all Etienne needed to hear to know how his meeting with the German ambassador would go. His mind turned to more personal matters. "When do you see him again?"

Lisle was stirring her Perrier, temporarily engaged with the bubbles. "Who?"

"The German."

Her eyebrow arched. "Etienne is interested in my days."

He pursed his lips. Lisle's other men were mere conversation filler, nothing to be treated seriously, never to be part of an inquiry. Her smile dimmed, his concern threatening to cloud her day. A shrug. "A few days, nothing definite."

"I would -." He stopped.

Her head dipped, Etienne not known for his shyness. "You would?"

"Nothing."

"You were going to say you would prefer I not see him."

A deep breath. "The Germans, they are dangerous."

"You are more dangerous to me than he."

Etienne blinked, her words confusing him.

She covered his hand. "My heart."

Lisle the romantic. It did not raise his heavy spirits. "He has not -." Another hesitation.

"Has not?" Lisle worked her lips, reveling in his discomfort, body wriggling as her sharpened fingernails tapped the back of his hand.

"Touched you."

"Etienne." The squeal caused those nearby to look up from their meal. A wink from Lisle had them settle back to their business. "You are afraid for my virtue." She slid her hand under his then began sliding her finger against the palm of his hand. "The German's mind has a solitary goal." Her eyes twinkled. "The plans of the French foreign ministry according to the Deputy French foreign minister."

Etienne blinked as Lisle spread her lips, nostrils flared, eyes offering a hint of moisture, an alluring look that calmed even the most savage breast. He nodded as Lisle brought her other hand over his. "I have told him little beyond what he would not have learned from the newspaper." Her tongue flickered, reptilian. "But he has told me so much."

Etienne could testify to that, as could his American paymasters. A shake of her head and the waiter was at their table, menus at the ready though unneeded. The rest of the afternoon would be pleasant, the Russians, the Germans forgotten, Lisle guiding Etienne back to her boudoir, a phone call placed to Francois to cancel all appointments. He could seek European peace the next day.

15

July 2, 1940   **Sychevka, Russia**

"Does Herr General wish to pilot this afternoon?" asked Waltraud Shriver as they walked to the Fieseler Storch tied down adjacent to a dirt track just outside Sychevka. Rommel had flown the aircraft earlier in the day, landing at Sychevka less than an hour after the 7th Panzer secured the now burning village.

"Nein, Lieutenant Shriver. I must focus on the positions of the retreating forces before us" replied Rommel. He gestured for Shriver to examine his map. "Let's follow this road from Sychevka to Gzhatsk and get a feel for the Red Army's strength."

"Jawohl, Herr General," agreed Shriver, following the red line on Rommel's map with his finger. He had flown almost daily with Rommel since early June and had become a disciple of the unconventional general. Occasionally, Rommel flew the aircraft himself, which was unnerving for Shriver. Rommel was certainly a good enough pilot, but observering rather than flying left Shriver little to do and did not eliminate his responsibility for the general's safety. Shriver enjoyed his job much better when Rommel rode in the back and snapped photographs with his camera.

Shriver could not help admire the general. After all, he was aware of Shriver's poorly kept secret. His maternal grandmother was Jewish, rendering him a quarter Jew and a *mischling* or mutt in the eyes of the Nazis. While not an absolutely disqualifying trait in the Luftwaffe, it certainly was not helpful. Rommel had advised him it was of no consequence to the general.

"The maps Army intelligence provided us are almost worthless," observed Rommel. "This road is nothing more than a dirt track."

"General, I would say we have about two hours before dusk and I am concerned about landing here in dwindling light. This track is pretty rough."

"What are our options?" queried Rommel.

"Land here before dusk or head to Smolensk. We have enough fuel for either."

"I prefer to reconnoiter the battlefield and land here to meet *Kampfgruppe Schmidt*," advised Rommel. "I have a special mission for them."

Shriver waited for Rommel to explain, but he did not offer more information. Shriver was certainly not going to pry. The general would tell him what he needed to know and Shriver expected nothing else. Instead Shriver gazed at the smoke from Sychevka, judging the wind direction to be from the north at 25 kilometers an hour. The road was east-west where the Storch was parked. Shriver would have a fairly brisk crosswind to contend with on takeoff. He proceeded to loosen the tie down ropes.

Rommel never spoke to Shriver about the massacre of Jews they witnessed near Orsha in early June. Shriver knew Rommel was unsettled by the event for he heard the general's outrage and could see disgust in his eyes. Whether Rommel took any action was simply beyond Shriver's consideration. For Shriver, the fact that Rommel allowed him to be his personal pilot when he knew of Shriver's partial Jewish heritage was more than generous and resulted in intense loyalty to the general.

Shriver confirmed Rommel was secured in the rear seat of the Storch and fired up the V-8 Argus engine. Whatever a detractor might say about the Storch, he would have to agree that it was more than adequately powered.

Shriver taxied onto the road and lined up for takeoff to the east. He stood on the brakes and applied power smoothly. Releasing the brakes, Shriver bounced down the rough track using less right rudder than usual due to the crosswind from the left. He was anxious to get off the pot holed road as soon as practical. As the tail raised and airspeed increased to barely over 50 kilometers per hour, Shriver eased back on the yoke. The Storch was airborne in seconds.

"Impressive Lieutenant...a full load takeoff in less than 50 meters," announced Rommel over the intercom.

"Danke Herr General but it is due primarily to the capabilities of the Storch," replied Shriver.

"Nonsense Waltraud, I couldn't do it," admitted Rommel. "Head southeast and let's see what we are facing. Our panzers have run into antitank guns 6 kilometers down this road. The *Flivo* has called in the Stukas but I want to see what's behind this position."

Shriver climbed to 500 meters and leveled off. He quickly performed the cruise checklist. They were flying low above a chaotic battlefield. Shriver needed his head to be outside the cockpit, alert for threats.

Five minutes later, they reached the tip of the spear. A handful of PzKpfw 38s lay discarded on either side of the track, turrets at awkward angles smoke billowing from open hatches.

Rommel tapped Shriver's shoulder and pointed to woods further south and several agricultural type buildings. Shriver rolled right 20 degrees to skirt to the west of the enemy stronghold. Below the Storch appeared another platoon of disabled Czech built panzers.

"Flanking attack failed," said Rommel flatly. "The Russian antitank guns have to be set up in that collective farm adjacent to the woods ahead."

Shriver nodded and banked left to allow Rommel a clear view.

"How many disabled panzers did you count?" asked Rommel.

"I see eleven," answered Shriver.

"I counted ten but regardless the division started this morning with only 75 operational PzKpfw 38s," stated Rommel. "We are going to have to dislodge this position without losing anymore panzers."

Dismounted motorized infantry were assembling in a shallow depression behind the burned out panzers. Rommel scribbled furiously on his notepad.

"Circle over the top of the command halftrack," commanded Rommel. Shriver instantly complied, bringing the Storch to level flight above the battalion commander. Rommel opened the side window and flung a message container overboard. It hurtled towards the waiting major, landing almost in the halftrack. Satisfied that his instructions were delivered, Rommel secured the side window.

"Fly west 10 kilometers and slip around behind. Let's pick up the road 7 kilometers south of this farm," ordered Rommel.

The evasive route took almost 15 minutes to accomplish. When the Storch reappeared over the road, Shriver was surprised to see it streaming with trucks, horse drawn carts and soldiers on foot. Only they were not reinforcements, they were heading in the opposite direction towards Gzhatsk.

"The Reds are fleeing, Herr General," pointed out Shriver.

"Yes they are. The antitank line is a rear guard, if we can get through we can rout the mob behind it," surmised Rommel. "Fly southeast another 10 kilometers and then let's return to Sychevka. I want to brief *Kampfgruppe Schmidt.*"

Shriver turned right and maintained position 500 meters above the ground, one kilometer west of the road. Further away from the collective farm the retreating Soviets thinned out, with fewer vehicles. No one fired at the Storch.

The town of Gzhatsk appeared off the nose of the Storch. Shriver observed a roadblock on its outskirts and turned to point it out to Rommel. The general nodded, "Commissars preventing further retreat."

Shriver circled the Storch to the west, avoiding the cluster of Russians. They spotted infantry creeping around the sides, not in attack but desperate to slip away from the Party's enforcers of discipline.

"I have seen enough, return along the rail line from Vyazma to Sychevka," ordered Rommel.

Shriver turned west initially blinded by the descending sun. He eased the Storch's nose away from the glare. Near Vyazma they received ground fire. Shriver banked sharply to the north, advanced the throttle and descended to the tree tops. The Storch was unscathed.

"The Red Army hasn't broken at Vyazma," remarked Shriver.

"Let them stay there, they will be trapped," instructed Rommel. "We slam the door shut at Gzhatsk."

Shriver proceeded north to their origin at Sychevka. As they approached the antitank gun infested collective, a flight of Stukas took turns flattening the stronghold.

"Lieutenant, it is time to get on the ground," said Rommel.

"Jawohl, Herr General it is slow going…the wind has picked up considerably," replied Shriver.

Inwardly, Shriver became concerned that the wind speed and direction were going to result in a difficult crosswind scenario for landing. He was not going to share his fear with Rommel.

Rommel sensed Shriver's stress. As a pilot he was aware of the crosswind limitations of the Storch. "Waltraud, this landing doesn't need to be smooth. Just get us on the ground."

Shriver wiped sweat from his brow and dried his hands on his trousers. He ran through the landing checklist. The smoke from Sychevka indicated a strong northeast wind. The dirt road lined up northwest. He was facing a 90 degree crosswind.

Shriver slowed the Storch adding 20 degrees of flaps. He was afraid to go anywhere near full flaps, the wind seemed gusty and he did not want to stall if it suddenly decreased in intensity. He crabbed into the wind, planning to kick the left rudder over just before he flared with his right wing lowered into the wind.

Into the wind, the Storch crawled at a ground speed less than 50 kilometers an hour. Shriver glanced back at Rommel, who smiled and gave him the thumbs up signal.

The sunlight was fading quickly. He picked a section of the road bent more to the north to lessen the cross wind. Committed, he increased flaps to 40 degrees stepped on the left rudder and dipped the right wing.

The small right tire kissed the dirt perfectly. The Storch rode on it while the left wing hung in the air. Slowly, the left wing sank and its tire thumped on the road.

Rommel began to clap when the unthinkable occurred. The left tire caught a pot hole and grabbed, spinning the Storch. It departed the dirt track and crumbled into a ditch, the wooden and fabric right wing collapsing instantly. The Storch rolled on its side and stopped, as its ground speed was less than 40 kilometers per hour when the mishap sequence began.

Shriver felt warm liquid on his face and rubbed it off, realizing it was his own blood. He whipped around to Rommel. The general was peering at his right arm, which was hanging limply, his hand bent back an impossible angle.

"General, are you alright?" gasped Shriver.

Rommel did not answer. His eyes were open but were unfocused.

"Mein Gott," exclaimed Shriver. "General Rommel! Can you hear me?"

Shriver struggled to unfasten his belt and render aid to the general. He was pinned, unable to move. Tears streamed down his face, his life was ruined.

Shouting and tools ripping into the fabric fuselage startled Shriver. Unsurprisingly, the rescuers focused on freeing General Rommel. Shriver closed his eyes and waited, recognizing that death from loss of blood might be his best current option.

"Is General Rommel injured?" inquired someone in an officer's voice.

A sergeant pressed his face to the cockpit glass, his face inches from Shriver's.

"The Jew is alive. I can't see General Rommel's condition yet," responded the sergeant.

Shriver felt movement in the aircraft. Perhaps Rommel was alive!

"My arm is broken but otherwise I believe I am intact," rasped Rommel in an authoritative voice. "The pilot is Lieutenant Shriver, do not refer to him in any other manner…do you understand sergeant?'

"Jawohl, Herr General… we will remove you immediately," replied the sergeant sheepishly. "Medical aid is on the way."

"Very well, please have Captain Schmidt and Lieutenant Kleime brought to me immediately," barked Rommel.

"Immediately, Herr General…may I ask what battalion they are with?"

"They are assigned to *Kampfgruppe Schmidt* and they should be here in Sychevcka now," announced General Rommel. "And make sure Lieutenant Shriver is cared for…he made a spectacular landing under very difficult conditions."

Shriver smiled as he lost consciousness.

16

July 3, 1940   **Roman, Rumania**

Noise. Ianu clutched at his ears to block out the noise that pressed him as tight as the heat in the rail car. There were the sounds of dying – men coughing, pleading for water, gasping for breath in the scorching heat – sounds of living – praying for release from a God that had forsaken them, mindless chattering that went along with the slow descent into madness, begging for food that no one had – all of it keeping pace with the background noise of the heaving train, moving ever so slowly.

Ianu had noticed the lurch toward the west, Lev's promise of freedom in Russia a myth. The movement followed hours of being packed inside, shouts and gunfire revealing the fate of those unable or unwilling to meet their death in the heat and darkness. Ianu pushed through, squeezed by neighbors and strangers, short and tall, all lacking the room to do more than squirm, flesh packed firmly against flesh. The middle of the rail car was the worst, the air leaden as odors stung his nose and lungs and he gasped for air. As the sun reached its zenith, the heat pressed tight on them.

Those who had been without water were the first to grow clammy, legs buckling as they slid to the wooden floor, existence ground out by the weight of those who remained standing. Sinking to the floor meant certain death, the air more pungent and rarer, shoes crushing bones and eventually the will to live. As bodies sank, space opened but Ianu did not notice. His breaths were shallow and painful, heat draining the last moisture from him. He struggled in the direction of rail car's far side. He focused on the thin line of sunlight that pushed through the slats. Stumbling, holding onto other bodies, some light, others heavy as below him arms and legs plied his feet trying to pull him down. He ignored them, focusing on the sunlight. It meant air and survival, lungs desperate for relief as the air thickened.

Ianu stumbled struggling to free his leg, heat gripping him, sweat diminished to a trickle. He drove down his foot, meeting resistance then collapse, the crack of bone freed him. He stumbled on, pushed past swaying figures, some tumbling to the floor. His feet touched flesh, a moan told him they were alive, silence meant the heat had claimed another victim. He blinked as the sunlight streaming through the slats hit his eyes. He struggled to adjust in the uneven light, his pause saving him. Others had noticed the light and the air flowing through the holes in the rail car sides. The herd struggled toward it, pushing aside the weaker, elbowing the stronger then wrestling as they struggled to place their mouth over the opening. A shot rang out, bullets penetrating wood and prisoner before lodging in the far wall. Bodies pressed against the hole then eased into a sitting position, blocking sun, air and the life flowing from it. The shots set off more jostling but little movement.

Ianu remained still, heat scorched his skin, sweat requiring a mighty effort, the previous evening's moisture already squeezed from him. He tottered, knees buckling, the cushion below offering sleep, escape, freedom, death. Survival meant suffering, pain, loneliness and likely death. Another shot echoed through the rail car, another body slumped against an open space. The sound sent Ianu shaking, Saloman had been shot, the image of his father grasping his bleeding throat, eyes flickering pride, determination, all of it toward Ianu. Saloman wanted him to survive, for Manu and Joni, to teach them about the store, counting change, maintaining supplies even though the store no longer existed.

His right leg gave away, knee touching soft flesh, other knee buckling, dropping him among the live rags. He peered up, a few slivers of light poking from the top of the rail car. Ianu's body went limp, another shiver, this as his skin went clammy, unable to cool itself, heat crushing him, bodies moving to block the light as his space was occupied. He dropped onto all fours, body trembling, growing cold, shivers wracking him, mind swirling, vision darkening. It was the end.

He had felt the same during a trek from the farm to the store
with Joni. Their horse had thrown a shoe, refusing to move. It had
been a hot June afternoon, the nine year old Joni watched her older
brother sag, tumbling to the ground, clothes drenched but skin dry.
She had diagnosed immediately, her quick read of the medical book
taught her about heat stroke. Her diagnosis was matched by a cure,
he needed water and Joni had rushed to the town well, filled one of
Saloman's leaky buckets and poured the water over him then down
his throat. The sickness had passed, Joni talking during the entire
trek to the store, Ianu barely listening, the ringing in his ears
drowning out much of what she said.

Water. Ianu needed water but Joni was not there to deliver it.
With Saloman lying in the sun, with Manu suffering the same in one
of the rail cars there was no one to dump it over his head. Without
warning, Ianu's question went answered, a thin stream, warm and
uneven tumbled onto his head. Startled, Ianu opened his mouth,
sucking and swallowing, shaking his head to allow the liquid to cool
his skin. The rescue lasted only a few moments, Ianu then blinking,
eyes adjusting to the source. There was movement above him, one
of the larger men in the mob who had consumed four shoes full of
rainwater then protected his large puddle with force including
broken limbs and bruises for those who dared approach him. His
water hoarding had kept him and Ianu alive. Joni's words,
seemingly unheard and forgotten, rattled in his mind. A last resort to
fighting heat stroke was could be one's own discarded moisture,
sterile water, unpleasant but life preserving.

There was another stream, an oversized bladder emptying,
the warm flow soothing Ianu's throat, flowing into his nose, his eyes
then down his neck, skin cooling, heat dissipating, muscles regaining
some strength. A third and final burst flowed then was swallowed,
dwindling to a trickle, Ianu drenched but happy, the odor nothing
compared to the reeking car. Swallowing and licking his lips then

his hands, sheering the liquid from his head and cheeks, Ianu felt normal for a moment, the stifling heat breaking for a flash before pressing against him.

He was up, a miraculous recovery allowing him to stand, death suddenly unacceptable though the cure would always be secret. On his feet, Ianu looked about for his unusual benefactor but the oversized body had melted into the darkness, another shot forcing the herd away from the splintered wood of the rail car. Temporarily blinded Ianu was beset by moans for air and water, calls for "mother," howls of despair that accomplished nothing. The Iron Guard had plans for them, having rounded up the Jews for the train. The pile of occupied clothing, the mass of flesh at his feet, all of them were expected to die, the train a moving camp different than the German camps but with the same result. There would be no Rumanian ghetto where they could live and work until the inevitable. Even if they were, as Lev had said, shipped to Russia, little of what remained of the human cargo would be able to work, mere survival a miracle that could not be repeated.

The jerk of the train alleviated some of the heat, the slats producing a slight breeze but the movement shifted all of the bodies inside, Ianu's face pressed against matted hair, another shift slipping it into his mouth, oil, sweat and grime threatening to choke him. From behind came a hand, part of the struggle to remain upright, Ianu's shoulder a ledge to grasp before tumbling into the abyss. He tried to shake free, the added weight weakening him but the grasp remained. He shifted, trying to slip between two bodies but his shoulder remained locked. Sucking in the scorching air Ianu swung his leg, foot connecting with bone, a knee cap, producing a howl, shoulder released, the car having a bit more room even as the floor rose by a single body.

The train moved, afternoon sunlight shifted from afternoon, slowly shifting to the evening but the heat remained as confinement spread the insanity. From the door came cries, howls demanding to be freed then pleas and finally threats. The wood and metal became sounding boards, smacking with a dying furor, escape coming only when the doors were smashed. The desire to escape continued when the train trundled to a halt. Voices from outside were followed by shots, bullets splintered the wood, bodies propelled back, smacked into others. Ianu bent back as flesh pushed against him. Rage followed, those who survived the initial fusillade crashed into the doors followed by more shots and a new pile of occupied rags.

When the pounding of the door stopped so did the shooting, the once upraised voice mere moans, adrenaline fueled bodies sliding onto the floor lifeless, their purpose served. Ianu turned away, fearful he might spot familiar faces and forced to mourn the dead.

More time passed, the light from the slats dimmed. Ianu shifted, trying to find air but also to keep his blood flowing. A jerk marked the restarting of the train and it gathered momentum. Ianu swung around, spotted the body of the man who had sucked air then bullets. It remained but sagged. Once the train was moving there would be no more guards to shoot through the holes in the wall. He stumbled over, squeezing past swaying bodies, reaching then tugging free the body and assuming its position at the hole. One eye closed he watched as the countryside passed. No guards. He settled on the body he had displaced, mouth pressed against the hole. Fresh air.

17

July 5, 1940   **Paris**

"Sir, the ambassador."

Etienne refocused, the announcement jarring him back to reality and the foreign ministry. "Yes, ten minutes," and 300 kilometers. He had been chased back from the Riviera and Fiorenza who was prodding him to join her in Nice then Monte Carlo where her family was awaiting them. Time on the beaches with Fiorenza and her lack of inhibition was the cure for his ennui. Spending any time with the raucous crowd that was genetically tied to her made Francois and the foreign ministry seem like paradise on earth. Fiorenza dancing, her brothers coughing, Fiorenza swimming, her brothers-in-law importuning, it was a mix certain to destroy his love of the Mediterranean beaches.

His lunch with Lisle had prepared Etienne for the Germans. He had her in mind when he made the request the ambassador be accompanied by his chief military adjutant. The day after Lisle told him the meeting held no hope he was shaking hands with the hard faced adjutant who had swept Lisle from her feet. Sporting an aggressive Aryan nose and deep set eyes with hard combed blond hair, the adjutant wore the field gray Heer uniform like a second skin. There was no sign of a wrinkle, a matching pair of iron crosses lined his chest along with several decorations Etienne did not recognize. He imagined "untermenshcen" slid easily off the cracked lips as the ramrod straight body straightened into an even more painful tautness at Etienne's entrance.

Ambassador von Hotzendorf clicked his heels with Prussian formality even as his eyes searched Etienne's face for an explanation for the summons. Etienne motioned for the ambassador to sit, but did not extend the courtesy to the adjutant, the thought of the Nazi's hands on the lovely Lisle grating on his senses.

"The French government has received a request from the Soviet representative seeking an end to the hostilities with the German government."

Von Hotzendorf blinked, the possibility not having crossed his mind while being driven to the foreign ministry. He turned toward the adjutant, the news deflecting off the stern face without effect, the request not to be considered, untermenschen not worthy of negotiations. Von Hotzendorf required a few moments to gather his wits then asked a question for further delay. "They seek to surrender?"

Etienne in his brief tenure as a diplomat had developed the skill to deflect the ridiculous without revealing his true feelings. "No ambassador," he said. "They seek an armistice." He waited for the German's reaction though there was only one that he expected. From the embassy reports he knew the Wehrmacht had continued the march east, the Red Army buckling, Moscow on the horizon, victory not far beyond. The Bolsheviks began their revolution speaking confidently of the inevitability of victory and history being on their side. It seemed that history had turned against them.

Von Hotzendorf motioned the adjutant to his side, a brief, quiet conversation yielding little emotion then the adjutant was waved back to his place. "Is the French government interested in negotiating an armistice?"

Etienne recalled the brief conversation with Laval. Under no circumstances was he to offer to negotiate. Instead he was to act as a mere messenger, his paramount concern was to maintain French neutrality in any effort to end the war. "At this time we are conveying the Soviet government's desire for an end to the hostilities." It was Etienne the messenger rather than Etienne the peacemaker.

The ambassador mulled, then offered a non-answer, a 24 hour delay though would not change the result. A day later, nearly to the minute the ambassador returned and rejected the offer. It neither surprised nor displeased Etienne. Von Hotzendorf meetings offered him little joy and the Soviet ambassador chilled him. A day after the rejection he replied to the third hurried request for a meeting from the Soviets. Etienne wondered aloud to Francois if the Russians were so naïve to believe the Nazis would remove the boot from their throat. The analogy had confused his assistant, Francois puzzling over it much of the day before asking for an explanation.

The ten minutes was gone and Etienne was fully girded for the meeting, Francois hovered outside the meeting room. "There are two of them," he hissed.

Etienne motioned to the bit of rebellious hair poking from Francois scalp. "There are always two of them."

Francois reached up, eyes wide as Etienne pushed open the door and his assistant's words took on real meaning. There were three of them, two NKVD men position in shadows, finding them or creating their own, with the ambassador standing in their crosshairs. Etienne approached warily, step slowed by the four eyes, suddenly concerned if his answers meant the end of their ambassador. The Russian extended his hand, it was sheathed in perspiration, protocol prohibiting Etienne from cleaning his skin. "I have spoken with the German-."

"They have agreed to a-." A throat clearing behind silenced the ambassador, who bowed his head and awaited his fate.

"The German ambassador conveyed his government's unwillingness at this time to discuss a ceasefire or make any attempt to end hostilities between the German and Soviet states." Etienne breathed, the memorized lines recited perfectly on the twenty eighth and final attempt. He waited for a reaction, surprised at what he saw.

The Soviet's head rose, eyes forcing Etienne to retreat a step. Instead of fear there was satisfaction or calmness, fatality, expectations fulfilled. "Yes, of course. The Germans will not end hostilities." He approached Etienne, drenched hand making the Frenchman's skin wriggle. A throat clearing halted his progress, arms dropping to his side. "The Soviet government appreciates the foreign ministry's efforts in pursuing peace." The flat tone and gaze locked on his shoes said otherwise. "Can we rely on the foreign ministry remaining open to other requests?"

Etienne clenched his jaw, the Russian's perspiration starting to set in the crevices of his palm. "Uh, yes, yes, we will be available." A check of his watch." I am afraid I have a critical appointment in fewer than ten minutes." A quick bow and he was out, flexing his hand, leaving the Russian to his fate.

Francois was raised on his toes. "How did you know." He chirped.

"Towel?"

"Pardon?"

"Towel." Etienne held up his hand. "The Russian. He was perspiring. I must cleanse my hand." Francois dashed off and returned to find Etienne in the washroom beside his office. A towel was proferred, a thorough rubbing followed, curses below his breath, Etienne wondering if Laval recognized the sacrifices he made for France. Francois watched then repeated his question. "How did you know?"

Etienne eyed his assistant's reflection. "Know what Francois?"

"The meeting in ten minutes."

The towel fluttered to the floor. "Meeting?" Beside a lunch with Fiorenza to discuss their Riviera plans his afternoon was free.

"The ambassador from London."

Etienne sighed as he bent to retrieve the towel. "British ambassador."

"Pardon."

"It is the British ambassador not the ambassador from London."

"Oh yes. They seek a meeting."

"In ten minutes?"

"In ten minutes."

A nod, movement dislodging the balky hair from the side of Francois' head.

"And you agreed?"

"They said it was urgent."

Another sigh. The British and their urgent meetings. At times they were worse than the Americans. The Anglo Saxons and their demanding immediate attention. Etienne checked his watch. "They should be arriving." He sniffed as he fluffed the towel. "Do as the Americans say and 'put them on ice.'"

A frown from Francois but a wave of the towel drove off the assistant to decipher the cryptic orders. Etienne completed his hand cleansing, studies his face, tie and collar in the mirror then considered his options. In half an hour he was expected at Fiorenza's side, excuses unacceptable, the "London" ambassador on important diplomatic business earning a disdainful sniff if it meant his late arrival.

Lord Bainbridge, the stiff aristocrat would have to be hustled in and out, protocol demanding rapid deference but little else. There had been few meetings since Etienne declined to draw France into a losing war with the Germans. Little had been accomplished. A blockade of the Baltic ports yielded little beyond protests from neutrals. A few skirmishes on the high seas between the Royal Navy and Kreigsmarine had proven the former's superiority if it were ever doubted. The Germans had surrendered their colonies after the Great War, the British expanding their empire to the chagrin of the rest of the major powers. It left nothing for the Anglos to gobble up and unless they launched a seaborne invasion of the north German coast, their "phony" war would continue to be the butt of the editorial writers.

Lord Bainbridge was waving off a sizable glass of ice water offered by Francois, Etienne's assistant taking his suggestion to heart. A nod and the two men were soon alone. The Brit, age carved deep into his face, trembled with diplomatic anger, finger waved at Etienne in an undiplomatic pose. "The French government has been aiding the German government in receiving shipments of oil, chrome and rubber." The tremor in his voice spoke of a man losing a war his country had not even begun to fight.

"Aiding?" Etienne had perfected the questioning tone for his infrequent visits from the British. "I am uncertain to what you refer."

A long breath drawn through Bainbridge's nose revealed several obstructions and provoked a round of coughing. Drawing erect he snapped. "Through your ports in Marseille, Nice, Cherbourg."

"They are open ports and receive commerce from around the world."

"Their commerce in oil has increased 60 percent in the last six month. In rubber over 100 percent and over 130 percent in chrome in the same period."

"The end of the economic slump has had a beneficial effect on our economy. Automobile sales have increased dramatically. I can call in our economics ministers to provide the data."

Bainbridge snorted away the offer. His wrinkles collected as he prepared for a counteroffensive. "The German Army's petrol requirements are considerable. They exceed the output of the Ploesti oil fields."

Etienne looked beyond the ambassador, Rumanian oil output beyond his purview.

"We request the French government take steps to halt petrol, rubber and chrome shipments across the French/German borders and through French ports bound for Germany."

Etienne was not surprised by the demand. Reports of British agents skulking about French ports had crept onto his desk. French companies were eager to profit from the German need for war materiel. The Nazis paid handsomely for quick delivery for all three resources to ensure their drive to Moscow continued. Some of those excess profits were deposited into the pockets of French officials who stamped the necessary export documents or fended off British complaints about the commerce.

"France is neutral," Etienne reminded Bainbridge. "We trade with all the current combatants." He nodded at the ambassador. "I doubt the British government would be pleased if France ceased trade with the United Kingdom at the request of the German ambassador."

"His Majesty's government would prefer not to take action to prevent improper trade with Germany."

Etienne raised an eyebrow. The British were desperate. "I believe I misunderstood the British ambassador."

Bainbridge's wrinkles smoothed as he said what he came to say. "Continued trade with Germany will be considered an act of hostility toward the British Empire."

"An act of hostility." Etienne allowed the phrase to roll around on his tongue. "It is an infelicitous phrase. Possibly you can explain."

"The deputy foreign minister is perfectly capable of understanding my words." Bainbridge's chin shot up, aristocratic bearing learned from generations of practiced snobbery. "The Empire will not allow Germany to trade freely for war materiel. Sanctions will be imposed on every state that refuses to abide by our trade limits."

Etienne allowed the threats to recede. "We have no agreement with Britain to limit our trade with Germany or any other combatant state. We expect the Empire to respect the freedom of the seas."

Lord Bainbridge was not listening, his message delivered. "The British government also wishes to register its protest of German warships using French ports in the Caribbean and Pacific Ocean. As a neutral state France must refuse access to all warships of belligerent states in its ports."

Etienne had expected the protest. "The warships were granted limited landing rights for obtaining humanitarian supplies."

"And the submarine base in Fort Dauphin."

Etienne frowned. "I am unfamiliar with -."

"The Royal Navy reports German U boats along the northern coast of Madagascar. There are further reports of German naval officers in the Fort Dauphin area."

Etienne shifted his weight. "I know nothing of this. I will speak to the colonial minister." He fixed the ambassador with his steeliest gaze. "It is unacceptable for the Kreigsmarine to use any French facility as a base."

For a moment the mask slid from Bainbridge, Etienne's sincerity convincing. Unfortunately for both men he spoke only for himself and not for the entire French government. After a few moments the frozen relations returned. "If the French government has not taken formidable and immediate action on these questions within three days His Majesty's government will be forced into stringent countermeasures to prevent further unrestricted trade with Germany."

Etienne nodded. "I will pass you concerns onto Minister Laval," he said. Bainbridge swung to leave. "Mr. Ambassador." Etienne stopped him. "I wish to convey a concern of this government that the British government is seeking to dictate economic and military policy of every country around the world. The French Republic will not be dictated to by any country, including Britain."

Bainbridge puffed out his chest. Etienne nodded and the two men parted. Francois rushed in several moments later. "He was angry."

"As am I," Etienne breathed. He checked his watch and realized he had a more dangerous crisis on his hands, he was late for Fiorenza.

18

July 6, 1940   **Roman, Rumania**

Nightfall. The passing of day into night was the only connection Ianu had with the world outside the rail car. Darkness descended on the trundling machinery, the early July days refused to die, driving the heat in the railcars, relief granted only when the next dawn beckoned.

Two days had passed, Ianu suffering through the heat and welcoming dusk, the early evening usually consumed by thunderstorms. As the rain poured he cupped his hands to catch the water as it rushed through the slats. He peeled the wood around the air hole to slip his folded palm through the wall to catch water flowing from the top of the rail car. He even used his good shoe to catch the water, its taste reminding him of when a small animal had fallen into the well and died. In better days he would have spit out the tainted water, but in the railcar he gulped it, then later in the day possibly urinate in his shoe for a second drink.

As darkness closed around him, he sat, mouth at the air hole. Each day there was more space, the train stopping, some of the dead tugged free. Those who remained were locked into their own world, hypnotized into silence by the swaying rail cars and the clacking of the rails. Occasionally one of the sick moaned, expending a final burst of energy to announce their existence. Ianu hunched over his hole, praying no one would notice his tiny window to the outside world. When the train slowed or stopped he fell away from it, the sound of guards bringing the threat of gunfire.

On his second day their first stop had been a town, the volume of conversations and the sounds of horses announcing civilization. He dared not peek. A Jewish eye peering at them might provoke the guards. He guessed they were in Roman, the second stop in the village in the last three days. He knew that moving left to right was toward Iasi, right to left away from it, but little else.

Sucking in the air as the train moved, he recalled dashing beside one of the monsters, keeping pace until the engineer pushed the engines, eventually leaving Ianu and his friends watching it skim down the rails, a wisp of smoke becoming the only proof of its existence. Ianu guessed at the pace of the railcars he could have remained running beside the train for several kilometers, the machine limping toward a new - and old – destination every day. Even the insects, the grasshoppers and cicadas seemed faster, their calls starting, finishing then restarting as the train struggled forward through the heat. Their irregular sounds soothed Ianu, reminding him of more normal days.

Ianu tried to nap in the day, the heat tiring him. The second day he was awakened by more voices, some harsh and official, others restrained, all of them moving around the train cars. He dared not look, a sharp eyed guard able to spot a Jew even from a distance. The voices receded, untethered sunlight, sanity and survival threatened by the gathering heat.

Even with removal of some bodies, those that remained began to swell, flesh liquefying as the gasses building up inside burst through. The scent ripped at his stomach, Ianu wanting to vomit, but the sunflower seeds from earlier long had left him.

The heat sped putrefaction, another word gleaned from Joni who explained the disintegration of a bird that had been trapped in their barn and died. The sight of the squirming worms – Joni identified them as maggots – sickened Ianu but not his sister who tossed off the usual female squeamishness and probed at the bird's remains with a stick. It had split open, the maggots spreading over the ground. Ianu hopped away and brushed off imaginary worms.

She trapped one of the squirmers between two sticks and held it up to a blanching Ianu as she explained the cycle of life. Ianu had barely listened, eyes closed until the worm was dropped on the bird.

The scent sharpened the memory, Ianu shuddered as he thought of the wiggling worms on the bursting corpses.

The voices moved to the opposite side of the rail car to where the door had been sealed shut to allow the squirming worms to perform their part of the life cycle. Ianu tensed, listening as locks were pulled apart, latches separated. Another removal or worse additions to the rail car. The growl of grating metal stopped, replaced by cursing, yelling then a gun shot. Metal and wood were scraped with more ferocity, the door slowly pulled open, light streaming into the car. It vomited out the occupied rags, producing more curses but no gunshots. No one appeared, prisoner or guard, only a rush of cooler air, fresh air, Ianu's hole losing its value.

The light and air drew protests, groans and shielded eyes. There was stirring, rags rising, their owners tumbling, days of lying leaving weakened legs. Some crawled, making their way through the mounds, toward the door. Ianu remained in place, doubting the door was escape. Instead he sank into the bodies, decay threatening his senses, making him bite his lip while pinching his nose.

"Water, water." The call came from outside. "Water, water." Ianu raised his head, squinting in the light and spotting the purported bane of every Rumanian's existence – gypsies. Silhouetted in the sunlight, they held branches toward the train. "Water, water."

Ianu's legs faltered as he tried to rise, joints balking at any weight. Crawling he approached the door, blinking and gaping at the sight of gypsies selling water to the prisoners. "Who has money," he thought, throat too dry to allow him to speak. Jamming his hands into his pockets he found nothing. Saloman and Manu had special pockets in their pants to hide money but his father was gone.

Manu. Ianu squinted in the sunlight, seized with hope. Manu was in the next rail car, he could pay for the water, he would survive. The gypsies selling briskly, a dirty rag drenched with water earning 50 Lei, a tin cup purchased with 200 Lei. Not all of those in the rail car were as unprepared as Ianu.

The rags went quickly. The torn fabric was held above the head, twisted, water dripping into gaping mouths. Ianu crawled to the side of one of the fortunate, hoping their shaky hands might spray water onto him. The prisoners, though, proved stronger, hands steady, water slopping into their mouth, rag twisted nearly dry then tossed to the gypsies to be resoaked. This set off a frenzy, those lacking Lei scrambling to touch the damp rag, snatch at it and try to twist out a few spare drops. The rags tore, infuriating the gypsies who smacked at hands with their sticks, drawing blood but not slowing the scramble for moisture.

Ianu was not one of them. Never big like Manu he had never won a fight as a boy and two days without meaningful food left him even weaker. He sagged, unable to watch the water so close but so far. Ianu clung to his stomach, plagued with the thought Saloman had been the fortunate one, taking the bullet. He could do the same, fight his way from the rail car and attempt escape. The guards would shoot him down within a few meters. The thoughts were pushed from his mind by a hefty body shoved against him.

It was Lev, nursing a cup of water, his money followed him no matter where he traveled. "Ianu." His voice was scratchy, worn, the moisture having little effect. A drop hung on his chin, teasing Ianu until Lev's tongue swept it into his mouth. "The gypsies," he gasped. "It is the first time I am glad to see them." He finished the cup, smacking the bottom to drive out the last of the water then using his finger to sweep away any stray drops. He lumbered back to the door, steps producing groans and the occasional snap as he struck something still living on the floor. Lev did not seem to notice, water livening him, his status in town remaining in the rail car. He returned, cup filled again, teetering over Ianu, hands shaking.

"They are loading more Jews, we are headed east again, to Russia." Lev tipped back the cup, water rushing into his mouth. Ianu cocked his head to catch a stray drop. One poised on Lev's gristled chin only to be caught on Lev's hand, his tongue sweeping it between his lips. Another speck escaped, briefly wetting Ianu's upper lip only to evaporate in the heat of the rail car.

"We are the lucky ones," Lev said. Ianu flinched, the bodies piled in the rail car, pungent odor burning his nose, throat raw. "One of them is from Iasi." He motioned with his cup to the pile at the far end. "The Jews were sent to the city square. The Iron Guard used machine guns on them."

Ianu choked as he tried to swallow. Iasi. Uncle Liviu was convinced he could survive the Iron Guard because of his barges.

"They resisted." The water had revived old Lev, his size allowing him to ignore food, draining fat from his system. "They should have -." Lev was interrupted by a burst of sound from the open door. One of the cups had been snatched from the gypsies without payment. A tug of war ensued, two pairs of hands pulling the liquid toward the rail car, another trying to keep it out. The single pair enjoyed an advantage, a weapon hidden by the glare of the sun. It was swung, a howl of pain marked it hitting flesh, one of the prisoners sinking back, head dropping, blood flowing. The hatchet was swung again, but the second pair of hands proved more resilient. Another blow then another, blood spurted but the fingers remained firm around the metal cup. The weapon was aimed with greater precision and a final blow found its mark. The ragged figure tumbled, hurtling past Ianu who spotted the rough hewn hatchet that had delivered the coup de grace. The hatchet remained, sitting crookedly in the skull.

The door closed, the sound of metal grinding metal ending any hope of escape. Ianu dropped to his hands and knees, needing to return to his air hole. He avoided the battle that had broken out over one of the damp rags, desperate hands tearing at it, trying to squeeze free a few drops of moisture. Ianu returned to his air hole, sucking in fresh air until voices sounded. He pulled away, the gypsies having returned with water not yet sold.

They settled at the far end of the car where a high mound of occupied clothing blocked a crack in the side of the car. A rush ensued, bodies dragged away, disintegrating as they were touched, bits of flesh smacking Ianu in the face. He turned and shivered at the feel of what had once been human.

Across the rail car fingers scrabbled at the wood. A small opening was created and a stick poked through, producing an exchange. Mildewed, bloodied and gnarled Lei were pushed through the hole, a rag jabbed inside and was ripped to shreds during another wrestling match. In the semi darkness feral instinct seized the moment, thirsty mouths open, bits of the rag jammed inside, hands scratching and pulling as the moisture was sucked greedily from the cloth.

Ianu watched through narrowed eyes, frightened by the sounds and the occasional flashes as the men touched the slivers of light from outside. For a moment his thirst receded, the burning in his mouth and throat temporarily calmed by the grunting then the sounds of bone meeting wood. A head flashed across a sliver of light then the sickening sound marked a skull being crushed, a head sliding to one side to join the disintegrating pile. Another exchange with the gypsies provoked more battling.

"They are losing their minds." Lev's voice croaked from the darkness. "It is best to stay away."

Ianu clung to his spot. Survival required a steady mind. He cast aside thoughts of Saloman, his uncle or even Manu, alone and suffering in a rail car only a few meters from him. He thought of

Joni, sensing she was free and teaching their mother one of her lessons of life. During Ianu's rides to Iasi, Joni pointed out the animals, irritating her brother, a streak of jealousy tinging their journeys. He had bristled at Joni the favorite, Joni the wise, Joni who could go to the university and not be locked into a life of drudgery in Letcani, counting change for elderly widows. Joni excelled even at that, able to run the counter – and the store – absent her two older brothers.

He tried to relive her words, difficult as Ianu had not always listened, filling in with his own. There had been words – Latin – which he could not understand or recall. Trying to fill in the gaps focused his mind, removed it from the aching and burning, the odors and noises that pervaded the rail car.

Angry shouts from inside ceased for a moment as an exchange was offered, except this time it was not the gypsies on the other side of the rail car. A scream, a hand withdrawn, more of a stump, the victim tumbling back, spared the bullets as a gun barrel was poked through the hole and fired into the darkness. Squeals and falling bodies marked where lead found flesh.

The train rumbled beneath him, stopping, starting, jerking, movement relaxing him. A few moans sounded from the far end of the rail car, some cursed because a bullet found its mark, delirium seized control, bloody infections, a brief burst of chattering, crying then silence.

A voice cried out, drawing shouts of silence. "They are here, shoot them, shoot them." The orders coming from a world no one in the car knew. "It hurts, cut it off, cut it off." A strangled gasp followed then silence.

Ianu jerked from the sound, flinching as his shoulder landed against the wall of the train car. Below him the bodies shifted as they swelled. The air hole, the breeze produced by the train moving kept his sanity. Morning was bearable, afternoon drawing retching, and the agony of death. The dirty rags had contained more than water, the temptation deadly for those already weakened by hunger and thirst. The retching came in waves though Ianu doubted they were vomiting anything, no food in three days leaving little to expel. As the heat built, the retching slowed then stopped, surrender to the inevitable more space to the survivors.

The sun bore down on the car, Iana wobbling, hand finding the wiggling worms that sickened him when he saw them with Joni. He allowed them to wriggle in his hand, the hunger stabbing and tempting him, a reminder of the cycle of life, protein according to Joni. He could not, tossing them aside. The train jerked, unusual during the daytime, the guards seemed to enjoy keeping them stationary, afternoon sun more torturous when sitting. Ianu sucked air then peered through the hole, trying to recognize the sliver of the real world. Nothing was familiar, fields worked, forests offering some shade and coolness, but no towns that might reveal their location or destination.

Ianu struggled with his new world, the train that traveled nowhere. They had no destination, Lev was wrong, the bearded dissenter was right. It was a train to nowhere, the tracks a means to keep them prisoners close to death. The gypsies had simply been additional torture, water little more than poison, those who did not drink learning the difficult lesson that help brought only death.

Afternoon to evening to night, but no rain as the train trundled to a halt. Mouth open, his throat growing rawer with every breath, Ianu struggled to flex his jaw, the lack of moisture stiffening the skin around his mouth and lips.

The open mouthed ghoul who had sucked air from a hole in the car did not move, did not notice the intruder that squeezed through the opening. The train had halted, the odor of decay penetrating through the boxcars, rural Rumania's smallest residents swept toward the train. The first entered Ianu's ear then his mouth and he jerked awake. Threatened with choking he clenched his jaw, teeth grinding the creature, the hardened body producing substance and moisture. The creatures struggled, wriggling as they cascaded down his throat. Ianu dared not spit out the protein, instead he bit harder, chewing them into a thick paste, the remains working down his raw throat.

Ianu's stomach rumbled at the unexpected treat, adrenaline flowed and he began flailing his arms, scooping up the creatures and jamming them into his mouth before it wriggle free. After several minutes his head cleared and he realized he was surviving off the scourge of Rumanian farmers – grasshopper. The train had halted somewhere in the fields where the pests congregated for their destructive efforts. The scent of flesh attracted them, much as they would consume dead animals at a furious pace, they could do the same to human bodies piled high in the rail car.

Ianu snatched the grasshoppers in both hands. He crunched down hard on one, the chewing drowned out the cries, except for one.

"Ianu." Only one person in the train knew his name. "Ianu." It was a mere croak but close.

"Lev?" Ianu choked down his meal, stomach churning.

"Ianu?" The large man, so determined to better his life, flapped his arm, striking Ianu's hand and rescuing several agitated grasshoppers. "What is it?"

Ianu did not know, could not know what was streaming through Lev's mind. He did know that the first food he had in day would soon escape if he did not continue scooping it into his mouth and suddenly balky stomach. He did not answer.

"What is it, what is it -?" Lev was cut off by a tremendous retch, the last sound he would ever make.

Ianu's meal would be interrupted, this time by the train which clambered into a slow jog. He rushed to find as many grasshoppers as possible, realizing as the train moved the grasshoppers would be left behind. His mouth and throat coated, he leaned against the side of the rail car, thirst returning but the night brought no relief.

He woke in the morning to a face full of water. The rain was coming in sheets, lashing at the sides of the railcar, Ianu's mouth nearly full, choking, water spilling from his face. He scrambled for his shoe, drinking without tasting. Time was another, the rain seeming to follow the train's path. Death, life, death and life again. Ianu dared not revel in his good fortune, the streams of liquid likely not to be repeated anytime soon if ever. The worst was the rekindling of a normal thirst, dehydration ensuring there was never enough water. It also unclogged his senses, reminding him through his nose, his ears, his tongue of his plight. Then as quickly as it began it stopped.

"You." Ianu jerked as his ankle was snatched. He looked down, spotting the veined hand and the craggy fingers that had wrapped around his bone. In the first hours of riding the train he would have stomped the fingers and shaken free but this day, so many hours into his journey he craved some human contact, a touch, a voice, someone to pour out his suffering, much like he would have to Saloman.

"You ran the store." The voice rasped, it owner sucking air into rebellious lungs. "The Cohnescus."

Letcani. The name rang in his ears. Home, normalcy, paradise. Ianu shuddered, closing his eyes to shut off the sudden threat of tears made possible by the rains.

"Your father." The hand began to creep up his leg.

Ianu swallowed, unable to say the truth – Saloman was dead. He reached to the wall of the railway car, steadying himself and tried to help his feeble companion to his feet but the old man sagged back to the floor of the railcar. Ianu's knees buckled, strength diminished, a burst of adrenaline worn off as the heat pressed onto him.

"Your sister." The croak from the darkness triggered a painful memory.

"Joni," Ianu said. "You knew her?"

"Smart." The croak had strengthened, Ianu's sister having that effect on many. "She always had something to say."

Ianu sucked on his lips. Embarrassed by past envy of his youngest sibling he would surrender much to hear her reveal some obscure knowledge.

"Were you at Iasi?" The fingers halted their assent just below the kneecap.

Ianu's ears perked up. Iasi was to be their savior, the urban Jew protected from the ignorant and superstitious rural Rumanian. This was the second time his uncle's home city was mentioned though again he held out little hope of reaching it. "No," he said.

"They are all dead." The fingers began slipping toward Ianu's ankle. "The Iron Guard gathered the Jews together and shot them." The finger's rolled onto his shoes. "Some of us escaped to this train."

Glancing about the rail car he had never imagined it as an escape. "You saw this?"

No response. Ianu shook his leg free of the man's grip and crawled away, feet cracking bones beneath him occasionally sinking into swelled flesh. He dropped to his air hole, sucking in the fresh oxygen, kicking at anything that touched him. The rolling, jolting train caused the random arm or leg to break free from the pile as if its owner were alive. Ianu created his own space, free of human contact and tried to make sense of the latest news.

The Jews had been killed in Iasi. Ianu struggled to believe his uncle and brother could bribe themselves free of the Iron Guard. Ianu wondered if any amount of money could keep the Iron Guard from their determination to eliminate the Jews of Rumania. Sucking through his air hole, reality hit him. He was alone. His uncle and older brother probably rounded up in Iasi, Manu might have survived in the rail car a few meters from him. His mother and Joni along with Saloman having disappeared into the maw that was the Iron Guard.

Voices shook him, raised voices that accompanied the return of the heat. Ianu backed from his air hole, pushing to his feet beside a raised mound of bodies, a buffer in case the soldiers decided to fire into the rail car. Balancing on the bones of the dead he strained to make out the voices. The last time he heard so much talking the gypsies had shoved tainted water in the direction of desperate men.

The sounds waxed and waned, men moving along the entire length of the train before crossing to the opposite side. The sound of groaning metal in the distance marked the opening of rail cars either to free those inside or to add more bodies to the suffering. Ianu listened for the doors to his car to open, certain to provide a buffer from those entering. The other survivors were more daring, edging toward from the light as the rail car door was slid open. They were confronted with the edge of the car, dropping to the ground only to be raised by their scalp as the bodies of the dead tumbled from the train.

"Get, get." The prisoners' heads were jerked and pressed close to the corpses, noses close to the valuables remaining on the dead.

Ianu edged forward. He watched the prisoner drop to his knees, fingers clawing at one of the bodies, fumbling with a watch hanging on an emaciated wrist. He struggled with the clasp, the metal rusted from perspiration. The prisoner tugged, fingers slipping from the metal, breath coming faster. He was an older man, one of the few his age to survive, skin an ashen gray, cheeks sunken. Ianu jumped as a shot ended his efforts and another prisoner was dragged by his ankles from the rail car and dropped at the wrist and the newly cooling body.

The new prisoner was younger and stronger. He planted his foot against the corpse's torso and tugged with youthful might but the watch remained hooked on the limp wrist. Another shot, the guards tiring of the ineffectual struggle. A third prisoner, this one realizing his fate had been decided, pushed aside the guards and dashed toward a crowd of gypsies watching the scene. The soldier aimed, poorly, one, two, three, four, five gypsies falling before the prisoner was hit. Several more shots ended the misery and the guards, faces grimy with sweat and marked with frustration sought another prisoner. The gypsies ranged over their fallen comrades, plundering their still warm corpses.

The next prisoner proved more difficult. The rail car offering safety where it had once offered only death. Shots echoed inside, soldiers determined to find a Jew capable of scavenging bodies. Ianu rushed into the darkness but it offered little safety, the soldiers jumping inside, firing wildly. Splinters and flesh flew, forcing Ianu to the floor, scooting among the bloated corpses, soon covered in blood and the detritus of death. He was soon exposed and tugged onto the ground to become the next prisoner to face the conundrum of the watch. Shoved face first into the much abused body, Ianu trembled, trying to blot out the sight of the guns aimed at his head and torso. At such close range even the poor shooting Rumanian soldiers could find their mark.

"Get, get." The demand set Ianu glancing about for a solution. He wrapped his fingers around the bony wrist holding the watch, skin flaccid almost as if ready to be pulled free from the arm. The skin remained, the guards beginning to shift their weight from foot to foot, a sign of losing their patience. Ianu then spotted one of the bodies, head split earlier by the hatchet thrown by one of the gypsies. He scooted toward it, not too quickly so as not to startle a guard then began wrestling with the tool that was wedged in the skull. He removed it and returned to the body and the recalcitrant watch.

He swung the hatchet, driving the blade into the wrist, a howl of pleasure circled the guards, pleased by the Jew and his eagerness to extract the gold from the dead. The first blow glanced off the wrist. Ianu fumbled, hand grimy and slick. Sucking in air he pressed the handle between his palms, interlocking his fingers and drove the blade into bone. A crack and the blade wedged in the slit. He wriggled it free, raised the hatchet and struck another blow, this one deeper, forcing him to press his hand against the blade to extract it. He lifted it again, the hand now hanging loosely by a single tendon and the suddenly tough skin. A drop landed on Ianu's cheek, he jumped, wiped it from his face then gaped at the red smudge on his fingertip. Blood. He jerked his head and noticed the trickle from the arm pooling in the dirt. The watch's owner remained alive.

"Get, get." A shove in his back led Ianu to drive the blade into the tendon, slicing it and tearing the skin. The watch was easily removed and handed over to the pleased guard who raised it toward the sky, nodding at his latest prize. The celebration was brief, there were more bodies, more gold to collect. Ianu was raised by his scalp.

He stifled his cries, pain soothed when he was dumped onto another body.

"Get, get." This time it was rings, fingers easier to loosen with the hatchet even as they were more numerous. Ianu raised the blade and lapped off the wrinkled digits, offering the gold to the guard. Four fingers, four rings, another body, the ease of his task blotting out reality. The next body was that of a woman requiring the removal of fingers and ears followed by a fourth and fifth, Ianu's rail car yielding an abundance of wealth.

He was not the only one as others from the cars joined the ranks of workers, the occasional shot marking failure. Ianu saw the bearded dissenter, the one certain they were not headed to Russia but rather a camp. He used a sharpened tool, a knife, requiring cutting rather than hacking, but he proved able, sliding across the bodies as the guards jockeyed to be close when he finished his task.

The day moved on, Ianu allowed to stop only when darkness made further plunder impossible. He was collected with the others, Ianu counting several dozen, who were herded into a field for sleep. He required nothing beyond the earth, the fresh air and the sky. He had survived, one of the few Jews of Letcani.

19

July 6, 1940   **Chicago**

Westbrook Pegler was not a fan of Chicago, but his job and a hefty expense account beckoned him to the windy city. His Philadelphia reporting earned him praise from above and a contract extension with Scripps Howard along with the assignment to cover the coronation of Franklin Roosevelt for what the Democrats believed would be a lifetime term in office.

It had been a confusing spring for the party as they struggled to read the Sphinx's mind. Roosevelt declaimed any interest in overturning Washington's two term precedent, but allowed his name be placed on primary ballots while giving the cold shoulder to anyone who dared run against him. Pegler commented on the scene, never fooled by Roosevelt's denials and knowing the president wanted to be carried to a third term on the shoulders of cheering public rather than be forced to sink to the level of dirty campaigner.

The third term movement was in full swing, offering the Republicans a campaign issue. The Democrats sneered "Better a third termer than a third rater," as the Republican convention closed. Pegler disagreed Arthur Vandenberg was a third rater but admitted the phrase enjoyed a certain cachet.

Chicago added to the feel of a coronation. Mayor Kelly received his title partly because of famed Rooseveltian luck. A deranged gunman in Miami shot at the president elect in 1933, missing the immobile Roosevelt, but killing Anton Cermak, newly elected Chicago mayor. With a major obstacle eliminated, Kelly ran the Chicago machine with the efficiency of the Capone gang but with less violence. In return for Roosevelt's "aid" Kelly was pulling out all of the stops, packing the Chicago convention gallery with FDR supporters, mainly municipal employees provided several days off to shout as instructed.

As with the Republican convention, Pegler joined other reporters on the train ride to Chicago though there were no presidential pools. No one was willing to flush their money by betting against Roosevelt or his first ballot nomination. There was some talk of a vice presidential pool but it was not the same.

Pegler and his colleagues arrived on Monday afternoon with plans to leave on Friday, their convention stories posted. Pegler's story left blanks for the delegate vote totals and the exact time of the nomination and speeches. Without real news to report, their days would not be spent in the convention hall or hotel lobbies, but rather bar hopping on Rush Street, reinvigorated nearly a decade after Prohibition. Unfortunately the preordained outcome also kept pols out of the bars, not present to buy drinks for reporters in return for a kind word in an article. Without the booze flowing, the celebration faltered, Pegler and his fellow scribblers reduced to paying for their own drinks, slowing the pace of sales while ensuring coherent conversations.

A gaggle of reporters were at the Lake Michigan tavern, its frosted windows and a variety of pool tables and dartboards attracting blue and white collar drinkers alike. Pegler was opposite Bennet, the two men holding court over younger reporters.

"Who you got for vice president?" Bennet asked the fair haired boys and single wizened face.

There was no consensus, some had Robert Jackson, a couple for Cordell Hull, others for Indiana Governor Paul McNutt – though Pegler suspected his unfortunate name would be ruthlessly heckled on the campaign front – while others had Jesse Jones or Jimmy Byrnes with Harold Ickes and Henry Wallace taking up the rear. Pegler laughingly offered up Cactus Jack Garner, the sitting vice president whose feuds with Roosevelt and attempt to succeed him had made the old Texan *persona non grata* with the New Dealers. The suggestion drew laughter but also offered an opening.

"Vandenberg has not been doing much," he said, more interested in the real campaign than the faux one playing out in Chicago.

The comment drew almost as much laughter as his Garner comment. The political press had written off Vandenberg, except for the few writers who were paid to say otherwise by their publishers.

Even Bennet, more open minded than most, could not stomach a President Vandenberg.

"That name," one said. "Reminds people of greedy old Cornelius Vanderbilt."

Another youngster, still sporting freckles as a stringer for the Associated Press, agreed. "Next thing you will say that old Joe Kennedy's boy will be president."

More laughter. Joe Kennedy had also hit the New Dealers shit list. As ambassador to Britain he had said too many nice things about the Nazis while his inherent Irish dislike of the British had shown through, irritating politicians on both sides of the Atlantic. His political future all but destroyed, Kennedy survived only because of his influence with the Irish Catholic vote.

"Vandenberg can't win," another youth said, this one writing for the Hearst syndicate. "He split the party with his isolationism. William Allen White and the Committee to Defend America have come out for Roosevelt."

Pegler sputtered at the mention of White, publisher of the Emporia Kansas Gazette who enjoyed little influence. The newspapers were filled with stories of the Wehrmacht descending on Moscow, the communists fleeing east and panic gripping the country. Pegler grunted. "Once the Russians are beaten the Germans will run Europe. We aren't going to take the American Army and chase the Nazis from the Rhine to the Volga even if the French are with us,"

"The French will be with us," another reporter murmured, the old man of the group, barely touching thirty and already bearing the reputation for leaking stories favorable to the White House. "They remember what we did for them in the Great War."

A groan sounded. There was much speculation across the pond about French intentions. Some thought a western war was inevitable, others suspected the French were waiting for the final Soviet collapse before joining the Axis. Few trusted its government much less its independence and loyalty to former allies.

"Maybe the Russians will halt them at Moscow." This from a reporter known more for his wine palate than his military knowledge.

Bennet was the first to shoot down the possibility. "Stalin is done, a lot of the leadership has been killed off. I heard as many as two million Russians have surrendered and at least another million have been killed in about two months."

Several low whistles sounded around the group. A million casualties were a lot to Americans who had not lost that in a century and half of wars. For the Russians it was just another zero in centuries of casualties from invaders east, west, north, south.

"The Nazis will kill every communist they can reach and I don't know who can stop them."

There was silence, Pegler having done the inexcusable, defending Hitler, or at least the Nazis or worse yet not defending Stalin and the Bolsheviks. None of the reporters knew of the exact offense, but it was one they were certain not to copy. Bennet, recognizing discomfort, switched to a more familiar subject. "What about the VP?"

The debate was rekindled eventually settling on Wallace and Jimmy Byrnes. Pegler only listened, distracted by a pretty face. He had caught the eye of a brunette sitting several feet away, listening to the boisterous reporters, nodding on occasion then focusing on the eldest of the group. Pegler knew the glance well, having seen it used by his colleagues during his sports writing days. Athletes had their female fans but only so much stamina and for some women, sportswriters were a satisfactory substitute.

"Hey," Bennet poked at Pegler. "Need a refill?" He nodded at Pegler's nearly empty glass.

"Hell yeah," replied Pegler as he shifted his gaze back to Bennet, ready to argue the merits of Henry Wallace. "This convention is like watching grass grow."

20

July 6, 1940   **West of Bryansk, Russia**

"Herr Hauptsturmfuhrer." Reichenau raised his eyes from the brown bread that was his midday meal. He and his men were in transit, sent south on an important mission in the direction of Bryansk. The mission required speed and little time for luxuries such as edible food, something he had missed in the two days he had been pointed south and east. Part of Einsatzgruppen A, Reichenau had seen his professional mission as well as his personal situation change dramatically in the previous weeks. A veteran of the Great War, Reichenau had retired to the family lands in East Prussia. He had remained a farmer until the invasion of Poland, but too old for regular duty he feared losing his last chance at military glory. His opportunity came with the formation of special groups raised for deployment in the east. The Einsatzgruppen sought experienced, capable men dedicated to the ideals of National Socialism and who would not otherwise be eligible to fight with the Wehrmacht,

"Ja, Rottenfuhrer?" Reichenau said. The corporal had repeated the captain's slip of the tongue in Velikye Luki that their task was the "extermination" of the Russians. Suddenly under suspicion for "unreliability," Reichenau was rescued by an unexpected ally, Strauss. SS Rottenfuhrer Strauss spoke loudly and fervently for his commander, declaring him dedicated to the Fuhrer Order to erase untermenschen from the newly captured eastern territories. Strauss' words helped end the inquiry, but placed the captain in the unwanted position of owing him. Reichenau realized keeping Strauss happy meant unleashing him on the populations in their path, the corporal killing without discrimination as the Einsatzgruppen cut a swath through Belorussia and the northwestern territories of Russia. They left villages burning, refugees fleeing for their lives and a civilian casualty total that further strengthened Strauss' reputation.

Strauss mixed well with the motley collection of Baltic Germans and others who joined the squads determined to cleanse the soil of "Ostland" for future settlement. Estonians, Latvians, and Lithuanians, all enjoying various mixtures of German blood, were combined with Poles and White Russians to carry out the mission. Reichenau's men offered the impetus and direction for the "volunteers" who conducted much of the cleansing. Strauss eagerly joined the small squads in their endeavor, much as he had in Poland.

Reichenau's unit's efficiency earned them the new assignment to the Bryansk Oblast, recently captured but not yet cleared of Red Army deserters turned partisans. Major Schmundt delivered the news to Reichenau at his command post near the Latvian border. Standing outside a former school house, Schmundt spread a map on a wooden table, plate with two sausages and slick of mustard keeping the paper in place against the wind. It was the first time the captain had seen the major use a map, his usual orders involving a particular village, forest or road. Facing a mostly disorganized enemy, Schmundt did not require the detailed tactical maps of his army counterparts. Misplaced orders might lead to the destruction of the wrong village but the correct one would suffer the same the next day. Strauss was another who did not need maps, he could sniff out the untermenschen and kill them regardless of their location.

"Attacks." Schmundt's stubby finger pointed to the Bryansk Oblast. The point was marked by a greasy smudge, the remains of one already consumed sausage.

"Terrorists," Reichenau murmured.

Schmundt was uninterested in labels. "The army is moving on Moscow. Its supply lines must be secured, the roads and railways must be protected. Our rail repair crews are regauging the railways but work has stopped in this area after several attacks."

Reichenau listened to Schmundt's words which could be trimmed to a simple command – unleash Strauss on the guilty and innocent between Smolensk and Bryansk. "Strauss," he murmured.

The major reached for his fork, poking at one of the two remaining sausages. "This comes from above. Our sector is the quietest in Russia."

"My sector is the emptiest in Russia."

The major had ignored the comment, instead focusing on sweeping enough mustard from the plate and onto his sausage, a yellow splotch dropping onto then spreading across the map. "Not all are pleased with men like Rottenfuhrer Strauss," he murmured, tearing at the sausage skin with his teeth. Schmundt chewed as Reichenau waited for an explanation.

The major motioned to the map, drops of grease marking his path. "There are groups, potential allies who share our views of the Bolsheviks. Berlin believes they would be helpful in pacifying the locals while securing our supply lines."

"These groups, they are Russians?" Reichenau asked.

Schmundt nodded.

"Einsatzgruppen B will be displeased by our appearance in their region." The SS was as territorial as any military command. "Can they not perform this operation?"

Schmundt had dipped a portion of his sausage into his mustard then chewed contemplatively. "Einsatzgruppen B is the cause of your reassignment. Their commander knows only one way of fighting partisans."

It was a surprising admission from Schmundt. The SS had a single official policy for dealing with partisans - swift and total annihilation.

"What of das Heer? They are better equipped to handle partisans." Reichenau chose his words carefully, not one to argue with his commander.

Schmundt continued chewing. "These are not questions we ask." He swallowed and jabbed another piece of sausage. "The move on Moscow has begun. Most rear army units are already fighting these bandits and every other available unit is heading east." Schmundt replaced the half eaten meat on the plate. "Then there is this." He wiped his hands on a rag then reaching into his jacket pulled out a much folded cable. He handed it to Reichenau who unfolded and read it. His throat tightened at the signature decorating the bottom.

"This is so?"

Schmundt nodded, returning to his sausage. Orders given, it was an informal dismissal that Reichenau knew too well.

During the long trek through the sandy roads leading from Lithuania through Belorussia then into the Bryansk oblast, the captain could not forget the name on the cable. There was no choice, his men asking no questions about their deployment, their success at cleansing the territories around the Baltic States heightening their confidence.

As their convoy swept past the devastation wrought on the Russians, Reichenau's men marveled at the efficiency of Einsatzgruppen B in eliminating the Slavs in the area. During one evening's stop, Strauss begrudgingly expressed respect for his comrades and rivals.

Only after turning directly east did it become apparent that the Einsatzgruppen's efforts had flagged. Whole villages remained intact, dull looking peasants glared at the black shirted invaders trundling through their lives. Reichenau paid little attention, but listened to Lieutenant Kassmeyer as he directed them on the quickest route to their area of operation. The captain and his lieutenant struggled to discern the dotted lines representing a Russian "road." Afternoon was waning as the convoy shuddered to a halt. Reichenau tried to contact his lead units on the wireless, any slowing or stopping threatened the schedule to meet the German forces.

The captain was out of the car in a single leap only to be slowed by one of his sergeants, a man approaching his forties. The SS sought out the mature, those who could handle the duties of cleansing the countryside without suffering an emotional breakdown. Boys in their twenties might be fanatical, but were too unreliable. The sergeant's report was to the point. The convoy had taken fire from the village to the east and the men wanted to know whether to bypass or to eliminate the threat. Usually there was no question, gunfire mean annihilation. The SS could not allow anyone to own firearms and defend themselves. With sunlight dipping below the trees, though, Reichenau considered bypassing the threat.

The village was the typical clapboard set of hovels, wood scavenged from sturdier built czarist era structures. A single electric line led into the village with a loose line connecting each hovel. The communists bragged they had brought the electric light to even the most isolated village even if it lit only a single flickering bulb. Reichenau's men had positioned around the paths leading into the forest, the railroad the road to the communal farm some six kilometers in the distance. The two dozen or so "houses" represented a problem. Machine guns could easily topple them but waste valuable and limited ammunition, the same was true of flamethrowers and limited fuel. House to house searches would take time, which they did not have in the gathering darkness, and yield casualties.

Rottenfuhrer Strauss offered a quick, efficient solution to their obstacle with a minimum of German casualties. "Burn them out." He flicked his lighter. Within moments the dry grass then wooden hovels were ablaze, dusk turned into daylight, villagers' silhouettes transforming them into easy targets for rifles. Three Russians shot back, but framed in the fire and shooting into the shadows they did not last long. It took less than half an hour and the fire provided Reichenau's men with enough light to make their way to night quarters at the communal farm as the village burned out.

The captain slept in his car, the safest place in the inhospitable Russian forest. The next day promised a meeting with German forces, the 281st Security Division, which had been in constant contact with the partisans since mid-June.

The roads in the Bryansk Oblast were mere tracks and the rail lines they followed were even more decrepit. The Russians, backward and suspicious, had rejected the European rail gauge for their own wide gauge unusable for German trains. Sitting in the command car, Reichenau considered his mission, while a blurry eyed Lieutenant Kassmeyer struggled to find their location on the maps, the Russian countryside a blank slate.

The armada stretched for a kilometer, gaps in the machines ensuring easy escape if attacked. Leading them was Strauss, his perception of danger even more refined than his sense of Juden. No matter where they hid, above or below or even in a crowd, the corporal discovered the Reich's enemies.

The convoy halted, Reichenau out of the car, Kassmeyer struggling with his maps. Shots were fired, yelling, men hustling to the rear, Strauss either stifling an ambush or shooting up a Russian farmer with a wagon. Returning to the car, they passed the shattered vehicle, on fire, horse in front so scrawny it offered no value to the SS. The owner was propped against a tree, body bloodied, victim of Strauss' eagerness.

Reichenau ran Major Schmundt's orders through his mind. Some anti-Soviet partisans had adopted the name Russian National Liberation Army or RONA. The RONA roamed the forests searching for Red Army partisans left to ravage the German rear. This "army" sought territory and an alliance with the German invaders that could provide them with the fire power to eliminate their rivals. Rosenberg's Ministry of Eastern Territories offered the RONA little and the Wehrmacht frowned at the existence of a Russian force in their rear. It was the SS Obengruppenfuhrer Reinhard Heydrich, always in search of a means to eliminate the useless Slav, who ordered the directive that sent Reichenau on his mission. One did not disappoint the ruthless Heydrich.

Another halt. This time the ambush could not be denied. The command car drove up to find Strauss and his men straddling a ditch fronting the road. Efficient as ever, Strauss found and eliminated the threat within half an hour. Riechenau slipped out to congratulate his men while commending the corporal's eagle eye. The convoy restarted, the slow drive lengthened when trucks sank into the sandy soil. The captain remained in the command car while Kassmeyer worked on his maps. The trucks were freed, another hour passed, the afternoon sun reaching its apex before another stop, this time a knock on the window announcing welcome news, a Wehrmacht encampment was ahead.

"Ahead' was in the eye of the beholder, motorcycle troops, daring and dangerous, had established a road block of sorts, the barricade the surest way to prevent a convoy of partisans from driving into the midst of the encampment. Beyond the obstacle Reichenau would find the 281st Security Division. Three hundred meters, 500 meters, the captain grew edgy. A second road block marked the edge of the position. Within moments Reichenau was skirting the edge of the forest led by two motorcycles.

He faced several, ugly, gray concrete mushrooms poking up from the earth, barely visible in the dim lighting allowed by the white pines. A smile flickered over Reichenau at the thought of German soldiers seeking refuge in a former Russian defense position.

The gray uniforms of the Wehrmacht served as perfect camouflage in the dim light and Reichenau, in the black uniform of the SS, was soon surrounded by his countrymen, their lined faces and tired eyes spoke of a difficult month of fighting. The 281st Security Division, like others spread around occupied Russia, was stocked with men in their thirties and forties if not older. He was not standing amidst the cream of the German forces in Russia. The captain was led to a wood shack, the only dwelling fully above ground, where he was greeted by another captain.

"Uwe Bremen." A military salute followed the introduction, Reichenau replacing the usual Nazi salute with the military greeting he had learned during the Great War.

"Captain Reichenau," he said, taking Bremen's hand. He studied the captain, nearly a decade his senior.

"It is good to see you." The Wehrmacht captain led the SS captain into his "command headquarters" in the shack. "It has been difficult." The 281st Security Division was a shell of its former self, eighty percent attrition with casualties and his best soldiers being called to the front as replacements. The division had been spread thin as the front lines moved east. While talking, Bremen led him to a map "table" and Reichenau realized the Wehrmacht's guides were as pitiful as Kassmeyer's.

Bremen wasted little time explaining his position. "We have found large groups of bandits, here, here and here." He tapped over a dozen red circles spread across the map. "A rail repair crew here." He jabbed at a point seemingly within walking distance of the shack. "It was attacked. We arrived during the battle, my men barely escaped. The engineers and workers were less fortunate."

Reichenau did not doubt the captain. Bremen's men's eyes and posture all told of suffering in firefights, the survivors shambling shells of their past lives. "We were directed to cooperate with another group of partisans."

Bremen's eyes, buried deep in their sockets, barely registered the captain's words. "The RONA," he murmured, more lines poking free from his face. "They may be worse than the partisans or the -." He stopped, suddenly realizing who was standing beside him.

Reichenau ignored the slip of the tongue. He was in no mood to report on those who believed the SS too vicious in performing its duties. The pitiful men who had watched him and the one standing before him, all closer in age to pensioners than front line soldiers, represented no threat.

"There has been contact?" He asked. The captain's slow nod revealed why Reichenau was there. Captain Bremen could not see beyond survival. "They are near?"

"They are here."

"Here?"

A slow nod, arm extended in the direction of the "road."
"They are everywhere," he murmured, chin sinking to his chest.
"We have been sent on an impossible mission. I requested
reinforcements but they sent you." Bremen closed his eyes, on the
verge of falling asleep.

Reichenau left the captain, who agreed to a pair of men to
accompany him, then went in search of Kassmeyer. The lieutenant
was valuable beyond reading maps. He had served two years as an
interpreter while training the Russians during the 1920s, overseeing
Luftwaffe practice runs along the Don River outside the Allies
prying eyes. Kassmeyer knew the Russians and their language.

The lieutenant had remained beside the car but was not
inactive. "The RONA," he said as the captain approached. "They are
in the forest, at the edge of the encampment."

For a fleeting moment Reichenau wished Strauss was nearby.
The corporal, unhappy with any orders requiring talking with the
Slav rather than shooting them, remained Reichenau's most
fearsome soldier. The RONA partisans would respect him.

"We will walk," the captain said. Stepping by the lieutenant
he motioned to the two soldiers granted him by Bremen and they
headed off in search of "friendly" Russians.

The RONA had marked their presence, several sentries
posted at the edge of the forest. They halted Reichenau, agitated by
his gun bearing soldiers. Outfitted in what appeared to be Red Army
uniforms, the sentries chattered at a pace that overwhelmed
Kassmeyer.

"They are upset," the lieutenant said, the captain frowning. "Their orders are to allow only commanding officers through."

Reichenau knew better than be dictated to about the size of his entourage. "Their orders are of no concern of mine," he said to Kassmeyer, who translated to the sentries. "The SS chooses its own forces." This earned a gimlet eye from the soldiers, but their unease at the sight of the sentries kept them quiet. "I will not come without these men."

"Herr Hauptsturmfuhrer." Strauss appeared, drawing the attention of the sentries who sensed the danger that accompanied him.

"Rottenfuhrer Strauss," Reichenau said. "You can return to your men."

"Sir." The corporal was out of breath, but even in his depleted state eyed the RONA sentries as dangerous vermin. "Hauptmann Bremen has ordered his men to return." Strauss sneered at the mention of "men," eyes narrowing as he considered the soldiers with their dirty uniforms and curved backs.

The captain motioned and the soldiers retreated. Strauss ignored them, having brought his own squad of five to protect his commander. "We will follow, sir."

Reichenau felt his efforts slipping away from him. The sentries had objected to two soldiers, a half dozen SS men were unlikely to be acceptable. A rustling from within the forest made Reichenau turn. He jerked at the sight of a Red Army uniform, the sentries stood at attention.

"What is this?" He eyed the SS men, gaze alighting on Strauss.

Reichenau blinked, German. The man was speaking German. A burst of Russian from the same lips confused him even as Kassmeyer translated, but the captain held up his hand.

The new arrival growled at the sentries, who stepped aside. "Branislaw Kaminski," he said.

"Captain Reichenau." Salutes were exchanged then hands shaken.

"You are surprised I speak German."

Reichenau nodded.

"My mother was German, she spoke it well but quietly. It is dangerous to speak the language of the enemy in Russia."

Reichenau agreed, still puzzling over Kaminski. "I have an interpreter if you prefer to be safe and speak Russian."

Kaminski, prominent nose seemingly perpetually raised, weak chin and gray hair making him a less than intimidating figure, smiled at the offer. "Very well."

Reichenau slid in his own demand. "My men wish to join me." He nodded at the eager Strauss. "For security purposes."

Kaminski's mouth flickered. "That one," he nodded toward Strauss. "He wants to put a bullet in my head."

The corporal blinked at the reading of his mind. Kaminski waved the sentries away and turned toward the forest, Reichenau beside him.

"It is good to speak to a military man," Kaminski said, Kassmeyer translating. "We talked with some of your civilians but they are only about paper." He waved his hand at the distant bureaucrats. "We need weapons, we will fight with help."

"We," Reichenau said. "My briefing on your RONA was sparse." His words were partly drowned out by the floundering SS men, tripping over bushes and smacking their faces into trees as they scouted the woods for ambushes.

Kaminski motioned Reichenau to a farmstead featuring a wood building and a cottage, its roof partly collapsed. Beside it was a barn, where Kaminski led Reichenau, Strauss' squad remained outside for easy entry and exit.

The barn bustled, armed men and staff stared at the black suited Germans. Kaminski waved them away then leaned over a pair of hay bales. A map sat on top, its detail making Kassmeyer's eyes glisten. Kaminski's knowledge of the area went far beyond the efforts of any German cartographer.

"This is Lokot." Kaminski swept his hand over the paper. "At this moment it is led by Konstantin Voskoboinik."

Reichenau eyed Kaminski, his unusual choice of words a warning of future change.

"Lokot will be an independent district within German occupied Russia."

Reichenau held up his hands. "That is a political matter, I can only answer military questions."

Kaminski continued, seeming not to hear. "Lokot is an enemy of Bolshevism and its Jewish leaders. We will have neither within out boundaries."

"That is also our duty."

"But we know the area, we know the people. My men can spot a partisan where your men would see only a civilian."

Reichenau showed his teeth. "The difference means little."

Kaminski nodded. "I have men who believe the same." He turned from the map. "How well do you know the Soviet Union?" The captain shrugged, puzzled by the change in direction. "Do you know the Uzbek Soviet Republic?"

"I know little of your country."

"They are Asians. I have three, they deserted when the Germans attacked. One of them is my company commander. He does not understand the difference between military and civilian."

Reichenau glanced about the barn. "What do you want from us?"

"At this time, nothing." Kaminsky strode to the open door. "Are you familiar with the Soviet T-34 tank?"

Reichenau had seen hundreds of tanks scattered about roads and fields but knew little else.

"We have one and some smaller tanks." He emerged in the clearing and eyed the forest surrounding them. "My men will work with your troops. My commanders, my men." He whistled and the suddenly the forest swarmed with RONA men, armed if a bit ragged. Strauss gripped his rifle, but the captain warned him off. He saluted Kaminski. "We will work with you."

21

July 7, 1940   **Chicago**

"Happy days are here again"

"The skies sing a song of cheer again"

"So let's sing a song of cheer again"

"Happy days are here again."

The bands at the Democrat Presidential Convention alternated between the Democrat theme song for the last eight years and Dixie, the southern Democrat song for nearly a century. Beside the musical entertainment, Tuesday was an uneventful day in Chicago, mainly consumed by nominating speeches for men with no hope of knocking off the champ. It was an opportunity for politicians to vent about a president who would not leave much like when, Pegler suspected, Catholic cardinals vented when a pope would not die. Sitting in the press gallery he saw the tension on the faces of Democrat pols, all wanting their man to challenge and defeat Senator Vandenberg but straining not to insult the man who held their fate in his hands for the next four or (shudder) eight years.

In the hotels surrounding the convention center there was much activity, all of it for naught. Cactus Jack Garner, the sitting vice president, well-funded by Texas oil money, but spinning his wheels, counted the days until he would retire from Washington and return to Uvalde to listen to the wind blow. The others held out false hopes, trying to place themselves at the same level as the champ, possibly to help their reelection bids or to capture a well paid lobbying job. In New Deal Washington access meant high commissions, and merely being mentioned in the same breath as the president translated into a sizable pay day.

The evening session also had little to offer. For once Pegler found something good to say about Roosevelt's push for war, not that he could ignore the drawbacks. Bennet eased in beside him in the press gallery, smacking Pegler's shoulder and producing a cringe. He grinned and bore the pain.

"Did you hear?" Bennet hissed, not that much could be heard over the droning of an earnest speaker with little of interest to say.

Pegler had heard a lot but doubted it was the same as what Bennet heard. "No," he mumbled, even his teeth hurting.

"The Germans are moving toward Moscow. They call it the last great battle for Europe. The Russians say they will fight to the death. I heard they might have as many as five million in there."

Pegler was not surprised and even less interested. The Russians were a cruel and barbaric bunch. A western government would surrender their capital city and allow the population to leave but the Russians made every Muscovite a target and Pegler did not doubt it was within the Germans' capabilities to eliminate each of them.

"I heard the Russians will be out of the war by fall."

Pegler knew this was not true. The Russians would never be out of the war. They would keep moving east and the Germans could not chase them all the way to the Pacific.

A nudge from his opposite side drew Pegler away from geopolitics and found his seatmate, a reporter of dubious morals poking at him. He flinched, the alcohol odor rushing from his mouth too much even for Pegler. "You see those girls at the bar last night?"

Pegler slowly shook his head, concerned a sudden movement might set off a burst of speech.

"These Democrat girls are the best, they know how to have fun."

His boozy seatmate leaned over and Pegler jerked, concerned he was about to be vomited on but instead the reporter jabbed his finger into Pegler's leg. "Those Republican girls you never know, they act all so nice, but you get them liquored up-." A nudge and a wink followed, a sign his seat mate was speaking from personal experience.

On the convention floor, nominations continued. Pegler paid little attention, Roosevelt certain to be nominated for a third term no matter what Jack Garner or Jim Farley believed. As FDR's vice president and Postmaster General were nominated, guffaws sounded in the press gallery, conversation turned back to speculation on the war.

"The British are talking to the Russians," one of the scribes said.

"What can the British do," Pegler huffed. "Stuck on that island of theirs." He closed one eye and squinted at the reporter. "They are waiting for Roosevelt to get reelected so he can send American boys to Europe to die for the communists."

"Peg's mad." This from one of the Pulitzer boys. He wiggled his cigarette toward the columnist. "Somebody's got to stop Hitler," he declared. "The Brits can't do it and Uncle Joe is on his heels."

Pegler grimaced, realizing he should have kept his suspicions about Roosevelt and the war to himself. He could not control himself. "The Germans will stop Hitler," he pronounced, flummoxing the gallery.

"Germans?" The Pulitzer reporter huffed. "The Germans love Hitler. He's got them more than ever."

"He can't stop," Pegler said. "Napoleon had Europe and couldn't stop so they got him." He raised his chin at the Pulitzer writer. "What's he going to do with a hundred million Russians?" He closed his eye again. "Chase them out, kill them?" Pegler shook his head.

The Pulitzer man looked around for help, a Hearst reporter, a waspish faced man with black eyes that revealed little as there was little to reveal, jumped in to defend his colleague. "They got allies, the French, those eastern European folks." His tongue flickered from his mouth. "Hitler can run Europe until he dies in bed. If we don't go over there every country goes Nazi then what do we do?"

Pegler sighed, having heard it all before. He knew further arguing only produced more arguments. He caught Bennet's eye, hoping for an escape and his friend was quick to help.

"Caught any of Vandenberg's speeches?" He asked, looking around the group. "Sounds more like Hoover than Hoover did."

The Pulitzer man was shaking his head, hair flipping out of place. "Willkie was the one who could beat him. Vandenberg can't win outside Michigan."

Bennet agreed even as Pegler gave him the evil eye. "He might be trying to bore all of the Roosevelt voters, put them asleep Election Day."

"They ain't too tired," Pegler grunted. "Spending all day leaning on their shovels, earning that WPA pay. Plenty of time for rest and to vote."

"Peg, Peg, Peg," the Pulitzer man chided the columnist. "Vanden-bore is just another Republican, born to lose, living too much in the past. He thinks Hoover was right but too liberal, people don't want to hear that anymore."

Pegler opened his mouth to respond but was interrupted by a voice from above – or below – a voice that copied the fervor of the Willkie delegates in Philadelphia. "We want Roosevelt," the loudspeakers boomed. "We want Roosevelt." On and on again the voice demanded a third term until the crowd below matched the decibels, some in the reporters' gallery covering their ears.

"Christ," Pegler groaned. "Here we go."

22

July 21, 1940   **Smolensk, Russia**

Hauptmann Johanns Franks reclined in the passenger seat of a captured Soviet staff car as his driver, Stabsfeldwebel Oskar Herrick, negotiated a path through the rubble of Smolensk. He had no idea what kind of vehicle it was but he was not concerned. He was looking for a particular medical unit.

"Slow down Staff Sergeant," ordered Frank. He pointed to a post on the right side of the dirt road. "Follow that sign to the 342nd Field Regiment Hospital."

"An Army hospital, Herr Hauptmann?" asked Herrick.

"An Army hospital, Sergeant," confirmed Franks. "I believe I know someone there."

Five minutes later the worn and damaged Red Army staff car stopped at a collection of tents and buildings just outside of the devastated city. It had the appearance of a former Soviet military installation. A wrecked multi turreted Russian T-35 pointed its many guns randomly.

Franks dismounted from the vehicle and straightened his

Fallschirmjager uniform, brushing dust from his sleeves. Satisfied with his appearance as an officer of Germany's elite airborne division, he motioned to Herrick, "Wait here, I hope to be no more than 30 minutes."

Franks had become fond of Herrick, a massive shouldered man from Kiel, blue eyed and blonde. Sergeant Herrick was not the fleetest of foot but he could literally carry anything on his back. Franks wondered how a parachute could adequately support Herrick's weight but was assured that the feat was within acceptable limits. Herrick just descended faster than the other parachutists.

Hauptmann Franks strode to the guard at the hospital unit's entrance.

"I wish to see Major Bluent. Is he still attached to this unit?" demanded Franks. After more than 30 minutes of waiting, Franks was led into a private examination room within a sturdy canvas walled tent. Another 20 minutes later, an older officer appeared toting the requisite clipboard.

"Back for more cream, Captain?" inquired Major Bluent of the 342nd Field Regiment Hospital. Major Bluent was an army doctor. "Or did it resolve the issue?"

Hauptmann Johanns Franks blushed, unusual for an officer but somehow appropriate for the situation. Dr. Bluent had treated him eight months earlier for a case of genital warts.

"Herr Major, that matter appears to have been favorably resolved. How can you possibly remember my embarrassing condition?" asked Franks. "With the number of men you treat and the trivial nature of my affliction."

"Honestly, I am not sure. Maybe it is the Condor Legion connection. Who knows?" conceded Bluent. "I'm glad it is no longer an issue. So, what you are here for today?"

"I am sure you have heard it is likely that the 7th Flieger Division may be deployed in the upcoming battles?" offered Franks.

"Captain, it would seem that the parachute forces would be of little value if they were not. This is the second war the Wehrmacht has fought in the same number of years and they have yet to see action," mused Bluent. "Lots of Reichsmarks spent for a mere threat."

"With all due respect Herr Major, we can only fight when we are deployed," responded Franks. "I am certain General Student will convince the OKW of our value and contribution for the final thrust."

Major Bluent held up his hands in mock surrender. He was a veteran of the Great War. He was not looking for an argument.

"We are on the same side, Captain. I am rather busy today, what may I help you with?"

"I am here today not for me but my men," explained Franks. "It is likely that we will be deployed at night or very early in the morning. I am concerned about their alertness during the battle. We may be behind enemy lines for an extended period. Sleep will be something to be avoided at all costs."

"Well you have Pervitin for that, Captain," stated Major Bluent. "It has been used quite effectively to keep our men alert and awake, sometimes for days. Although I will say there are clearly risks involved with continuous use."

"Of course, Major. But I am concerned that we do not have enough of the pills for such an extended operation," advised Franks. "I would like more."

"Well then go through the proper chain of command. Don't come to me directly," warned Major Bluent.

"I apologize Major Bluent. I am only trying to do the best that I can for my men and the Fatherland," replied Franks. "I don't know how much time there is before it is needed."

Major Bluent considered Hauptmann Franks for a moment. He took a step back. "I wonder about Pervitin's long term effects but we are fighting a war. Come along with me."

He took Franks by the arm and steered him back into the sunlight. The temperature was rising as the sun continued on its path to its now overhead station. It was noon.

Bluent moved quickly for a man in his mid-fifties. Franks was forced to quicken his step. There was no chance that he would ask Bluent to slow his pace. They saw Sergeant Herrick leaning against the staff car.

The major stopped short of a remarkably intact storage building. Graffiti was scrawled across the wall in white paint. Major Bluent pointed at the Cyrillic script. "Do you know what this says?"

"I have no idea," shrugged Franks. "You speak Russian?"

"I do, quite fluently actually. This says…" Bluent hesitated but not because he was uncertain of the translation. "Death to the Fascist Vermin!"

Bluent led Franks inside. As far as the eye could see, boxes were stacked from the floor to ceiling. "Pervitin" was clearly printed on the side of each box Franks was close enough to read.

"Gott in Himmel!" exclaimed Franks.

"That's right Captain. We have almost 500,000 tablets right here. The upcoming battle will not be as easy as Herr Goebbels suggests." Bluent gestured to the entrance, where the graffiti exhorted the Red Army. "You will need every advantage."

"How many tablets does the Wehrmacht have?"

"My colleagues in Berlin have shocked even me with their information. The war against the Bolsheviks is unlike anything the Fatherland has ever attempted." Bluent hesitated and then spoke softly. "35 million Pervitin tablets have been shipped to the front since April."

Franks was too stunned to respond immediately. He walked over to the nearest stack and turned his back to Bluent.

"Major, how many boxes may we take today for my men?"

Bluent grinned, "As many as you and Max Schmeling's bigger brother out there can carry."

Franks laughed at the reference to the German heavy weight boxer from the thirties. Staff Sergeant Herrick was indeed a large man.

Franks reached for Major Bluent's hand and shook it. "Schmeling is a member of the division but as far as I know they are not brothers."

Franks hefted a box of tablets of the methamphetamine Pervitin on his shoulder and went to find Herrick and his strong back.

23

July 25, 1940   **South of Shakhovskaya, Russia**

Lieutenant Rudi Kleime dried his worn body with fragments of what was once a towel. His makeshift platoon of captured Russian BT-5 tanks were positioned at a bend on a dirt track adjacent to the headwaters of the Ruza River, less than 5 kilometers southeast of Shakhovskaya, Russia. The flowing waters of the river were cool and invigorating.

Rudi surveyed their position, a temporary respite from the battle. The morning sky was clear, perfect for the Stukas. They were still part of *Kampfgruppe Schmidt*, which had grown to include not only Rudi's unit of Soviet tanks, two platoons of Czech PzKpfw 38(t) panzers and a company of motorized infantry but a battery of four 50 mm antitank cannons and a motorcycle platoon. All were under the command of newly promoted Hauptmann Schmidt, which seemed insane to Rudi but the speed of the advance and the vast distances of Soviet territory already conquered generated shortages of everything, including officers.

The main units of *Kampfgruppe Schmidt* had re-positioned to Shakhovskaya from Mozhaysk two days earlier in anticipation of a Bolshevik counterattack. Soviet deserters had informed Army Intelligence that three entire Russian armies were planning to attack north of the Ruza River along the Moscow rail line to Volokolamsk. Rudi had the unpleasant experience of witnessing the initial stages of a brutal interrogation of a young Russian by Boris, the White Russian assigned to his platoon. He tried to somehow intervene when Boris sliced off one of the teen's fingers but Captain Schmidt had already arrived and was not even remotely interested in humane treatment of the hapless prisoner. Rudi felt his respect for Captain Schmidt weaken. He did not agree with the captain's indifference to the peasant soldier's suffering.

Rudi was pleased to learn that the added antitank battery and the motorcycle platoon were also formed from remnants of his old unit, the Third Panzer Regiment. More men had survived the battle of Smolensk than he originally believed. The antitank guns were under the command of the capable Lieutenant Lunge, who was instrumental in the Third Panzer Regiment's slaughter of counterattacking Russian tanks at Shklov only two months earlier. Rudi's current command consisted of Russian BT-5s captured at Shklov when their original crews ran away.

Rudi shook his head. He was discouraged that his platoon was still saddled with operating the captured BT-5s. They were fast but thinly armored. His men had very limited ammunition or spare parts. Captain Schmidt had promised they would receive replacements, German or Czech made panzers but nothing happened.

Satisfied that he was as dry as he was going to get, Rudi pulled his trousers up and synched his belt. He was losing weight rapidly. Rudi longed for his mother's cooking. At least the Russian dust that had caked his body was mostly gone.

Rudi grimaced when he thought of Lieutenant Groesbeck, the commander of the motorcycle platoon. As far as he was concerned, Groesbeck was evil. Rudi did not like the Nazi before the war and was revolted by Groesbeck's execution of a Soviet Commissar at the border. Rudi wondered if Captain Schmidt was traveling down the same dark path.

Thunderclaps pierced the morning calm, jolting Rudi. He scanned the sky, not a cloud in sight. The thunder increased in frequency. Rudi's arm caught in his undershirt sleeve, it was on backwards. Abandoning the struggle to right his shirt, he grabbed binoculars off his folded tunic and scrambled atop the BT-5 command tank, avoiding the bed spring antenna contraption that dominated its superstructure. Standing erect on its turret, he trained his binoculars to the northeast, towards the railroad tracks leading to Moscow. Black smoke billowed from numerous, seemingly equally spaced sources. A low rumbling noise joined the louder, sharper retorts.

"Lieutenant, Hauptmann Schmidt wants you on the wireless," called Corporal Adolf Brauch.

Rudi maneuvered to the front hatch of the light Russian tank and leaned his head into the hull, grabbing the German made headset from Brauch. It was his platoon's only radio, as the Russians did not equip their tanks as the Germans.

"Lieutenant Kleime, Herr Hauptmann," announced Rudi.

"What can you see from there Rudi?

"It looks like massed artillery fire across a wide area north of the tracks, towards Volokolamsk," responded Rudi. "I hear tanks. Who's up there?"

"General von Wiktorin with the 20th Motorized Infantry Division has been there a few days," replied Schmidt. "They are light on panzers and artillery. They have a platoon of Stug IIIs and a handful of PzKpfw IIs. Fairly strong with anti-tank guns but nothing that can tackle the monster KV-1 or this new T-34."

"It looks like they are facing a strong attack by the Reds. What are our orders?"

"Get your Russian tanks ready to move out. We will move out from Shakhovskaya at noon and rendezvous 3 kilometers east on the railroad tracks," commanded Schmidt. "We have a little surprise for the peasants."

Rudi waited for Schmidt to reveal the subterfuge, but he did not receive clarification. He handed the radio gear back to Brauch and slid off the hull of the BT-5. The third crew member, the teen Gunther Reiner, was looking busy but not doing anything useful.

"Panzerschutze Reiner, get our shit packed, we are rolling in less than an hour," snapped Rudi.

Startled, Reiner flinched, immediately enhancing his display of industriousness.

"Where are we going, Herr Lieutenant?"

"Reiner, are you serious? Do you not hear the artillery?" Rudi waved his right arm northwards. "Where do you think we would be going, to the zoo?"

Moderately disgusted, Rudi stomped further down the dirt track, calling out to commanders of the other captured BT-5s.

"Schnell! Crank up your engines! Schnell! We are moving north in 30 minutes."

Rudi watched with approval as his small command rushed to carry out his orders, preparing the four captured BT-5s for action against their own makers.

24

July 25, 1940   **Shakhovskaya, Russia**

Lieutenant Waltraud Shriver scanned the horizon in front and to the sides of the dark green Fieseler Storch Fi 156C-2 spotter plane, searching for Russian fighters. Cruising at an altitude under 500 meters, the Storch was vulnerable to ground fire from any Russian weapon that could be pointed upwards. Shriver followed the railroad tracks east towards Shakhovskaya, where he expected to find *Kampfgruppe Schmidt* assembling in preparation for a counterattack to relieve the 20th Motorized Infantry beleaguered at Volokolamsk.

Shriver felt a hand grasp his shoulder. He turned and acknowledged his observer, who spoke over the intercom.

"Lieutenant, are you ok?"

Shriver knew he was not a pleasant sight. He wiped blood away from the bandage over his eye. Another dressing protected a similar wound on his neck. He certainly did not appear like an image on a Luftwaffe recruiting poster. The injuries caused by the landing accident three weeks earlier looked much graver than they were. But they were not healing. Perhaps he should have listened to the doctors and received more extensive care, but he had refused. Shriver had something to prove. He had a burning desire to redeem himself to his brethren.

"God dammit, Rolf it shouldn't have happened. I shouldn't have even tried to land on that road," responded Shriver.

"Lieutenant, no one blames you. Even General Rommel said you weren't at fault," replied his observer, Junior Officer Rolf Auchen.

"Rolf, General Rommel had his right arm amputated last week. Did you know that?"

Rolf demurred and looked out the window.

"Waltraud, it was an accident," offered Rolf. "Accidents are unavoidable in war. It is not like peace time."

Shriver shook his head negatively.

"I am already known as the Flying Jew, for the sole reason that one of my grandparents was Jewish. I barely remember her, she moved to fucking Amerika with her second husband, also a Jew," gushed Shriver. "And now General Erwin Rommel has lost his arm because of me."

Rolf Auchen could think of nothing to say that would help and he certainly did not want to make his pilot's attitude any worse. They were heading into enemy territory in a robust but still tiny spotter plane. And the Storch would be within easy range of virtually anything the Red Army had in its inventory.

"Well you didn't get much of her Jew blood, that's for sure," was the best Rolf could come up with at the moment. "You are tall, blonde and the frauleins worship you."

Shriver grunted in disagreement. He renewed his scan, aware that he was nearing the enemy.

"There's Shakhovskaya," said Shriver, pointing ahead and to the left. "The Ruza River will be to the right. This Volokolamsk shithole should be another 15 kilometers, just north of the tracks."

The Storch was slow and it took another five minutes to reach the village. They could see Russian artillery detonations in the near distance. At 300 meters above the ground, it was easy to identify the PzKpfw 38(t)s of *Kampfgruppe Schmidt* forming into a wedge at the edge of the village. Behind the panzers was a SdKfz 251 Hanomag halftrack with several long radio antennas and a bright red Nazi flag draped over its rear section.

"That would be their Flivo, Oberleutnant Wheilerd," advised Shriver, referring to the Luftwaffe Fliegerverbindungsoffizier or forward air controller typically assigned to advancing Army units. Shriver greeted his friend and fellow air force officer Wheilerd by wagging his wings as the Storch passed over the Hanomag.

"Wheilerd is with the 7th Panzer now?" asked Rolf, watching Wheilerd perform obscene gestures in their direction. "He certainly remains very talented."

"Who knows what division *Kampfgruppe Schmidt* belongs

to? The survivors of the 3rd Panzer Regiment were slapped together to form it after the battle of Smolensk," explained Shriver.

Rolf whistled lowly into the intercom and pointed to the rear "Well what do we have here?"

Shriver glanced down and was greeted by the distinctive silhouette of heavy anti-aircraft guns, mounted on four wheel carriages. Shriver banked the Storch 45 degrees and made a tight turn over Shakhovskaya's town center.

"Rolf, those are our Luftwaffe comrades about to paste the Bolsheviks with 88 mm shells," answered Shriver. "I heard General Rommel advise Guderian himself that he planned to use the 88s against the Russian monster tanks."

"Do you think the 88 mm shell can pierce the armor of this KV-1?" wondered Rolf.

"Rolf, an 88 mm armor piercing shell can slice through anything, and I mean anything," responded Shriver. "Like a hot knife through butter."

"And that unit is manned by Luftwaffe guys, not army apes," added Rolf.

Shriver leveled his wings and ordered Auchen, "Raise Wheilerd and tell him we will continue towards Volokolamsk to find out where the artillery is firing from."

Unteroffizier Rolf Auchen complied with Shriver's command, radioing the Flivo and reporting their intentions. As the exchange ended, the Storch was buffeted by gusty winds. Shriver climbed 50 meters and seemed to float above Groesbeck's motorcycle platoon, now advancing east along the tracks. The counterattack was forming. *Kampfgruppe Schmidt* needed Shriver's eyes above.

25

July 25, 1940   **Smolensk, Russia**

Hauptmann Hans Oswald was as tired as any of the pilots in his *staffel* of Junkers Ju-87B Stuka dive bombers. The frequent sorties were draining but the repeated moving of their unit forward to airfields closer to the front was yet another challenge. Their present base, a captured airfield at Smolensk, was far from adequate. The buildings that remained standing were crude at best and none of the Russian hangars had survived the Luftwaffe onslaught. Repairs and maintenance were performed in the open. As a veteran of the Condor Legion, Oswald had operated from less than ideal conditions. However, nothing in Spain was as primitive as Russia.

The relocations were necessary because the panzers had advanced so far, so fast. The range of the Ju-87B was limited to less than 800 kilometers with a bomb load substantial enough to cause appreciable damage to the Red Army.

Presently, Oswald stood before his pilots, finishing yet another briefing. He decided not to warn them that the unit was moving further east the next day, to Vyazma. The men would certainly be motivated by its proximity to Moscow but they had barely set up camp in Smolensk. The news could wait until after today's primary mission.

"The Red Army peasants have somehow assembled a significant number of artillery guns west of Istra and south of the rail line." Oswald pointed to the map attached to the side of the tent. "They are pouring rounds onto our boys at Volokolamsk. We are going to take out this threat."

"Are we expecting Soviet fighters?" asked a young

replacement pilot from Stuttgart.

"*Ja*, Krauss, the area is thick with *Ratas*," nodded Oswald. "But we will have cover from a *staffel* of Me-110 heavy fighters."

"*Ratas*?" queried Krauss. What are *Ratas*?"

"Lieutenant Kraus, did the Luftwaffe not provide you with any training? The Polikarpov I-16 is a short and stubby fighter that doesn't look very modern," answered Oswald. "We called it the *Rata* in Spain. Don't be fooled. They are very maneuverable and almost 100 kilometers per hour faster than our Stukas."

Oswald concluded the briefing as strongly as he could muster.

"Men, this is the real thing. The Bolsheviks are throwing whatever fresh troops they have at us to stop the drive on Moscow. This is everything for them, the whole war. You know what our part is. The Russians are hitting the 20th Motorized Infantry hard at Volokolamsk. We have to be better than good today."

Satisfied that his pilots understood the gravity of their mission, Oswald shifted his gaze to appraise each of his pilots. They were a collection of worn out veterans and eager replacements.

"New guys, stick with the veterans like you are fucking them," concluded Oswald.

The pilots shuffled past, heading to their Stukas, maps marked in red pencil, target areas identified. Oswald grasped Lieutenant Mueller's shoulder as the men filed out of the command tent. Oswald had flown with Mueller since the formation of the *staffel*. Mueller was a competent flier, one of his most accurate dive bomber pilots.

"Lieutenant Mueller, you ready for today?" Oswald

continued to hold Mueller's shoulder, squeezing lightly. "The *Landsers* on the ground need us badly. Our panzer and motorized units are strung out thinly. The infantry is still days away."

"Jahwohl, Herr Hauptmann," responded Mueller automatically, but without conviction. "We will do our duty."

Oswald spun Mueller partially, to face him. He looked into Mueller's eyes, which were dull and cloudy. Mueller's pupils were large. He seemed much older than his 23 years.

Oswald knew immediately. "How much Pervitin have you been taking?"

Mueller appeared confused. After a moment, he feebly held up his map, doodles in red scribbled on the bottom. "These maps are shit. Nothing on the ground is even on them."

"What are you fucking talking about? I am not asking you about the quality of your charts. Did you even hear me?" barked Oswald. "How many Stuka pills have you been taking?"

Mueller nodded at the Luftwaffe slang for Pervitin. "I am falling asleep in the cockpit without them," responded Mueller. "I can stay awake without a problem with the pills. I am flying fine."

"I understand Lieutenant, but too many and you lose connection. The mission won't feel real," warned Oswald. "Do I need to ground you?"

"Not at all," replied Mueller. "I will take less."

"No more than two a mission, spaced out by at least two hours." Advised Oswald. "Any more than that and you lose focus. Do you understand?"

"I do and I will cut back," agreed Mueller. "We've all been

pushing."

Satisfied that Mueller could control his methamphetamine intake without further intervention, Oswald moved his hand to Mueller's elbow and nudged him out of the tent and into the sunshine.

"It is a beautiful day for flying, Mueller," exclaimed Oswald. "Let's go get the army out of a jam."

Mueller smiled and flashed a thumb up signal to his Captain. Oswald had wasted too much time with Mueller and hustled over to *Jolanthe*, his Stuka. Named after the Stuka Oswald had flown during the Spanish Civil War in 1938, *Jolanthe* was a pig character from German children stories. The pig emblem was painted on the wheel pants on Oswald's Stuka, serving notice to all Luftwaffe pilots and enlisted alike that his war began not with the invasion of Poland but years before.

As Oswald arrived at *Jolanthe*, ground crew completed ordinance loading supervised by Sergeant Sandmann, his rear gunner.

Oswald motioned Sandmann to the starboard wing, where he unfolded the map. The Austrian sergeant had initially been the target of open scorn from Oswald but things were changing. Sandmann had essentially stopped eating, replacing food with regular Pervitin intake. He was no longer fat, now merely overweight. While the long term effects were certainly unknown, Oswald felt the results of the pills were far more favorable with Sandmann than Mueller. At least Sandmann was no longer lazy.

"Feldwebel Sandmann, we have an important mission today," said Oswald as he pointed towards Volokolamsk. "The Bolsheviks are attacking in force here. The 20th Motorized Infantry is in their way."

Sandmann peered at the map without really looking closely. He was alert but unfocussed. He nodded his head. Eventually, he straightened, saluted in the Nazi manner and bellowed "Seig Heil!"

Oswald shook his head wondering if his entire unit was hopped up on Pervitin. He folded his map and snatched his flight gear from a young corporal. Oswald pointed to a canteen and the corporal responded instantly. Cracking open a 30 roll of Pervitin, he swallowed a tablet, washed it down with the offered water and climbed into *Jolanthe*.

Moments later, Oswald taxied his Stuka into position, facing into the wind. The Smolensk airfield was more a large field than an airport. A strip of un-cratered turf, perhaps 100 meters wide, was marked by small flags. Mueller took position off his starboard wing. The remainder of the *Staffel* taxied into position behind them. Oswald pointed two fingers down the runway. Mueller grinned back at him.

Oswald pushed the throttle forward and skipped down the turf, straining to get airborne before one of his main wheels dug into an unforeseen hole. Free from the earth, Oswald lowered *Jolanthe's* nose, building airspeed. Satisfied that he had sufficient velocity, he climbed to 1,000 meters in altitude. He pulled back the throttle and allowed the *Staffel* to form up on *Jolanthe*, into three *Kettens* of three aircraft each.

26

July 25, 1940   Moscow

In the Soviet paradise the Party controlled everything for the benefit of the people, including memories. The Party, though, had yet to learn how to control dreams. Alexei's sleep was haunted with memories of a name he had not mentioned since his school days. He had excelled in his youth, parroting turgid Marxist theory to impress his teachers and their masters. Professor Vatutin was a dynamic Marxist who could place every economic activity instinctively within Hegel's dialectical materialism. The shift from land to paper money, from agriculture to manufacturing, from serfdom to wage slavery, all were explained with such cunning that Alexei felt as if Marx was teaching the course. The professor and his student bonded, even a potential Protopopov-Vatutin family on the horizon as his seventeen year old daughter Tatiana attracted Alexei's eye. Their first summer together, the two walked the city, watching the people return from the shifts in the Kharkov steel plants, pleased their lives would be easier than that of the slumped and grungy figures hobbling home for a morose dinner.

Tatiana finished her secondary school and moved onto the university, the celebration of her womanhood saw Alexei present her a family heirloom and the promise to never leave her. The summer of 1930 was to be the best and last Alexei would enjoy in Kharkov. July nineteenth was the height of his happiness, the day that was the dawning of adulthood. Tatiana had accompanied him on a Sunday afternoon to Shevchenka Park and the lake near the zoo. They enjoyed the ducks skimming the water, a warm breeze from the steppe making the day bearable. Alexei had brought vodka, satisfied Tatiana could not hold her liquor.

They had sat in the grass withered by a dry spring, rough to the touch, but shaded from the sun. Curious eyes were blocked by low hanging branches and a pair of bushes. Alexei had started slowly, holding back the vodka and soothed her with talk of their future.

"Comrade Bergoyen will bore you to death in his Marxist philosophy class. He used to be a White, but now he reads from

notes prepared for him to teach. He never looks at the students."
Alexei warned her.

Tatiana giggled. "He is too afraid of the NKVD."

It was a joke that could only be told and enjoyed by those who had never received the ominous knock on the door in the middle of the night. The laughter led to intertwined fingers, a rarity as physical displays of affection were not part of the new communist man's image. Behind the trees and bushes, though, no one could object.

"Comrade Zebayev is much more interesting and difficult," Alexei reached around her back, snapping her bra. Tatiana shrieked.

"Why did you to that?" She feigned indignation, wiggling under Alexei's touch.

Alexei grinned. "If you let Comrade Zebayev do that he will give you good marks."

"Dirty old man. If he touches me I will tell my father. He knows the director. They will put a stop to Comrade Zebayev."

Alexei chuckled at the furrowed brow and curled lip, the same expression that greeted borscht at the local eatery. Tatiana floated on the cloud of her father's influence. She enjoyed the benefits at a time when influence could get her whatever she wanted.

"What is so funny," she demanded, folding her arms across her chest.

"Just the way you look when you are angry."

"It is not funny." She struggled to rise but Alexei gently shoved her back. The pouting descended into giggling as they tottered onto their side, dirt and grass sticking to their clothes.

When Alexei allowed his hands to wander, Tatiana scooted from him. "Not yet." She slapped his hand then squeezed it when he made a second attempt. "I don't want it yet."

Alexei froze. Tatiana recognized his intentions and rejected them. Her father described Tatiana as a willful child, a will Alexei worried was beyond even the reach of vodka. He settled back to staring up at the trees and the scattering of blue pushed between the leaves. "You need to join the Party by the time you are twenty one," he murmured.

Tatiana flopped down beside him. "I don't like the Party. It is filled with fools and boot lickers."

Alexei half rose, legs pulled tight against his chest. "The Party," he began his defense only to be interrupted as Tatiana pointed at him, laughing.

"You look cute when your nose is like that."

Alexei had felt his face grow warm as her words rattled around his mind. "Yes, yes, the Party." She flicked his left ear. "What about the Party?"

"The Party is the best of everything," Alexei explained. "It is the controller of our destiny. We would be nothing without the Party. Old Russia was a mass of superstitions and exploitation. The people were crying for leadership and the Party rose up and provided it. You want to live a full life, one dedicated to a great cause then you must join the Party."

His earnestness was greeted by a giggle. "Your nose, your nose, it looks like a little pig. All pushed together like that." She reached up but he avoided her.

"You must listen."

Tatiana was in no mood to listen. "Where's our party?" She craned her neck, eyes searching for the package Alexei carried with him to the lake.

"What?" Alexei froze.

"I saw the vodka bottle." Tatiana's eyes twinkled. "What did you think, I was going to sip and take off all of my clothes?"

"No," he lied.

"Where is it, where is it?" She reached around him.

Alexei surrendered, realizing what he intended to control her instead would control him. They took their first tentative drinks watching to ensure the other emptied their glass. The second was easier - vodka was a much part of the diet to a Russian as potatoes were to an Irishman - and by the third they were racing each other to down it. Relaxed, inhibitions smoothed, desires and self- control fighting a pitched battle, they began. It was not Alexei's first time. Tatiana, fumbling with her clothes and afterwards blushed behind a satisfied smile. Alexei offered only determination for another.

Their afternoon assignation remained a secret though Professor Vatutin could not ignore his daughter's sudden mood shift. Her emotions ran the gamut from depressed, even for an eighteen year old, to ecstatic. Summer turned into fall but their July Sunday afternoon together would not be forgotten, even a decade later as Alexei sat in the Kremlin.

Memories of Tatiana were dangerous and shoving them deep into his consciousness saved Alexei embarrassment during his waking hours. His dreams, undeterred by party control, were a different story and awakening with a start, hand on his chest he moved from the Kharkov park to the dark little room where he was being summoned by his NKVD guard rattling his door.

"Alexei Mikhaelovich" sounded through the heavy wood, forcing Alexei from his bed, sheets sticking to his body. Moscow heat was unbearable without the benefit of electricity. A blackout prohibited nighttime electricity and sleep became a rare commodity. Screen less windows only allowed in pests, leaving Alexei to remain on the roof of the building until the darkness cooled his place from sweltering to stifling, a distinction without a difference when it came to sleep.

Alexei stumbled in the dark, toe stubbed, elbows nicked. He no longer feared late night visits from the NKVD. The Nazi invasion had ended the purges. Loyalty was assumed, division more deadly than potential treason.

Alexei tugged open his door, locks offering less resistance than usual. He faced a pair of flashlights pointed into his eyes. "You are wanted," Uri his handler grumbled, squinting into the dark apartment. "You have a girl?"

"No," Alexei said, tiring of the questions about his personal life. As the adjutant to the Soviet Communist Party's Secretary General, he enjoyed little time for things as inconsequential as a woman.

Uri grinned. "I have someone for you."

Alexei glanced at his watch, the radium dial the only light seeping into the apartment other than the flashlights. It was four thirty, not the best time for discussing dates with his secret police shadow. "They want me now?' Alexei was brusque, an attitude he learned working for Comrade Stalin. A word from Alexei and they could be headed east or to the western front to die in a German prison camp.

"Yes." Uri handed Alexei his flashlight. "Get dressed."

Alexei's clothes were always at the ready beside a pair of small cedar boxes holding family heirlooms from Voronezh. Once free of the overheated apartment he struggled to make sense of the early morning summons. Smolensk had fallen weeks earlier. The fight for the city barely slowed Guderian's panzers pointed toward Moscow. There had been talk of the Soviet government moving east to Kuibyshev, baiting the Germans to overextend before smashing them west of the Volga.

Many Muscovites heard the same rumors, hustling to apply for internal permits to visit relatives in distant cities safe from the swastika. Alexei was not worried. He would travel where Stalin went, the general secretary the only one who mattered in maintaining the Soviet system.

The drive was quick, the early summons putting speed at a premium. The city streets were empty, even the July heat insufficient to tempt Muscovites to escape into the night air for fear of arousing suspicion. Everything appeared normal within the Kremlin walls, no suggestion the government was fleeing. Even at four in the morning it was eerily still, a forced quiet that chipped away at his confidence.

The walk to Stalin's corner office was no different, his NKVD escort silently menacing, Alexei too tired to talk. Entering Stalin's office, Alexei was jolted by the sight of Molotov behind the general secretary's desk, smoking a cigarette. He jumped at Alexei's entrance. Beria was nearby, small eyes fluttering, agitation lining his face. Seated and facing Molotov was a uniformed man.

Beria waved for the door to be closed. "There has been a disaster."

Alexei eyed him. The sweat dousing his face, the quiver in his lips and hands replaced the usual menace associated with the NKVD chief. Molotov approached Alexei. "The army generals attempted a coup, led by General Voroshilov. Comrade Stalin was wounded.

Alexei's grabbed the back of a chair to steady his wobbly knees.

"He is alive," Beria said. "But he will be unable to work for weeks, maybe months." Beria grabbed Alexei's shoulder and squeezed. "We need your help, Alexei Fedorovich." Fingernails dug into his flesh, a signal he was being ordered rather than requested.

"If the soldiers should discover this news they might throw down their arms. Traitors at the top level of the Red Army. Who could be trusted to battle the Germans?"

"Voroshilov?" Alexei croaked.

Molotov and Beria exchanged looks, the NKVD chief nodding. "He is of no concern. The danger has been eliminated. We have rooted out the traitors in the army. General Chernyahovsky is now the War Minister." He motioned to the man sitting quietly in front of Stalin's desk.

Alexei squinted at the man who did not appear much older than him. "How many were involved?"

"That is not your concern," Beria growled, steel returning.

Molotov's eyes widened, a quick nod moving the NKVD chief. "Comrade Stalin will need rest and recuperation. The Party has ordered it. We must not allow this information to reach the ears of ordinary people."

Alexei nodded and swayed, imagining the peoples' reaction to the news. "You want me to help Comrade Stalin in his recovery?"

Molotov sighed. "Comrade Stalin is in excellent hands." A queer little smile crossed the foreign minister's lips, joined by Beria. "No, Comrade Protopopov, we require your assistance here. You are the one link to Comrade Stalin, the one who can speak for Comrade Stalin as the Politburo makes difficult decisions."

Alexei's eyes widened. "You want me to join the Politburo?"

Molotov's face tightened and he wandered away, as Beria returned his grip to Alexei's shoulder. "The Politburo will issue the order in Comrade Stalin's name. You will follow those orders to make it appear Comrade Stalin is issuing them. You will carry on here as if Comrade Stalin was working in this office." He squeezed.

Alexei flinched. He was in danger and sensed the same for Stalin. His protector was gone, his return unlikely in the near future.

"For the Party, for Comrade Stalin I will do this duty."

Molotov slumped into Stalin's chair, relieved. Beria snatched Alexei's hands, the NKVD chief returning to old form. "You are wise for your age, Alexei Fedorovich, you may survive this crisis."

The vote of confidence did not make Alexei feel better.

27

July 25, 1940   **South of Moscow**

NKVD Major Natasha Anatolievna Merkulkov climbed carefully off the horse drawn cart, rebuffing her traveling companion's outstretched hand.

"Dmitry, I do not need your help," stated Natasha. "I think I can handle dismounting from a farmer's wagon."

"I am sorry Major Merkulhov. I merely wanted to assist as much as possible," replied the young engineer Dmitry.

Natasha considered Dmitry for a moment. Since her aggressive physical attack upon him in the abandoned peasant hut outside of Smolensk, he had catered to her every need. He was afraid for his life. Not because she had a gun and might kill him but because she was a major in the NKVD, the Soviet secret police. Such status threatened his entire family lineage.

Natasha nodded to the driver, a stooped shouldered peasant probably much younger than he appeared. Discharged from duty, he turned the medieval conveyance in the opposite direction. He waved and departed south down the dirt track, delighted to take his leave of the NKVD officer and her pistol.

Dmitry waved back to the peasant without enthusiasm. He was now alone with Natasha. He kicked a series of rocks across the road like a small child, causing dust to rise into the humid air. He coughed.

Natasha let him carry on. She walked 10 meters further north, where the dirt track joined a larger, paved road.

Natasha grinned. "Where do you think we are now, Dmitry?"

"I don't know Major. We have been traveling for over a month. Close to Moscow?" suggested Dmitry.

Natasha laughed and pointed to the pavement and then to the north.

"Yes, Dmitry, we have reached the outskirts of Moscow. It is over that rise, not more than 15 kilometers."

Natasha and Dmitry had walked, crawled, ran and floated for six weeks, evading the Nazis by day, moving only at night. Three days earlier the pair had unwittingly slipped through a gap in the chaotic front line. They simply walked through an area that was not yet occupied by the Germans, between the disorganized Russian strongholds. After another two days of walking and the commandeered cart ride they finally reached the southern outskirts of Moscow. No longer in enemy held territory, they chanced daylight travel.

Natasha found an empty trunk in the weeds by the road. She dragged it to the side of the intersection and turned it over. After testing its sturdiness, she gingerly eased her tired frame into a sitting position.

Dmitry started towards Natasha, as if to sit next to her on the trunk. She raised her hand to stop him. "There's not enough room for two."

Dmitry sighed and slumped onto the ground next to her. She smiled again, which was unusual. She had smiled more today than in the last sixth weeks.

"Why do you think Moscow will be so grand?" asked Dmitry.

Natasha shrugged her shoulders. She alternated her attention from north to south, peering down the highway.

"I will be back with my people, the leaders of the Revolution. I will be away from all of the unwashed peasants. No more walking or sleeping on straw covered floors. Perhaps I can eat something other than the shit we dig up in the fields," reasoned Natasha. "I can find out what is really going on in this war."

"But you were not posted in Moscow. You live in Kharkov."

"Dmitry, for an engineer you really aren't that smart," replied Natasha. "I am not from Kharkov."

"Mikhail Koshkin is your uncle. He is the head of the design bureau in Kharkov,"

"Of course, I almost forgot about dear Uncle Mikhail," laughed Natasha. "Dmitry it does not matter what you believed. It only mattered what the American James Reilly thought was real."

"Reilly meant nothing to you?" asked Dmitry with hope.

"We have covered this topic," said Natasha. "Reilly was my job. I did not love him and do not love him. He is a capitalist. He cares only about enriching himself from the labor of the workers. And if you haven't figured it out by now, Comrade Koshkin is not my uncle. It was all part of the ruse."

Dmitry moved closer to the trunk and looked up at Natasha. He motioned to the empty space.

"So what do we do now?" wondered Dmitry. "If we find another ride we shall be in Moscow before nightfall."

Natasha looked into Dmitry's eyes. She studied his face, concluding Dmitry was unusually unattractive, even by Russian standards.

"No we do not want a ride. It is too dangerous, the situation is too chaotic. Tonight, we will walk to Moscow along the side of the road, hiding from bandits and patrols," instructed Natasha. "When we arrive in Moscow, you are released from my service. If necessary, you may discretely use my name. I will confirm your account of our heroic fight against the Fascists and you tireless efforts to assist the Red Army and the NKVD major you saved from certain execution."

Dmitry was relieved but not satisfied. While deathly afraid of the NKVD major, he had grown attached to her. He wiped the sweat from his brow with the back of his hand. The groan of aircraft engines caused him to turn his head to the north.

A pair of Messerschmidt Me-109s hunting for targets zoomed low along the highway. They passed over the intersection and opened fire further south on the dirt track. Natasha did not have to see the results to know the cart driver and his horse were gone, ripped apart by the staccato bursts of machine gun fire. The strafing attack caused Dmitry to take cover, lying flat on his stomach. Natasha did not move an inch, but watched in disgust. As quickly as they appeared, the Luftwaffe fighters were gone.

Natasha's mood turned, she began to cry.

"Where are our planes Dmitry?"

"Gone, destroyed or grounded, who knows which," said Dmitry. He remained prone on the ground but lifted his head to speak. "They certainly aren't in the sky."

Natasha sat in silence. She placed her head in her hands.

"Natasha, where will you go?" asked Dmitry, risking much by using her first name after her clear instructions prohibiting him to address her by anything other than her rank.

Natasha wiped her tears and smiled.

"I will go to the Kremlin and report. I will be assigned a new task."

Dmitry frowned, "the Kremlin? Is it still there?"

"I am sure it is," replied Natasha. "At least I hope it is. I don't know anymore. Perhaps, Comrade Stalin has a plan to counterattack."

Dmitry froze, as there was nothing Natasha could have said that would have been more terrifying than the mere mention of the Soviet leader.

"The one thing I know for certain is that the Red Army is equipped with far more tanks than the Nazis and ours are much better," continued Natasha, her voice gaining strength. "This war is far from over."

Dmitry struggled to his feet and walked over to Natasha. She shifted slightly, allowing him room to join her on the trunk.

"I'm very hungry," advised Dmitry.

"Well, we will find plenty of food in Moscow," suggested Natasha. I'm sure it has been stockpiled since the attack."

28

July 25, 1940   Volokolamsk, Russia

Waltraud Shriver nudged the little Storch spotter plane higher, for a better view of the battle taking place at Volokolamsk. The entire village was covered in black smoke. Artillery detonations exploded almost continuously. Two kilometers further east, Shriver saw a mass of Russian tanks advancing rapidly towards the inferno. Infantry ran alongside the tanks, somehow keeping pace.

"Rolf, there's at least a hundred tanks down there. T-26s, BT-5s and some bigger ones, KV-1s or T-34s," advised Shriver over the intercom. "Looks like some are hugging the rail line and are going to bypass Volokolamsk. Radio down to Lieutenant Wheilerd and let them know mechanized forces with infantry are heading directly for their position."

"How many of the heavies?" asked Rolf Auchen.

"I see twenty. Their hulls look about the size of the PzKpfw IV. I'd say they are T-34s," said Shriver. "I'd say brigade strength."

Unteroffizier Auchen peered over Shriver's shoulder and exclaimed, "Shit, it looks like the whole Red Army."

Shriver pointed out the right side of the windshield, "See the flashes? The artillery is south of the railroad, another five kilometers. That's where the Stukas need to drop their bombs."

"Ja, they won't be able to do much against tanks moving that fast," agreed Auchen.

Auchen radioed Wheilerd, confirming *Kampfgruppe Schmidt's* fears. Wheilerd reported that the Luftwaffe ground coordinator attached to the 20th Mechanized Infantry Division had already called in a *Gruppe* of Stukas to take out the artillery.

Shriver banked to starboard, lining up with the Ruza River. He flew south to the town of Ruza, observing German infantry digging in, preparing for the onslaught. He wagged his wings as the Storch passed over the tired *Landsers.*

"I don't see anything this far south," stated Shriver. "Do you see movement?"

Rolf scanned east of the river and, finding nothing, joined Shriver's observation. "Nein, looks like their thrust is north of the railroad. The only activity I see south of the tracks is the artillery."

Shriver initiated another turn to the right, crossing the Ruza River to the west and rolling out on a northerly heading.

"Agreed, we will fly back to Shakhovskaya and then north towards Kalinin," explained Shriver. Enroute, the Storch passed over the position of *Kampfgruppe Schmidt*. The 88 mm antiaircraft gun crews were unlimbering the *Flak* guns. Shriver wagged the Storch's wings slightly and this time Wheilerd did not offer obscene gestures. The battle was too near.

North of the railroad, Shriver spotted more Red Army tanks and infantry at the west edge of the Volga Reservoir. He pointed the nose north towards Kalinin. His focused his gaze on the horizon, straining to measure the breadth of the Soviet counterattack.

The staccato of the Fieseler Storch's rear mounted 7.92 mm MG 15 machine gun interrupted his efforts. The recoil vibrated through the tiny plane's frame.

"Indians!" shouted Rolf Auchen between bursts of defensive fire, using Luftwaffe slang for attacking fighters. "Two I-16s above and on our tail.

The attackers screamed by the Storch passing less than 50 meters above. The Russian I-16s pulled straight up, gaining altitude but losing airspeed.

"I'm going to slow us to a crawl. We'll see how good their gunnery is," responded Shriver. He was well trained and knew that tests had proven it was very difficult for experienced fighter pilots to hit a Storch flying low and slow.

Shriver pulled the throttle back to idle and dropped the nose. He engaged full flaps. His goal was to get down to tree top level and slow the plane to an anemic 55 kilometers per hour.

The Storch was configured to land and Shriver searched for a suitable spot to put the plane on the ground. Auchen unleashed another salvo from the MG 15, signaling the return of the I-16s. Shriver banked the Storch hard to port, careful to maintain sufficient airspeed to avoid stalling a wing. The I-16s shot past again, still unable to hit the Storch.

Shriver continued turning until he reached a southerly heading. He raised the flaps and added power in an attempt to put distance between the Storch and the I-16s. If he could get back to Shakhovshaya, *Kampfgruppe Schmidt's* anti-aircraft guns could provide some measure of defense.

"Rolf, where are the Indians?" demanded Shriver.

"Turning and gaining altitude," replied Auchen. "They'll be back quickly."

"We're still 10 kilometers from Schmidt's flak," warned Shriver. "We're not going to make it."

"Their aim is shit. Keep going," encouraged Auchen. "Where the hell is the Luftwaffe?" We could use a few Me-109s right now."

Less than two minutes later, the I-16s were back on the Storch's tail. The lead *Rata's* aim had improved. It descended on the little Storch, raking the fuselage with 7.62 mm rounds from its four Shkas machine guns. Shriver pulled the throttle back, dropped flaps and bank hard to starboard. Auchen desperately returned fire with his sole MG 15.

"I'm hit," exclaimed Auchen.

The *Ratas* flashed by again. With flaps extended and throttle at idle, the Storch sunk to the ground.

Shriver felt liquid on his face and wiped it away. He looked at his hand, finding it covered in blood. He was also wounded, but not incapacitated. He added power to stop the descent. The Storch's engine stopped abruptly, the propeller slowed.

"Hold on Rolf, the engine's dead. I'm putting it down in that field," shouted Shriver. "Can you move?"

"I think so, it's my arm," advised Auchen.

"Be ready to run for those trees," said Shriver. "We have to be fast."

The field was tilled but nothing appeared to be growing. Shriver lined up to land with the grain of the rows, to avoid flipping the stricken plane. Mercifully, the direction he intended to land was into the wind.

Shriver held the Storch off the ground as long as possible, slowing to stall speed. He flared and set the plane down with each main tire snugly at the bottom of a tilled row. He kicked opened the side canopy and exited.

"Rolf, let's go," yelled Shriver as he grabbed Auchen by the collar and yanked him forward. "The *Ratas* are coming back."

The wounded pair hobbled quickly to the edge of the field into the woods. As they slid into a drainage ditch, the Storch's remaining fuel exploded, ignited by a final volley from the I-16s. They watched the Russians fly off to the north.

"How badly are you wounded?" asked Shriver.

Auchen pulled off his jacket. His left sleeve was soaked with blood. He struggled to remove his shirt. With Shriver's assistance and after much cursing, Auchen's wound was revealed.

"I don't think it's a homeland shot Rolf," concluded Shriver, referring to Wehrmacht slang for a wound that was not permanently crippling but sufficient to require the recipient to be evacuated from the front.

Auchen peered at his wound and looked at the gash above Shriver's right eye. Blood seeped out freely.

"Mine is worse than yours Lieutenant," observed Auchen.

Shriver wiped blood from his brow and examined his hand.

"Ja, this isn't new. It's the old one opening up again. I'll be alright."

"What now, Lieutenant?" wondered Auchen, pointing at the burning Storch. "We're not going anywhere in that."

Shriver surveyed the plowed field and the wrecked Storch. A dilapidated structure was at the north end.

"Well we can't stay here Rolf. They'll be bandits at night," said Shriver. "I have my Luger and as far as I can tell, you are unarmed."

Rolf nodded affirmatively. "What should we do then?"

Shriver climbed from the drainage ditch and walked over to the smoldering Storch, searching for useful items thrown from the aircraft. He picked up a piece of plexi-glass and tossed it aside.

"We will bandage your wound and then we walk south towards Shakhoyskaya and the train tracks," ordered Shriver.

"That's where the Red Army is attacking," countered Auchen.

"We'll have to be cautious," agreed Shriver.

29

July 25, 1940   **East of Shakhovskaya, Russia**

Rudi watched as the 88 mm flak crews prepared for the onslaught. His captured BT-5s were positioned ahead but not as far forward as the rest of Schmidt's panzers. He was the group's ready reserve, to be thrown into the fray if a weak point developed.

Schmidt's PzKmpfw 38(t) panzers were arranged with half on either side of the train tracks. Lunge's 50 mm antitank guns were north of the tracks, hidden in a stand of woods. Groesbeck's motorcycle platoon was dismounted and provided modest infantry support for Lunge. *Kampfgruppe Schmidt* did not have artillery support other than the 88's.

Schmidt motioned for Rudi to join him at the Flivo's halftrack where he found the combined unit's leaders. Rudi stood next to Groesbeck and behind Lunge. Wheilerd gestured to the east.

"The Stukas will target the artillery batteries south of the tracks. Once they are destroyed, they will look for appropriate targets north and west back towards our positions," explained Lieutenant Wheilerd.

"What is the status of the 20th Motorized Infantry at Volokolamsk?" asked Schmidt.

Wheilerd shook his head. "I have nothing from the air to report."

"Not good," replied Schmidt. "They have been frantically calling for reinforcements."

The assembled officers looked at each other.

"We have to hope they can hold on. Our job is to prevent a deeper penetration here along the tracks. We fought hard to get this far east. Let's not give territory back." Schmidt paused and looked at each in turn. "We have to hold on for 24 hours. Two panzer divisions are driving northeast to relieve us"

Luftwaffe Staff Sergeant Albert Beyer waited until Captain Schmidt was finished, "Herr Hauptmann, I may be a mere Stabsfeldwebel but it seems we do not have anywhere near enough men, artillery, anti-tank guns or panzers to face such a large force. Our 88's are very valuable and shouldn't be unnecessarily risked."

"Staff Sergeant, the 88s are the only weapon we have that can stop the KV-1s and the T-34s. Without them, we will be slaughtered," barked Schmidt.

Chastised, Beyer rebounded, "We will light up their tanks, Herr Hauptmann."

"How many anti-tank shells do you have for the 88s? asked Schmidt.

"Plenty, we haven't used any since we were re-supplied in Smolensk," replied the Staff Sergeant.

"Lieutenant Wheilerd, why are we not hearing anything from the Storch?" asked Schmidt.

Wheilerd replied immediately. "It appears that it may have been shot down. We have not heard from Lieutenant Shriver since he passed over us headed north."

Groesbeck, the ardent Nazi, could not stop himself from offering a disparaging comment.

"The Flying Jew is worthless. He almost killed General Rommel and now he's disappeared."

"Shut up Groesbeck, Shriver is as German as you," said Wheilerd. "It's not his fault he had a grandmother he didn't even know was Jewish."

Captain Schmidt raised his hand to quiet the squabbling.

"Enough of that shit. We have a battle to fight and it is not going to be easy. Sergeant Beyer, focus the 88s on the heavier tanks as soon as they are in range. Lunge, pound the light tanks from the flank. Kleime, be ready to move with the captured BT-5s to buttress Lunge and Groesbeck if they need it. We will keep the Czech panzers in the center." Schmidt paused and pointed to the map outstretched on the hood of the halftrack. "At all times, target any tank with aerial contraptions like that on Lieutenant's Kleime's captured BT-5 command tank. The Red Army is unable to function without their officers. We break up the tanks and we stop the infantry assault. If the Bolshevik hordes get to the 88s, we're done."

The assembled leaders saluted and dispersed to their units. Rudi stopped Staff Sergeant Beyer and pulled him aside.

"What kind of range do the 88s have against tanks?" asked Rudi.

"Let's put it this way, Lieutenant. We will start firing as soon as we can see them," replied Beyer.

"Let's not be so formal Albert," grinned Rudi. "I was a Staff Sergeant myself a month ago. Call me Rudi."

"Well Rudi, you did something heroic to get a medal and a promotion," remarked Beyer, pointing at Rudi's Iron Cross.

Rudi shook his head.

"I blew up a Russian KV-1 with gasoline I poured on it from a can. It was the first one we had ever seen," explained Rudi. "It destroyed about half of my battalion, my Panzer PzKpfw III and killed most of my crew first. Afterwards we counted 50 hits from our 37 mm and 50 mm guns, which barely dented it."

Beyer put his arm around Rudi, which was somewhat awkward as he was several inches shorter. He saw wetness in Rudi's eyes. He was inspired by Rudi's devotion to his lost crew members. They walked to the 88s.

"I understand that our 88 mm shells should easily pierce the armor of the KV-1 and the T-34," boasted Beyer. "But we haven't fired at Bolshevik tanks yet."

"Why not?" asked Rudi.

"We've been in the rear, providing flak defense for Minsk," advised Beyer. "It was a waste of time and the 88s. There were no Russian aircraft targets and frankly, the entire deployment lowered morale."

Rudi glanced at Beyer quizzically and said, "Explain further please."

Beyer lowered his voice.

"I don't know if you are aware what is happening in the areas we have occupied. The Fuhrer Order requiring elimination of the Bolshevik commissars and other undesirable elements is being carried out, shall we say, aggressively."

Rudi's shoulders slumped. He had hoped the atrocities he had witnessed with the SS were an aberration.

"I have seen similar things with the SS," offered Rudi. "I don't like it. There has to be a better way."

"I agree, but what are we going to do?" Beyer stopped and swiveled his head to confirm their conversation was not being monitored. He continued, "My men were outraged when we saw women and children being herded like cattle to who knows what fate?"

Rudi was torn internally but knew there was no point to discussing it further. He changed the subject.

"How long to button these up and make them ready for transport?" inquired Rudi, pointing to an adjacent 88 mm anti-aircraft gun.

Beyer laughed, reached up and patted the barrel.

"What's so funny?" asked Rudi.

"If we have to retreat, that will mean we haven't stopped the Red Army's counter attack," reasoned Beyer. "It will be too late for us to save the guns."

Rudi nodded and reached into his pocket, retrieving a roll of Pervitin methamphetamine tablets. He offered the roll to Beyer who declined, raising his hand in a halting motion.

"I don't want any of that shit, Rudi," said the Staff Sergeant. "It messes up my brain."

"I agree but it does keep me alert and awake," replied Rudi. "I don't take it all the time."

Rudi left the four 88 mm flak guns and headed for his own unit, confident that he made a friend with a like-minded soldier.

30

July 25, 1940   **East of Ruza River, Russia**

"I think I can see Moscow, off to the east," exclaimed one of the radio operator/rear gunner's to the rest of Oswald's *staffel* of Ju-87B Stukas as they crossed the Ruza River.

"Sandmann, tell them to stop the unnecessary chatter," instructed Oswald of his own backseater. He did steal a glance off the starboard wing, in the direction of the Soviet capital. At an altitude of 5,000 meters, it was possible to make out irregular shapes on the horizon to the east. Oswald was inspired. The end of the war was literally in sight.

Five kilometers to the north, Oswald observed flashes on the ground revealing the position of their target, the Russian artillery that was torturing the 20th Motorized Infantry Division at Volokolamsk. Above the emplacements was a tangle of cartwheeling aircraft. He could the easily see twin engine Messerschmitt Bf-110s and stubby Polikarpov I-16s locked in melee.

As the Stukas closed on their target, Oswald determined that the big and heavily armed Me-110 *Zerstorer* was ineffective in a dogfight against the tiny I-16s. Even though the Luftwaffe crews were far better trained, the *Ratas* were considerably more maneuverable, turning hard when threatened from behind. Conversely, the *Ratas* were lightly armed with only four machine guns and their pilots' gunnery skills were weak. The air battle was proceeding but without significant results other than the loss of a handful of I-16s flown by novices. Oswald tightened his seat belt and harness. He knew from his experience in Spain that the Ju-87B would be a much easier target for the *Ratas*.

"Sandmann, I got the radio," advised Oswald. He then broadcast to the entire flight of nine Stukas.

"It's a hornet's nest. We are attacking three abreast, set contact altimeters at 1,300 meters," radioed Oswald, using his best estimate of the ground elevation plus 1,000 meters. He believed their target was on ground that was 247 meters above sea level, but he added a few meters for safety. Releasing their bombs at 1,000 meters was standard against a defended target.

Oswald ran through the pre-dive checklist. He confirmed the pull out altitude was set at 1,300 meters on the contact altimeter and turned on his reflector sight. He closed the radiator flaps and opened the ventilation air supply for the windscreen to avoid misting as they descended to the warm, moist air below. Me-110s and I-16s streaked by ahead and below. The Stuka was vulnerable to attack from virtually every nation's fighter aircraft and it was clear the Luftwaffe had not achieved local air superiority.

Oswald encouraged the pilots for the attack. "There's a lot of Bolshevik artillery down there, so make it count."

Oswald peered through the small window on the floor on *Jolanthe*, waiting for his target to appear. Sporadic anti-aircraft fire rose to greet the *Staffel*. Oswald spotted a line of 152 mm howitzers. He pulled back on the throttle, engaged the Jericho siren, opened the dive brakes and began his dive.

Established in the standard but exceptional 80 degree dive, *Jolanthe* lost altitude quickly but did not increase its speed beyond 300 knots. The massive dive brakes prevented the gull winged dive bomber from blasting through its maximum structural airspeed. Oswald established a Russian howitzer in his reflector sight and kept it centered. Smaller caliber anti-aircraft guns fired ineffectively. The Jericho siren screeched its demoralizing scream. The Red Army artillerymen scurried for cover.

Barely two minutes into his attack, the dive bombing system's horn sounded indicating the imminent arrival of the release altitude. When the horn ceased, Oswald released the SC-250 high explosive bomb. It swung on its trapeze, cleared the propeller and hurtled to the ground.

Oswald rode through the incredible gravitational forces instantly created when the automatic recovery system engaged. He had experienced the violent pull out so many times over the years that it was no longer uncomfortable. It was something to be endured, not feared.

"Scratch a Red Army artillery battery," exclaimed Sandmann. He hesitated and added, "I see more large guns by the embankment north of the woods."

"We'll give them our 100 kilos," replied Oswald, swiveling his focus to the Stukas forming up on either side. He announced to his flight, "keep climbing and turn south to 180 degrees."

"Mueller, there's a *Rata* diving on you!" warned Sandmann.

Lieutenant Mueller continued a climbing turn as if his radio was off. He did not take evasive action.

Sandmann pleaded for help from the Me-110 fighter cover but they were busy fending off the pesky *Ratas*. Smoke billowed from Mueller's cowling and he increased his pitch angle dramatically.

"He's going to stall!" exclaimed Sandmann. The rear canopy opened and the rear gunner attempted to climb out.

"Mueller, get out!" barked Oswald over the radio but it was too late. The stricken Stuka began to spin and burst into flames. The rear gunner fell away from the crippled bomber.

"Eindstall got out," yelled Sandmann over the intercom. "Chute is opening."

Oswald turned his attention back to maneuvering *Jolanthe* into position for another attack on the Red Army artillery. Sporadic cumulous clouds were moving in above the target, rendering the melee even more confusing as aircraft darted into their thick billowy cover. A pair of dark olive painted Me-110s dove past his nose, diving on the nimble *Ratas*. He spotted the battery adjacent to the river embankment through a gap in the clouds. Oswald initiated his dive from a much lower altitude, decreasing his dive angle accordingly.

The *staffel's* attack was productive. Oswald could see twisted metal and multiple fires. He aimed for the unscathed 152 mm howitzers spotted by Sandmann on their pull out from the first attack. The Russian guns were not firing, their crews having fled for cover. He aimed for the middle howitzer and dropped his two remaining 100 kilo bombs.

After the pull out, Oswald turned southwest and leveled off in the midst of the cumulous clouds passing a *staffel* of Heinkel 111 medium bombers, their bomb bay doors open. He knew the clustered Red Army artillery was doomed. He set their course for the airfield at Smolensk. The ride was bumpy in the clouds but they offered safety from the *Ratas*. They were not chased as they left the battlefield.

The cost had been high. He scanned his unit as they formed, climbing above the thickening cloud deck. Three were missing. He knew about Mueller, but who were the others?

"Sandmann, find out who's missing," ordered Oswald.

"Mueller and Eindstall are dead," replied Sandmann.

"I though Eindstall got out?"

"He did, but he was burning. When his chute opened, it was also on fire," answered Sandmann. "He didn't make it."

Oswald shook his head, unable to think of a response. He checked his heading and surveyed his instruments, all appeared in the green. They were back over German held territory.

Several radio communications later, Sandmann reported their battle losses. One other Stuka shot down, one crashed landed behind lines with possible survivors. A third of their *Staffel* was destroyed in 15 minutes.

"The Bolsheviks are not giving up yet, Sandmann," commented Oswald over the intercom.

"Moscow is going to be a shit storm, Herr Hauptmann."

31

July 25, 1940   **East of Shakhovskaya, Russia**

Shells from Staff Sergeant Beyer's 88 mm flak battery whistled towards the onrushing Russian tanks. Rudi watched with his binoculars from the turret of his captured BT-5 command tank as round after round tore into the larger of the approaching Russian tanks. The range was still too great for smaller caliber weapons to engage. With nothing more to prepare, the men of *Kampfgruppe Schmidt* could do nothing but wait and watch the effect of the lethal 88s.

"What's going on out there, Rudi?" shouted Corporal Adolf Brauch from the driver's compartment. The BT-5 was hull down behind a stone wall, obstructing Brauch's view from the hull.

"There are at least 100 Russian tanks driving right at us, of all different sizes." Rudi lowered his binoculars. The roar of the 88s was constant. "It's incredible Adolf. Beyer's 88s are accurate and their rate of fire is incredible,"

"How many they light up so far?" questioned Brauch.

"At least of 20 the bigger ones, some KV-1s and some smaller turreted ones, which must be the T-34s," replied Rudi.

"Are they retreating?

Rudi scanned the battle before him, adjusting the focus on his binoculars.

"No, they are still coming, with lots of infantry running alongside." advised Rudi. "They'll be in range soon. Reiner, get ready to load. Be fast, the Russians only made room for two in this turret."

Rudi turned back to the battle. He felt like it resembled a spectator sport, rather similar to the Olympics. Most of the T-34s and the KV-1s were smoking. The 88's turned their attention to the Russian command tanks with their elaborate antenna contraptions.

"They're pretty close to in range for Lunge's 50 mm guns now," announced Rudi as Lunge's anti-tank cannons opened up. T-26s and BT-5s burst into flames as 50 mm antitank shells ripped into their weak armor. Several Russian rounds passed overhead Rudi's position, long range volleys randomly launched by the attackers.

A hundred meters ahead, Schmidt's Czech PzKpfw 38(t)'s joined the battle. Their 37 mm shells were small but sufficient to pierce the weak armor of the BT-5s and T-26s.

"I aim and fire, you load," directed Rudi to Reiner. He lined up an advancing BT-5 in the rudimentary aiming system and fired the 45 mm main gun. In seconds, his target was burning. Reiner slammed another shell into the breach.

Rudi quickly acquired another target, a fast moving T-26. He fired and missed to the left. Surprisingly, its turret shot straight into the air and landed behind the still moving tank.

"Damn, an 88 got that one," exclaimed Rudi. He scanned for another victim. A dozen BT-5s were charging Schmidt's position.

Rudi fired at the lead BT-5, scoring a hit on its tracks, causing it to stop dead in 10 meters. A second round finished it off. MG-38 machine gun fire from Groesbeck's dismounted motorcycle platoon sliced into the Red Army infantry.

Half of the attacking tank force was disabled or burning, but the Russian tanks and infantry pressed on. BT-5s were almost to Schmidt's Czech panzers. The infantry swarmed into their position. Rudi raked the Bolsheviks with his Degtyaryova Pekhotny DP 7.62mm co-axial machine gun, confident any stray rounds would not harm Schmidt's panzers.

"They're on top of us!" cried a radio from one of Schmidt's panzers. Without supporting infantry nearby, they were in real trouble. Rudi's BT-5s continued to spray machine gun fire but the Russian infantry took cover, shielded from certain death.

The Czech 38(t)s and the BT-5s traded blows at point blank range, with equal success. The Red infantry tossed crude petrol bombs on to the stranded German panzers. Beyer's 88s and Lunge's anti-tank guns effectively stopped the attack north of Schmidt's position but were unable to impact the close quarter melee.

Rudi did everything in his power to help Schmidt other than approach the tangled brawl. He knew his thinned skinned platoon of captured BT-5s would not last 5 minutes tangled up at close range. He was able to destroy two more attacking BT-5s with his main gun and fired all of the ammunition for the co-axial DP machine gun.

Twenty minutes later the firing stopped. There was no word from Schmidt over the radio. Rudi did not deem it wise to approach the stricken unit without supporting infantry. *Kampfgruppe Schmidt* waited to learn the fate of its leader.

A Russian BT-5 tried to flee the field but was demolished by shells from Lunge's 50 mm guns. From the rear, Rudi heard the groan of motorcycles. The recon platoon of the 7th Panzer Division rolled into their position, followed by a platoon of more Czech PzKmpf 38(t)s. Motorized infantry dismounted and gingerly advanced to Schmidt's position. Submachine guns chattered dispatching the surviving Russians. Medical personnel were called up to tend to the wounded Germans.

Captain Schmidt was not among the wounded. Adolf and Rudi found him, slumped atop the turret of his Czech 38(t). His upper body was burned badly, his face covered in soot but otherwise remarkably intact.

Corporal Brauch put his arm around Lieutenant Kleime. They had been with Schmidt from the beginning.

"Well looks like he will get his Knight's Cross, Rudi," whispered Brauch, alluding to their common belief that Schmidt was desperate to receive the coveted version of the Iron Cross.

"Adolf, Schmidt was a good leader and certainly a faithful National Socialist," agreed Rudi. "He died fighting for his men. He gave his life for the Fatherland and for the Fuhrer."

The 7th Panzer and the 10th Panzer divisons sped by, heading for the gap created beneath the failed Russian counterattack and the Ruza River. The gates to Moscow were open.

32

July 26, 1940   **Berlin**

Reilly thumbed through the packet of technical explanations and drawings he had prepared. Almost 300 pages in length, they had taken him several weeks to compile. Most of the materials related to Russian tanks that he worked on in Kharkov. Captain Scheller had returned his initial work product with a list of almost 100 questions relating to the KV-1 and the T-34, tanks he had only briefly mentioned. After five days, he was finally finished with his answers.

Reilly pulled the sheets together and stacked them repeatedly on the long table in an effort to arrange them in a uniform pile. Success eluded Reilly, as some of the engineering drawings were on oversized paper. He stood and stretched his arms high above his head.

The sounds of traffic drew Reilly to the open window. He was in the same room as he had been every day since his arrival at Abwehr headquarters in Berlin. During the initial meetings with Captain Scheller, Reilly expressed enthusiasm for cooperation with the Germans. Apparently, he had been convincing as Scheller ordered the removal of the shackles after the second day. Reilly knew that his voluminous work product thereafter had kept the cuffs off.

Reilly observed an attractive brunette stride on the sidewalk below. The afternoon temperature was certainly above 90 degrees Fahrenheit. The brunette was dressed for the weather, her light yellow dress fitted and clinging to her voluptuous form. She did not look German to Reilly but Eastern European. Reilly closed his eyes, his thoughts drifting to Natasha. The odds of her remaining alive were low. Reilly sighed, recognizing that it was very unlikely that he would ever see Natasha again.

The interior door opened as Reilly muttered, "Forgive me Natasha, I should have stayed with you."

"What was that James?" asked Captain Scheller as he entered followed by two civilians.

"Nothing Karl, I was admiring a young lady on the *strasse*," admitted Reilly. The two civilians appeared to be related, possibly father and son.

"May I present Professor Ferdinand Porsche and his son Ferdinand?" announced Scheller, solving Reilly's suspicion.

Reilly stepped forward gingerly to shake Professor Porsche's extended hand, "Pleased to meet you sir."

The elder Porsche smiled as Reilly shifted attention to his son.

"Everyone calls me Ferry," explained the younger Porsche as he shook hands with Reilly.

"Professor Porsche, I have been in the Soviet Union much of the last decade but I am familiar with your Volkswagen design," gushed Reilly. "It is masterful and reminds me of the Model T concept of Henry Ford. I worked at Ford for a number of years in the twenties. "

The elder Porsche turned to Scheller for translation. Scheller immediately launched into a five minute explanation in German. Reilly was confident Scheller had provided more than the German version of his simple sentences. Professor Porsche replied to Scheller in the same language. He turned to Reilly and pointed to the chairs arrayed around the table.

"We sit, Herr Reilly?" gestured Porsche.

"My father's English is not so good," said Ferry as he took a seat across from Reilly. "However, I can understand if you speak slowly."

Scheller translated Professor Porsche's words for Reilly.

"Professor Porsche said that you have much in common. He has visited the Ford factory with Ferry. Mr. Ford's idea that the workers at the factory should be able to purchase the cars they build is very similar to our Fuhrer's concept for the Volkswagen."

Reilly expressed surprise, "You have visited the Ford factory?"

"Yes, several years ago and it was most helpful," replied Ferry. "But now with the war…we will probably not build Volkswagens as we wished until it is concluded."

Professor Porsche spoke to Ferry for several minutes in German. Captain Scheller placed his hand on Porsche's sleeve, the universal sign for caution and then translated.

"Professor Porsche wanted you to know that in the early 30's, the Bolshevik Josef Stalin invited him to Russia and offered him much money and a *dacha* to develop cars for the Communists. Obviously, he declined but he admits it was somewhat tempting. At that time cooperation with the Soviets was not discouraged. He understands why you would have taken their offer."

"Thank you Professor," said Reilly. He felt as if the trio were warming him up by building common ground. He also knew their plan was working.

"Our High Command is very interested in the new tanks the Soviets are building," explained Scheller. "I will be blunt. The information you provided on the BT-5 tank series establishes your credibility. However, we are not afraid of the BT-5, as our panzers have slaughtered them in the field. We want to know everything about the KV-1 and the T-34."

Reilly nodded, he understood their fear of the new Russian tanks. His safety depended on the value of his information. It was time for Reilly to exaggerate. "I know little about the T-34 but I have been directly involved with the KV-1 project."

Ferry Porsche retrieved a tablet and poised, a mechanical pencil ready, "Herr Reilly, the Wehrmacht has requested proposals for a design that is capable of defeating these tanks. We intend to win the design competition. We would like your help."

Reilly turned to Captain Scheller and raised an eyebrow, seeking direction.

"My superiors would like you to assist the Porsches in any way possible," advised Scheller. "This project is a priority. I have been told the Fuhrer himself will monitor progress."

Scheller paused and looked at each man, calculating the impact of his words. The Porsches appeared excited and Reilly seemed bewildered.

"Have any of the Russian tanks been captured intact?" asked Reilly. "A working example will be of enormous value to such an effort."

"Regrettably, we have only acquired a handful of each, all of which were knocked out by our brave *Landsers* on the Russian front," admitted Scheller. "Unfortunately, none were destroyed by direct fire from a panzer."

"Thus the need for a better panzer and this competition," said Ferry Porsche.

"Where are they now? Are they still in Russia?"

Scheller grinned, "James, you know German efficiency better than that. They arrived yesterday and are in a warehouse outside Berlin."

"May I see them?" inquired Reilly.

"Better than that James, you will be moved there tomorrow morning," answered Scheller.

"We will join you for the inspection," added Ferry.

"But that is for tomorrow. Now we will have an early dinner," stated Captain Scheller, pointing to the window. "At an outdoor café not ten minutes from here."

"You mean outside this building?" said Reilly. Since his arrival in Berlin, he had not been anywhere other than his sparse cell at night and the conference room at Abwehr headquarters.

Ferry laughed, "If we are work together we shall as colleagues."

0

Reilly sat back and patted his extended stomach, "I have not eaten such food in many months."

"Better than the Soviet Union?" asked Ferry Porsche.

Reilly took a long pull on his Beck's, "I really like German beer."

"The whole world likes German beer, James. The area my family is from is closer to Prague than Berlin. Czech beer is also very good," added Ferry.

"It is too bad your father could not join us for dinner," remarked Captain Scheller.

"Ugh, duty calls… there are many demands on his time," replied Ferry. "Now I must also go gentlemen."

Reilly stood, displaying as much respect as he knew how. Regardless of politics, the Porsche family was respected in the automotive design world.

"Ferry I enjoyed meeting you and look forward to our work together," said Reilly. "Please give my regards to Professor Porsche."

Ferry smiled, waved and was gone. Scheller summoned the waiter and ordered two more Beck's. They sat in silence for several minutes.

"Better than your prison cell?" Scheller asked.

"Of course Karl, I really don't want to stay there anymore," pled Reilly.

"Oh, James, your days in the cell are over," stated Scheller. He pointed over Reilly's shoulder. "What do you think of that?"

Reilly spun his head slowly. The girl from the street below the Abwehr, with the yellow dress, sat at the bar dangling her foot.

"Would you like to meet her?"

"Are you kidding with me Karl?"

Scheller left his chair and set his beer down. He flipped Reilly a full pack of Lucky Strikes. "She's all yours James. Behave yourself. She will know where to drop you off."

The brunette was smiling at Reilly. He lamely shook Scheller's hand and made his way to her stool. The bar was not crowded.

Reilly contemplated an opening statement, but she beat him to the punch. "I'm Gertrude, and you are James Reilly, the American."

It was obvious to Reilly that the entire matter was arranged by Scheller to encourage his cooperation. Reilly did not need prodding, he had spent too many nights alone in his cell.

"I am. It is a pleasure to meet you Gertrude," announced Reilly. He openly admired Gertrude's smooth legs, encased in nylons. "Where did you learn to speak such good English?"

Gertrude made a motion with her hand, as if flicking away a pesky insect. "It does not matter, Jimmy, does it?"

Reilly chuckled, "I suppose nothing could matter less."

"I will make you happy, James," warned Gertrude. She took his hand and placed it around her shoulders. Her yellow dress revealed substantial cleavage. He could easily see a third of her breasts.

"I like happy," mustered Reilly.

Gertrude pulled Reilly's face to towards her and placed her cheek upon his own. She whispered in his ear, "I will do whatever you ask."

Reilly pulled back slightly and appraised her smooth skin. It was shade darker than what he would expect from a German. Reilly held his hand to her bare neck and examined the contrast between her coloring and his own pale reddish hue.

"The tint of your skin is perfect," said Reilly, leaning closer and kissing Gertrude's forehead gently. "You are intoxicating."

Gertrude frowned, "I do not know that word."

Reilly laughed, "It is a good word."

Gertrude's crystal blue eyes lit up. "Shall we go James?"

Reilly stroked her dark brown hair gently. Her thought fleetingly of Natasha.

"She is dead," escaped from his lips.

"Who, James? Who is dead?"

Reilly continued to stroke Gertrude's hair. "Just someone I knew from another time, another world. Let me go to the loo and I am ready to leave."

Gertrude reached for her cigarettes and pointed to a dark hallway, "It's over there."

Reilly took her lighter and flicked a flame. Once her cigarette was lit, he headed to the back. The light in the hallway was burned out and an old drunk partially barred the door to the bathroom. He wore a German Army blouse from the Great War, medals haphazardly attached. Reilly tried to squeeze by without touching the veteran, but his path was blocked.

"Excuse me sir," offered Reilly as he slid to the drunk's left.

"No need to apologize James," replied the drunk in American accented English.

Reilly froze as the vet grasped his arm.

"What the fuck is going on here?" demanded Reilly. "Who are you?"

The drunk brought his face to within an inch of Reilly's. His breath stank of schnapps.

Reilly blinked and stuttered, "Edwards? Is that you?"

"Yes, James. I must be quick. We know you are here. We know what you are doing."

"I had no choice. It was help them or die," explained Reilly.

"Unless the brunette fucks you to death, it looks like you will be fine," spat Edwards.

"Can you help me escape?" asked Reilly in desperation.

Edwards chuckled. "Why would we do that? Many in our government want the Nazis to defeat Stalin. We want you to help them."

"They already have! They will be in Moscow before the summer is out," stammered Reilly.

"The Red Army isn't dead yet James," reasoned Edwards. "You reported yourself that the Communists possess 20,000 tanks, most of which are better than anything the Germans can field."

"They don't know what the fuck they are doing," said Reilly, his voice rising. "It's a complete mess. The Russians are losing men and ground on a scale that's unimaginable."

Edwards held his hand up, silencing Reilly. "We shall see James. Go take a leak. Enjoy your night with Francine."

"Francine? What the hell are you talking about? Her name is Gertrude."

Edwards shuffled towards a door at the end of the hallway. "Is that what she is calling herself nowadays?"

Reilly relieved himself and returned to Gertrude or Francine, he was no longer certain as to what was real.

"It took you awhile, James," said the brunette with the flawless light brown skin and yellow dress.

Reilly thought about questioning her but changed his mind. Why look a gift horse in the mouth? "There was a long line, one of the commodes was *kaput*...let's get out of here Gertrude."

Later Reilly performed as expected by his new masters. He had not lain with a woman in months. He decided to forget Natasha and Scheller and Edwards. Reilly did what he always did well. He pulled her dress off her as soon as they entered her apartment. He mauled her nipples with his teeth. Entering her from behind, he drove deep into her, biting her shoulder, leaving marks. She pushed back, panting, "Yes Jimmy, harder. "

Reilly hooked his arms under her shoulders and bore down, losing control, ejaculating. He remained in Gertrude for several minutes before withdrawing and rolling to his side. He verified that the condom had remained intact.

Gertrude slumped until she was prone. She placed her hand on his chest and then traced her fingers along the edges of the tattoo of the 4 nines, slowly touching each and announcing the suit in English.

"Spades... hearts... clubs... and my favorite...diamonds."

Reilly asked her, "Don't you want to know the significance of the nines? I was born on September 9, 1899. 9-9-99."

"Jimmy, my briefing was very thorough," whispered Gertrude. "I already knew."

33

July 27, 1940   **Minsk, Belorussia**

Operation Typhoon. The name had been chosen, important to the
generals in Zossen and Rastenburg and possibly to some of the
grenadiers preparing to launch toward Moscow, but of little notice to
Colonel Gunther Blumentritt. Chief of Staff for the 48th Panzer
Corps and General Manstein, he had watched the medium German
and Czech tanks outmaneuver their heavier, faster and more
numerous opponents, blasting their way from the Latvian border east
and leading Fourth Panzer Group to Novgorod, the ancient city once
the capital of Russia. They had come to rest not far from the odd
geographic formations known as the Valdai Hills. Behind this break
in the stultifying flat Russian terrain were the endless steppes that
would take them to the Volga then the Urals. But they were not
moving toward nothingness, instead the panzers were heading south,
toward Moscow.

A month had elapsed since the meeting with the Fuhrer and
the decision to take Moscow rather than shifting forces to the north
and south. The drive toward the Soviet capital was decided with the
belief that Ukraine and much of European Russia would collapse
once the Bolshevik government was beheaded. It was gamble,
ignoring flanks for all out drive toward the Soviet capital.
Blumentritt had played a small but pivotal role, defying the
deskbound generals and placing his career in the hands of front line
leaders.

The general decision made, the operation details were next.
Blumentritt joining the Army Group Center staff, the Fourth Panzer
group to be transferred from Army Group North to join Operation
Typhoon. He soon learned the fighting among the generals was not
yet over.

The first battle came with the northern army group. The departure of Panzer Group Four left only two infantry armies in the north, the Eighteenth, which had fought its way from Estonia to the outskirts of Leningrad, and the Sixteenth, which had been led by the panzer group to Novgorod. Without the panzers slicing through the Red Army rear, the two armies would be static, their contribution to Operation Typhoon to tie down as many enemy divisions as possible. The protests were ignored, though a question was raised, would the Red Army notice the movement of an entire panzer group to the south. The solution was simple. The panzers would turn south, but the group's telegraph operator would remain outside Novgorod, continuing to send orders to nonexistent divisions. The operator's cadence with the telegraph would be known by the Russians, who would assume the panzer group remained near Novgorod. A small but clever deception to protect the start of Operation Typhoon.

The next debate was an old one as a request was made for General Guderian to turn his Second Panzer Group to the south and clear the Ukraine. The drive in the south had been slowed by the largest Red Army concentrations. The Sixth and Seventeenth Armies had battled to within striking distance of Kiev. General Kleist's First Panzer Group had swept up the Red Army divisions blocking the eastward movement of the Rumanians and driven to the Dnieper and crossed it. Kleist was prepared to strike north, over 100 kilometers east of the main Russian forces around Kiev.

The southern arm of the pincer, though, needed a northern arm to close the trap. Kleist and the Army Group commander von Rundstedt, wanted Guderian to turn south and become the second arm. They guaranteed the destruction of up to one million Red Army soldiers if they acted immediately. Kiev and the Ukraine, though, would have to wait.

The plans were presented to von Bock, Army Group Center's commander and after his changes were added they were sent to Rastenburg for approval. After a week, von Bock was returning to Smolensk and army group headquarters either with approval of the plans or with major changes. Blumentritt joined his commander, Manstein. The 48th Panzer Corps staff had been careful to place their machines at the front of the northern pincer.

Army Group headquarters in Smolensk was located at an old Red Army air base. Now fitted with Luftwaffe planes, their sorties blasting at the Red Army, it was the center of activity, drawing in staff and battlefield leaders. Blumentritt arrived with the others, six army commanders and several corps commanders, all with their staff. They were familiar faces. The florid Hoepner, who had driven the Fourth Panzer group through the remains of the Red Army as they retreated from the center thrust. The Third Panzer commander, General Hoth, one of the older battlefield leaders known as Papa Hoth. Talking with him as they walked to the ugly concrete buildings that represented Bolshevik architecture was General Guderian, whose shredding of the Bolshevik defenses had brought them to the verge of Operation Typhoon. General Kluge of the Fourth Army and General Strauss of the Ninth Army were also present. Their staff was even more familiar, Blumentritt spending hours with them hammering out the details of the Moscow attack.

Into the conference room, concrete walls and floors, pain peeling, cracks from bombs and tank shells that hit close enough to shake it foundations, Blumentritt took his position behind Manstein, who was at the concrete table with the others. He had been briefed on the location and ending point for the 48th Panzer Corps, approving of the daring and refusal to remain still under Russian fire.

Field Marshal von Bock stood among the leaders, maps spread across the table, lines and number marking Russian and German dispositions. "The final phase of the operation will begin in the center." Bock poked his finger at a spot west of Vyazma. "The Third Panzer Group and Fourth and Ninth Armies will continue to advance along the Smolensk-Moscow highway."

Blumentritt contained a smile. Labeling any Russian road as a "highway" was a distortion of the word. "We seek to draw in Konev's Western Front and reserves from the wings, compressing the Western Front into a narrow zone. Five days after the start of the campaign." A jab at a point north and south of the offensive. "Fourth Panzer Group west of Toropets and Third Panzer Group, west of Orel, will launch their assault on the flanks. A massive counter attack at Shakhovshaya was successfully repulsed. Follow up probes have been met with limited resistance. North of Moscow, it appears the Red Army may already be broken."

A throat clear from Strauss. "East," he motioned to a point 120-140 Kilometers west of Moscow. "Can we not turn at Maloyaroslavets and surround the Western and Vyazma fronts. Moscow would be defenseless."

A rustle from the staff behind Hoth and Guderian. Strauss' staff had protested the two tiered offensive from the first conference. They saw the Ninth Army slogging with the Red Army's deepest defenses, taking casualties while Hoepner and Guderian sliced through open space, certain to reach Moscow first.

"We do not want them at Maloyaroslavets." Guderian brought his hand down on the map. "We want them here." His palm covered Moscow."

Strauss, much like his staff, was not easily swayed. "If the West and Vyazma fronts are pinched at Maloyaroslavets, Moscow can be taken by one or two divisions."

"The Fuhrer does not want to capture Moscow. He wants it to burn."

Bock's words drew confusion in some quarters, disdain in others. The man who had embarked them on the eastern campaign had expressed the wish to level Moscow with bombing and artillery, raze the remains and create a massive reservoir along the Moscow River. It was not a militarily feasible plan. Destroying a city the size of Moscow would take months, wasting men and munitions. Then there were the millions of Muscovites trapped in the inferno. No man at the table wanted to issue the orders for their prolonged and unnecessary deaths.

Bock cut off further debate. "The Fuhrer believes if the Russians retreat to Moscow, their fate will be the same as if they are surrounded outside of the city." Bock had just arrived from Rastenburg, having presented Operation Typhoon at Fuhrer headquarters. Dissent and argument was acceptable, but would not change the plans.

"The Second and Fourth Panzer Groups will advance to a point 100 kilometers east of Moscow and turn, cutting retreat and the path of reinforcements."

Hoth, the only other commander to feel the shudder of machinery beneath him, closed one eye at the map. "How many days are predicted for the pincers to meet?"

"Seventeen to twenty one days."

"To move over 300 kilometers?" A stir around the table.

"We will not stop," Guderian promised.

"It might not be your choice," Strauss interjected. The map rustled as he leaned over it. "We are expected to hold one million Russian troops in place while two lines of panzers sweep hundreds of kilometers around Moscow?" A sputter. "It cannot be done."

"It will be done."

"The Russians will snap your supply lines."

"The Luftwaffe can provide us fuel as we need it"

Papa Hoth had another concern. "The Leningrad, Kuibyshev and Voronezh rail lines can move reinforcements into place. The Fourth and Second Panzer Groups lack the forces to defend the rail links and prevent reinforcement or retreat."

"The Second and Sixteenth Armies can extend their zone of control to cover the rail links." This from Kluge, the Fourth Army commander.

Bock found the armies on the map. "The Second Army will hold the Orel Region. It must defend against an attack from the south." The map did not include the Ukraine.

"The Russians, the Russians," Guderian sneered. "We should be less concerned with the enemy and more concerned with our forces. He had repeatedly berated the infantry generals and their obsession with flanks, lines of communication and logistics. He had express contempt for the old way of war.

"There must be more than panzers and motorized forces." Hoth, who was Guderian's partner in driving to Smolensk, could not be easily dismissed.

"They will slow the drive." Guderian looked at Hoepner, who nodded, their grand drives to Moscow about to be slowed if not halted by the plodding of infantry boots.

"What if they came from above." Blumentritt was jolted as Manstein interjected.

"From heaven?" Guderian laughed.

"The Falschirmjaeger."

Rumblings at the table and behind it. The parachute troops were the Fuhrer's pride and joy, an exotic and modern weapon that could be used only with is explicit approval. Manstein leaned over the map. "They can be dropped near the railway bridges at the rivers, where the rails are at their most vulnerable. They would hold their positions until the panzers arrived.

Bock followed Manstein's finger as it ranged across the Russian steppes. "General Student is in Germany. He is lobbying hard for use of the airborne forces. The Fuhrer is enthusiastic about their deployment."

The drive around Moscow and the railroad bridges a problem for the future, Bock continued. "Once the Second and Fourth Panzer Groups path has been cleared, the Russians will either disperse to Moscow, where they will be trapped, or fight in place and be destroyed by Army Group Center. Once the Western Front has been eliminated, the Ninth and Four Armies and Third Panzer Group will drive down the highway and invest the city. There will be two rings around Moscow, our infantry in the first ring, our panzers in the second ring. We believe with the collapse of the Red Army's command and control centers, forces in Ukraine and Leningrad will become independent of central authority."

"Those are high expectations," Strauss grumbled.

"It is the view of Fuhrer headquarters." That ended the discussion of the remainder of the Red Army. Another half hour was taken, Bock explaining zones of control, target dates and enemy dispositions. Blumentritt paid little attention, the details worked out over weeks of meetings. He had focused much time on ensuring the 48th Panzer Corps remained the schwerpunkt of the northern pincer.

The conference ended, grumbling having ceased and Blumentritt walked with his commander. "Do you believe the parachutists can hold back the Soviets?"

A smile from Manstein. "If the Fuhrer's pride and joy is threatened, there will be no limits to the materiel and men granted those who are to rescue them."

Blumentritt marveled at his commander's strategic vision. His suggestion had ensured the 48th Panzer would reach its destination and his name would be written with the German greats.

34

July 27, 1940　　　　**South of Smolensk, Russia**

"Misha, Mother can't go any further," exclaimed Tonya her hands on her hip.

Big Misha sighed and motioned his sister to the side of the encampment, away from the others. He took her arm and propelled her gently forward. Once they were alone, he began the conversation he had been avoiding for two weeks.

"Da, Tonya what you say is true. She can no longer walk. Mother is weak and can only continue if she is carried. "

Tonya began to weep. Misha put her arms around her and drew her near.

"Misha, how can we carry her? It is not possible."

"I can do it," replied Misha automatically, stepping back and standing erect. "I am strong and she is light."

Tonya was openly crying. She turned and leaned against a fallen tree trunk.

"Nyet, Misha." Tonya wiped her eyes. "Could we stay here until the Red Army beats the Fascists back?"

"Tonya, tell me what you have seen in the last month that suggests such an event is even remotely likely? Have we seen a single one of our tanks or airplanes?"

Tonya shook her head negatively.

"Tell me again why we couldn't go to Rogachev?" Tonya questioned, although she knew the answer.

Misha moved to her and sat on the tree trunk. It croaked and settled but held. He placed his hand on Tonya's shoulder. He appraised her condition. Her red hair was matted and filthy. Her face was shrunken due to weight loss. While once lively and robust, Tonya was now a shell. She was starving.

"You heard what Comrade Volodya reported. The road south was thick with Nazis."

"What about the others that were heading to the Pripet Marshes?"

"Tonya, there is no food there. We discussed this. The marshes would be a death sentence. East is the only way we can go."

"Into Russia?

"We are already in Russia. I think we must go towards Bryansk."

Tonya sat staring at the forest floor. She was exhausted and dejected. "Big Misha, perhaps I should stay here with Mother and you should go on with the others. You could bring us help."

Misha rose abruptly. He pulled Tonya up by her arms. "If you stay here, you will die. Mother will die. I will build a stretcher and Sasha and I will carry her."

"The others have been talking. I do not think they want to continue east. They want to go to the marshes. Russia means nothing to them. They no longer fear Stalin."

"I am aware. Sasha and Marina have told me this information. Let us go back to the camp and discuss our situation."

Misha led Tonya back to the clearing where their meager belongings were clumped. The little food they had started with was gone. Their numbers had dwindled to no more than a dozen. Some had slipped off in the night in small groups. There was no talk of fighting the invaders.

Misha waved his hand, motioning the group to assemble. He watched them struggle to drag themselves to the center of the encampment. Misha's mother was unable to stand. With few weapons and little ammunition, they were more refugees than anything else. "Comrades, we have reached the point in our journey where we must consider our situation. It is not good. I know many of you do not wish to continue into Russia. We are southwest of Smolensk. We have no food. There is no one coming to help us."

"Big Misha, won't the Red Army return to save Belarus?" asked Sasha, the young man from the beet collective. He had his arm around Marina's waist. Marina was listless, her body struggling to fend off a virus.

"They are not coming, Sasha. Yesterday, Comrade Volodya scouted the route to Smolensk. It too has fallen. The Red Army will be lucky to save Moscow."

"It is true Sasha. Smolensk is gone," added Volodya.

"I see three options," continued Misha. "Number one, we stay put here and wait."

"We have no food, shelter or medicine here," observed Tonya.

Misha held up his hand, silencing his sister. "We can discuss the merits of each option afterwards. Number two, we try to make it to the Pripet marshes where we hide. We will still have very little in the way of food but we will likely meet up with others that have already chosen this option. It may be worse than staying here."

Misha looked into their faces. No one said anything, waiting for him to finish the choices. He was still the unchallenged leader. "Option three is to continue east to find our lines and sneak through. This will be very dangerous and we have no real way to defend ourselves."

One of the older conscripts spoke quietly with a fourth option. "Or we could surrender."

The ensemble immediately hissed.

"Yuri, the Fascists would surely kill us," shouted his companion.

"I will rather die than bow to the Germans," exclaimed Volodya.

"I have seen the leaflets. All of you have. They promise to treat us well and to free us from Moscow." Yuri was on his feet, animated.

Volodya jumped up and picked up is rifle. "Yuri, you old fool. They are trying to trick us into giving up. Those papers are only good for wiping your ass."

"How would you know Volodya?" asked Yuri. "You can't even read."

Misha stepped between the two men, stopping the discussion from erupting into a brawl.

"Stop this now," demanded Tonya. "We must decide now what we are going to do. It may be time for us to go off in smaller groups. Everyone is free to do as they wish."

Misha re-took control of the meeting. He was covered in sweat. The shade of the trees did little to lessen the effects of the July heat. "Here is what I have decided. Tonya and Mother will go with me east. Others are welcome to join us. It is the best option. We will leave at first light."

Misha picked up a sturdy but thin branch. He brought it over to Tonya and placed it at her feet. "Tonya, I will gather the materials for us to build a stretched for Mother."

Sasha did not wait for the others to decide. For the second time in his life he decided to trust his life to Big Misha. "Misha, Marina and I will go with you."

Misha nodded and turned to Marina. "Is this your decision as well?

"Da, Big Misha," whispered Marina. She was weak. Marina knew she was running a high fever but she could not think of a future without Misha leading her.

Volodya nodded his head affirmatively. No one expected a different result. The others moved to the side in small groups to discuss their plans.

"We will not go with you," stated Yuri, pointing to the remaining members of the group. "We are going to head for the marshes."

"That is fine Yuri. We will spit the food, weapons and ammunition equally."

Sasha and Tonya spent the remainder of the day preparing the stretcher. Misha and Volodya kept their rifles ready and watched the others readying to depart. Misha did not expect trouble with the exiting men but it wise to be cautious. The situation was desperate.

35

July 30, 1940   **Rumania**

"What will happen to us? What will they do?" The hissed questions dug at Ianu, his head in the grass, dew collected on his cheek.

Weeks had passed and Ianu had come to know some of the train survivors, their work habits, their rest habits, all of it except their names.

"They are coming," the hiss warned.

Ianu closed his eyes. Sometimes when they were asleep the guards passed over them. Sleeping prisoners were easier to handle than those who were awake and milling about with nothing to do.

"Up, up," the order came with a sharp kick to the back or leg. Ianu judged when to shift so the foot glanced over him.

The others were not so lucky. Groans and cries for mercy sounded across the meadow. Ianu was up, swaying on his feet, blood inching its way to his brain. He bent, hands on knees as the dizziness passed.

"Up, up." The order drowned out the moans. One of the guards, weighed down by a gun, swung his foot, missed his target which remained still. Another kick found its mark, his prey rolling onto his back crying in pain. Suddenly he launched up, arms grasping the guard around the waist then slipping to his legs.

Ianu jumped as a shot rang out, the grasping arms dropping to the ground. There would be more work for the survivors. Ianu waited, the guards would be herding them in the direction of their work. The survivors of the train, the few who stumbled free from the heat and scent of death, clung together, eating and speaking in whispers when the guards were at a distance.

"This way, this way." The orders jerked Ianu into action, stumbling, but remaining upright. A boot to the midsection or a rifle butt to the hamstring was punishment for malingerers.

"Where are we going?" The question was hissed by the usual suspect, an older man, somewhere in his forties, shirt ripped from him, body burned a deep red.

Ianu ignored him as he had for three weeks, focused on his shoes as he picked his way through the gullies that cut across the meadow. His left shoe had remained whole, his right flapping free until he found a length of bailing rope and fastened to prevent it from splitting into two. They were headed in the direction of the cemetery and their workplace, though instead of digging a single grave they were responsible for the pit and filling it with the remains of Iron Guard prisoners.

"Stop, stop." Ianu slid to a halt, glanced toward the leader of the local guard. Burly with a permanent half beard, the leader was the oldest of the four guards. Face cut with a permanent frown, unhappy with his lot in life, Grigore calmed his frustrations with frequent and unexpected beatings of the prisoners. In the weeks since stumbling from the train, Ianu learned to maintain his distance and never look directly into the chief's watery eyes. Matching Grigore's squint meant a beating and on one occasion, a shot from his weapon, which sat crookedly on his waist, attached to his body by a leather sling.

"Down, down." Grigore carried an unusual gun, shorter and with a barrel that had holes as if to cool the weapon after it had been fired. When fired it caused all to leap and Ianu covered his ears. The bullets poured from it as if propelled by a giant fan. Ianu had not seen such a gun before.. Gun ownership by Jews was viewed suspiciously by the authorities.

Ianu dropped onto the damp ground, focusing on a ragged weed, bent, leaves torn, looking much the way he felt. His stomach ached, diet mainly limited to brown bread and the occasional piece of meat. This was usually rabbit or squirrel captured in a snare. Such a treat produced a frenzy among the prisoners, the fur torn first then the meat from the creature gobbled down untasted, blood covering the mouths of those lucky enough to receive some protein. More than one fist fight had broken out though the few punches thrown rarely left a mark, the battlers too weak to cause much damage. Ianu scrambled to safety when the battle began, careful to watch when a bit of meat flew in his direction. On those few lucky times he felt briefly better. This morning his stomach, meatless for three days, rumbled as only bread moved through his system. He noticed his flesh hanging from his bones.

In the distance, Grigore was greeted by three men, black uniforms fit as if tailored to their bodies. Ianu tilted his head, greasy hair flipping from in front of his eyes. Usually it covered his face, a trip to the barber long overdue but unlikely to occur in the foreseeable future. He squinted, the dark uniforms highlighting the pale faces and blond hair of their wearers. When they opened their mouth Ianu strained to catch their words but could not understand German. Ianu shuddered. It was his first glimpse of Nazis.

The Germans motioned toward the collection of Jews. Grigore nodded, eager to please. Several minutes passed, Ianu shifting as the earth grew hard below him. He shivered, the presence of Nazis unwelcome news. Grigore and the Rumanian Iron Guard worked them hard, fed them little but mostly kept them alive. The Nazis killed Jews without even thinking.

Grigore turned on his heel and headed in Ianu's direction. He began pointing, the guards snatching members of the group and collecting them off to one side. Ianu remained on the ground, trying to be as invisible as possible. The Germans passed over him and accompanied the Jews from the meadow.

Time passed, the sun burning off the morning fog and drying the dew laden grass. Grigore marched around the remainder, head down, watching his feet, kicking at loose clods of dirt. He stopped at the sound of shots, one after another, deadly, final.

"Up, up." The remainder scrambled to their feet. Ianu glanced through clumps of greasy hair, the gaps in the ranks meaning more food but also more work. The other guards returned, laughing and cursing, duty done.

They were herded back to the cemetery, toward the rail line. Ianu tried to ignore it all focusing on the grimy man in front of him. He recalled the slack figure, never a customer but always importuning those in Letcani for scraps of food or a handful of change. He was a gypsy, darker than most though the thickening layer of dirt coating their skin made all the prisoners resemble gypsies.

The trek to the cemetery was short, uneventful, their duties not so much. A train had arrived, three sealed cars, ominous beyond their appearance. Ianu shuddered, memories fresh. On one side, he heard retching, glancing over he spotted the agitated prisoner, head close to the ground, unable to ask his usual list of questions.

The grinding of metal marked the opening of a door. Ianu could not control his stomach, clenching as he retched when the stench of death rushed over him from the car's interior. His throat burned, teeth aching, stomach empty even as it revolted from the odor he hoped he would never experience again.

"Up, up." Back to their feet, legs wobbly, face taut as they were herded toward the car. The ragged creatures who appeared in the open doorway were familiar, eyes blinking at the burst of light, mouths open, lungs ravenous for fresh air, they stumbled to the edge of the rail car, knees bent, unable to straighten.

"No." The cry came not from the rail car but from behind Ianu. He remained fixed toward his task even as sounds of a struggle offered the possibility of escape.

"Down, down." Grigore motioned with his sidearm, Ianu dropping flat on his stomach. One of the guards cursed, earth moving as he hit it hard. "Stop." Grigore yelped then pointed and fired. "Get it," he ordered the guards, partly out of disgust, partly out of triumph. The escaped prisoner was dragged to the edge of the rail car. It was the agitated one. No longer talking or retching, he clutched his calf, hand red with blood. Crying he pawed at Grigore. The weapon was raised, the prisoner stiffened, eyes closed. A shot then a howl, the prisoner clutching his foot, the bullet pushing through flesh and bone and lodging in the earth.

"Up, up." Grigore motioned, a thin trail of smoke wiggling from the barrel. "There, there." The gun was pointed at the rail car. Ianu and the others were quick to their task. He avoided their former comrade, the others were less sympathetic, stepping on and even kicking the bleeding man.

"Down, down." The order confused the newly arrived prisoners, their bodies swaying at the edge, the drop to the siding meaning a form of freedom, something they had dreamed of while trundling down the rail line. Ianu recalled his own hesitation on the edge of escape. "Down, down." Grigore yelped. He aimed, a quick shot into the huddled mass. Lead struck bone and one of the ragged figures tumbled onto the ground. The shot sent some scrambling back into the car while others followed the path of least resistance to the earth.

Ianu and the others were on them, tearing at their clothes in search of valuables. The scuffles sometimes ended with a gunshot, but mostly the guards watched, laughed and pointed. The new prisoners were weak and disoriented, some surrendered willingly, others fought, and small number turned the tables. Their defeated opponent was dispatched by the guards, the victor replacing the old prisoner.

Ianu learned the lesson well, choosing the weakest prisoner and swooping in, valuables taken and offered to the guards. Others were more aggressive. The bearded prisoner, so certain they were not headed to Russia and freedom, always found those prisoners with the most to take. A blow across the face stunned his prey and he was liberal with his use of the rusty knife allowed him by the guards. Fingers and hands were torn free from the struggling bodies along with ears. Jewelry was prized by the guards to impress their women. Those who struggled against the amputations were ended with their head being driven into a rock, the train wheels or the sharp edge of the rail car. Ianu had lost count how many had suffered this fate. It did not matter. They scrambled for valuables purely for the guards' amusement, the new prisoners dispensed with a bullet, their journey ended after surviving hell.

The emptying of the rail cars dragged into the afternoon, three times the bodies inside then those who tumbled to the ground. The afternoon heat burned Ianu's skin as he hauled bodies by the ankles, dropping them into the landing below. For all the lifting and carrying he had done at the Cohnescu's store he never carried anything as heavy as a body.

"There, there." Grigore jabbed his finger in the direction of the cemetery and the pit beyond it. Once the remainder were in a mound outside the rail car, the carts were brought, the bodies loaded on them, ten to fifteen piled high. Four men took the two ropes in the front of the cart while a single prisoner guided it from the rear. Ianu was always among the four, the bearded prisoner the guide. Back aching, legs cramping as dehydration threatened. Ianu dug his feet into the grass and dirt. The slight incline from the rail line to the cemetery slowed the journey as did the rickety axles. An overly slow pace brought pain, ire directed at the prisoner guiding the cart then at the four men pulling it. Screaming, kicking and firing over their heads was the motivation. Shooting one of the four only slowed the trip, a lesson the guards learned quickly.

Once the wagon was moving the momentum allowed it to bounce over the ruts made during the weeks of transporting of bodies. The descent toward the pit was more dangerous. The overloaded carts tended to careen out of control. If those pulling the cart did not scatter they would become its next victim, crushed beneath the wagon wheels. This would attract the guards, a bullet dispensing with those too injured to continue. Ianu and the others learned how to slow the wagon, able to unload without attracting the guards. Back and forth, three wagons transporting the entire content of the train cars. The pit, dug to a depth of five meters, was partly filled with burnt remains. As a smaller member of the group, Ianu was pushed into the pit, forced to rearrange the bones and burnt flesh that remained. His first journey into the pit set him retching, the odor and the fell of burnt skin, ash covered bones, brittle and crackling beneath his feet. The bodies were tossed into the pit, and he arranged them for easy incineration. Ianu lost count, out of breath, body growing clammy, food and water long out of his system.

With the flesh arranged, his next task was spreading the fuel, scrambling from the pit as the torches were thrown into it, his clothes dripping with petrol. One time the flames had attacked his shirt, forcing him to roll on the ground to the delight of the guards. He was luckier this afternoon, escaping without incidence then stripping free of his clothes, sniffing as the flames rose from the pit, smoke and the odor of burning flesh hanging over them.

Their job complete, Ianu and the others sat, heads down, trying not to think of those dragged from the rail cars. Each day was a reminder of their "fortune" at not being stripped and piled high in the flaming pit. Ianu shook the thoughts from his head, reaching for his clothes and sniffing. The petrol remained. He needed a puddle to clean it, knowing he had succeeded when a thin layer of "grease" clung to the top of the water

The burning continued, the wind taking the smoke and human detritus in the opposite direction. Free of remains they faced Grigore and the guards, who always remained a safe distance from the pit. They were happy only when their prisoners were moving.

"Up, up." Ianu gathered his shirt, holding it as he drew on his pants. His last day in Letcani had been a fortunate one. Saloman had planned a day of wood and water gathering, the work requiring tough clothes that were also flexible. Never guessing he would wear them for a month, Ianu watched them disintegrate as he unloaded bodies, dragged the cart, and dodged the flames as he scrambled from the pit.

A shove made him stumble forward, snatching at his pants and keeping pace with the others. Ianu realized they were returning to the rail line even though the cars were empty. They never cleaned them. The train instead traveled up the line for a new load of prisoners as the odor of death lingered in the sealed chambers.

The train remained, though, a single car open. Ianu's legs ached, hunger and thirst swept away by the image of the waiting car. It was death, long and painful with a hint of hope glimmering through the slats in the wood. Ianu knew he would never survive a second trip.

"In, in." Grigore swung his sidearm in the air, directing them toward the rail car.

The prisoners remained in place, memories of the train cars too fresh, too painful. Their freedom, the work, the fresh air, the rations, all was paradise when compared to being locked in the rail cars.

"In, in." Grigore's voice rose and he swung the gun with the holes on the barrel.

None of them moved. They preferred death in the meadow, quicker and less painful than death riding the rails. A burst of fire from Grigore, followed by the other guards, convinced one of the workers.

"Up, up." The order came from behind Ianu. It was the bearded one, the confident worker, hand driving into the small of Ianu's back then his comrades, propelling them to the train car. The shove had the desired effect, their paralysis ended and they shuffled to the open car and climbed inside, numb to what they were doing, accepting their fate that made sudden death welcome. Ianu stumbled to the far wall, flopped onto the floor of the rail car, his arms clasped around his midsection and began to sob.

36

August 1, 1940   **West of Bryansk, Russia**

"Where is this?" Lieutenant Kassmeyer wrestled with the multipaged map. Kassmeyer was a map-obsessive, preferring to eye the much folded papers, marking their progress north and east, than watch the countryside. Captain Reichenau preferred the actual over the perceived as drawn by the distant cartographers in Zossen. Where the map authors found a road, marked as if it were the paved autobahn to Frankfurt, Reichenau discovered a mere track, sandy, bumpy and with enough hidden protrusions to send a German force into circles. This day their path on the map was another of the sandy tracks, the roughest patched covered by a corduroy road of pine logs, bumpy, tooth rattling but passable.

"It does not matter," Reichenau murmured. Their convoy, split into two pieces, had started north prior to dawn. Three hours later they remained in the dense forest, unable to penetrate the dampened floor of the unending lines of trees. It was bandit territory, dangerous territory, but where Berlin wanted them. The captain's contact with the anti-Bolshevik partisans was to be expanded, forging a relationship then an alliance, failure meaning more than disappointing his superiors but likely his death and the slaughter of his men. They were outnumbered and in enemy territory.

"D'yatnovo" Kassmeyer muttered, his finger moving along the length of the Desna River, north of Bryansk where the Bolva and Snov rivers met the Desna. "It is not on the map."

Reichenau was not surprised. The Russian countryside was beset by unmarked villages, hiding places for Soviet bandits. It was the reason the captain was risking his men and accompanying a rag tag Russian force into a forest to a village no one knew for certain existed.

According to the RONA men, D'yatnovo was the central location for the partisans who had butchered the railroad repair crews. Strauss proposed storming the village and wiping out all of its inhabitants. The Uzbek leader had refused, drawing the corporal's ire and suspicions. Reichenau had only Berlin's orders to restrain Strauss, who he put at the head of the column. If it were a trap, the captain wanted his most ferocious killer to meet the partisans and slow them, allowing the others to escape.

"It could be a trap," the lieutenant warned, taking a few valuable moments from his map to glance at his commander.

Reichenau waved away his concerns. The Russians were being cautious. As Slavs they were considered enemies of the Reich, to be shot on sight. Offering the SS an exact location of their positions would be suicide and Reichenau did not believe Kaminski, the RONA leader, was suicidal. The captain, though, remained cautious. His men had roamed the forest around the track, watching for an ambush. Half of his men were half a kilometer away, a sufficient distance to prevent an ambush from overwhelming the entire force, but close enough to provide reinforcements against any attack. Reichenau's wireless operator worked overtime, his men on the fringes reporting no massing of bandits.

Hunched in his staff car, Reichenau had another reason to be pleased. His memories had begun to recede, including the many false familiar faces which plagued him since crossing the Russian border. Central Russia held few females who might resemble his sisters, an absence of familiarity calming Reichenau, memories of Etta, Mena and Tilda pushed deep into his consciousness. Three days in the company of the partisans, though, had a different effect on his men, as they grew more agitated by the hour. They entered the SS determined to eliminate the Slav not accommodate them. Diplomacy and negotiation were not the strength of the SS, but Reichenau's age and experience had earned him the assignment and could add a new chapter to the brief history of the SS. Meeting with and allying with the Slavs would earn Reichenau either commendation or condemnation, but he did not care. He was performing his duty as ordered, no bureaucrat could erase that fact from his record.

"Sir." The lieutenant jerked in his seat beside Reichenau, map sliding onto the floor at his feet. "The convoy is halting." It was an unnecessary warning but potentially welcoming. Without the sound of firing it was unlikely the partisans were preparing an ambush. Instead the halt meant they had reached their destination.

The sound then sight of horses complicated matters. The Russians had refused to ride in German vehicles – not that riding beside Strauss was a possibility – and instead remained on their horses. Their approach was unsettling but also humorous, their ragged Red Army uniforms stained with dirt, creases and rips which exposed reddened and scabby flesh. Their hats sat askew on their heads, ill-fitting as if taken off the corpses of their enemies who had also been their former colleagues. Their weaponry was less diverse, a bandolier of bullets fitting loosely over the shoulder of one of the approaching men. Their rifles were strapped to the opposite shoulder, sidearm within ready grasp of calloused and bloodied hands. The sound of the horses shook a memory from Reichenau's childhood, his grandmother's stories of the Book of Revelations, the Russian horsemen arriving not from the depths of hell, but from the nether reaches of Stalin's "paradise."

SS guns were raised as the horses were heaved to a stop, a half dozen pointed at the pair of Russians, their death guaranteed if the captain was harmed. Reichenau was not bolstered by the knowledge his death would be revenged swiftly. The Russians were unaffected by the weaponry trained on them, instant death a constant possibility in war or peace in Stalin's Russia.

"We are here." The leader of the pair, his high cheekbones and slitted eyes revealing his Uzbek origins, waited patiently for his words to be interpreted by the lieutenant.

Reichenau, struggling to contain his nerves at being confronted by a modern version of Ghengis Khan, wet his lips. "Here," could mean only thing. "D'yatnovo?" He asked as if ordering an attack.

The Uzbek partisan squinted then laughed. "Nyet."

Reichenau glanced about, SS rifles steadied in preparations for a fusillade. If it was not D'yatnovo, it had to be a trap.

"The road to D'yatnovo." The Russian twisted in his saddle pointed toward the western fringe of the forest and another track that curved from the path taken by the convoy. "There." He motioned and for the first time Reichenau noticed the thin trail of smoke inching into the sky from behind a long row of pines.

The captain squinted at the smoke, wondering how it could be anything. His ruminations ended at the sound of more horses approaching, three in fact, two riderless. The Russians pointed again. "Ride, ride."

Reichenau relaxed. His youth had been spent on the back of horses, riding always calmed his nerves and cleared his head, the first time he would feel normal since finding the Russians. The captain pointed at the other horse for Kassmeyer. Unfortunately the snorting animal he faced, its fiery eyes and agitated limbs were something new to him.

"Sir," the lieutenant squeaked, an uncommon sound among SS troops. "I have never ridden a horse."

Reichenau was already eyeing the surrounding forest from the back of his steed. "Lieutenant," he grunted, pointing to the other animal.

"Sir." The lieutenant's face had paled as the horse pawed the ground in preparation for throwing its rider. "I cannot ride."

It was an embarrassing admission for the lieutenant and an astounding one for the captain. Riding was as much a part of his life as eating and shitting. "Attempt." Reichenau jabbed his finger toward the horse. "Think of the Fatherland."

The next several minutes amused the watching Russians and would be recalled by the lieutenant, but much worse by his fellow SS soldiers. He clambered onto the animal, flopping stomach first, arms and legs hanging ineffectually like an overturned turtle. Eventually the Russian released the reins and pushed the lieutenant upright onto the steed, handing him the bridle then slapping the beast on its flanks, sending it snorting in the direction of the smoke, the lieutenant clinging to the mane for his life. The Russian followed at a gallop, the captain at a trot, his men double timing behind their commander. Before reaching the trail leading through the forest, Reichenau spotted another horseman, a fierce rider leaning forward until his chin nearly touched his steed's head. It was Strauss.

"Herr Captain." The corporal was red faced, breaths coming in shallow gasps possibly from the struggle to remove one of the Russians from his steed then mounting it. "It is too dangerous for you to go alone." He unstrapped his shoulder weapon. "I will go. If it is an attack, it is best they shoot me."

Reichenau squinted at the corporal and his sudden burst of concern about his commander mixed with discovery of an unexpected vein of courage. Strauss was quick to storm an enemy when its forces were unarmed women, children and old men, but wading into a forest controlled by Russian partisans was a signal there was more to Strauss than Reichenau had suspected. Or not.

"The Slavs must die." The gun shook in the corporal's hand. "They cannot live among us."

Reichenau managed a grim smile. Killing the untermenschen rather than protecting his captain was prime on the corporal's mind. The captain motioned to Strauss who kicked at the horse as if it were a wayward Juden and rushed into the forest. Reichenau followed, continuing his trot, listening as his men crashed through the underbrush behind him.

The journey lacked the expected danger. Reichenau's horse picked its way over tangling roots, downed limbs and over the barely visible path in the darkened forest. Reichenau's nose wriggled under the weight of the odor of approaching death, forcing him to snatch his handkerchief and cover his mouth and nose. A clearing beckoned, a burst of light quickly dimmed as the captain was surrounded by a smoky haze. Reichenau blinked, adjusting his sight and searching for the lieutenant. He spotted the younger man's riderless horse then after a few moments noticed the hunched figure, head dipping toward the well worn grass about the village. A gray mass was close by, the results of either the odor or the frantic dash through the forest.

Shifting from the lieutenant, Reichenau eyed the remains of the village and the marauders who had destroyed it. The thatch and wood houses were mere smoldering piles, their occupants scattered bumps in the single dirt tracks that cut through the village. Unlike the villages cleansed by the SS – which collected the bodies – the Russians left the fleshy lumps lying in the sun, swelling from internal gases, plump targets for the scavengers waiting unseen until the humans disappeared. Reichenau felt a catch in his throat.

"Herr Hauptsturmfuhrer." It was Strauss, upright in his saddle, unaffected by the remains of the villagers. "The Slavs want you." He sneered.

The Russian horsemen were at the single stone building that remained standing, its thatch roof eviscerated, a few feet outside a fire burned in what appeared to be a spit. Strauss again took the lead ostensibly to protect his commander but more likely to catch sight of the little figures spread across a square of worn grass. Reichenau realized the village's youth had been collected and his corporal was riding at full speed to reach them. Reichenau kicked at his horse. A Strauss shooting spree would make quick work of the fragile arrangement with the RONA. Worse the captain might find himself in the midst of a firefight where he would be outgunned and surrounded.

The youth were sitting, some with their hands clasped around their knees, eyes staring forward as they struggled to comprehend the destruction of everything and everyone they knew in their brief lives. Others were fighting against it, crying, howling, tossing clumps of dirt in the air, all with little effect. The RONA guards were unrestrained in keeping order, their hands, boots and rifle butts downing all who attempted to leave. The desperation was replaced by pain and finally acceptance of their fate.

Strauss had dismounted, gun unhooked from its holster. Pushing aside a raggedly clad partisan, the corporal stepped to within a foot of the head of one of the crying teens. The shot ended her pain, body going limp as sections of her head scattered to the wind. The others around her jumped, pawing at the blood, brains and bone sprayed onto them. They skittered away but Strauss proved quicker, left then right, left then right, tiny bodies their arms and legs bent and twisted in a bloody artistic pattern. Only the Mauser's clip offered a respite from the killing and allowed the partisans to rush toward him, arms reaching toward Strauss, a volley of "nyets" but no gunfire.

"Corporal." For the first time Reichenau sought to restrain Strauss. He was on the man, smacking the gun from his hand and onto the ground, scattering bullets into the worn grass and earning a flash of anger from the corporal.

"Captain." Strauss eyed the gun at his feet and the rapidly advancing partisans. "The Slavs are SS prisoners.'

"Corporal." Reichenau pointed to the Russians, eight of them within a few meters of the two SS men. "I want your weapon." He held out his hand.

Strauss hesitated, as close to insubordination as an SS corporal could come. He slid the rifle from his shoulder and presented it to Reichenau. "Long live the Fuhrer and the Fatherland," he bellowed.

Lieutenant Kassmeyer, nerves settled after emptying his stomach, hustled to his commander's side. The partisan leaders were already gathering, issuing orders to corral the frantic youth then turning to Reichenau for an explanation. It was quick and apologetic, Reichenau recognizing the teenagers were the partisans' prisoners and offering a promise no more would be killed.

The Russians seemed unconcerned even as they talked among themselves and jabbed agitated fingers in the direction of the corporal. The guards eventually returned to their posts, calming their prisoners with kicks and cuffs to the ears. Reichenau realized the youth had no more value to the partisans than they did to Strauss though their quick corralling was an ominous turn.

A hurried conversation among the Russians ended with the partisan riding off to the stone building. Reichenau had discarded his horse and followed more slowly on foot. Toting Strauss' rifle, he glanced in the direction of the corporal who remained fixed in his salute until standing alone in the bloody morass of his own creation. Eventually concluding this would not be the day he would die in glory for the Fuhrer and the Fatherland, he relaxed, returning to a normal posture before bending to retrieve his sidearm. Reichenau no longer cared as he approached the stone building and tried to make sense of the fires burning behind it. The three fires each sported several metal pokers pushed deep into the coals. A few feet from the fires four of the prisoners, tame and uncertain, were herded into the stone building, guards pushing and kicking them until they were inside it.

Standing at the entrance, the Uzbek motioned for Reichenau to join them inside the stone building. Reichenau was cautious entering. Three RONA partisans guarded the little ones while another trio stood at the opposite end of the structure. The Uzbek leader pointed and a girl, fourteen or fifteen, blond haired, round faced was pushed forward. She reached out with chubby fingers to regain her balance, but was immediately snatched by three partisans who spread her against the wall, feet clamped down by heavy boots, arms splayed tight against the wall. The third one pressed his hand against her forehead to hold it in place.

Reichenau heard the sound of metal clinking from outside and another partisan entered, the metal pokers red at the end. Holding it steady with both hands he approached the girl, her dark eyes blinking, uncomprehending as the hot metal approached. Watching from the doorway, the Uzbek partisan laughed and yelped something which forced Reichenau to wait for the lieutenant to enter and interpret. "The first one is the quietest."

The poker was lunged forward. The girl struggled but the six hundred pounds of weight holding her down had no problem controlling a mere 100 pounds. Anguished cries sounded from the opposite end of the stone structure, the others mourning the girl while realizing what awaited them.

The lieutenant tapped at the captain's shoulder and Reichenau dismissed him with a quick motion, his subordinate never enjoying the strong stomach required an SS officer. The girl's cries choked away, head flopping once it was released, body struggling with the evisceration of one of her senses but she was not to be released.

One of the remaining three, a boy of 15 or 16, was the next to be summoned to the bloody wall. His struggles proved more successful, his appendages slick from sweat and the girl's secretions making it more difficult for the men to hold. A blow across the head turned him more compliant, closed eyes not seeing the approaching pokers. Reichenau exited, the boy's squeals following him into the grass and dirt outside and into his dreams for the next several nights. Once reaching the fresh air the captain drove down his emotions. He could not allow Strauss or the lieutenant to witness any reaction. Instead he turned to the Uzbek partisan with a single question. "What will you do with them?"

His response turned the already pale lieutenant nearly transparent. "Them," he began. "The ones who survive will be sent to D'yatnovo. They will serve as a warning to surrender the communists in the village or theirs will suffer the same fate." The lieutenant gasped for air, drawing a glare from the hovering Strauss. The true Nazi forced him to straighten and contain his emotions.

Strauss stood for a moment then noticed the stumbling, crying girl who ran free from her captors. Strauss followed her only to return a few moments later touching his eyes. "Herr Captain," the corporal squinted, the sole sign of an emotion other than hatred, demonstrated by Strauss. "What is in there?"

"You must witness it yourself," the captain murmured. "The Slavs may teach you something." He walked away with direction, leaving a perturbed and disbelieving Strauss.

37

August 3, 1940   **D'yatnovo, Russia**

"Comrade Volodya, sit and calm down," commanded Big Misha. "What have you seen?"

Volodya would not remain still. He was shaking.

"D'yatnovo is under siege!"

"What do you mean?" demanded Misha.

Volodya stopped pacing and collapsed on the forest floor. He removed his cap and wiped his forehead dry with a rag. He sighed.

"It is a really bad there, Misha."

"Explain please," demanded Misha. "Do they not have food?"

"The comrades we met were correct. There are many defenders in D'yatnovo. But they are surrounded." Volodya took a breath.

Sasha approached and sat next to Volodya, placing his hand on the troubled soldier's shoulder.

"They are surrounded by the Nazis and Red Army deserters that have changed sides!" Volodya stopped and continued in a voice too low for the women in their group to hear. "They are called

RONA. The Fascists and these RONA scum have been torturing children."

"How do you know this?" asked Misha. "Did you see the RONA or the Nazis? Did you see any of the victims."

"Yes I did," exclaimed Volodya. "On the dirt track to D'yatnovo I found a girl, not more than two years younger than Marina."

Volodya stopped again, hesitant to continue the narrative. He checked on the proximity of the women. Convinced they could not hear his words, he spoke slowly.

"Her eyes were gouged out by a hot poker. She was dying. She told me our own countrymen did this to her. They are with Germans, demanding the surrender of communists."

Misha and Sasha sat motionless.

"How would she know of RONA if she was but a child?" asked Misha.

Volodya shook his head negatively. He grabbed Misha's arm and looked in his eyes.

"Misha, I also came across two Red Army conscripts. They were fleeing D'yatnovo. The RONA has demanded that the village give up or they will all be killed. They believe the villagers are going to comply so they fled. They insist the entire village will be slaughtered anyway."

Misha placed his hand over Volodya's and squeezed it. He glanced back to his mother and sister. They were comforting Marina, who was recovering but still with fever. At least she was able to walk. Misha's mother had to be carried in the litter.

"The RONA are working with the really bad Germans, the SS. There's going to be a battle Misha and it is not going to go well for our side," warned Volodya. "We cannot go any closer to D'yatnovo."

"I agree Comrade," replied Big Misha. He sighed. The hopelessness of their plight was overwhelming. They were not partisans. They were six refugees with no food or supplies. They had no realistic way to defend themselves. They had not eaten in days.

"What will we do, Big Misha?" asked Sasha. He was loyal to his leader but was clearly frightened.

"We will not give up, Sasha," answered Misha immediately. "We will go further south and then east."

"Your mother is not doing well," observed Sasha.

"I am not leaving her under any circumstances," shot back Misha. "You and Marina can go alone if you wish."

"No, of course not. We want to stay together. It is just hard and we have nothing to eat."

Volodya grinned and produced a previously unseen sack.

"I did find this near dead soldiers," announced Volodya. "I don't know if they were partisans or RONA but there are two tins of meat, a few potatoes and half a loaf of bread."

"Well there you go Comrade Volodya!" said Misha. "We will eat later. But now we must pack up and leave this area immediately."

"In the day light?" asked Sasha.

"We have no choice," observed Misha. "We need to get away from D'yatnovo as quickly as possible."

38

August 4, 1940   **Moscow**

Alexei hated the nights when deep sleep evaded him. In the warm darkness of an August night he was alone with memories from his youth. The Nazis were closing in on Moscow and no one could stop them. Doom was spread on the faces of those around the conference table as they studied the military maps. With his world on the verge of collapse, Alexei took comfort in his past where he faced disaster only to survive.

As the heat pressed upon him, Alexei's mind wandered back to his second year in Kharkov, early November as the school prepared for celebration of the thirteenth year of the Soviet revolution. Alexei was called into the director's office on a Wednesday evening, the summons unexpected and puzzling. Dr. Shapsinikovo was a veteran of the Russo-Japanese War, his right side – eye, fingers and leg – torn by shrapnel from a Japanese shell during the Port Arthur siege. The incompetence of the czarist regime with two naval fleets sunk and defeats at Port Arthur and Mukden transformed a loyal czarist officer into a dedicated Bolshevik with a hint of Social Revolutionary in his words. His early dedication to the cause and ability to straddle factions earned him the director's position at Kharkov University.

Mandated to root out traitors, saboteurs and dissenters, Shapsinikovo had removed two thirds of the faculty for counter revolutionary thought. His success at uncovering hidden Whites and capitalists had earned him the respect of the Ukraine Communist Party and he was given control over the entire city's schools. He proceeded to purge eighty percent of the faculty and cowed the rest into following his directives.

Students were no safer. The director chose "junior commissars" to monitor the speech and thoughts of their classmates. No one knew the identities of these spies. Everyone was cautious, even when talking with friends, anyone a possible Shapsinikovo spy.

The summons to Shapsinikovo's office, located in a cold, white building at the edge of campus, had come from his assistant Vlad. A veteran of the 1878 Russo-Turkish War, he sported a wooden leg to prove his loyalty to mother Russia. Only sixteen when drafted into the army, Vlad was an old sixty eight as he clumped his way to the unheated single room, triple occupancy for the fortunate students. Alexei could not miss the uneven sounds of hard sole and wooden leg on the floor as Vlad approached.

His message was distorted by the phlegm that at times bubbled from his mouth, possibly another result of his war wounds. Alexei heard that the director wanted him in his office that evening at seven, but could not make out whether it was on the hour or half hour. He had not taken the chance of being late. Shapsinikovo was obsessive about tardiness and the summons suggested he was already angry at the little revolutionary hero of Voronezh. Making him angrier by being late was tempting fate. Alexei arrived at the whitewashed building ten minutes before seven.

He sat alone in the outer office for over half an hour. He was relieved to be alone rather than with the director's emaciated secretary with the runny eye and the habit of clearing her throat into the same handkerchief as the one that she used to wipe her eye. He was forced to abide the ticking wall clock, each second marked by a piercing click. Alexei had spent his time recalling every word and expression of the past week. He was always so careful, never laughing at some of the anti-Bolshevik jokes repeated by his classmates. Every question to a professor was carefully weighed, written out and memorized, the paper burned to prevent prying eyes from detecting some hidden counterrevolutionary meaning. There had been the one time he had made a face during a lecture on the capitalist imperialist exploitation of Africa and Professor Berezov saw him, but it was made in preparation for a sneeze, which the professor had seen and heard. Surely Berezov had not interpreted the momentary lapse as a full-fledged Trotskyite deviation from the anti- imperialist line.

Shapsinikovo had been cracking down. Some of the students gossiped he was under intense pressure to find more traitors. His early success at removing counter revolutionaries raised expectations of his abilities. According to the newspapers in 1930, treason was everywhere even at the highest levels of the Party. Every loyal communist was responsible for reporting traitors and examining their own non-existent soul for hints of Trotskyite or rightest tendencies.

Alexei had not discovered his anti-Bolshevik behaviors by the time Vlad limped from the director's office and eyed the young student. It was seven minutes prior to the apparent appointment and the old Russo-Turkish war veteran looked surprised to see Alexei.

"The director -," the remainder of the sentence was cut off by phlegm.

Alexei hesitated then rose and followed Vlad to the well lit room at the end of a long corridor. Years later Alexei would note the similarities of the director's entryway with his Kremlin duties. The hallway was similar to that leading to the General Secretary's corner office. However limited the director's power, to a twenty year old he seemed as powerful as Stalin.

Shapsinikovo was upright in his chair, his office a monument to socialist austerity with a single shelf of books and pictures of Lenin and Stalin, the former slightly higher than the latter. He sat, fingertips on the edge of his desk, primed for something important. Alexei stood, barely inside the office, arms at his side, waiting to be told to sit. The order would never come.

"A request has come to me from Moscow," he began unexpectedly. "They are seeking a top student to attend Moscow University starting in the spring."

Alexei had swallowed, relief rushing through him. He had done nothing wrong. This was an opportunity rather than an interrogation.

"Comrade Protopopov, I was thinking of recommending you." Shapsinikovo barely looked at him. Instead he lit one of his toxic cigarettes, the smoke burning even the healthiest lungs.

Alexei remained silent, uncertain whether he was expected to accept the offer. He thought it best for Shapsinikovo to ask him.

"But there is a difficulty."

There always was in Stalinist Russia.

"Comrade Alexei, you are a student of Professor Vatutin?"

Alexei felt the blood chill in his veins. It was an odd question as the director assigned all of the students to classes and would know Alexei's instructors.

"Yes sir."

"Do you enjoy his course?"

Lying in his bed ten years later Alexei recognized the question was a trap and offered a bland, "I take his course as part of my training for serving the state." At age twenty Alexei did not sense the danger and answered truthfully "Yes."

Shapsinikovo's fingers had continued to tap the edge of his desk. "You agree with everything Professor Vatutin offers in class?"

Alexei sensed danger. He hesitated and mulled his response. "I am not sure I understand."

Fingers on both of Shapsinikovo's hands began to tap the desk as he repeated the question. The delay allowed Alexei to offer the right answer, "There are certain things I do not completely agree with."

Shapsinikovo edged forward in his chair. "Certain things? Be definitive comrade."

Alexei thought quickly. The Bukharnites were unpopular. Denouncing any part of Vatutin's lectures on the New Economic Policy would please the director. "His defense of the Kulaks," Alexei murmured, gauging the director's reaction.

His finger tapping ceased. "Professor Vatutin defended the Kulaks?"

Alexei felt his stomach sink. It was the wrong answer. The Kulaks had been small farmers who owned their land and sold their produce in the open market. They "had been" because the Kulaks fought communalization and became the enemies of the state. Any word supporting them would classify that person also as an enemy of the state.

Alexei's mouth immediately went dry. If he did not change his answer he could not continue. "No, no, he said it was proper policy to exterminate them."

Shapsinikovo's frown deepened and Alexei realized he had not given the correct answer. The student wobbled on his feet. If only the director told him what to say he would say it.

"And what about the rightest deviation of Bukharin?" Bukharin had been a friend of the Kulaks and was considered rightist as it supported private property and deviated from true Leninist teaching. Deviation was always bad unless it was a deviation from the deviationist.

"He said they had not deviated from the party." Vatutin had said no such thing, but the finger tapping had resumed and Alexei's legs had firmed as he realized what the director sought.

"Comrade Alexei Protopopov, do you believe he is a right deviationist?"

Alexei did not hesitate. "Yes, sir."

The director leaned over his desk and lifted several papers from the blotter. He held it out for Alexei who approached with trepidation. "A commissar was monitoring Professor Vatutin's lectures and found deviationist teachings that suggested he supported Bukharin's treasonous attacks on Leninist theory. Read these and sign you heard Professor Vatutin poisoning the minds of his students with Bukharanite treason."

The paper listed thirty four quotes from Professor Vatutin, none of them familiar to Alexei. One had Professor Vatutin denouncing Lenin as a Social Revolutionary. Another had him claiming Stalin provoked a famine to eliminate the Kulaks. Any one of them was grounds for dismissal from his teaching position, the three pages of them ensured the severest of punishment.

Alexei hesitated. Faced with the papers, reality set in. Professor Vatutin was not a right deviationist. The paper he signed would extinguish a good man.

Shapsinikovo noticed his hesitation. "You are friendly with Vatutin's daughter, Tatiana."

Alexei could not conceal his surprise.

Shapsinikovo nodded. "She has been under surveillance for several months, the daughter of a traitor. It is the reason I had you summoned." Shapsinikovo stopped tapping on the desk and raised his hand to his chin. "Comrade Alexei, you are one of our brightest students, but I fear you have become influenced by this family of traitors." He reached for the papers. "I had hoped you would sign and I could recommend you for Moscow University, but if you prefer to defend those who attack the state."

Alexei did not resist. "No," he took the paper and scribbled his signature. "Professor Vatutin is a right deviationist. Tatiana wanted me to join their plans for sabotage, but I refused. I will not betray the Revolution."

Shapsinikovo was pleased. "You are a loyal member of the Party." For the first and only time Alexei noticed a smile cross his lips. "You will need to prepare for your journey to Moscow." Alexei was dismissed with a quick nod and then hurried out. Euphoric at the time Alexei remembered being so bold as to smile at Vlad, startling the old veteran, who only blinked in response.

For the next weeks Alexei had tried to eliminate all memories of the Vatutins. The professor disappeared, replaced by a humorless instructor from Rostov. Tatiana disappeared. Alexei could never admit knowing them. A relationship with a right deviationist was a permanent mark on the record of a Party member. Several years later the Vatutins were raised by Beria when Alexei was considered as the General Secretary's adjutant. Fortunately everyone in the Party, young and old, had connections with those who had deviated from the ever changing Party line. Stalin picked him, Beria could not object and Alexei learned to remain silent, never offering an opinion other than firmly rejecting the Bukharin-rightist deviation.

Lying in the slowly dying heat, Alexei could remember the decades old faces clearly. He could even feel Tatiana's touch on his arm. He tumbled into sleep only as the first rays of an early summer sun wiggled above the city. It was barely four in the morning and the heat began to again build in his room. Once the heat had pressed tight against him, Alexei jerked awake, ears ringing from a lack of sleep. Forced from his bed, he managed a hunk of stale bread for his breakfast, then dressed and headed downstairs. A call summoned the car and driver to take him to the Kremlin and the officials' gate. Barricades sat several meters away, soldiers bearing heavy guns ready to defend against the always feared German paratroopers landing in Red Square.

The guards knew him and his car well, but had suffered from sudden onset of amnesia or paranoia that the adjutant to the General Secretary had been replaced by a Nazi spy. Twenty minutes elapsed between his entry into the Kremlin gate and arrival in his office. Poskrebyshev was waiting, grim as usual but unusually nervous. The meeting had begun, Comrade Alexei was to join it immediately. "The meeting" could only mean a military conference, which had become more frequent and lengthy, the news from the fronts growing more desperate.

Alexei slipped into the conference unseen, Marshal Rokossovsky motioned to a map covering the conference table, yellow stars represented the Wehrmacht positions, red the Red Army. A.glance at the table revealed a flood of yellow in a three quarters circle, north, west and south of Moscow pinning in the smaller clutch of red stars.

"The Western Front is holding." Rokossovsky pointed at two clumps of red nearly overwhelmed by two masses of yellow. "General Konev seeks reinforcements to hold the Maloyaroslavets line."

"The Siberian divisions," Beria yelped. The civilian members around the table had dwindled, with Molotov, Beria and Kaganovich the mainstays. New Politburo members had risen, Alexei recognizing none of them.

The marshal brushed aside the question. Outnumbering the civilians two to one around the table at most conferences, the generals had become more brusque with their civilian masters. "The Siberian divisions were deployed on the Bryansk Front after Tula was captured."

Molotov raised on his toes and jabbed his fingers at a blob of red near the great bend of the Dnieper River. "What about these divisions?"

"Under heavy pressure." Rokossovsky turned to another decorated general at the end of the table, uniform so loaded with metal he appeared on the verge of tipping face forward onto the map. "General Simonov may explain."

Alexei suppressed a sigh. Commander of the Southwest Front, the general was known for his never ending explanations which confused, bored and silenced the civilians into acquiescence. After fifteen minutes, Alexei gleaned troops in the Dnieper bend were the only men holding back the German Army Group South. Six hundred miles from Moscow they would not arrive in time to defend the capital. If removed there were no Russian troops to stop the Germans from driving to the Volga. It was the end of the civilians offering suggestions, leaving them only to ask questions. "What can we do?"

"A hard shell around Moscow." Rokossovsky pointed to a spot 50 kilometer outside the city. "The people are digging anti tank trenches. We can draw the Germans into the defenses while collecting forces beyond the perimeter to the east." The Marshal waved vaguely around the Volga River to the north of Moscow.

"With the Germans tied down before Moscow we can prepare a counteroffensive."

Molotov and Beria exchanged glances. "Allow the Germans to surround Moscow?" The NKVD chief asked.

The tone of the question drew caution from the marshal. Less than six months from being locked in an NKVD prison cell after being swept up in the 1937 military purge, he understood the power and fury of the secret police. "Possibly," he said.

Beria pursed his lips, little eyes blinking. "Comrade Stalin finds that unacceptable."

The marshal glanced down the table at his colleagues, nods and knowing glances bolstering his confidence. "We would like to speak directly with Comrade Stalin. We are concerned with his continued health problems."

Alexei swallowed as the NKVD commissar's lips peeled into a cruel smile. "Marshal Budyenny and Voroshilov and Commissar Khrushchev expressed similar concerns," Beria said. "I believe I settled their worries sufficiently."

The menace was unmistakable. The marshal was of the army, large and better equipped than the NKVD. The army though, was locked in a death grip with the Germans while the NKVD was ten meters away. Alexei watched the marshal pale, wobble, straighten and regain his bearing. "Yes, of course, Comrade Stalin will decide on the final defense of Moscow."

Comrade Stalin. For a moment Beria's malevolence flickered, focus moving from the marshal to Alexei, from hatred to confidence. Comrade Stalin, according to what Alexei put on paper, according to what Molotov and Beria told him to write.

August 5, 1940   **West of Bryansk, Russia**

Operation Typhoon was proceeding to the east of Captain
Reichenau. His men and the members of the 281ˢᵗ Security Division
were dug in not far from the Desna River. Their task was twofold,
tracking the partisans who had been attacking the railroad repair
crews and keeping a suspicious eye on the RONA partisans pledged
to help the Germans in their search. Lieutenant Kassmeyer had
recovered from his tussle with a partisan horse and the Russian
method of "diplomacy." He spent much of his time in the Russian
forest collecting wireless reports on the Moscow advance of the
three panzer groups and three infantry armies comprising Army
Group Center. He maneuvered lines of strings tacked to a map of
central Russia to mark the competing armies, red for the Soviets,
green for the Germans. Some of the troops had protested the color
but the lieutenant had only two choices and red could never mark the
progress of the Wehrmacht.

A full day sandwiched between two quiet nights had passed
since the partisans had distributed their ultimatum to D'yatnovo in
the form of "well marked" fifteen year olds. Not all had survived
their transformation, Reichenau demanding their burial as a health
precaution in tandem with the bodies of the village adults. The
RONA dragooned a score of nearby commune workers to dig the
holes then fill them, their payment to be shot last and buried on top.
The Russian efficiency pleased even Strauss who clutched his
holster as the workers were dispatched. He was less pleased with the
proposed D'yatnovo surrender terms. Only the lieutenant's map in
the command tent kept the corporal from leading a squad to
D'yatnovo and eliminating the Slavs.

A frequent visitor to the tent, Strauss probed the map with his
dirty forefinger, scabbed from overuse, jabbing at the towns swept
over by the panzers. There was Klin and Kalinin north of Moscow,
Maloyaroslavets in the center and Tula south of the capital. Others

watched with more personal interest, focused on specific divisions or brigades if possible, male relatives fighting in the region. Reichenau's men knew they were to clear the rear areas of Slavs to provide land for the very infantry who were risking their lives for Lebensraum. Fighting for Fuhrer and Fatherland was one thing, fighting for a family member tended to extract that extra bit of brutality from the Einsatzgruppen.

Unfortunately the energy generated by the sight of pincers closing around Moscow went to waste as Reichenau as his men waited for the Russian partisans to pacify the area. The captain struggled to restrain Strauss and the others.

It was in the midst of the second afternoon of waiting that news arrived from D'yatnovo. Lieutenant Kassmeyer was stretching the green string further to the northeast, marking the severing of another rail line to Moscow when a cry sounded as a Russian horseman penetrated the camp. With German rifles pointed at his head and chest, he delivered the news to the lieutenant, who translated to Reichenau. D'yatnovo had been liberated, a phrase that enjoyed ominous vagueness. The captain and a squad could view the results.

The days in the presence of the RONA had the salutary effect of removing German concerns about an ambush. It allowed Reichenau to make the ride to D'yatnovo in an efficient trot. The lieutenant managed a sweaty and uneven gallop, his confused steed shook his head and resisted the reins as they were alternately pulled and released. Strauss was fluid on his mount. He looked about, his free hand alternately fingered his side arm then his rifle, the Slav never able to earn corporal's trust. The forest cleared, undergrowth peeling back as the path widened. Unlike the village where Reichenau had established camp, D'yatnovo boasted stone buildings, once bearing tile roofs. Soot coated the stones, broken tiles scattered along the rutted lane that ran through town. Only the buildings remained, wood walls sitting in a criss cross patter. There were no livestock – ownership of such animals banned under communist dogma – nor were there people, their surrender total. Reichenau pressed his horse forward, pleased and surprised at the Russian's skill. They might prove to be useful allies. Berlin would be pleased.

After a few minutes trot, they reached the center square, a small stone toppled, some paean to the Bolsheviks bearing a hammer and sickle but diminished by the new rulers of the town. Reichenau halted, turning his horse in a circle to survey the rutted roads. He wondered how the army moved so swiftly through Russia on such roads.

"Herr Hauptsturmfuhrer." The lieutenant sat more comfortably on his horse, reins no longer cutting into his hands. "The Russians."

The Uzbek leader was charging toward them in a cloud of dust, riding hard and for a moment the captain's stomach sank, the ferocity of the Russians on the battlefield a frequent topic among wounded soldiers. The "Hurrahs" of Soviet infantrymen as they charged German forces curdled the blood of Werhmacht soldiers all along the Eastern front. Hearing about it was much different than having the Uzbek creatures bearing down on him. Strauss had his rifle ready but the partisan ignored him, a different type of Russian peasant, not fearing the German soldiers around him.

The words rushed from him, the language and its speaker animated. The lieutenant cocked his head, working his mouth as if hearing something distasteful. Reichenau waited, his focus on Strauss, the corporal determined to shatter the peace between the German forces and the RONA. Sudden pressure on the trigger of his rifle would be the death of them all.

"Herr Hauptsturmfuhrer." The lieutenant had digested the eager Uzbek's words. "D'yatnovo has been cleared of the enemy."

It was not a dramatic pronouncement.

"They have captured communist soldiers and are interrogating them." Reichenau glanced at the Uzbek who nodded as if understanding every word coming from the lieutenant. The glint in the Uzbek's eye was all the captain needed to explain "interrogation." The captain would never forget the red hot pokers and their use on the teenaged "enemies." He did not want to imagine their use on adults.

"The people surrendered the communists the moment they saw their children."

"The townspeople," the lieutenant hesitated as if struggling with the correct word. "Resettled." Another nod from the Uzbek added ominous overtones to the word.

The Uzbek rattled off another long phrase, the lieutenant nodding then following the Uzbek's gaze until it fell upon Strauss. "The partisans have captured men who will not talk. They ask if the corporal would like to 'resettle' them."

Strauss sat up straighter in his saddle, his reputation having penetrated deep into the Russian forests.

"Corporal Strauss." Reichenau said. "Would you be willing to perform this duty to cement the alliance with our new Russian allies?"

Strauss' eyes shifted in their sockets, his mind struggling with the paradox. He could join the Slavs in eliminating the Bolsheviks. The Untermenschen were allowing him to perform his duty. He eyed the Uzbek, gauging whether his expression was one of pity or respect but decided refusing the offer would demonstrate weakness.

"Jawohl, Herr Hauptsturmfuhrer." Strauss saluted, nodded at the Uzbek and steered his horse toward the forest, kicking it.

"Resettle, sir?" The lieutenant was lost without his maps. "I don't recall any other villages where they could be resettled."

"The Russians created their own villages," Reichenau said, waiting for the lieutenant to untangle the hint.

"I do not understand sir. They destroyed this village, why would they build another?" He shook his head. The irrationality of their Slavic allies was incomprehensible. Destroy, build, build, destroy.

"It does not matter, lieutenant." His subordinate's obtuseness was amusing and depressing. Spurring his horse, Reichenau headed toward camp, the opposite direction of Strauss and his resettlement plans.

The men greeted their captain eagerly, concerned when their commander left with the partisans but also seeking news after almost two days of silence. Reichenau's announcement of success drew cheers then a gathering of weapons and supplies for the march. The captain returned to his tent, ordering his wireless operator to send the good news to the major. Reichenau then settled onto his cot and found an envelope that had not been there when he had left.

Mail delivery was an irregular event on the eastern front, a bare reminder of how different life had been before crossing the border. Carbon monoxide trucks, "resettlement" and red hot pokers applied to children were his new life. There had been death at home but always explainable, the enemy was the hideous Jew, a creature lacking morality and conniving against those enjoying pure German blood.

The straight lines and precise lettering on the envelope told Reichenau it was not from his family. His uncle, a man of considerable wealth but little formal education, relied on his housekeepers to compose personal letters. This produced a range of handwriting from barely formed letters to sweeping script that Reichenau treasured even though he never met the writer. The letter quivering in his hand could have only one author, Frau Crump. Tearing open the envelope he slid out four folded slips of papers and immediately flipped open to the bottom of the second page.

"Frau Crump" drew a smile from the captain. Elena Crump had been the same age as his youngest sister and partly took Mena's place after the Jew had taken her life. Elena's father had been displeased when learning she had spent an afternoon at the Reichenau's farm, storming onto the property on the back of his favorite black mare then dragging Elena, strapped face down on that same mare, back to his land. A week later her father had relented but only after a sobbing Elena had threatened to make his life an unending torture. A young Reichenau had been just as dramatic, his cries convincing his father to allow Elena to see his son but only on Crump land. Reichenau would visit, stumbling down the muddy lanes until reaching the edge of the Crump farm, the furthest she could travel without igniting a paternal tirade.

Four years of visits saw Reichenau enter adolescence, a dangerous time according to Elena's father, who halted the visits. He had been unable to stop Elena, and the fourteen year old Reichenau had learned the joys of platonic love. Then tragedy struck, the eldest Crump killed in a riding accident, leaving her an estate she was too young to handle. A man was required and if he had been older Reichenau would have enjoyed a different life but Elena was swept away by the unmarried son of a small farmer. Single and in his thirties, Tetra had been the object of rumors until marrying Elena. The relationship lasted less than a year, Tetra killed during the Battle of the Marne. Reichenau had been away, pushed into a military school to prepare him for war once he reached the age of seventeen. When he returned, Reichenau found Frau Crump, a full grown woman who protected her emotions with a façade of formality. The tenderness she had displayed with her young charge only a few years earlier had melted away, appearing only occasionally when her eyes glistened as she talked to Reichenau.

Elena never remarried, death and disappointment driving the passion from her. She had remained in contact with Reichenau during the quarter century since their first separation. She kept the SS captain in touch with his home. Unfortunately the letter would have to wait, Reichenau's reading interrupted by the sound of horses, more RONA members demanding his attention. Sliding through his tent flap, the captain was awash with trepidation. Less than half an hour after leaving Strauss with the allied partisans they had returned, riding hard. He imagined the worst, the corporal deciding all Slavs had to die. The lieutenant joined him but had little to interpret.

"A communist was broken, he is revealing all about the Red Army troops in the region."

Reichenau rose up on his toes. The Russians' interrogation may have been even more effective than the SS and Strauss, an admission he could never make before his own men. Reichenau returned to D'yatnovo at a faster pace, sensing his mission would become easier with the Russian's information. Knowing the identity and the location of the enemy ensured success. The two partisans, faces sculpted by years of cold winters and murderous summers, led him to a far outpost of D'yatnovo, a fenced home where a fire awaited him as did the Uzbek. Nothing was said, the captain entered to find another intimidating sight.

The communist was strapped to the wall, head lolling to one side, right eye blinking furiously. His left eye was a mass of melted flesh and Reichenau spotted a bit of singed bone poking from where his fleshy cheek had once been. One of the partisans smacked him, speeding the blinking and forcing his head to loll to the opposite side. Reichenau spotted the shriveled and blackened remains of his ear, a trickle of blood inching down the side of his neck and coagulating on the shoulder of his uniform. For all the dirt, grime and blood on his shirt, enough remained to reveal his Red Army origins.

The Uzbek partisan entered bearing a poker. The communist screamed when he approached, struggling to wriggle free but to no avail. He shut his eye, bracing for the inevitable. The partisan twirled the poker before him, brushing the communist's nose, head jerking, cry bouncing around the stone walls then drowned out by the laughter from inside the structure. Reichenau watched, holding his breath, heart thumping in his ears. The poker was drawn back, its presence merely for entertainment purposes. After several moments the communist opened his eye, blinked at his continued eyesight, relief sweeped across the remains of his charred face. His scream brought in the lieutenant, reticent about entering as he sensed the horror that was inside the building.

The Uzbek partisan tossed away the poker, slapped the prisoner and demanded answers. The man's head lolled again, mouth sagging open to reveal bloodied gums holding in a few remaining teeth. He was not talking. The partisan reached to one side, another poker removed from the fire outside and thrust into his hand. The glowing red end focused the communist's attention.

"I talk, I talk," he squealed, the desperation in his voice requiring no interpretation. Talk he did and for the next twenty minutes Reichenau collected more intelligence on central Russia than the Abwehr had for an entire year. The story was simple. When the Germans pushed through Minsk and Smolensk, the Russian high command had organized six groups of partisans under the direct control of a Red Army general. Several thousand troops enjoyed food and weapon caches hidden when the Red Army retreated. Their orders were to slow the German advance with sabotage, attacking convoys and killing as many German soldiers as possible while punishing any collaborators. The troops operated under their commander and had little contact with others so that the Germans could not destroy all of them in a single operation. The broken figure standing before Reichenau was a supply officer and he surrendered all knowledge of villages where supplies were hidden and troops allowed to live. His surrender came with a request.

"A quick and painless death," a tear rolled down from his one functioning eye. The request set off howls from the partisans and Reichenau turned to leave. Before he could escape, the captain stepped inside carrying three pokers. Death, yes, but quick and painless was not part of the eastern front. He exited to find a wide eyed lieutenant waiting, mouth gaping.

"Be careful," Reichenau warned. "The Russians might just fill your mouth with one of those." He motioned to the remaining pair of pokers.

"But sir," the lieutenant gasped. "What are they doing to them?"

"They are Slavs," Reichenau attempted to explain. "They have neither morality nor fear of pain or death." He mounted his horse. "It is best if we allow them to kill each other. It saves the lives of our men for more important duties." He was cut off by a yell from afar and the captain nodded in the direction of Strauss, heels digging into his horse as he shot at something below him but out of sight.

Reichenau ignored the scene, uninterested in what his corporal was doing and turned his horse, galloping to the far end of the village where he could circle its remains without exposure to more death. He would not be so lucky. Approaching the fringes of the town, he spotted barbed wire stretched across a copse of trees. Confined inside were the village's children, some sitting, others milling about eyeing two fires and the long metal rods pushed deep into the red coals.

40

August 6, 1940 **Southwest of D'yatnovo, Russia**

Tonya gripped her mother's arm and whispered in her ear.

"Mother, can you hear me?"

Marina crouched behind Tonya, her hand over her shoulder. Big Misha, Sasha and Volodya huddled around the three women, uncertain and confused.

Tonya gentle placed a rolled up blanket under her mother's head and stroked her cheek.

"Please Tonya, the Germans are close," implored Volodya. "We have to go."

Big Misha fell to his knees, tears streaming down his face. He reached for Tonya and drew her into his bear like chest. They had not hugged in many years.

"She is dying Misha," wailed Tonya. "Our dear mother is dying. Oh, I hate the Germans."

"I will stay with her until the end, Tonya," replied Misha. "You must go with the others."

Sasha, small and boyish compared to Big Misha stepped closer. He looked at Marina and smiled slightly. He pulled Misha away from the group.

"Misha, there is another way. Please do not be offended by my suggestion," offered Sasha. "If you mother will die perhaps we should not lose you as well."

Misha peered into the younger man's eyes. "What are you saying, Sasha?"

Marina and Volodyna joined them by the small fire they had built. All eyes were on Sasha.

"Maybe we can ease her suffering without sacrificing any of our group," offered Sasha.

Misha grabbed Sasha by the lapels of his conscript uniform. "You want me to kill my own mother?"

"Nyet, Big Misha," sputtered Sasha quickly. "I do not suggest that at all. I'm just saying this whole war is horrible and we serve the Motherland and ourselves best by fighting Germans. Not dying senselessly."

"I will kill any Germans that come near while I sit with Mother," exclaimed Misha. "I will take many with me if they are so unlucky to happen upon us."

"Of course Big Misha, we all know that and are certain of your strength," agreed Sasha.

Marina placed her hand on Misha's chest and nudged him away from Sasha. Misha released Sasha's tunic and stepped back.

"Sasha is only trying to help, Misha," said Marina. "We need leaders in this fight against the Fascist pigs. We need you. We will take care of your mother, she will not suffer."

An explosion startled the group. It was no more than a kilometer away. Volodyna grabbed his rifle and crouched into a firing position.

Misha stared at Marina, unable to accept her plan. Tonya rose from her mother's unconscious body and walked to Misha's side. She placed her hand in Misha's and moved him towards the small pile of supplies past the fire.

"Big Brother Misha, Sasha and Marina are right," explained Tonya. "Mother will not survive the night. She is very sick. We must say good bye and leave her."

Misha was crying openly, his massive frame convulsing. He hugged Tonya and squeezed her tightly. "How will we bury her?"

"There's no time Misha," answered Tonya. "It must be now."

Tonya led Misha to their stricken mother. They knelt in unison by her side. In turn they whispered in her ear. Tonya helped Misha to stand and led him to collect their supplies.

Marina pushed Sasha forward.

"Use your knife and be quick," urged Marina.

Sasha stumbled to the old woman and knelt. Her breathing was labored. He unsheathed his knife and placed his body so the view of the others was obstructed. He wasn't certain how to accomplish the task. He knew he must do it so she would die instantly.

He glanced at the blade. It was very sharp. He placed the point on the side of her head at the softest part. Sasha pushed with as much force as he could muster. There was not an excessive amount of blood. He confirmed her breathing had stopped.

Sasha wiped his knife clean and pulled the head scarf over her face. He removed the blanket. It would be needed later. He gathered the body in his arms and carried it over to Volodyna. Together they placed the mother of their leader under a small tree and left to join the others.

41

August 6, 1940   **Bogdanovka, Rumania**

Bogdanovka. The name meant nothing to Ianu when he and the other prisoners were prodded from the enclosed rail car. He knew nothing of the town, though a boy in Letcani had borne the name Bogdan. It was a miracle birth according to Saloman, earning the boy the name "given by God." Little of what he saw of Bogdanovka seemed God-like. This included the clapboard shacks and the thousands of hungry of prisoners poised behind the barbed wire fence that comprised the main section of the camp. They had watched Ianu and the other workers rush by, the new arrivals clenching at the stifling odor of excrement, intimidated by the massed numbers who saw them not as prisoners but as captors.

Grigore was nowhere to be seen, neither was the Iron Guard, Bogdanovka seemingly controlled by the Rumanian Army, a camp filled with the enemies of the state. The soldiers stood, rifles hooked around their arms, eyes trained on the mass of prisoners who could overwhelm them in a bloody rush. They paid little attention to the small group detached from two rail cars of new arrivals.

Ianu and the workers were halted outside the shack. It had been three days since the nearly dozen men had eaten. They remained a few meters from the guards who spoke in lowered tones that eventually rose in volume. Ianu cocked his head even as he looked elsewhere. Spying on the guards would get him sent behind the barbed wire.

"Why are they left outside?" This from the best dressed of the soldiers, pudgy but with a vengeful expression. The prisoners were delaying his enjoyment of what Ianu imagined would be a sumptuous dinner.

"These are the workers." The oldest of the group, older even than Saloman, and thin with a hawk like nose, advocated for them. He glanced at the huddled humanity while his superior ignored Ianu and his comrades.

"There are plentiful Jews in the camp," the pudgy commander hissed. "They can do the work, we don't need these." His arm shot out, finger pointed at them to resemble a cocked rifle.

"They are dependable. They did not attempt to escape in Roman. Grigore sent them, the Germans said hundreds of bodies were eliminated."

"Grigore." The commander's cheeks reddened. "Iron Guard scum. It is their responsibility, these Jews." He spat. "The army is in Russia, we are trapped with this vermin."

"It is our duty."

Ianu bent his head as one of the soldiers passed close, leaned over and smacked the Jews kneeling in the wet earth. He missed the dispute over where to send the new arrivals. The older soldier won, convincing his commander the workers were a special breed and they were locked in one of the clapboard huts.

Barely five meters by five meters it offered even less room than the rail car. Windowless wood walls fit together tightly to block the sunlight, the shack required several moments for their eyes to adjust. Ianu settled into a corner, pulled his legs tight against his chest, the shack did not allow them to stretch. Splinters dug into his uncovered arms, earth hard beneath him, but for the first time in weeks he felt protected from the elements and the guards.

"You saw them." A croak in the darkness made Ianu jump. "It is a concentration camp."

Ianu shifted, flinching as the splinters scraped offer a layer of skin. The Nazis ran concentration camps. Rumors of thousands murdered penetrated into even isolated Letcani. Ianu had paid little attention. The Nazis were far away. Pressed into the shack he wished he had listened to the warnings.

"We work," a croak responded. The long trip to Bagdonovka had made throats raw, nothing swallowed in three days.

"All of them?" Everyone in the shack knew what was meant. The train had brought mainly corpses, the few living ones usually too weak to fight.

"We cannot talk of it." Ianu recognized the voice of the confident man, the one who knew they were not going to Russia. "We do the work or they put us on the other side of the barbed wire."

It was reality. They were in a covered place, the others were penned in the open air, treated like animals. Ianu hugged his legs, suddenly chilled even as the heat built in the shack. Within moments he was asleep, three days without food having its effect.

The next days proved to be the best of their captivity. Two meals, bread in the morning, softer and absent mold, and meat for the evening. It was enough to keep the dwindling Ianu alive. Most of their day the workers dug pits, the guards choosing some of the stronger prisoners for the same duty. The prisoners were isolated from the workers, who knew the real use for the pits. The prisoners heard they were building a lagoon to empty the overflowing latrines in the camp. They dug with eagerness, the sooner the pit was finished, the sooner their lives would be better.

Two pits were ripped from the moistened fields nearly two hundred metres apart, seventy five metres across and twenty metres deep. Ianu would never forget the triumph after days of digging, the prisoners tired and hungry but proud of their effort. They were lined upon the edge, food a reward for work but also a distraction. From the far side of the pit Ianu and the workers watched the soldiers line up behind the hungry prisoners, rifles aimed at heads. The firing squad squeezed off their rounds, though in typical Rumanian Army fashion several missed. A few lucky prisoners scrambled to escape, using the only path available, the pit.

The scene descended into the comic incompetence, prisoners dodging and ducking, rushing to the opposite side of the pit, scrabbling in the dirt, sometimes climbing several metres before the clods gave away and they slid back to the pit. After several minutes of fruitless firing the guards followed the prisoners into the pit, ending the chase with metal pipes, heads smashed in their fury and leaving a residue of blood, brains and undigested food to coat the pit bottom. Then it became Ianu's and the workers' time.

As the guards used ropes to escape the death chamber, they tossed in knives, hatchets and pliers. The sprawled bodies became Ianu's workplace. Metal was removed with the usual hacking and splatter. The worst for Ianu was retrieving wealth from the mouths of the dead. Rusty pliers, the same type he used to pry off hinges in the store, shook in his hand.

His first was a lad, a few years younger than Ianu, skull split, right eye staring at him as if seeking an explanation. His dark features said gypsy, who were known for swallowing valuables. Ianu'a fingernails scrabbled through human waste, the odor unnoticed.

Ianu cleaned his fingers on the lad's shirt then raised his hand to display the found valuables – the few diamonds which had wriggled through the intestines prior to death and were the main source of money for the guards. He was careful to empty his hands and ragged pockets that remained in his pants as hiding contraband was the quickest route to death.

Duty sent him to the next body, an older man, his beard gray. Unlike the lad who was a gypsy and had no dental work, older prisoners usually had some gold or silver wedged into their teeth. It was a valuable corpse. He found rings jammed in hidden compartments in his clothing. His mouth, though, held the best – gold teeth. Pliers shaking, Ianu pressed the metal against the teeth, struggling to wriggle them free. Pliers scraped the enamel as he tugged the teeth one by one. A shot sounded. Ianu did not look. It was only another dead prisoner.

"What are you doing?" The growl sounded, its proximity making Ianu jump.

"Here, here." He raised his hand, unclenching his fist to reveal what he had taken.

The guard held out an oilcloth sack. Ianu emptied his hand into it before receiving a cuff on his ear. "What takes you so long? We have more." The guard, grimy from sliding into the pit, raised his sidearm. "They are finished, you remain."

At the sight of the gun Ianu dropped the pliers, the tool settling into the prisoner's mouth. He snatched them up. "The teeth, the gold, so many."

The guard, pressed between the choice of killing prisoners or filling his oilcloth, settled on the latter." Faster, faster, or-." A shot rang out. Ianu tightened his grip, tearing flesh, teeth ripped by their roots, material covering his face.

"Faster, faster." The guard snatched each filling. "That one." The pistol wriggled, pointing at a sizable filling at the back of the mouth. "Take it." He flexed his hand, eyes shining at the possibility of gold.

Ianu jammed the pliers into the back of the mouth, the remaining teeth cutting at his flesh. The tooth resisted, right to left, front to back, little movement.

"Why are you messing with the Jew?" The call came from above and the edge of the pit. The guard waved off the question then cuffed Ianu again. "Out." The gun barrel was pressed against Ianu's neck.

Both hands gripping the pliers, elbows and arms locked, he tugged. Movement. Another tap on his neck and a click. Taking a breath, Ianu summoned his strength and the tooth was free. He jerked, tooth and filling clamped between the plier head. At that moment he bumped his elbow, nerve pressed, fingers releasing the plier handle, tooth sliding free and plummeting into the prisoner's throat and disappearing into its owner.

"Bastard." The gun butt caught Ianu's ear sending him tumbling among the corpses. "Dirty Jew, stealing." He stepped over Ianu, straddling him, pistol poked between his eyes. "You -."

A shot interrupted him, Ianu's eyes closed, body tensing for impact. He flinched then realized the shot had not come from above. More sounded, then shouts, forcing his eyes open. Bodies tumbled into the pit, the dead ones flopping with little direction, the live ones scrabbling at the dirt to slow their descent, tumbling then dashing further into the pit, believing escape beckoned from the far walls.

"Shoot, shoot." Desperation sounded from above the pit, the poor aim of the barely trained Rumanian soldier creating a crisis. The soldier straddling Ianu turned, facing another choice, kill the Jew who cheated him or follow orders and eliminate the prisoners trying to escape.

"I come back for you." The guard planted his foot between Ianu's legs, pain followed by a cry then a curling into a fetal position. More shots, more bodies tumbling into the pit. Once the pain subsided Ianu climbed over the dead and joined his comrades in the corner of the pit. The guard, still seething over loss, took out his anger on the escapees, emptying his pistol into them until his gun clicked ineffectually as life bled from his victims.

Ianu counted several dozen bodies, mostly new arrivals that would have to be "cleansed" of their valuables. The guard, kicking at the bodies, was distracted by the soldiers above and used one of the ropes to climb free, never looking back at Ianu. Unfortunately for the workers most of the new corpses were from rural areas, barely able to survive much less afford luxuries such as dentistry or jewelry. It was the city dwellers who offered a gold mine of dental work and rings, all of which pleased the guards.

The bodies continued tumbling into the pit, more than Ianu could count after the firing squads improved their aim. The Rumanians had learned their lessons well. Instead of leaving the bodies to rot in the open to stir panic or leave witnesses who could spread stories, they had learned to conceal their crimes. Ianu sensed the Germans were involved – an orderly people even in the messy task of mass killing. The Nazis he had seen elsewhere had been ordering the Rumanians like children, their appearance followed by the digging of graves then pits. The solution had its own problems. The scattered bodies made movement difficult, then the vermin and flies, the heat attracting both as the cooling bodies offered a feast. The rats were less aggressive then the flies, recognizing that live flesh was more dangerous to them. This became a problem only as the pit filled and if the bodies were allowed to sit overnight.

More shots, more bodies, more work for them. Ianu no longer paid attention, work meaning another day alive.

42

August 14, 1940   Moscow

The Germans were coming. Panic swept eastward to Moscow, thousands of refugees from Mohaisk, Klin, Tula and other towns around the capital city clogged the roads and packed the trains, slowing troops moving west. Alexei Protopopov was aware of the rumors swirling through the population spread by tens of thousands fleeing the Nazi hordes. Their stories clashed with the official line of the Wehrmacht checked 200 kilometers, then 150 kilometers from Moscow. Alexei knew better, sitting in on the daily briefings, writing reports and sending them to the recuperating Stalin. Watching the members of the Politburo dither, delay then decline he wished for the return of the one man who could steady the government, the army and the people. A month had passed since Alexei's early morning summons and much had changed.

War Minister Voroshilov had been killed by German artillery while visiting the front near Vyazma. The Communist Party leader in Ukraine, Khrushchev, had his plane shot down, killing him and

General Budyenny near Kiev. Trade Minister Mikoyan was captured by a fast moving German column and in true patriotic fashion had shot himself rather than reveal state secrets. It had been a difficult four weeks for the Soviet government, several dozen high ranking officials and Red Army officers cut down by the enemy or in war related accidents. While the population bemoaned the run of bad luck and superstitious Russians saw it as a sight of impending defeat, Alexei was heartened. He recognized a purge of the rotten elements of government, a purge only Comrade Stalin could have ordered. Alexei would have preferred trials, an airing of the conspiracy, but during war danger was all around and people must be united rather than divided. He kept repeating this as he released documents under Comrade Stalin's signature and issued verbal orders in his name.

Ultimate victory drove him to work for the Party until he visited the map room, the pins and arrows on the table map showing not victory but a Fascist wave, Moscow surrounded on three sides. He had not been able to sleep that night, the heat keeping his mind racing. Instead he had snatched a flashlight, packing his belongings after having unpacked them under Pravda's soothing reports of Red Army victories.

The lies were quickly revealed with the August order for the evacuation of all essential officials to Kuibyshev, eight hundred kilometers to the east. The order had also been soothing, promising it as a temporary arrangement until the danger passed but Alexei knew better. He had overheard the generals speaking about the potential loss of the capital. Moscow was the key, everything passed through it, the railways, the paved roads, once it fell everything west of the Volga was gone.

Then in the midst of a normal evening, eating soup with a hint of strained meat for his dinner, Alexei was carted off by the NKVD. Three agents, none he knew, one taking him, two others his essentials which they searched first for weapons or anti-Soviet tracts. It was to be a quiet removal of all essential personnel, but word had leaked out partly from those left behind, partly from a wave of refugees fleeing from a battle that was one hundred kilometers away. When Alexei was driven from his apartment he noticed soldiers patrolling with their tanks and automatic weapons at the ready. Even at six in the evening there was a curfew. Civilians remained in their sweltering apartments as anyone on the streets would be considered a potential saboteur or spy. Riding through the empty streets, Alexei pointed in the direction of the Arbat, revived as a market as people sought to sell their belongings to speed their escape.

"That has to be the first time I have seen that street empty."

The NKVD agent did not respond. The two agents in the front were eying the street and sidewalks, unnerved by the possibility of Muscovites rushing into the streets to stop the car. There had been much talk among the Politburo about security of government officials, sometimes crowding out discussion of the military situation and how to halt the Germans.

"When is the train leaving?" Alexei asked.

"At 4:30 am," replied the NKVD agent reluctantly. Train schedules had been declared a state secret. As most Muscovites lacked cars, the train was the only path to escape. Publishing schedules would only lead to crowds and there were not enough seats to let all citizens escape, much less the tens of thousands of refugees parked in the outskirts. Herded together by the NKVD, they were isolated to prevent the spread of wild rumors about the approaching Germans.

"Why are we going there now?" asked Alexei.

Before the NKVD agent answered, air raid sirens blared. The driver drove recklessly, oblivious to automotive safety.

Searchlights blazed into the night sky, as anti-aircraft fire unleashed. Bombs generated massive explosions.

Alexei was overwhelmed by the fury of the aerial assault. He cowered in the back seat, trying desperately to make his body smaller.

The car slid to a halt, slamming into a lamppost. Instantly, the NKVD agents exited the vehicle. Alexei was muscled from the car to the street and into the foyer of an old governmental building.

Alexei stole a glance to the street. His eyes detected bright lights and fire, his ears a deafening crescendo of thunder. He turned his attention to his NKVD entourage. They were crouched on the foyer floor.

The NKVD leader grabbed Alexei by the arm, dragging him to the tile. He screamed, to be heard over the explosions.

"We wait until the raid ends."

"Then what?" asked Alexei.

"Then we walk."

0

Natasha loved trains as a girl. She remembered her first ride, with her Uncle the Party big shot. She was eleven. The speed and the freedom to move over large tracts of barren landscape generated enthusiasm and energy she had not felt earlier.

Now she was petrified. The Luftwaffe bombed Moscow indiscriminately all night. Fires burned out of control.

Natasha had connived orders to board a train east, away from the city. It was scheduled to depart at 4:30 am. She stumbled through the streets with Dmitry toward the station. It was hours before dawn and there was a curfew. Crossing Moscow was dangerous and the likelihood of the train leaving unscathed was not high.

"Dmitry, we have to hurry. If we miss the train to Kuibyshev, we may have no other chance," implored Natasha.

"You have too much for me to carry," responded Dmitry as he tossed her bag to the side of the lane atop a pile of rubble. "I'm done carrying this shit."

Natasha fetched the bag and forcibly slung it back over Dmitry's shoulder. She smacked him on the back of his head with the palm of her hand. Not particularly hard but as a reminder.

"Don't be a fool. I need everything in my bag," ordered Natasha. "It is not heavy and it is important that I look attractive."

Dmitry grumbled incoherently and trudged along. The eastern sector of Moscow was as badly damaged as the center. Collapsed buildings encroached upon the street. A trolley was lying on its side, smoldering. Dead horses were as common, certain to be sliced up by the starving populace at sunrise. The stench of death invaded their nostrils.

"You said there would be food and shelter in Moscow," complained Dmitry. "This is worse than where we came from."

Natasha continued walking without comment. Dmitry was right. Moscow had been a disaster since they arrived. There was nowhere to stay and nothing to eat. She was able to contact her superiors but their information was ghastly. The Fascists were approaching the city and Comrade Stalin was strangely silent. She eventually acquired a uniform and directions to an underground subway station where NKVD officers were billeted.

Natasha was debriefed by uninterested colleagues. She requested an assignment, but received no direction. Moscow was truly struggling. There was no electricity. The morale of the citizens was somehow holding but balanced on a razor thin wire. Then the dreaded Luftwaffe began the air raids. She became desperate.

After two weeks, Natasha was given orders directing her and her "aide" Dmitry to board a train east. Natasha shivered and almost vomited recalling the disgusting sex she traded with a pockmarked NKVD general to obtain her orders. She rolled up her sleeve and examined the bite marks he had left on her arm.

"What are you looking at? Are you injured?" asked Dmitry.

"Da! The asshole general bit my arm," spat Natasha. "Do you understand what I had to do to get these transit orders, Dmitry? Do you have any idea?"

Dmitry lumbered along silently, sweating in the August heat. Poor Natasha, but how was screwing a general worse than her actions with the American, James Reilly? At least the general was Russian. He kept his thoughts to himself because Natasha's willingness to trade sex for favors had benefited him. He did not want to stay another minute in Moscow.

Dmitry watched her walk from behind. The replacement uniform was small, fitted to her body. She wore the insignia of a NKVD major. Fires from buildings destroyed in the massive air raid silhouetted her figure. Natasha was certainly attractive.

Closer to the rail station they were stopped by a Red Army patrol. A burly lieutenant demanded papers. Natasha immediately produced her hard gained orders.

"Fleeing the city, eh," commented the lieutenant as he inspected Natasha's offering. "There is a curfew."

"Lieutenant, it would be wise for you to remember I am a NKVD Major and your superior," stated Natasha.

The lieutenant laughed, "of course you are. There's still a curfew."

"Are you unafraid of your superiors now?" inquired Natasha as rudely as she could muster.

"Why would I be afraid of political officers running from the front?" replied the lieutenant, his hand moving to his holstered sidearm. Other men began to move in their direction. "There have been hundreds fleeing officers and Party members. Why should we fight the Fascists when the Party leaders save their lives?"

"What is your name and unit?" demanded Natasha.

Dmitry was near panic as the situation deteriorated. He moved to Natasha, taking her arm. Natasha pushed him away. It was clear the unshaven lieutenant and his men were drunk.

The lieutenant stepped closer to Natasha and reached for her lapel. She brushed his hand off her uniform and stepped back.

"My name is Lieutenant Fuck Your Mother," cursed the drunken officer. He considered Natasha. "Perhaps my men would like to be motivated by a whore major?"

Natasha's eyes glared as she considered her options. She counted seven soldiers, all brandishing rifles, some waving bottles of vodka. She and Dmitry were unarmed.

"Lieutenant, we understand the stress of the situation," said Natasha. "But the war is far from lost. We must regroup and fight back for the Motherland."

The lieutenant laughed and grabbed Natasha by the shoulders and pulled her close. His face was inches from hers. Natasha could smell the vodka on his breath. Lieutenant Fuck Your Mother smiled and withdrew.

"Let the whore and her faggot pass," he ordered to his men.

Dmitry and Natasha hustled past the soldiers. After they were past, the lieutenant staggered into the street and yelled.

"Please give Comrade Stalin our regards."

43

August 14, 1940   Vyazma, Russia

Captain Johanns Franks' eye patch was pulled snug against his head, causing it to bow outwards. He removed the distinctive round helmet of the Fallschirmjager airborne troops and fidgeted with the strap that held the black patch in place. Satisfied that he had reached maximum comfort, Franks replaced his helmet.

Franks confirmed that his gravity knife was tight against his chest, ready to cut away the parachute's harness should he become entangled in the trees. His MP 38 submachine gun was similarly strapped to his torso, loaded and ready for immediate action. It was almost midnight and it was difficult to recognize his men. He walked over to his non-commissioned officers for his final words of encouragement.

"Get free of the parachutes as quick as possible and get to the canisters," reminded Franks. The officers and NCOs jumped with MP 38s but the enlisted were armed with nothing more than a pistol and two grenades. Large metal canisters were dropped with the men, obtaining the weapons and ammunition inside immediately was critical to their survival. Franks surveyed each leader, satisfied they were ready.

"Confirm every man has at least a 30 roll of Pervitin," commanded Franks. "We will not be relieved for a minimum of 48 hours. Sleep is forbidden."

The sergeants nodded, acknowledging receipt of the message. Their men would not have to be coerced to take the methamphetamine infused tablets. Franks moved to a group of enlisted, boys no older than 19 years of age. "This is it men, at dawn the battle for Moscow begins."

The young paratroopers grinned but were quiet. They checked each other's straps, confident in the knowledge that they had packed their own RZ 20 parachutes.

An hour later, Lieutenant Gottizner approached Franks and saluted. "We are ready to board the aircraft Hauptmann Franks.

Franks returned the salute. He was very impressed with Lieutenant Wilhelm "Willy" Gottizner, an original from the Regiment General Goering before the official creation of Germany's airborne forces. He had received an officer's commission on the eve of the Polish campaign. No soldier in the second company knew Fallschirmjager tactics better. Franks smiled and took Gottizner by the arm. He squeezed it fraternally and spoke firmly, "Let's close the noose on Moscow!"

At 2:00 am, the first of the Junkers Ju-52 tri-motor transports lumbered down the grass strip and lifted off. The transports swung south of Moscow, avoiding the heavy anti-aircraft screen surrounding the Russian capital. Once past Moscow, the aerial armada turned north to the drop zone. They were escorted by dozens of Me-110 long range heavy fighters.

The entire 7th Flieger Division would be dropped on the main rail line connecting Moscow to the east. Every available Ju-52 transport in the Luftwaffe was assembled for the effort. Goering had guaranteed to the Fuhrer that not a "single Mongoloid peasant" from the far flung republics of the Soviet Union would "step foot in Moscow." The panzer divisions had already cut the southern and northern entries to the city. The Luftwaffe's paratroopers would seal the trap.

As a diversion earlier in the evening, the Luftwaffe launched its largest aerial bombardment of the Russian capital to date. Scores of Ju-88s, He-111s and Do-17s pounded the center of the Soviet government. The anti-aircraft fire was murderous and bomber losses were high. Their sacrifice was not only expected but almost welcomed. It confirmed that the Bolsheviks were distracted. The lumbering transports flew unhindered and unharmed to their target.

The 7th Flieger Division was untested in battle. But it was a fresh formation. Its aggressive leader, General Kurt Student, promised it would prevent re-supply of Moscow from the east. He maintained that the presence of an entire airborne division in the rear would cause confusion and chaos among the defenders.

The massive bombardment of Moscow and the airborne assault on the re-supply and retreat route from the city were to be combined with an all-out assault by the panzer divisions to the north and south. The entire offensive might of the Wehrmacht was concentrated to overcome the stiffening Soviet defense.

Hauptmann Johanns Franks grabbed Stabsfeldwebel Oskar Herrick's knee and stood. It was time. He attached his parachute to the static line. The door was opened. The roar of the Ju-52's three engines and the air rushing past the fuselage was deafening.

Franks bellowed to the men in his aircraft, "Heil Hitler!" and jumped into the early morning sky from the lead Ju-52, clutching his MP-38. Cold wind slammed into his face, momentarily obscuring the sight in his good eye. He panicked briefly before regaining his senses. The earth approached rapidly. He confirmed his chute was fully open, with the single tether untwisted.

He hit the ground hard but on all fours, as trained. He landed in an open field, bordered by thick woods. There were no man-made structures. Franks looked skywards to witness Staff Sergeant Herrick's textbook collision with Russian soil, east of Moscow. He rose and pulled his chute towards him.

Herrick was beside Franks almost instantly. He already had his used parachute bundled. He motioned towards the woods.

Franks nodded and said, "The canisters are 100 meters north, by the woods. They didn't drift."

"I'll organize the men," replied Herrick. "This doesn't look right."

Franks grunted affirmatively and pulled his map from inside his paratrooper's smock. He scanned their surroundings. He had expected to see agricultural buildings to the east and a railroad embankment to the south. There had not been small arms fire. Franks slung his MP-38 over his shoulder and carried his folded chute in the direction of the woods.

The field was not plowed or planted. Franks grumbled as it was clear they were not in their designated landing zone. Lieutenant Gottizner hustled over to him with Sergeant Herrick at his heals.

"Herr Hauptmann, we have assembled approximately half of the company. The same with the canisters," reported Gottizner.

Franks motioned Gottizner to draw closer. "What's that mean, Lieutenant?" Franks pulled a stray twig from Gottizner's helmet. "I need better information. Where are the other men? Where are Lieutenant Ericksen and the non-coms? Have we reached them by radio?"

Gottizner straightened. "The rest of the company including Lieutenant Ericksen are not in this area. We are unable to raise them. We have recovered one radio. We do not believe it is working correctly. It appears to have been damaged in the drop."

"What have we recovered from the canisters?" demanded Franks. "Provide weapons first, then provisions."

"Six MG-34s, demolition charges and plenty of MP-38s, rifles and ammunition," answered Gottizner. "We're weak on food and water, decent on medical supplies."

"Any idea where we are?" wondered Franks aloud.

"Ja, I believe we were dropped short, significantly short," responded Gottizner. "I base this on my observation of other Ju-52s continuing north while we floated in our chutes."

"So the railroad is north, the bridge to the northeast?" surmised Franks.

Gottizner shrugged but it was not an indication of complete certainty. Instead, Franks read Gottizner's body language to suggest that was his conclusion. Franks agreed with his lieutenant and waved the men over. Dawn was soon to be upon the paratroopers, the sky to the east began to brighten. He surveyed his company. Most appeared intact, only a handful leaned on makeshift crutches.

"Men, we appeared to have been dropped short of our designated landing zone." Franks held his map to the side and continued. "We are not exactly sure how far we have to march. We will remain on the offensive. We will march north hard until we reach the railroad."

The men on crutches appeared worried. Franks would let Sergeant Herrick figure out how to transport them. Determining their location and moving into position to participate in the battle was his mission.

44

August 15, 1940   Moscow

Security was tight at the station. Soldiers had shut down the area around the station, using barricades, light tanks and troops behind sandbags and barbed wire to allow the trains to run. Several minutes passed before Alexei and his group were allowed through, somewhat frightened soldiers studying his papers as the NKVD agent tried to explain he was a very important person.

Once inside the perimeter, the agents rushed him into the station where he was left to sit and wait like the other refugees fleeing to Kuibyshev. He settled in, his agent remaining beside him and preventing any conversation with the others. Each had their own agent as a buffer, more rumor prevention. The high ceilinged station, a mix of czarist and Stalinist architecture was both beautiful and intimidating, a reminder to the average citizen that the Party could crush resistance beneath the weight of marble and concrete.

Sitting in the middle of the long bench, his closest fellow passenger a good ten meters from him, Alexei eyed those who were fortunate enough to be considered essential personnel. He again tried to squeeze information from his NKVD companion.

"Did they tell you when we were leaving?"

"There's a delay. Politburo."

The agent did not add to his cryptic reply but looked forward. Alexei wondered if he was among the fortunate or would be left in the city to fend off the German hordes. Alexei shook his head. The movement stirred his companion to glance in his direction as if Alexei were sending a signal about some Trotskyite conspiracy.

Alexei settled. The NKVD turning on their masters was too horrible to consider but events in July convinced him that all he knew was about to change. There was the meeting between the generals, Beria and Molotov, one of several but the only one of two Alexei had witnessed. Instead he was ordered to issue a statement in Comrade Stalin's name about the inevitability of victory and the determination of all Soviet citizens to throw the Facists from their villages.

The generals began with a proposal to declare Moscow an open city, ensuring it would not be destroyed, its citizens not slaughtered in a siege or months long street battles. The politicians were unimpressed. Moscow was a prize and prizes must be earned not plucked like ripe fruit.

Then there was the generals' request for NKVD troops to fight with the Red Army. Molotov, knowing the NKVD was the only barrier between him and the howling mobs scoffed at the idea as did Beria, the sweating little man in a fervor about traitors and saboteurs as the Germans approached. Alexei had heard rumblings about a Red Army purge and only an intact NKVD would allow Beria to do that.

The debate in Stalin's corner office had lasted for hours even as papers, archives and maps were toted through the office and hauled onto trucks bound for Kuibyshev. Then the scientists had been brought in to handle the most delicate of subjects, Lenin. Removing him from the mausoleum was necessary. He was more important than anyone living in the Kremlin. Without Lenin the Soviet state would cease to exist, but transporting him was tricky as deterioration was both unacceptable and certain. Alexei listened as the scientists offered differing opinions, no one but Stalin's adjutant seeming to realize the oddity of old men arguing about the handling of a corpse as danger closed in on three sides.

Eventually they agreed Lenin would be transported in a refrigerated rail car where he would remain until a new mausoleum was built or Moscow was retaken. If and when that occurred Alexei doubted there would be much left except ruins. He imagined the remains of the Red Army's western army group and a contingent of NKVD agents – trigger happy and conscienceless – destroying the city and its residents in a fanatical last defense. Alexei suspected they were a worse danger to Muscovites than the Nazis.

Alexei followed the German advance closely, his sister and mother were hundreds of kilometers south of Moscow in Voronezh on the Don River, a city lacking any strategic importance. He kept in contact with letters, always on innocuous topics as they were opened and read by the NKVD to ensure he was not sharing state secrets such as the collapse of the Red Army and the Soviet state. Then the contacts ceased. Weeks had passed without a letter, a worry but not overwhelming, as Alexei knew the Germans were far from Voronezh.

There was movement in the Moscow train station, large wagons pushed by scraggly looking porters who tugged the luggage with verve, their efforts potentially getting them out of the city on what might be the last train. Alexei eyed them, not too long as contact stirred his agent. Enemies were all around and exchanged glances might reveal information about train departures, a signal to potential saboteurs. The wagons passed and the scene settled, Alexei returning to the surprise visit from Beria.

The NKVD chief was sweating that day, rubbing his hands, up on his toes trying to look taller. "There are problems in Voronezh," he had announced while Alexei stood in the hallway between the lobby and the corner office. "Some people in the city knew of your connections to Comrade Stalin and thought getting to your family would speed their departure from the city."

Alexei trembled at the news, hands reaching for the wall. What had once made his family untouchable – his working in the Kremlin – had suddenly become dangerous.

"I made certain they are safe, especially your sister." Beria wet his lips at the mention of the teen, hands flexing with anticipation. "When I see her again I will send her your greetings."

Alexei murmured thanks then watched the NKVD chief head to the corner office, chin pointed high, a man fully in control the situation. With Alexei's family in his power, Beria ensured Stalin's adjutant would remain loyal.

More activity in the train station, a low murmur feeding down the benches, partly relief, partly fear. They were leaving, the guard tugged at Alexei's elbow, the younger man rising and following the others to the train platform. Alexei did not recognize any of his fellow passengers as they were pushed up the stairs and stumbled to their seats. The train was only about half full as Alexei settled into a seat facing a couple, his riding mates to Kuibyshev or possibly spies testing his loyalty.

Alexei recognized mid-level bureaucrats, assistants and deputies, men whose career and lives depended on their usefulness to a government that needed qualified men after years of purges and three months of war. Most of the men were alone. A few had wives but no children. Luggage was also sparse, personal possessions frowned on by the Party. Alexei eyed the couple across from him, facing the rear. The man was in his fifties, a careerist, possibly an old czarist bureaucrat who had switched sides at the right time. A faceless, colorless man never noticed by anyone above, he was willing to stamp papers and mouth the right phrases to ensure survival.

"Alexei Mikhaelovich," the man offered his hand.

Alexei blinked, surprised at being recognized, embarrassed at not recognizing the man. "Yes."

"Leonid Georgovich." He took Alexei's hand and gripped it.

Leonid, a Pravda worker. They had spoken about articles for publication, businesslike conversations that were not unpleasant. Leonid realized who had written the articles Alexei was bringing with orders not to change a single word. Alexei glanced at the girl beside him.

"Kuibyshev," Leonid exclaimed. "I just thought it was all rumors spread by the Trotskyites or saboteurs. The last I heard the Germans were halted at Vyazma."

Alexei nodded slowly. Vyazma had fallen weeks earlier with barely a fight. He heard Beria denouncing the generals and the Eighth Shock Army for fleeing at the sight of a single German tank, tens of thousands surrendering to a panzer regiment.

"They are preparing something," Leonid said with a nod. "Comrade Stalin is drawing them in. The further they move from their supply lines the easier it will be to surround them." He swung his hand. "By next summer we will be in Berlin hanging Hitler from a lamppost."

Alexei closed his eyes at the bravado. He studied Leonid's face, ruddy and fleshy with acne scars and oddly shaped boils, a not uncommon face, a peasant's face. Naïve, stupid and fanatical until bullets started whistling by his head, Leonid was convinced of Soviet greatness, not just frothing patriotic for Alexei's benefit. His timeline for capturing Berlin might be moved back, but his absolute belief in the Soviet cause would remain, as hard as his head.

The girl beside Leonid wiggled her arm beneath his, head sliding onto his shoulder and Alexei suddenly understood his calm. Leonid enjoyed some influence, a fact that did not escape attractive girls who wanted access to dachas, food, clothes, comfort, escape, all in exchange for access to them. The corruption of capitalism, always the subject of Soviet propaganda, thrived among the lucky few who enjoyed real power at the top of Soviet society.

"They have moved the presses to Kuibyshev," Leonid said. "Pravda will be printing again within three days of our arrival." He jerked his shoulder, the girl's head bouncing then straightening. "I wonder if Comrade Stalin has already left."

Alexei wet his lips. He did not speak of Stalin with others. "That is an interesting question," Alexei murmured.

Leonid did not press his question. Alexei relaxed, staring out the window at the platform, only a few NKVD agents standing and waiting, steam occasionally hiding them as the train prepared for departure. Alexei did not stare for too long, too much attention paid to the secret police suggested something to hide though ignoring them suggested the same. It was a delicate balance, but working in the Kremlin he learned how to work it.

Leonid unhooked himself from the girl. "Irina, go find us something to drink, the car, a babushka selling things." He looked at Alexei. "There should be a dining car, all the way to Kuibyshev would be hard to take without refreshment."

Irina was on her feet, confusion in her eyes as if this were her first train trip. Alexei would not have been surprised if it was true. Travel was restricted in the Soviet Union except for Party officials and extremely important business, such as fleeing to Kuibyshev. Irina toddled off, glancing back in confusion at Leonid, who waved her on.

"Not bad," the older man said with a leer. "Her mother works for me, introduced us a few weeks ago." His head wobbled. "She heard all of the rumors."

Trade your daughter for safe passage, Alexei thought.

"Must be careful. The Party frowns on men having wives and girlfriends."

"So do wives," Alexei murmured.

Leonid laughed. "Yes they do but she does not know."

"She's not on the train?"

"She is remaining in Moscow with the children."

Alexei froze. Moscow was soon to be a charnel house. Leonid disgusted him. He had abandoned his family with the knowledge the city would fall to the Nazis.

0

The train was overloaded with fleeing Party leaders and high ranking soldiers. Natasha was shocked by the amount of luggage the elite attempted to load onto the train. The NKVD guards simply discarded the trunks and suitcases in a massive pile on the platform. There was no room and Party rank was losing its value quickly.

Natasha and Dmitry squeezed into a car jammed with complaining self-important minor Party functionaries. Through the open window, they watched as a bespectacled official grabbed the arm of a NKVD sergeant, demanding his attention.

"I must take this trunk on the train," demanded the indignant man, pointing to his rank insignia.

The sergeant barely glanced at him and spat, "Nyet."

"Do you know who I am?' demanded the once important official. "What is your name and unit?"

The sergeant spun, raised his rifle and smashed the butt into the face of the demanding pest. The conversation was over as the slight man fell to the concrete platform, unconscious. Dmitry gasped as Natasha dug her fingers into his side.

"Be invisible, Dmitry," she whispered. "We cannot get off this train. We have no other way."

Dmitry moved his mouth to her ear and spoke as lowly as he could and still be heard.

"How can this be, Major? The world is falling apart."

Natasha urged, "Quiet, the train is moving!"

She stole a further glance out the window and saw people running to somehow get aboard, trampling the fallen official with the broken spectacles and smashed face. The train jerked forward, the NKVD men leaping onto it as the cars passed them. It began to crawl, leaving the city to its fate, millions of men, women and children, left to the whims of the NKVD and the Nazis.

45

August 15, 1940   South of Orekhovo Zuyevo, Russia

Johanns Franks trudged north through the woods with Staff Sergeant Herrick at his side. Throughout the night, they gathered stragglers from his company and other units of the 7th Flieger Division. There had been skirmishes with disorganized Russian groups. It would not be fair to refer to the firefights as battles. Instead, they were chaotic bursts of gunfire and random yelling.

Dawn was gradually approaching. Franks raised his right hand, ordering a halt of the group of paratroopers. The sound of chirping insects seemed to intensify. Franks turned to Herrick.

"Herrick, we will stop in this clearing and assemble our force. Find Lieutenant Gottizner and bring him here."

Jawohl, Herr Hauptmann," replied the large Sergeant. "Good news, Lieutenant Ericksen and twenty five men from his platoon have joined us."

Franks nodded, dropped his gear on the forest floor and sat on a tree stump. The trees were impressive and thick. He stretched his back. His missing eye socket ached. To the west, he saw a reddish glow on the horizon with his remaining eye. He grinned, Moscow was definitely burning.

Herrick returned with Lieutenants Gottizner and Ericksen, along with three other non-commissioned officers.

Franks smiled at Ericksen. "So our Swede returns, eh?"

Ericksen smiled. His family had lived in Kiel for generations and was intensely loyal to the Reich. Nevertheless, he was known by all in the regiment as the "Swede." He began to salute but Franks stopped him. He pointed over his shoulder towards Moscow.

"Gentlemen, we have things other than formality to worry about. Salutes draw snipers, not that the Bolsheviks are organized well enough to effectively engage us," explained Franks.

"They definitely know we are here," offered Lieutenant Ericksen. "We have had several small unit encounters."

"What type of units are we facing?" asked Franks.

"We are not certain. There have been very brief exchanges in which we had the upper hand due to the superior firepower of our light machine guns," reported Ericksen. "We have also come across civilians."

"We cannot allow anyone to report our presence!" barked Franks.

"They were liquidated as planned," said Ericksen.

Franks nodded and directed his attention to his surviving leaders. "How many men do we have right now?"

Lieutenant Gottizner replied, "We have almost 150 men, Herr Hauptmann. There are many from our company but also from other units. We have a dozen from the pioneer battalion and they have a large amount of explosives."

"It appears that we were dropped several kilometers south of our planned area," added Herrick. "The advance patrol reports the railroad is less than a kilometer further north. There are two bridges over a creek with high banks, one for rail and the other a road bridge. They saw a dozen Bolshevik soldiers guarding the bridges. They appear alert."

Franks paced away from the group, which remained standing and ready to receive his orders. He placed his map on the tree stump and examined it with his torch. He drew the men near.

"I believe we are south of this village, Mtankov," said Franks pointing to his map. "The scouts said it appears to be nothing more than a coaling station. Lieutenant Ericksen, take a third of the men and swing left. Gottizner, you take another third and advance along the creek bed."

Franks paused and surveyed the face of each of the leaders. Satisfied they understood, he continued.

"Herrick, you will join me in the center with the pioneers, the mortar and the rest of the men. We will provide suppressing fire with two of the MG-34s and the 81 mm mortar will target the station building. Ericksen, advance into the village when we begin firing. We need to be in position before noon. We will start the attack with the mortar. As soon as we have control of the bridges, we will blow them with the pioneers' explosives."

Franks straightened and concluded the meeting.

"Do you have any questions?"

Ericksen asked, "How many mortar rounds do we have?"

Franks turned to Herrick who replied, "Fourteen HE and five smoke."

"That's what we have gentlemen, let's make it work," ended Franks.

0

Alexei settled in, focusing out the window, hoping to avoid Leonid's eye, knowing any glance in his direction would bring out more blather. Instead he tried to take pictures of the Moscow he would never see again, a city on the verge of destruction, the hammer and sickle to be replaced by the swastika though the Soviet government promised it would be planted on rubble once the Nazis arrived. With every blink he took a snapshot with his mind, cameras a luxury and a danger not allowed even to the highest Party members, any of whom might be spies intent on providing visual guides to the enemy.

But his view was interrupted as the train stopped before it had even cleared the station. NKVD men ran through the car and tugging on the shades, blocking the windows without explanation. Facing grimy curtains that cut off the flow of emerging sunlight, the car bearing only two lights, one at each exit, Alexei drifted to sleep. It was a dangerous decision, one's dreams could be considered treasonous particularly if he spoke in his sleep.

His eyes were closed only for a few minutes when a crash sounded against the side of the train. Alexei blinked in the darkness then noticed Irina had returned and was gripping Leonid's fat arm, fear in her eyes. He struggled to clear his mind as there were more sounds from the outside. The car was being pelted, at first he thought of hail, but the skies had been clear when he left his apartment. He jerked up straight. There had been talk about German paratroopers landing about the city, cutting off the rail and road link.

An NKVD sergeant rushed down the aisle, the pounding of his heels sending vibrations through the floor. The pelting of the railroad car became a roar and Alexei realized their source. It was not hail nor bullets but hands, hundreds of hands beating on the train, trying to halt it so their owners could climb aboard. Muscovites knew what awaited them once the Germans arrived, the Soviet government had not hidden Nazi brutality. Desperation at escaping rather than determination at remaining had overcome Muscovites, who understood Alexei's train was one of their last hopes for survival.

"Bastards," Leonid growled, lip rising on one end. "Traitors. They are traitors attacking their own people instead of fighting the

Nazis." He clenched his fist in anger. His eyes widened as the pounding reached a fever pitch.

Alexei recalled little of the next moments as he was thrown to the floor, landing on the young woman, Leonid lurched across the aisle, shattered glass tearing into his scalp and blood running down his reddened face. The floor began to shake again and lying face down on it Alexei saw the worn work boots of a Muscovite and the polished shoes of the NKVD. There was another explosion, this one closer but less powerful, followed by several others. Alexei recognized gunshots and plugged his ears.

A body landed on him followed by another. He wriggled free as the NKVD dragged one of them down the aisle. After a few moments he raised his head and saw the blood trail running along the wooden floorboards. Below him the girl was screeching, face smeared red. Alexei pulled her to a sitting position and helped her to the seat. She screamed again at the sight of Leonid, his eyes fluttering as blood ran down his nose. She pushed toward him only to be grabbed by a NKVD agent.

"This way."

Alexei knew better than to argue. He was jerked to his feet, turning to see the window and curtain had been ripped open and outside was the chaos he feared. There were hundreds of deranged faces, bloody hands clawing at the openings, skin torn apart by the glass shards. A child was tossed through the window, a desperate parent trying to save him, but he only sailed through the air, head hitting squarely against the wooden bench, squeals of fear followed by sudden silence.

Alexei was propelled through the car, toward the next, the NKVD man shouting curses, though he did not know at whom. Suddenly their path was blocked, a bearded, bloodied man in dark work clothes shouting gibberish while holding out his hands.

Another explosion, Alexei flinching at his closeness then at the sight of the bearded face ripped apart by a bullet. Irina screamed, holding up her hands at the sight of blood and brains that had splattered onto her. Another push, Alexei stumbled over the dead and bleeding worker the Soviet state had been created to protect. They reached the end of the car and pushed toward the next. The opening between was jammed with clawing hands, mouths open, screaming, Muscovites halted in their escape by three NKVD men who punched and kicked at them. When that failed more shots, the smell of gunpowder would remain with Alexei for days. But even with bullets striking bone and muscle they kept coming.

"Do not stop," the NKVD agent hissed, pushing them to the next door. Alexei hit his head, stunned for a moment, then fumbled for the door latch as Irina and Leonid were pressed against his back. More shots, more threats from the agent and Alexei was able to slide open the door to the next car. It was little better. There were three more NKVD agents striking at those who had boarded. Windows were shattered, arms and legs spread across the benches, mouths open and dripping blood, fingers, ears, eyes missing.

The NKVD agent pulled out his pistol and began firing, Alexei cringed on his knees as the car was cleared of invaders. More pushing followed as Alexei stumbled down the aisle, cringing at the feel of bones snapping beneath his shoes. Twice falling to his knees, he managed to push through the mass of bodies and to the next train car. This one was also filled but with passengers, all clinging to their benches, car intact.

The NKVD man pushed him and the others to the rear bench then returned to the other car. Irina sobbed, Leonid cursed while the others wailed. Alexei clutched at his ears, the car resembling the sanitariums he had heard about in Siberia, filled with the insane spending their days and nights howling at imaginary monsters.

But he could not blot out the next sound, the clanking of machinery followed by even worse screams of desperation from outside. Pulling aside the curtain at the window, Alexei felt his stomach cringe at the sight. Tanks rumbled outside the train, their crews not waiting for the clawing mass around the train to part but instead crushing them beneath their treads. Machine guns sounded, hitting those who escaped the several tons of metal bearing down on them. Alexei flicked the curtain closed and huddled on his bench seat. He looked down at his clothes, ripped by broken glass, stained with blood, his fingernails, torn and bleeding, his hand drenched and dripping.

The train lurched and the NKVD men returned to the car, grease mixing with the blood covering them. Alexei realized they had unhooked the cars that had been attacked, leaving the crowds behind them, the shorter train better able to escape as the tanks crushed all resistance in the rear.

"Cowards, traitors," Leonid sputtered, bravery returning with the passing of danger. "Are these the great Russian people that we have heard about?" He motioned to one of the NKVD men, signaling for something to wipe his arms. The political soldier stared for a moment then motioned to another, who pointed to the curtains protecting the windows.

Alexei eyed his arms, bits of glass poking from them, a trick of blood meandering among the sparkling pieces. He pulled at them, the pain at its worst when one was tugged free. Leonid was not as self-sufficient, holding out his arm for Irina, her manicured nails able to unwedge them.

"Watch it," Leonid grumbled as he jerked his arm free and rubbed it. "I am not a piece of cattle."

Irina blanched, hair having fallen free from their constraints, strands pressed together with dried blood. Her face was smeared, clothes rumpled and stained. She did not notice the remnants of former passengers dotting her clothes.

The train picked up speed, the clacking of the rails drowned out most sounds in the railroad car. Alexei slid the curtains and watched the scenery as it pushed past. Leonid grumbled, his pain little in comparison to those at the train station. Alexei cringed, stomach churning. Sitting comfortably in the Kremlin he had an inkling of Soviet tactics, the elimination of those who sabotaged the great Soviet experiment, the move toward pure communism. Alexei considered it all sterile killing, only the guilty were eliminated, a necessity for the welfare of the state. There was nothing necessary at the station, desperate people shot down then crushed as they scrambled for their lives. He could not forget the desperation of a parent throwing a small boy into the railroad car.

"We need water," Leonid howled. "Can't we get some water." He raised his arm, bleeding and still sparkling with the glass remains.

Alexei focused harder on the window. The pane was smeared with sweat, handprints still visible, even scratches from desperate nails trying to break through, all of it mixing with the sooty haze that had hung over the city for a week. There had been the massive Luftwaffe raids, destroying entire sections of Moscow. The smoke from the burning oil tanks had hung over the city, greeting Alexei every morning as he scrambled toward work. During one walk he overheard an elderly couple discuss how the daytime darkness was a sign of Armageddon. Alexei knew of the stories of the end of the world, superstitions from the Orthodox Church, not replaced by the rational, economic man of communism.

The cityscape receded, replaced by the few czarist era clapboard houses not destroyed as part of the communist war on private property. The only hint of modernity in these houses was the single strand of electrical wire attached to each. It was communism's gift to the people, light to shine reason against their czarist past.

"Hey," Leonid lashed out, palm smacking Irina across her cheek. "My hands are my life." He flexed his as if writing for Pravda resembled carrying a gun or driving a tank at the front.

Irina sat, own arms still marked by shattered glass, hands unwashed, sweat forming on her forehead and gumming up the dried blood around her face. One of the babushkas, having survived the angry mob, had brought a cistern of water and tore a swatch from her skirt for Leonid. He had used it to remove the blood from him then waved her away.

"These people." Leonid allowed his finger to run along the ridges on his arms. "Barbarians. Worse than the Nazis. Attacking their own people when they should have been using that energy to fight the enemy." He flinched when his finger poked at an offensive piece of glass. Irina reached over to remove it, her own fingers quivering with the stinging memory of his blow.

Alexei held his breath. He had little sympathy for the girl, trading on her body and condemning a family to death. He had less for Leonid, the one who made it all happen. The pair sickened him and he needed to escape them as quickly as possible.

"They don't love the Motherland," Leonid's chin jutted skyward, revealing a pair of bloodied boils on his neck. "Attacking the very people who are working hard to improve their lives."

Alexei wondered how copying articles for Pravda improved ordinary citizens' lives but did not ask.

Leonid was on a roll. "This is the reason the war has not been going as well as it should." He licked his lips. "I really do need something to drink." He looked about then continued. "The last few weeks have been difficult, our leaders dying at the hands of the Nazis. It is sheer incompetence by some, I am just pleased Comrade Stalin remains in control, he will guide us through this dark time."

Alexei smiled weakly, throat growing sore.

"People complain about the NKVD having too much power, but I say we need it to maintain control. It was the NKVD that protected us from the peasants." He waved at the slowly diminishing cityscape as the train reached cruising speed. "They are filled with czarist ideas, superstitions. Only the firm hand of the NKVD can contain them."

Alexei clutched harder at his stomach. The NKVD meant Beria which meant his family. Kuibyshev was further from Voronezh than Moscow and if the capital was consumed by riots he could only imagine the fear in a provincial city.

"It was a tragedy when we lost Voroshilov," Leonid said.

Alexei had stopped listening. The man was different than others who worked at Pravda, less self-aware that the paper was something less than the truth. His paper was the opiate for the masses with its uplifting, revolutionary message.

"Trotksyites," Leonid said, reaching the proper explanation for the carnage at the train station. "They were stirred up by the rightist and leftist factions that will not stop in trying to prevent Comrade Stalin from succeeding.

Alexei could not remain silent. "They are going to die," he croaked.

Leonid's eyes narrowed. "What?"

"Those people back there, they are going to die and they know it. There won't be many more trains and once the Nazis surround the city they will kill everyone."

Leonid's mouth sagged, tongue poking at his cheeks as he struggled with words. "Treason," he hissed. "Defeatism. The Nazis will never take Moscow, the Red Army will never retreat, never surrender." His voice carried through the car over the sounds of the rails. It was the faux patriotism intended to impress the authorities with the speaker's loyalty. But the other passengers greeted it with silence, too tired and bloodied for a bout of revolutionary propaganda.

Alexei bit his lip. The Red Army had done nothing but retreat and surrender the past months. His traveling companion had to know. Even Pravda noted the fall of towns and cities though with inflated Nazi casualties numbering in the millions of men and thousands of tanks.

"We are retreating now," Alexei reminded him. "We are heading to Kuibyshev, out of the reach of the Nazis for now."

Leonid puffed out his chest. "They will never get to Kuibyshev, they will never survive Moscow."

Alexei noted the treasonous little smile curling on Irina's lips, emboldening him. "We said the same thing about Moscow six weeks ago and we are here now."

Leonid snarled, Alexei's words suffering from the misfortune of being the truth. "I will listen to nothing more of this." Jerking his arm free from Irina, he lurched to his feet and down the rail car, muttering about needing a drink.

0

Johanns Franks studied the small group of buildings that were the town of Mtankov. It appeared that the only hard structure was the rail station. Everything else appeared to be constructed of wood. He pointed to Herrick, signaling to commence firing of the mortar. Seconds later, the unmistakable thump of their lone 81 mm mortar began the battle.

The confused Russians fired wildly from Mtankov in all directions. Moments later, the zip of a MG 34 light machine gun countered from the creek bed. Alerted to the apparent direction of the assault, the Russians centered their fire at the source. Mortar rounds found the range and exploded on and around the Mtankov station building. A Russian DP-27 light machine gun opened fire from the hamlet's sole stone structure.

"Suppressing fire on that machine gun," demanded Franks. His center group immediately joined the fight with their two MG-34s, peppering the station building and forcing the DP-27 gunner to seek shelter. MP-38 submachine gun fire burst from the west, signifying the advance of Ericksen's group.

The defensive fire from Mtankov diminished. Franks raised his hand, "No more mortar fire, Herrick."

"Jawohl, Herr Hauptmann," responded Herrick. "We are down to the smoke rounds anyway."

"Keep the MG-34s on the station building until Ericksen gets closer," ordered Franks.

Five minutes later the skirmish was over. Ericksen's men were in Mtankov and other than an occasional sporadic MP-38 burst, there was silence. Franks and his men collected their gear and proceeded to the village.

Franks gathered his officers and senior non-coms in the station building. The war had come to Mtankov. The smell of death and urine was strong but not overwhelming.

The station building was essentially demolished by the 81 mm mortar. Franks ordered the pioneers to set demolition charges on the two bridges immediately. Herrick motioned Franks to the southern corner, where the DP-27 gunner was crumbled in a heap.

"What is the significance of this?" requested Franks. "It appears to be a dead peasant."

"I'm not sure, Herr Hauptmann," responded Herrick, rolling the dead soldier to his back. "Look at this man's face. I don't think he's from European Russia."

Franks bent down and inspected the soldier's face. He was not Caucasian or Slavic.

"Ja, he is Asian," concluded Franks. He pulled his gravity knife from it sheath and cut the dead soldier's insignia off his tunic. "We will give this to Army Intelligence."

Franks returned to the unit's junior leaders, who were gesturing and pointing to the sky. Franks raised his only eye to determine the basis of the distraction. Four German DFS 230 gliders descended rapidly. One was pursued by a Russian I-16 fighter, which in turn had a Me-110 heavy fighter behind it. The wing of the target DFS-230 broke away and it rolled on its back, doomed. The men groaned but then cheered as the Me-110's heavy armament exploded the I-16 in a fiery ball.

Anti-aircraft fire exploded around the climbing Me-110. The remaining gliders disappeared from view behind the woods further down the tracks.

Franks interrupted the spectators.

"Men, we clearly will face counterattacks from all directions. Those gliders are the 22nd Air Landing Division. Lieutenant Gottizner, send a patrol to locate them and bring them here. We need everything they have. Hopefully they have a 37 mm antitank gun."

"It will be a long way to drag a Pak 36," offered Gottizner.

"We don't have a choice, do we Lieutenant?" replied Franks. "The Red Army will be on top of us in a matter of hours. Find a mule."

Two deafening explosions interrupted their planning. The bridges were blown by the pioneers. Black smoke billowed upwards. Franks turned and pointed to the destroyed bridges.

"That's a creek, not a river. There will be fording points the Bolsheviks can easily use. All we have done is stopped the trains." Franks paused and encouraged his leaders. "We have a working radio now. Our brothers in the Luftwaffe will give us air support. We will hold this shithole Mtankov until we are relieved."

46

August 15, 1940   Mtankov, Russia

Clear of Moscow, the train to Kuibyshev picked up speed as the passengers watched the realities of war pass by them. The roads into the city were clogged with tanks, trucks and soldiers heading into battle, dust stirred, hiding their faces and the faces of the train passengers who watched with awe.

Alexei understood their feeling, having seen the maps marking the German pincers as the ring of steel threatened to close east of the city and leaving those trapped inside at the mercy of the Nazis. He knew his escape marked the capitulation of the party leadership. As the Kremlin emptied, Alexei sensed his importance was diminishing. Stalin was either dead or captured, though his escape meant the Politburo and men like Beria and Molotov continued to believe he held some value to them. As the countryside passed by him, Alexei wondered if a future awaited him in Kuibyshev.

Irina and Leonid returned, the former Pravda writer having regained his senses after several vodkas. Irina clung to him, sensing she would need his connections even after escaping Moscow. Alexei maintained his distance, too tired to bear another Leonid outburst. He could not avoid the furtive glances from Irina when her consort pointed to some sight beyond the windows.

Eventually the combination of the swaying train and generous doses of vodka fed him by Irina sent Leonid into a deep sleep. She wriggled free of him and slid next to Alexei, hedging her bets, the younger man offering more opportunities if she needed them. "What are we to do?" She asked, head tilting onto his shoulder.

Alexei glanced over at the slumbering Leonid. "Are you sure he won't awaken?"

"I have seen him sleep after his vodka. I gave him twice his usual dose, he will not awaken until we arrive in Kuibyshev."

Alexei was uncertain but the feel of her body and the blinking of her eyes swept away his doubts. "I don't know," he said. "We should be safe in Kuibyshev, the Germans cannot go that far. Moscow will hold out for a long time." He hissed the last observation, even the slightest hint that total victory was not around the corner would attract the NKVD to his side.

"What about us." She flopped her leg over his.

Another glance at Leonid, who had not moved. "I don't know what you mean."

"Us. We can be together when we reach Kuibyshev."

"And Leonid?"

The question drew a sputter from the girl. "Him? I don't need him, he is nothing to me."

"He was enough to get you on this train. He could be helpful if you want to leave the country."

"I don't want Leonid." She slipped her hand onto his leg. "I want you."

0

The rhythmic motion of the train soothed Natasha. She felt secure enough to raise her head and look around at the somber faces. The chaos of the mob's attempt to board the train had unnerved her. Natasha had not felt as powerless in many years, since her alcoholic husband's beatings.

Natasha studied her surroundings. The floor of the rail car was covered with debris, broken glass and pools of blood. She noticed the obese civilian accompanied by an alluring young woman. Natasha was unsurprised when the girl shifted her attention to the young official while the fat man snored. Natasha was not the only Russian willing to trade her beauty for survival.

Most of the men in the rail car were in uniform, adorned with a variety of ranks and medals. Clearly, the cowards believed it critical to prove one's importance to gain a spot on the last train out of Moscow.

"I'm just as much a whore, just as much a coward," muttered Natasha to no one but loud enough to stir Dmitry. "I'm on the same train."

"What?" inquired Dmitry. "What does that mean?"

"Nothing Dmitry, just be ready to move when I say," replied Natasha. She laughed lightly. Despite Dmitry's heroic effort to haul their luggage across burning Moscow, it was all left on the platform. But Natasha knew she could always obtain more material items. All that mattered was getting out of Moscow in one piece. If that included Dmitry, all the better as she could likely put him to some use. Natasha somehow drifted to sleep, her head resting on Dmitry's scrawny shoulder.

An hour later, Natasha was jolted awake by the angry staccato of 37 mm anti-aircraft fire. Natasha looked out the window. She could see several light green automatic cannons firing skywards at unseen targets. A woman in their carriage begged God for mercy and was instantly hushed by her husband. God did not exist in the Worker's Paradise. The train did not stop, instead it actually picked up speed. Natasha re-confirmed the location of the nearest exit.

Dmitry implored, "What is happening?"

"Luftwaffe," replied Natasha. "Be ready to follow me."

"Why aren't we stopping?" whined Dmitry. "How can this be safe?"

"The further east we get, the better Dmitry," said Natasha. She saw a burning aircraft crash less than a kilometer from the train. Holding hands, a man and woman jumped from the train but the speed was too great. They bumped and rolled like sacks of grain for a long distance. They did not get up.

Then Natasha heard the Jericho siren of a diving Stuka.

0

Hans Oswald sensed this was the most important sortie of his life. His under strength *staffel* lumbered south of the Moscow defenses, escorted by Me-109s. They were joined by another *staffel* of Stukas, equally shorthanded. Together, they had ten Stukas, slightly more than one full strength *staffel*.

It did not matter. Their mission was crucial to the success of the battle for Moscow. The Luftwaffe's entire airborne force, the 7th Flieger and 22nd Air Landing Divisions were on the ground east of Moscow, interdicting the reinforcement of the Bolshevik capital and preventing its leadership from fleeing. The men on the ground were not Army, they were Luftwaffe brothers. They needed help from above.

"Here we go Sandmann, this is it," said Oswald to his backseater. He had changed his opinion of the Austrian since he began taking the methamphetamine Pervitin. Sandmann was now acutely alert.

"There are planes everywhere, Herr Hauptmann," replied Sandmann. "The whole fucking Luftwaffe is in the air."

"The guys on the ground are our boys, Luftwaffe men," reminded Oswald. "We are going to hammer anything moving in or out on the railroad."

They were at the limit of their combat range even with leaving the wing racks bare. They had less than a full load with one 250 kilo bomb under the belly. There would not be time to loiter.

"We're getting in then out, we don't have enough gas to wait around," said Oswald aloud but mostly to himself. Sandmann was not involved in the mission planning.

While understrength their *staffel* was compromised of veterans. They were skilled at dropping their bombs on target. Ahead, Oswald saw a straight line running east to west. It was not a natural feature. It was man made. The railroad tracks from Moscow. Oswald's heart skipped a beat. There was a train heading east, a passenger train.

"We caught them Sandmann!" exclaimed Oswald.

"Who?" asked Sandmann.

"The Bolshevik scum fleeing the sinking ship!" announced Oswald as he ran through the pre-diving checklist automatically. He made sure to engage the Jericho siren.

Oswald rolled his Stuka *Jolanthe* into an 80 degree dive from an altitude of 5,000 meters. He picked an aiming spot 100 meters ahead of the locomotive, certain his SC-250 kilogram bomb would hit the train somewhere along its substantial length.

Small caliber anti-aircraft fire rose from the side of the tracks. Seconds before releasing, *Jolanthe* shuddered. Sandmann screamed in anguish.

Oswald grasped the yoke as the warning horn sounded. He immediately released the SC-250 bomb and braced for the engagement of the automatic recovery system. The bomb swung on the trapeze and fell towards the Soviet train below. *Jolanthe* did not climb as usual, the gravitational forces were not as severe. Oswald felt 37 mm shells impacting the underside of his Stuka. The controls were not responding properly. Smoke began to pour into the cockpit.

Oswald was far too occupied to monitor the accuracy of his bomb. He struggled to keep his wings level. He released the canopy lock.

"We are fucked Sandmann," yelled Oswald. "Get out!"

Oswald heard nothing from Sandmann. He rolled his canopy back, banked slightly and climbed from *Jolanthe*. Hans Oswald felt for his pistol and jumped.

0

Irina was preparing to change consorts even as Alexei doubted his own future. Staring out the window, gloom deepening, he was jolted back to reality by the screech of the Stukas. The NKVD also recognized the danger, striding through the cars – the NKVD did not ever run, they had no need to run – clips fit into their machine pistols. Humid air rushed through the car as doors were opened, armed men settling in to maintain order on the train.

"What is it?" Irina's nails dug into Alexei's arm, the pain diverting him from the death hurtling from the heavens.

"Luftwaffe dive bombers," he murmured. "There is a bridge ahead. They are going to destroy it and stop all the trains. They are trying to prevent the Red Army from retreating."

"They are coming to kill us?"

"We will get there first," Alexei murmured, sounding even less certain than he felt.

Leonid, bottle in hand, was awakened by the commotion and stumbled toward them, choking on the smoke, reddened face revealing he felt no pain. Dropping into the seat next to Irina, he tipped over, head pointing toward his lap.

328

Leonid grabbed Irina by her hair, raising her to eye level. "You want him, is that it? You want him?" He shook her head, trying to rattle an answer from her.

Leonid swung his arm. "You can have her." He released Irina and she tumbled to the floor. "She's nothing but a little whore, a tramp, a slut, a -."

The window exploded. Glass cut through the air and flesh with equal ease, Alexei's arm was suddenly on fire from fingers to his shoulder, body thrown, head clipping the wooden bench across from him. Face flat on cold metal, eyes blurred from smoke and the concussion he turned and looked up. Leonid swayed above him, hands grabbing at his face, a mass of flesh and bone, hands bloody as he reached to steady himself. The train lurched and rolled on its side, the Luftwaffe finding its mark.

Leonid toppled, head bouncing on the metal floor. He lay, face a few feet from Alexei, the remnants of his mouth offering a gurgling sound, the last he would ever make. His one remaining eye blinked as if trying to send a final message, then nothing.

Alexei had no time or desire to mourn Leonid's passing, he had to get out of the burning railcar. He tried to right himself and stumbled, foot planting on the sprawled Leonid, pot belly offering support and a pushing off point. Alexei crawled, ignoring the arms and legs scattered about or the occasional grasping of his shirt or shredded trousers. It was not the time to stop and help others, death was everywhere, a few more bodies would go unnoticed. Reaching the end of the train car, Alexei was forced to his knees.

The train was destroyed, metal, wood and glass ripped apart, mixing with Russian blood into an unsightly stew. The Stuka sirens melted away, Alexei tugged himself back to his feet. Grasping the handle to the door at the end of the car he yanked. Alexei was blocked. Peering through the small window, the only piece of intact glass in the car, and saw the impediment, the NKVD. The agent's arm was wedged between the door and the wall.

"Shit," Alexei muttered. Once again, possibly for the final time, the NKVD was blocking him.

He sagged, arm now numb, limp at his side, train slowing further. Taking a deep breath Alevei tugged at the door, full weight against it until he heard the snap, the NKVD bone breaking, offering a narrow escape path.

Alexei looked down and recoiled, his foot firmly planted on the face of the NKVD agent. He stumbled backward then stared, the agent's eyes open, mouth curled in a peculiar grin, a combination of smirk and terror, possibly his life having flashed before his eyes as he bled from his ripped out neck. Alexei could only hope Marx was correct and there was no afterlife, the NKVD agent likely committing enough sins to send several men to hell.

Alexei stared past the grinning corpse to the countryside. Using his good arm, he grabbed the bar used to pull onto the train and pulled himself to an upright position. The rail car was on its side, hanging precariously on the embankment. The carriage rocked, it was unlikely to remain on its perch.

Alexei braced himself, legs bent, taking long breaths as if preparing to jump into water. The earth was likely three meters below. He saw the people stumble away from the cars, some were on fire, others scrambling for safety. Alexei ducked his head, leapt and landed poorly, rolling down the embankment unconscious.

0

Franks watched the Stuka attack with excitement. His ad hoc force needed all the help it could get. Several of the attacking Stukas were lost to anti-aircraft fire. He rubbed his eye and scanned the tracks to the east. A black locomotive came into view. It was pulling a passenger train. It was less than a kilometer from Mtankov.

A Stuka released its payload while under heavy anti-aircraft fire. Franks followed the path of the bomb to the ground. It did not land directly on the train, but south of the tracks. It exploded with massive force, midway down the length of the long train. Its concussion split the train in half, causing the rear half to roll off the embankment. His men shouted encouragement and pumped their fists skyward, jubilant.

A parachute opened north of the tracks, floating in the direction of the gliders and the 22nd Air Landing Division. Herrick appeared, startling Franks.

"The Stukas destroyed the train," said Herrick.

"Yes, but they paid a heavy price," agreed Franks. "At least four Stukas were lost and I only saw one chute."

Herrick nodded. "It looks like he'll come down right on top of the gliders."

"That will be immeasurably better than being captured by the angry peasants," suggested Franks. "How many men do we have?"

"We have been collecting stragglers from the division, plus some of the 22nd Air Landing men have shown up," reported Herrick. He smiled and continued, "Including Max Schmeling."

Franks grinned, "How is our famous boxer?"

"He's fine, showed up with two of the three sections of an 81 mm mortar," answered Herrick. "He's a brute."

"No less than you, Stabsfeldwebel Herrick," reminded Franks. "What's our total strength?"

"Close to 300 fit men and about 50 with various levels of wounds," detailed Herrick. "Some of the 22nd men pushed a 37 mm Pak 36 into town."

"That will help if we run into Bolshevik tanks," said Franks. "Let's prepare our positions. We are going to put our main force in the woods north of Mtankov in an ambush position. Move the Pak 36 there with most of the MG 34s. The town itself will be a magnet for counterattack. Take two squads to the train wreckage immediately, before they can recover."

Herrick moved off to carry out Franks' orders. Johanns lit a cigarette and sat, observing survivors climbing from the destroyed train.

0

Natasha could not breathe. She pushed Dmitry off her. She was stunned to see blood pouring out of his mouth and ears. Part of his skull was caved in. Dmitry was not going to be part of her future.

The carriage was on its side, dust and smoke clogging her nostrils. Moans and cries for help created a chorus of misery. Natasha struggled to get free from under the lifeless Dmitry. With a surge of energy, she extracted herself and sat up.

She climbed above and around bodies, eventually reaching a gap in the severed car. With a burst of energy, Natasha was able to pull herself out and away from the smoldering wreck. She rolled down the embankment. Satisfied that she was not seriously injured, she stumbled over to a group of survivors.

A colonel covered in medals stopped her before she reached the assembled men. He raised a pistol and commanded, "Stop, come no further."

Natasha looked at the man without comprehending his words. She continued walking closer, swaying with each step. The colonel fired a shot in her direction, creasing her tunic but not striking flesh.

Natasha crumbled to the ground as if she was hit. She played dead.

Satisfied that his marksmanship was better than he ever scored on the range, the colonel returned to his group of officers. Natasha was close enough to hear.

"We must go back," pleaded a general.

"We are not going back," replied an unseen figure. His accent was not Russian, but the voice was vaguely familiar. "Moscow is burning."

Natasha fought back the urge to sleep. Her body ached. Sleeping would be as effective as pretending to be dead.

"We are going east now!" demanded the voice. "What is that town?"

"Mtankov," answered the colonel who had accosted her. "We do not know if it is still in our hands."

"Find out now," ordered the clear leader.

Natasha felt movement around her, but she dared not open her eyes. For a moment her mind cleared. She knew the voice. The accent was Georgian.

Sergeant Herrick and the two hastily collected squads rushed the train. Speed was more important than caution. Russians milled around in confusion, clutching battered limbs and limping. Some carried suitcases. There were men and women, but few children.

Pistol and rifle shots rang out, an inaccurate attempt to stop the Fallshirmjagers' progress. Herrick pointed north and south of the wreckage, ordering the men to fan out. The paratroopers set up a MG-34 on a fallen log and zipped a salvo at the windows of the lead cars. The mob screamed and turned to run.

"These are not soldiers, they are Golden Pheasants!" bellowed Herrick, using the Wehrmacht derogatory slang for high party officials. "Fire above their heads and let's round them up."

The MG-34 peppered the rail cars with sustained fire as the squads split and swarmed the survivors. A Russian colonel aimed a pistol in their direction but was cut down before he could pull the trigger. The Bolsheviks were not a young or fit group and they were not hyped up on the methamphetamine Pervitin like the Germans. Herrick spotted a gaggle fleeing to the rear.

"Stop them," yelled Sergeant Herrick. He ran as hard as possible, his chest pounding. When he was within 30 meters, he took a knee and emptied the magazine of his MP-38 submachine gun at the officer leading the escape. His target jolted and danced as rounds tore into ribs and internal body parts.

The runners stopped and raised their hands in surrender. More of Herrick's force surrounded the prisoners. It was silent.

Lieutenant Ericksen appeared with another squad. He approached Sergeant Herrick.

"What the shit is going on, Sergeant?" demanded Ericksen. "You were supposed to recon the train, not fight the Red Army on your own."

"It just kind of happened," shrugged Herrick. "A flock of Golden Pheasants were flying away. It seemed right to snare them."

Ericksen nodded and appraised the situation. "Let's get them all in a tight group and see if there's plunder here that is of use."

The men reacted like children at Christmas when ordered to search for booty. As in all armies, there was nothing they enjoyed more than stealing the enemy's riches, other than perhaps appropriating the valuables of the enemy's officers. They took to their assignment enthusiastically.

Ericksen and Herrick inspected the captured Russians, who had been ordered to lie prone on the ground. The paratroopers were not able to take prisoners.

"We have to get out of here and back to the station," announced Ericksen.

"What do we do with the Bolsheviks?" asked Herrick.

"There's no choice, Sergeant. You know what our orders are," replied Ericksen.

Herrick nodded without conviction. He was more concerned that they were exposed at the wrecked train. A seemingly dead woman moved, causing him to jump. Herrick raised his MP-38 and pointed it at her chest.

"Nein! I can help," pleaded the woman.

Herrick hesitated. "You speak German?"

"Jawohl, Herr Lieutenant," insisted the woman. "I am an officer, I can help you."

"First, I am not a lieutenant but a sergeant. What can you possibly do to assist us?"

"If you spare me, I can identify an important prisoner," replied NKVD Major Natasha Merkulhov. She sat up and brushed off her uniform.

Herrick motioned for Lieutenant Ericksen to join him.

"What? We have to move on as soon as possible," responded Ericksen when he reached Herrick.

Herrick pointed to Natasha, who remained sitting in the dirt.

"This one speaks German. She claims she can identify an import person," offered Herrick. "All we have to do is not shoot her."

In accented German, Natasha made her sadistic offer. "I can tell you who is worth keeping alive and who should be shot."

"We can't take prisoners," answered Ericksen.

Natasha stood. "You don't need to. Kill them all but me and one other."

Lieutenant Ericksen considered Natasha. She brushed her hair back off her smudged face. She was beautiful.

"Herrick, go with her and find this important prisoner. If she fails to identify someone that meets your approval, shoot her," commanded Ericksen. "She has five minutes."

0

Franks now had over 500 men. More men of the 22nd Air Landing Division were brought to Mtankov by Lieutenant Gottizner. Most importantly, he had found another Pak 36 antitank gun and dragged it back to their position with a small horse. Franks positioned it where it could cover the approach from the east as well as be quickly deployed to face a threat from the south.

He observed the firefight at the train wreckage with his binoculars and sent Lieutenant Ericksen with more men to assist. He did not flinch when the sound of the subsequent execution of the survivors interrupted the mid-morning calm. Franks was agitated, but not because he cared about the unlucky Russians. He needed his men back to strengthen his position. One of the 37 mm anti-tank guns had already destroyed a lone T-26 tank that had approached on the road east of the destroyed road bridge. Of one thing he was certain, there would be more.

Franks was waiting for the return of the wayward marauders in the shell of Mtankov's rail station. When he saw them meandering back he turned his attention to the radio. It was working and he was preparing to send a report.

Sergeant Herrick and Lieutenant Ericksen stepped into the small room and saluted with precision.

"What's that all about?" demanded Franks, confused by the formality. "Are you men overusing Pervitin?"

"Lieutenant Ericksen reporting Herr Hauptmann. We secured everything we could locate of military value at the train."

"Well done, Lieutenant," answered Franks. "Did you secure anything of use to our mission?"

"No weapons larger than souvenirs," said Ericksen. "We brought back significant quantities of food and drink."

"Do not allow the men to drink spirits!" demanded Franks.

Franks paused as the roar of aircraft engines interrupted their conversation.

"Of course not, Herr Hauptmann," continued Ericksen. "But Stabsfeldwebel Herrick located something very valuable."

Franks turned his attention to the large sergeant. "What Herrick, I do not have time for foolishness."

"I must show you," explained Herrick as he left the room, oblivious to protestations of Franks.

Moments later, Herrick returned with two prisoners, one obviously female and both with sacks covering their heads. Their hands were tied behind their backs. The male was short by European standards.

"No prisoners!" shouted Franks.

Herrick raised his hand, silencing Franks who was astonished by his display of disrespect for an officer of the Reich. Herrick stood behind the male and Ericksen behind the woman. They grinned at each other and simultaneously pulled the burlap sacks from the prisoners' heads.

Franks stared at the Russian male. His face was pockmarked and adorned with a bushy mustache. He ignored the woman.

"Herr Hauptmann Johanns Franks I present to you the Bolshevik criminal Josef Stalin," announced Sergeant Herrick.

Franks slumped into a chair, the only place to sit in the small room.

"Are you certain it is him?" croaked Franks.

Ericksen prodded Natasha, who spoke up instantly. Her life was at stake.

"It is Josef Stalin," confirmed Natasha in German.

The prisoner spoke softly in Russian in a menacing tone.

"What did he say?" asked Franks.

Natasha looked away. She clearly was not enthusiastic about translating his words. Ericksen jabbed her in the ribs forcefully. Natasha cleared her throat and spoke without inflection.

"I will live to see your mothers fucked by divisions of the Red Army."

Sergeant Herrick stepped back and launched a massive right jab to the prisoner's face, collapsing his nose. Blood spurted from his nostrils as he fell to the ground.

Herrick pulled the Russian to his feet and held him steady.

Ericksen blurted, "I wish Max Schmeling has a jab like that, he would've killed Joe Lewis!"

47

August 15, 1940   **North Atlantic Ocean**

Maria Updegrove, nee Romanov, future Duchess of Braxtonshire, self-declared claimant to the Romanov throne, stood at the railing of her berth, a six room suite squeezed into the upper third of the American steamship Expedition. They were a day's sail from New York harbor and a short car ride to her first American destination, Connecticut, leaving little for the Russian princess to observe beyond whitecaps formed as waves dashed against the boat.

The cross Atlantic journey was the first leg of a trip to Japan and beyond, the fast moving German invasion of Russia spurring her to leave England. Destruction of the Bolshevik government was finally coming to fruition after two decades of prediction of its ultimate fall. When the Bolsheviks fell there would be a vacuum and Maria was determined to lead the triumphant return of the Romanovs to Russia.

The proposal had been offered by Lord Rothmere, whose *Daily Mirror* and *Daily Mail* had been loudly reporting every Soviet defeat and predicting the fall of Moscow and with it the communist government. Maria, daughter of the deceased Cyril Romanov, was the most visible member of the surviving Romanov dynasty. Rothmere encouraged Maria during several weekend parties, the flow of vodka making the publisher even more voluble as Maria remained pensive. Listening to the newspaper magnate, Maria understood her return to Russia would be a boon for the duke's broadsheets. The duke proposed Maria be accompanied by his reporter, offering regular daily stories on her trip to the Far East and holy Russian soil.

Maria was uninterested in profit, wishing only to return to her country in triumph, presiding as Russian peasants rejoiced at the new Romanov dynasty. She listened to the duke even as he mistook Alexander II for Alexander III, the Greek and Russian Orthodox churches and repeatedly calling St. Petersburg, Leningrad. The newspaper man would be the vessel she would use to be crowned the first Czarina since Catherine the Great.

Several weeks of quiet thought and planning followed made easier by Fergus, the valet, being dispatched to the eighth lord's estate after Exner was exiled to Bulgaria. A letter to Anastase Vonsiatsky in Connecticut, the leader of American Russian emigres, received an enthusiastic response. A visit by a former Romanov was considered an event demanding a celebration. A letter to Konstantin

Rodzaevsky in Manchukuo earned a more circumspect response. Maria had read reports from other Russian emigres in Japanese occupied China that Rodzaevsky was more concerned with his business interests in Hsinking and bowing to the Japanese than overthrowing the Bolsheviks who had killed so many of their people. Partly bolstered by these responses Maria attended an early August party with Lord Rothmere and agreed with stipulations. The primary one joined her at the railing of the steamship.

Antonov – Anthony according to his new English masters – failed the royal blood test that was so important to Maria. Born in the midst of the Great War to a former czarist general, he had been carried through the snowy passes of the Caucasus Mountains as the White armies collapsed at the end of the Russian Civil War. While enjoying safety in the Turkish city of Manzikert, Antonov's family was destroyed by a bomb, some claimed a deliberate act or an anarchist plot intended merely to sew anarchy. The result the same for Antonov – he was an orphan. Raised English by another military family, he delved into his Russian heritage and came to worship English and Russian nobility. A mere twenty years old, he swooned at the opportunity to accompany the princess.

Maria had her own plans for Antonov – she preferred the Russian variation of his name – ensuring he would not report anything to London without her approval. Barely out of Liverpool, she had included him in dinner, Antonov expecting a scoop but instead prodded to talk of his interest in astronomy and the constellations so bright in the sky above the ocean. Maria responded with stories of fleeing Russia, her marriage to Exner and her father's lonely wanderings then his early death. Antonov offered a mix of sympathy and awe. As the ship sailed into the horizon, Maria and Antonov became conspirators, offering drab bulletins about the future czarina's return to her home. They reveled in the secret, playing the duke for the fool as Maria deflected the sensationalizing curiosity that was the British press.

"Have you been to America?" The sun swept over the balcony on their tenth day at sea. Antonov's dark skin glistened, suggesting Tatar blood flowed through his veins.

Maria sniffed, never understanding the British desire to travel the world. "It is nowhere I want to see." She turned from the heavy seas. "Russia is where I must be."

"I do not remember Russia. I have seen photographs," he shook his head.

Maria turned from him, avoiding any reminders of England, Exner or his troublesome family. The princess had left a letter to her father–in–law explaining her departure and doubting he would be upset at her leaving England.

More days passed, New York coming into sight in the morning sun. Maria took her breakfast while reading over the details that were to be published when they reached land. Antonov had been composing a story about their American arrival and meeting with Vonsiatsky. Maria sliced at his manufactured quotes which had the Russian princess praising the aggressive Americans with their materialism and base moralities.

The harbor was busy as the steamship entered, the city hazy, buildings enveloped by factory smoke and car exhaust, the sun struggling to be noticed. Most on the boat stood on the deck cheering the Statue of Liberty as they sailed by it. Maria hustled her maids to complete packing then the porters to include every case and trunk for transport to Connecticut. A princess, past and future, did not travel lightly even if the duke complained about the costs. A wireless to Antonov had demanded "news" to spark interest in her trip and build circulation.

Maria was unworried. Connecticut was her entry point to America, whose money centers would approve the loans a new Romanov dynasty required to revive the country. Unpleasant as the country was, its money was welcome to old and new governments.

Anastase Vonsiatsky was awaiting them in Connecticut. An émigré, he had married into wealth in order to survive. It was the worse of America. The country lacked nobility and forced men like Vonsiatsky to marry a woman who inherited her wealth from a father who took advantage of the unrestrained chaos that was American capitalism.

Vonsiatsky used his wife's money to remain in contact with Russian exiles and prepare for the return. A journey to the "estate" was the cost of receiving American support and Maria, convinced by the duke it would be helpful to the cause, agreed.

Disembarking from the steamship was a lesson in logistics. A princess did not mix with the rabble as they rushed down the gangplanks to screeching families. A princess left before or after the mob departed, the dockside cleansed of commoners. Maria was left sitting in her suite, maids scurrying to meet her demands. It was to be a quiet wait until the Americans interceded, a visitor representing the duke arrived, the *Daily Mail*'s New York correspondent pushing his way onto the ship.

Haley Cantrell was a bulbous man with uneven edges, body lurching from one side to the other, oily hair, flabby face, all the worst physical characteristics of the American. He entered the suite, tie askew, slacks rising above his ankles to reveal white socks, the perfect figure to irritate the princess.

"Lady Braxtonshire." The greeting came through his nose. He extended a fleshy hand toward her but Maria only stared, nose wriggling with distaste until Cantrell withdrew the loathsome part.

"The boss wants me with you. We Americans are touchy about our Russians. Old Roosevelt loves them communists."

Maria remained stony faced. Such creatures as Cantrell would have been dismissed from her English estate and would have been barred from Russia for his impertinence and familiarity. When one of the maids approached, he snatched her arm.

"Youse got some of that good Russian vodka?" He held two fingers apart. "'Bout that much." The maid, eyes wide, the princess a terror when irritated, waited for her mistress to agree. A flicker of her eyes and the maid was off, returning shortly with one of the suite's cut glasses. Cantrell snatched it and downed the vodka with barely a breath. He wiggled the glass, a signal for a refill and the maid was off after another look from the princess.

Disaster was averted only when Antonov scurried in from the balcony, communique in hand. He slammed to a halt at the sight of the beefy Cantrell.

"There's the boy." Cantrell wiggled swollen fingers at the Russian turned English reporter. "What you got there?"

Antonov glanced at the princess, who snubbed him like the mere servant he was, then approached Cantrell. "My latest on the trip," he murmured. "The visit."

"Let's see, let's see." The fingers wiggled again.

Antonov hesitated, glancing at the princess, who remained stoic. The papers trembled in his hands, the young man trapped between two immovable forces, the louder of the pair succeeding.

"Here, here, now." Cantrell scooted forward in his chair, snatching the papers, crumpling then straightening them. Lips smacking as he read Antonov's words, Cantrell's face darkened. The paper crackled on his knee. "What the hell is this?"

Antonov blinked, confidence he had built with the princess disintegrating as he faced the American. "It, it, it is a report of the princess' arrival in New York."

"No, no, no." A ripping sound wilted Antonov, scraps of paper tossed into the air, a single bit floating onto the princess' lap. She eyed the invasion of her person, the expression drawing a maid to her, fingers removing it without touching Maria.

"It will not do." Cantrell reached into the folds of his clothing and yanked out a coverless notebook, pages bent, pen jammed into its midst. "This is the way to announce the arrival of a personage." He cleared his throat, reading aloud as he wrote. "Ignoring assassination threats, heir to Romanov throne lands in New York."

"Assassination," Antonov squeaked. "What do you mean?"

Cantrell waved away his question then continued. "Under the threat of Bolshevik hit squads, Princess Maria began her American visit to secure commitments for her quest to replace the tyrannical Bolshevik regime in Russia." He coughed, clearing his throat with a quick swig of vodka. "When pressed by this reporter about the threats to her life, the princess declared, 'The Bolsheviks have murdered millions of my subjects. I am willing to surrender my life if it contributes to the end of their tyrannical rule.'"

Antonov's lower lip quivered. "The princess never - there are no assassination attempts - the communists -."

A grunt interrupted the young man. "I say there are and you will too if you want to continue writing for the *Daily Mail*." Against all odds the flabby face hardened, a warning to the Russian turned English journalist. It returned to its over the top joviality as quickly. "Princess, you doubt the Bolsheviks would kill their opponents?" He tilted his head, double chin swinging in the opposite direction.

"Trotsky was one." The Trotsky assassination had dominated the news as the princess was crossing the Atlantic.

Maria's face creased. "Trotsky." Her fingers gripped the arms of her chair, the first sign of any emotion generated by the American. "A pig, his death will go unmourned by good Russians. They killed him like they killed the Czar's children, they will kill anyone who challenges them."

Cantrell held out his notebook. "There's your lead. Write it up but do not send until I see it."

Antonov departed, Maria sitting alone with the reporter. An incident was narrowly avoided with the arrival of the purser. He informed them the boat had cleared and her car was parked on the dock. Cantrell rose but Maria remained seated. "After you." He offered his hand again, pudgy fingers wriggling as if demanding her presence.

A cold stare, one that would have frozen a Cossack, convinced the gregarious American danger was near. A weak smile creased his fat face and he left without another word. Antonov reappeared moments later grasping his handwritten copy. He stopped at Cantrell's empty seat. "I have the report."

Maria was on her feet, irritation melting from her face, "It does not matter."

"But he was lying, writing things you did not say."

The cold stare returned though focused past Antonov in the direction of the departed American. "His insults to the Romanov family will be repaid." She swept past him, maids hustling to keep pace with their mistress. Antonov followed, body chilled in the August heat.

The next crisis came with the single passenger car available for transport to Connecticut. It would be trailed by a truck used for the princess' luggage and her maids. Cantrell stood at the open car door, nodding as Maria entered followed by Antonov then the American.

"Nyet." The Princess' lips barely moved though her rejection of his presence reverberated through the car and onto the docks. Cantrell pulled up, bumping his head on the edge of the car door.

"There is room." he said, humor remaining even as his patience with the Russian princess dwindled.

Maria waved at Antonov to close the door, smacking the American's knee before roaring free. Cantrell was left on the dock, forced to hobble after the truck as it lurched forward to follow the princess.

Maria paid little attention to the scenery of the city, with its skyscrapers and bustle, instead she focused on Antonov. The young man wiggled under her gaze, worried about Cantrell and her threat against him. The princess, though, had already swept the American from her memory, thinking instead of the Russian exile community she had abandoned after her marriage to Exner. Her occasional letters had been circumspect, Maria certain the British were reading her correspondence. The Romanovs were dismissed as poor cousins who refused to accept their fate while engaging in ludicrous plots. While Maria appeared to surrender to permanent exile, she maintained some contact with Vonsiatsky, who was unabashed in his desire to challenge the Bolsheviks' claim to power.

The drive took less time than expected, the car halting before a stone wall fronting a one story, peaked cottage. A sign announcing their location as "The Russian Bear" featured little of interest except for the peeling paint that threatened to transform it into "Th ssian ar."

"What is this?" The princess demanded, squinting at the building.

"This is the address," the driver said. "The Vonsiatskys own a restaurant."

The door opened, Cantrell standing, a grin exacerbated by the cigarette in his mouth. "Welcome to Quinnatesset. "You will feel like you have already entered Russia."

Maria blinked as she emerged from the car. "Russia?" She glanced at Antonov, who shrugged and Cantrell who smiled.

The trio walked around the stone fence, approaching the cottage/restaurant. Its door swung open to reveal women bedecked head to toe in traditional Russian peasant clothing. Head scarved, the women were covered by a long blouse, lace flowers decorating the bodice and stretching to their waist. The skirts extended to their shoes, lace serving as the hem. Antonov counted at least eight colors from white to a putrid orange and a light azure, none of it memorable. Maria recoiled. From the inside of the restaurant came the sound of violins, their strings prodded with a growing fervor.

Antonov hesitated, not wanting to step in front of the princess, but Cantrell had no such scruples, grabbing one of the waitresses and performing his version of Russian dance with her as she stomped into the restaurant. A grimacing Maria followed, Antonov close behind her. They found three more waitresses boasting a kerchiefed head and long skirts, with two men, each with a kerchief on his head and baggy shirts with pants, violins on their shoulders.

The moment the princess entered the entire staff launched into their full act. For the next ten minutes Antonov and Maria were treated to an American version of traditional Russian entertainment, with the Barynya transformed into more of a Charleston dance while the tropak descended into a soft shoe routine that would have made Al Jolson proud. Antonov managed a smile, moving ever so slightly to the music. The princess offered only a scowl, the performance a mockery of Russian tradition.

The dancing and music eventually ended and the trio, Cantrell was determined not to be excluded, led to a corner table. An overhead beam held a light, several flies clinging to the metal edge. The peasant clad waitresses, breathing heavily from their entertainment, lowered bowls in front of the three.

"Borscht." Cantrell said, digging his spoon into the dark soup, lapping it up like a man who had never tasted it.

Maria stared as Antonov downed a spoonful and shook his head. The peasant waitresses seized the bowls after only a few moments, though Cantrell had emptied his and eyed Antonov's. The waitresses returned with plates, the princess's nose wiggling at the fare while the young reporter picked at it with his fork before catching the eye of one of the waitresses. "What is this?"

"Blini," came the reply. "And Stroganoff."

Maria nibbled before washing down the fare with the offered vodka, face tightening as the liquid rushed down her throat. Cantrell had no such qualms, cleaning his plate then lighting a cigarette in celebration. The princess sat, arms across her chest, lips pushed tight, dislike of America growing.

The waitresses cleared the table after an acceptable time then without warning the dances were renewed, every stomp on the floor, every swirl of a skirt met with the princess' ever narrowing eyes.

Back and forth, clockwise and counterclockwise they threaten to make Antonov dizzy. Cantrell was quick onto his feet, hooking his arm with one of the women, assuming the role of the male in the Barynya. He lacked rhythm, his only graceful movement being when he jabbed his head forward to sneak kisses from the waitresses.

It came to an end with the arrival of Vonsiatsky. He bore dark and deep set eyes, made more ominous by the heavy bags beneath them. His fleshy head fit well on his chunky body which he maneuvered with remarkable grace. Seeing the princess he headed to the table, large feet quiet as he trod.

"Your majesty." He bowed with a flourish, breaking the princess' grim expression. "My eternal gratitude for your visit." He motioned to the "peasant" waitresses. "We have struggled to maintain the aura of traditional Russia here in Connecticut."

This produced a weak smile from the princess. She rose before another celebration could commence. "We must talk," she said, heading past Vonsiatsky and from the restaurant. Cantrell had learned his lesson and remained inside, the waitresses better company than the icy princess. He ordered another vodka and a dance, the last words uttered as Antonov and Vonsiatsky followed Maria from "The Russian Bear."

The drive from the restaurant to the "estate" was short, less than a kilometer. Once the car stopped in the driveway of a two story house, Antonov and the princess surveyed something less than a Russian nobleman's estate. Vonsiatsky was effusive, swinging his arms in the direction of the vast open ranges with lines of trees and what appeared to be pits of sand.

"This is the golf course and our home." He grinned. "We call it the nineteenth hole."

She sniffed. "Golf. The English play it."

Vonsiatsky's head bobbed. "A wonderful sport. I have taken it up." The smile dissipated. "Your father would have enjoyed it; he was a great man, we mourned his death here."

"My father hunted," Maria grunted. "He did not engage in childish games." She turned from the offensive course. "We must talk, there is little time."

Vonsiatsky did not react to the dismissal. Even after two decades out of Russia he was unoffended by the natural imperiousness of the Romanov clan. Reaching the princess' side he guided her away from the house and into a brick building several meters distant. He pushed open the door, flicking on lights which required several moments to illuminate the room. During the interregnum, Vonsiatsky hurried about making space and arranging a chair for the princess. Maria remained standing.

"What is this?" Her eyes fixed on the red and black flag with the instantly recognizable symbol on it. She turned to find Vonsiatsky wearing an armband with the same Swastika prominently displayed. He offered a Nazi salute to the princess.

Vonsiatsky beamed. "It is the All Russian Fascist Party." He jabbed a finger at the swastika on the wall then the armband.

Maria glowered. The irritating and presumptuous Cantrell, the ludicrous dancing, the poor imitation of Russian food burned in her. The Swastika uncorked the fury on the hapless Vonsiatsky.

"What is this?" She reached for the armband, tugging it from him and nearly taking Vonsiatsky's arm with it. "This." She held out the swastika. "You consort with the enemy, you honor them with this?" Her fingernails tore at the cloth, ripping it into indistinguishable pieces. "The Nazis kill Russians and you wish to be like them?" She jabbed at the flag. "Remove this."

Vonsiatsky's mouth sagged. "Your majesty, I believed you knew." He rushed to unhook the flag before her fingernails could strike again. He began folding and smoothing out wrinkles. "I meant no offense, the All Russian -."

"Burn it."

The deep set eyes widened, sweat thick on Vonsiatsky's forehead. "Burn the flag?"

"If you are a true Russian you will burn the flag of the enemy which has invaded our soil, killed our people and destroyed our land."

Vonsiatsky clutched the flag to his chest. "I do not understand. The Fascists will help us regain power. They will defeat the communists and we can reclaim our rightful places with you as czarina. The Romanovs will rule again in Russia."

"Rule? As a German puppet?" She reached for the flag but Vonsiatsky pulled it closer to his chest. "The Russian people will defeat the Bolsheviks then we shall band together and drive the German hordes from our soil." She jabbed a finger toward Vonsiatsky. "I will not work with you unless the flag is destroyed."

Vonsiatsky was adamant. "It cannot be destroyed," he said. "It is the only way to regain power."

"Traitor." The princess turned on her heel and left him to clutch the Swastika. Antonov remained inside, stunned and worried his adventure was about to be cut short.

Vonsiatsky reached out to him. "Speak with her, try to make the princess understand."

Antonov shrugged. Defending Nazis was not part of his duties and he knew he was no match for Maria. He had learned to follow orders, mainly out of fear of being discarded. He followed Maria to the car, where she stood, scowl deepening as she waited for him to open the door. Once inside she snapped to the driver, "Return to New York," then curled into a corner to brood. Antonov paid her no attention realizing he had witnessed the story of a lifetime.

48

August 16, 1940   Smolensk, Russia

Colonel Blumentritt pulled down his cap, jacket lying beside him, a machine pistol on top of it, thoughts divided between personal safety and Operation Typhoon. He was in a staff car bouncing toward the latest conference on the drive to surround Moscow. The trek took him from corps headquarters located south of Kalinin back to Smolensk. He represented the 48th Panzer Corps, General Manstein remaining near the front as he tried to ignite the drive around Moscow. The panzers had slowed, the chaos east of Moscow and uncertainty over fuel supplies had slowed the pincers before they could close around the city.

Intelligence reports revealed a startling development that complicated their strategy. Previously unknown divisions had been encountered east of Moscow and headed toward the city. These new forces were from the Soviet Union's Far East. Instead of open spaces, the Second Panzer Group and the 48th Panzer Corps faced armies approaching from two sides, their destination and orders uncertain. According to some reports the Russians were fleeing the Moscow cauldron, a panicked retreat that had soldiers throwing down weapons and ignoring their commanders all in a race for survival. Blumentritt had even received reports of fighting among the Russians, those entering the city firing at those who were fleeing.

Russians killing Russians was nothing new to the colonel. During their drive from the Baltic States they had come across bodies of Red Army soldiers and commanders with bullets in the back of their heads, not combat wounds, but "friendly fire" that was an instant court martial for cowardice or incompetence.

Blumentritt sighed, the trek west to Smolensk seemed more dangerous than the army's assault to the east. His mission important, he dragooned a ride on a Storch to the west, the "airfield" where he landed on a bumpy field used by the Luftwaffe as the army moved east and outran paved airfields. The flight was uneventful, the drive from the airfield to the conference point was more dangerous. Partisans, mostly Red Army deserters, had been active. The solution was to strip the car of all official markings. The colonel only shook his head at the ploy. Soldiers walked or rode on trucks, only officers enjoyed cars. The partisans would not be fooled into believing an elderly Russian couple was driving to market when they saw the unmarked car, they would know it held an officer and attack it.

The rutted roads slowed the drive. Yawning holes, some filled with rain water that hid their depth and danger, required detours from the track. Then there was the traffic moving east, mostly supplies but some reserves, presenting an even larger target to the partisans. Fourteen kilometers required two hours, but Blumentritt arrived, machine pistol cool in his hand.

He was the last to enter the tent which contained the main ingredients of a military meeting: a map and a table. It was a typical conference except for the options being offered. His entry went unnoticed as a battle raged between the commanders of the panzer groups. Erich Hoepner, the colonel's commander, was pecking his finger at the map. Face red, voice carrying outside the tent walls, he was arguing a point with the commander of the second group, General Guderian, who had also traveled from the front lines.

For the first time, Blumentritt heard the size of the current gap between the two groups, 60 kilometers, barely a day's drive in the early days of Operation Typhoon.

"Reinforcements are pouring into Moscow," Hoepner snapped. "We must stop them or it will become a bastion."

"They are pouring out of Moscow," Guderian returned fire. "We will have to fight the same soldiers again after we take the city."

Back and forth, confusion as deep in the tent as on the battlefield. It was finally halted by an unfamiliar face. "My men are here." A hand smacked the map, palm covering Moscow, index finger pointing to the east of the city and only a short distance from where Manstein's panzers sat waiting for fuel. "They have two days' supply at most."

The Falschirmjaeger, a point of amusement and amazement among Blumentritt's grenadiers. Men who jumped from planes and landed ready to fight seemed unbelievable to them, wasteful to Blumentritt. He had opposed the plan for the parachutists to seize the railroad bridges to block the Russian's retreat or resupply. Blumentritt had discussed it with Manstein, both men preferring orders for general direction of advance to be determined by staff rather than the predetermined route, all to connect with the parachutists. The colonel did not care what direction the Russian troops took. Retreated soldiers lacked supplies and order, easily swept from the battlefield by an organized force. Those who piled into Moscow would be as secure as a Red Army soldier in a prisoner of war camp.

"Your 48th Panzer Corps is within 25 kilometers of my men, but they have stopped." A Luftwaffe colonel representing General Student stared at Hoepner. "My men are dying, attacked on both sides."

Blumentritt caught his commander's eye before an explosion, the colonel's accusation bordering on a claim of cowardice. He was summoned to the table, the only one of those standing around the map who had witnessed the chaos of the Red Army retreat and attack. He tried to explain under present conditions 25 kilometers might as well be 100. Student's man was not listening.

"Attack east." He drew a line from where the panzer corps sat to another one east of it. "Then follow the rail line west to where my men are fighting."

Hoepner snarled. "And turn our back on the Red Army to attack the Red Army?" A nod toward the figure at the end of the table. "The Luftwaffe flew them there, they can fly in supplies."

It was an army challenge to the air force, General Joschenek suddenly on the spot. "Most of our forces are bombing Moscow. The rest are breaking up counterattacks. We do not have the planes or means to supply scattered forces."

Hoepner straightened, the Luftwaffe to take the blame for inaction.

"Does it matter?" This from General Strauss. His Ninth Army was holding Kalinin to the north of Moscow and blocking any Russian force that might attack the Fourth Panzer Group swinging to the east. "It does not matter where the Russians are." A nod in Blumentritt's direction. "If the Russians are fighting Russians that is good news." A sweep of his arm. "Drive around them, further east and trap more of them." A nod at the panzer generals.

The parachutist retreated a step from the table as General von Bock stirred. The commander of Army Group Center, he would be responsible for making a recommendation to Fuhrer headquarters. "Twenty kilometers east?" It was a question for both panzer commanders, neither Hoepner or Guderian willing to agree, not wanting to be upped by the other.

"Thirty," Guderian said, gaze matching Hoepner's, which drew a nod.

"Start immediately," Bock said. "Forty eight hours to close the gap.

Bock raised his hands as the generals turned on their heels to leave. "There is the other matter," he said.

"The rumors," Hoepner said.

"General Student has sent information about the possible capture of a high value target."

Hoepner squinted. "It is true?'

"What?" Guderian, on the southern pincer, was separated from rumors.

"A high value target may have been captured by our troops and is en route to interrogation." The colonel of the parachutists was unblinking. "It may be him."

"What high value -." Guderian stopped. "Gott im Himmel."

Blumentritt stared in disbelief. There was only man they could be speaking of. He could not resist. "It is true then, we captured. -."

Bock raised his hand. "We simply do not know for certain. The prisoner is still in the field in the custody of the Fallschirmjaeger. They are in enemy territory. Colonel what is the current status?"

"The prisoner is being transported from Mtankov to Orekhovo Zuyevo to meet up with General Student's main force. He is being held by a small detachment of the 7th Flieger Division led by a Captain Johanns Franks. His identity has not been verified."

"Where the hell is Mtankov?" demanded General Bock. "I do not see it on the map."

"It isn't on any of our maps. It is nothing more than a coaling stop on the rail line." The Luftwaffe colonel stopped speaking. He did not have further information.

"Well there it is. I can assure you the Fuhrer's interest in the possibility that this prisoner may be the greatest criminal the world has ever known is rather, shall I say-intense. Close the gap, save the Fallschirmjaeger, and bring Stalin to the Fuhrer."

49

August 16, 1940   West of Orekhovo Zuyevo, Russia

Lieutenant Rudi Kleime surveyed the fields to the south and east with his binoculars, his body half way out of his replacement panzer, a Czech built PzKpfw 38(t). The sun was barely above the horizon, signaling the start of yet another day in the struggle against the Red Army. His unit's captured BT-5s were gone, abandoned with their guns spiked. They simply ran out of ammunition and spare parts for the Russian tanks. Now they were of no use to anyone.

The 7th Panzer Division needed replacement crews for panzers that had been recovered from the field and repaired. Rudi and his platoon needed panzers. The two were connected and Rudi was given command of a reconstituted platoon of three Czech 38 (t)s and a single PzKpfw II. While not as capable as Helga, the PzKpfw

III he started the war with in Poland, the Czech panzers were much better than the thinly armored BT-5s.

For three weeks since the Red Army's failed counterattack at the Ruza River, Rudi and his platoon advanced in the wake of the panzer thrust north of Moscow. Together with the survivors of *Kampfgruppe Schmidt* they had occupied villages behind the main thrust, moving further east when the infantry caught up. Their unit no longer had the support of the 88 mm flak guns, which were sent forward to support the panzers leading the charge. To Rudi's disgust, they also had a new name and leader.

Rudi was pleased with the panzers they received from the repair depot. He was amazed at how quickly and efficiently the maintenance crews were able to bring the damaged panzers back to life. More importantly, the German and Czech panzers were familiar to his men and also their comrades. The threat of mistaken identity that was constantly present when they sped around the Russian countryside in captured BT-5s was gone.

He assembled his panzer commanders, directing them to a map he had spread across the rear deck of his re-conditioned panzer. He wiped sweat from his forehead. It was already hot and would be getting hotter. While the villages they encountered as they closed on the Russian capital appeared more prosperous, paved roads were still rare. The dry dirt tracks generated thick clouds of dust, which fouled everything mechanical. Rudi did not like Russia. He spoke to his unit.

"Men, the situation remains the same. We are continuing to bypass Moscow. Thirty kilometers east and southeast are our parachute forces. They were dropped almost two days ago. They are desperate for relief."

Rudi looked at each sergeant. They were mostly men returning from recovery from wounds with a sprinkling of replacements that somehow made their way to the battlefront. They had been together for two weeks, alternating between firefights with motivated but poorly led Russian units and the slaughter of disorganized stragglers passed up by the advance. He only knew Sergeant Colhaugen from before the war.

Dietrich Colhaugen was also a veteran of the Third Panzer Regiment, but from a different platoon. He had commanded a PzKpfw II during the Polish campaign and the early days of the war against the Soviet Union. He was tall and thin with an oddly substantial stomach, which he used to store the enormous quantities of beer he drank whenever possible. Even more unusual was his small head. The normal sized soft *Schiffchen* side cap simply would not fit properly. Colhaugen spent the majority of pre-war parades constantly adjusting his cap to keep it from blowing off or obscuring his vision. He actually employed folded strips of newspaper inserted in the band to keep his hat on his tiny head.

Dietrich was a prankster and very popular among the men. He had sustained a facial wound from small arms fire during the Battle for Smolensk while he was riding in his PzKpfw II unbuttoned, upper body exposed. Fortunately, there was more blood than serious damage. When asked about the wound, Colhaugen shrugged claiming he traded a substantial scar on his right cheek for a week away from the front. It certainly did not qualify as a "homeland shot" sufficient to send him back to the Reich.

"I recognize that we are not experienced as a unit," continued Rudi. "We have not trained together. But most of you are veterans. There are German soldiers dying out there and we are going to help save them."

"Are we going south towards Moscow?" inquired Colhaugen.

Rudi pointed to a river on the map. It did not have a name.

"We will drive further east 10 kilometers past the defensive ring and then turn south. We are heading for a village at this river on the rail line leading out of Moscow."

"I don't see the village on the map," responded Colhaugen.

"Sergeant, it's not big enough to be on the map or our maps are shit, take your pick," barked Rudi. He fumbled into his case for the orders. "It is called Mtankov. I don't have a name for the river. I am told it is more of a large creek. There were two bridges over it that were blown by our paratroopers."

"What's the major hurry all about?" asked Colhaugen.

"Enough Colhaugen. I follow orders. Now they are provided by Hauptmann Groesbeck. I do know the Fallschirmjaeger there faced repeated assaults last night but are holding on. The Luftwaffe will do what they can to protect their own during the day but the situation is dire."

Rudi took a breath after his outburst. He realized he was unusually adversarial because of his dislike for Groesbeck, the ardent Nazi who was recently promoted to captain and given command of their unit of understrength remnants. It was not that Rudi wanted the command, it was more rooted in his concern that Groesbeck did not care about anything other than promoting himself.

A flight of three Messerschmidt Me-109s buzzed overhead, heading east. They were a welcome sight, confirming the men's belief that the Luftwaffe retained control of Moscow airspace.

Rudi pointed skywards at the Lufwaffe fighters.

"Make sure you have your recognition panels displayed. We will be out front."

The men nodded. Sergeant Colhaugen asked yet another question.

"Who's going with us?

"*Kampfgruppe Groesbeck* consisting of Groesbeck's reconnaissance platoon, two panzer platoons including us, Lieutenant Lunge's antitank platoon, a platoon of motorized infantry with a mortar squad and a couple of 20 mm flak guns. Plus, the *Flivo* will be with us in his halftrack."

Rudi held up his hand to stop Colhaugen before he could launch another inquiry.

"We roll in one hour. We will be behind Groesbeck's motorcycles and in front of Lunge's antitank platoon. Tell your men not to take Pervitin until we are moving,"

The men began to disperse. Rudi took hold of Colhaugen's elbow, holding him back.

"What's the problem, Stabsfeldwebel Colhaugen?"

Colhaugen grinned awkwardly, looking down at Rudi. He was more than 10 centimeters taller.

"No problem, Herr Leutnant."

"Dietrich, I understand. We were both sergeants a few months ago. You don't like taking orders from me," observed Rudi.

Colhaugen shifted his gaze over Rudi's shoulder towards his PzKpfw II, 25 meters further down the dirt road. He sighed.

"Rudi, I suppose you are right. I will stop being a swine."

Rudi smiled and patted Colhaugen on the shoulder. He wanted to conclude the conversation positively.

"Are you happy with your panzer? It is just like your old one from the Third Panzer Regiment, eh?"

"It has many scratches and dents. The engine needs to be overhauled but it will be fine. I wouldn't mind a 37 mm cannon like the 38(t)s," responded Colhaugen with a grin, referencing the inadequate 20 mm cannon of the Pzkpfw II.

Rudi nodded, realizing Colhaugen would no longer question him. Attention and respect from his former peer was an effective remedy.

"Good luck, Dietrich."

Colhaugen jogged over to his command. Rudi motioned for his crew to return to their panzer from the shade of a tree they had been lounging under, waiting. The temperature was rising rapidly. Corporal Adolf Brauch led Reiner and the replacement Adolf Blaumann. Although similar in age to Reiner, he seemed much younger. Rudi knew the reason. Reiner had seen shit and had aged.

The Czech PzKpfw 38(t) carried a crew of four. Blaumann was the radio operator who also manned the 7.92 mm bow machine gun. Unsurprisingly, Adolf Brauch was delighted that the new man had the same first name, claiming that the platoon would be invincible if only all its members were Adolfs. The platoon referred to Blaumann as "New Adolf."

"We ready Adolf?"

Brauch straightened and saluted.

"Absolutely, Herr Leutnant. You have to love this Praga engine and the transmission is perfect. Other than the rivets, which will be missiles inside if we get hit by anything, I'd say the Czechs know how to build panzers."

Corporal Brauch guided Rudi to a bedroll and pulled off its fastening rope. "Take a look at what New Adolf and I accomplished yesterday afternoon while you were off with Hauptmann Groesbeck planning our mission."

Rudi laughed when he saw the white painted letters underneath.

"Helga II. Sure, why not?"

50

August 16, 1940   Mtankov, Russia

Hauptmann Johanns Franks removed his helmet and rubbed his scalp vigorously. He was hungry, thirsty and exhausted at the same time. His empty eye socket itched fiercely. He doubted he slept more than an hour, if at all. He raised his head and stared at lieutenants Gottizner and Ericksen, who were standing before him waiting. An artillery round exploded 50 meters from the collapsed rail station in Mtankov. No one ducked or even moved. Not after what they had been through.

"How bad is it?" asked Franks.

"Real bad, almost hopeless," replied Lieutenant Gottizner. "I do not know how we weren't overrun last night. There are two large tanks stuck in the creek bank. I believe they are the T-34s we've been warned about. If they had made it across, we would have been defenseless. "

Franks pondered the information before responding.

"They can't climb the bank? It does not seem that high."

"It seems they are stuck in the mud," reported Gottizner. "They have been abandoned but our efforts to retrieve anything useful have been frustrated by machine gun fire from the far bank."

The scream of Stuka sirens announced the return of the Luftwaffe. Lieutenant Ericksen raced outside to witness the attack. Bomb detonations followed, close but on the east side of the creek. He returned to the meeting.

"All kinds of Luftwaffe planes are hitting the far side," rasped Ericksen, his voice hoarse from exhorting his men to repulse the infantry attacks the prior night. "They are throwing everything at the Bolsheviks but they won't be able to help us tonight."

Franks stood and peered at the sky through a massive hole in the roof. Me-110 heavy fighters strafed the Russian positions east of the river.

"Lieutenant Gottizner, provide the situation report."

"We have 700 men from the 7th Flieger and 22nd Air Landing divisions. At least 100 are wounded and incapable of participating in our defense. Last night, we repulsed an organized assault from east of the bank. I estimate the enemy's force was a regiment supported by several T-34 tanks. The tanks were unable to cross the creek. Several hundred Russians made it over and were slaughtered by our MG-34s. A few, perhaps squad strength, infiltrated our strongpoints and were neutralized meters from here."

Gottizner halted, catching his breath. Franks surveyed the lieutenant, a man of courage who had risen through the ranks. Gottizner was not a defeatist. He motioned for the report to continue.

"The attackers were not European Russians. They were Mongolians or some other Asiatic soldiers. The dead outside this building wore the same insignia as the defenders we found here yesterday. "

"What have the prisoners revealed?"

Lieutenant Ericksen responded to Franks' question.

"We had the whore Russian translator question them. Who knows if is she is exaggerating or truthful."

"Where is the interpreter and the prisoner?" demanded Franks.

"With Sergeant Herrick in a dugout north of the tracks," replied Ericksen. "The prisoner is gagged and bound."

Franks asked, "What does the interpreter say of the men captured in last night's battle?"

"That they are skilled fighters from the Far East and that there are many more behind them, including countless tanks. They are here to save Moscow and Comrade Stalin. They have fought and defeated the Japanese before."

Franks snorted, "What the hell does that mean? They fought the Japanese? So fucking what? I've fought the Spanish Bolsheviks? And good luck saving Stalin."

The lieutenant shrugged, uncertain as to the appropriate response to Franks' outburst.

"Is our prisoner really Stalin?" asked Gottizner.

Franks raised his hand. "Possibly. It is not for us to say. The interpreter says he is. He acts like he is. I think he looks like Stalin but it is not as if I've met him before. His identity is a strict secret. We will only refer to him as Prisoner 1. We will discuss his disposition afterwards. Continue with your report, Lieutenant Gottizner."

"From the west, it is better. We did not face a professional effort last night. Instead, we encountered party officials fleeing with valuables, bandits and small groups of drunken conscripts. They were dealt with relatively easily by the men from the 22nd we set up at the train wreckage."

"I agree with your appraisal," concluded Franks. "What are our current capabilities and challenges?"

"I believe the translator. Many more Orientals are coming. We passed a riverbed no more than two kilometers south on our way to Mtankov. It is flat and rocky. Their tanks will be able to cross there easily. They will find it. Our two Pak 36 anti-tank guns are 37 mm. Fine against the BT-5s and T-26s but I doubt their shells will do much against the T-34."

Franks and Ericksen nodded. Additional aerial bombs exploded across the river. They waited until the thunder subsided for Gottizner to finish.

"We are heavily outnumbered and our ammunition is dwindling fast. It hinges on whether the Luftwaffe can break up the counterattack from the east and how quickly the panzer divisions get here."

"We can't hold Mtankov more than 24 hours," blurted Ericksen.

Franks paced the debris strewn room. He picked up a discarded Red Army helmet and studied it.

"Gentlemen, we have orders from General Student. We have two objectives. We must hold Mtankov. Retreat is not possible. Secondly, we must move Prisoner 1 north immediately. Nothing can happen to him. We are to meet elements of the 7th Panzer Division advancing from the north."

The lieutenants looked at the floor. They knew the next words were a likely death sentence for one or both of them.

"I must escort Prisoner 1 myself. I do not like abandoning my post, but General Student specifically ordered me to bring him out personally. I will take Sergeant Herrick, twenty men and the translator. We will leave before noon."

No one said anything. Franks concluded the meeting.

"Both of you will remain here and hold Mtankov until the panzers break through." Franks stopped, visibly shaken by the gravity of his orders.

"Dismissed."

0

Franks stood behind the crumbled rail station and directed his gaze east of the river. Short stubby winged Russian aircraft dodged German fighters, disappearing and reappearing in the partly cloudy sky. Their position in Mtankov had escaped attack so far that morning. The night would be different. The Luftwaffe would not be there to break up the Red Army formations.

Lieutenant Ericksen approached with a Luftwaffe officer wearing flight gear, clearly one of the downed pilots. The flier waited a few steps away. He looked familiar to Franks.

"Herr Hauptmann, we have rescued one of the Stuka pilots. Perhaps he should go with you. There's nothing for him to do here and the Reich would be better served if he doesn't die in this Godforsaken land needlessly."

Franks was saddened. He was always fond of Ericksen. It was not likely he would survive Mtankov.

"Of course, Lieutenant. There's no reason he can't tag along." Franks waved the pilot over.

Before he was close, Franks leaned in to Ericksen and whispered.

"Svein, I am sorry about this. Do not surrender, the Bolshevik animals will torture you."

"Of course, Johanns," replied Ericksen. He reached into his pocket and produced an envelope. "Gertrude Ericksen" was printed on its face, with an address in Kiel. "Please give this to my mother."

Franks clasped his arm.

"You know I will. Good luck, Svein."

Lieutenant Ericksen saluted in the military style, turned and left as the Stuka pilot reached the pair.

"That was pretty emotional," stated the pilot with a hint of sarcasm.

"What is your problem? These men are likely to die for the Fatherland in the next 24 hours," replied Franks sharply. The men recognized each other simultaneously.

"Oswald," blurted Franks. "Still an asshole."

"Franks, still an invalid," countered Oswald, referencing Franks' missing eye.

The men looked at each other with disgust and hatred. They did not shake hands.

"Get your kit Oswald. Even though you are a pathetic excuse for a Luftwaffe officer, we will allow you to accompany us on our mission."

"Mission?" asked Oswald. "Or do you mean your retreat?"

"Fuck you Oswald. We are leaving now with or without your diseased prick."

Franks turned and spotted Sergeant Herrick with Prisoner 1 and the whore translator standing near the train tracks. He turned his back to Oswald, reached for his MP-40 and walked to the embankment.

"What was that all about?" asked Herrick, aware that there had been an argument between Franks and the Stuka pilot.

"Sergeant, the Luftwaffe teaches us a very important lesson. We must work together with men we do not necessarily like to accomplish the mission."

Franks paused and made a smirking face.

"I knew that Stuka pilot while I was in the Condor Legion. We came to blows in a crappy bar in Spain. He's a complete asshole. But the Fatherland needs trained pilots more than I need revenge."

51

August 17, 1940   Mtankov, Russia

Lieutenant Ericksen knew the situation was grim. They had suffered from constant artillery bombardments most of the night. He met with Lieutenant Gottizner at dusk in the trench north of the railway embankment where Prisoner 1 had been kept until his departure with Captain Franks. The Mtankov station building had long since been demolished.

Lieutenant Gottizner had been in charge since Franks left. During the daylight, remnants of the 22nd Air Landing Division were able to repulse disorganized attacks from the west. They were eventually overwhelmed and they fell back from the destroyed train to Mtankov.

Gottizner whispered to Ericksen that the situation was no longer tenable. They were out of ammunition. The end was near.

"Svein, we can't defend any longer. I am notifying headquarters that we will be overrun shortly."

Artillery shells smashed into the smoldering rail station. It was already flattened.

"I don't understand. Our orders are to hold Mtankov until relieved by the 7th Panzer."

Gottizner shook his head sadly. He had risen from the ranks. He would do his duty until the end.

"Yes, Svein but we must remember that we can't be captured. We possess too much information regarding our order of battle."

Ericksen stared at Gottizner. He knew what was going to happen.

"Don't do it. Relief may be here soon."

"Svein, I will not order you to do it, but do not be captured."

Lieutenant Gottizner, stood erect, stepped back and saluted in the Nazi fashion.

"Heil Hitler, long live the Fatherland!"

Ericksen watched in horror as Gottizner raised his Luger, placed it to his temple and ended his life. He turned around and saw a number of the men watching.

Ericksen knew they would disintegrate as a fighting force once word spread Lieutenant Gottizner had committed suicide. He had to act quickly.

He ordered the radio destroyed and all maps burned. He summoned the only other unscathed officer in their group, Lieutenant Jacob Murz from the 22nd Air Landing Division.

Murz jumped into Ericksen's hole ten minutes later during a lull in the relentless Russian artillery fire. He stared at the Lieutenant Gottizner's corpse. Stukas dove on the far side of the river. Heavy smoke crawled across Mtankov.

Murz removed his helmet and wiped his brow. His voice was hoarse.

"We are done. We are out of everything. Half the men are wounded and we have no way to treat them."

Ericksen nodded. "Our orders are to hold Mtankov at all costs."

"We are going to die here," shrugged Murz. "The 7th Panzer isn't going to get here in time."

Several men rushed by heading north, towards the woods. Lieutenant Ericksen climbed to the lip of the dugout, preparing to fire his MP-40 at the fleeing paratroopers. Murz pulled him back by the collar of his Fallschirmjaeger smock.

"Fuck it, let them go. We can't hold any longer. We can re-group in the woods."

"What about the wounded?" asked Ericksen, but he knew the answer.

"A grenade and a pistol," replied Murz. He shook his head. "There is nothing else we can do."

Ericksen knew Murz was right.

"Agreed. In 30 more minutes it will be dark. Throw down all the smoke we have and we will move to the north woods. Spike the antitank guns. Let's take as many of the wounded as we can move."

Murz nodded and clawed his way out of the dugout. He turned and confirmed the plan.

"In 30 minutes, we lay down smoke and head to the north woods."

0

Franks sat with his back to the trunk of a massive tree and surveyed his group of travelers, which consisted of twenty-two German paratroopers, a rescued Luftwaffe Stuka pilot, Prisoner 1 and the female Russian translator. Their offensive capability was seriously deficient. Their equipment consisted of a MG 34 light machine gun, a dozen MP 40 submachine guns, pistols and two dozen hand grenades. Importantly, they had a short range radio.

At noon the prior day, Franks had reluctantly left his command at the tiny village of Mtankov, ordered by General Student to escape with Prisoner 1 at all costs. They had crept through the woods during the daylight, staying far from paths or tracks. They had made limited progress but had not crossed paths with the Red Army.

During the darkness, Franks pushed harder and they covered more ground. They were hampered by the sole reason for their mission. Prisoner 1 was gagged with his hands bound and a sack over his head. Not to mention, he was clearly not a young man. He did not move quickly.

Hans Oswald ambled over to Franks. Dawn had announced its arrival, forcing the band to seek concealment.

"Who is he?" asked Oswald, pointing to Prisoner 1. "I thought the Fuhrer Order discouraged taking of commissars as prisoners."

"I am unable to reveal his identity," responded Franks. "Do not ask me again."

"Obviously a high ranking Soviet," observed Oswald. "But I do not see fancy stripes or medals."

Franks said nothing. Prisoner 1 was facing away from the group. The Russian translator sat next to him, holding his arm but not talking. Sergeant Herrick had the captive's hood raised slightly, waiting while the translator tilted a canteen to his mouth. Prisoner 1 coughed and spat the warm liquid to the ground.

"That Bolshevik is an old man, he won't be able to take much more of this," suggested Oswald.

"That's why we are going to rest here until noon."

"That is basically suicide, Franks. Even you can see that. We are maybe 10 kilometers from that shithole Russian rail station. You saw the air battle over it all day after we left. Every airplane they have that can still fly was in the air. The artillery bombardment lasted all night and your rag tag force didn't have any howitzers. No one could have survived that onslaught. The Red Army is throwing everything at that pathetic village to open a path to Moscow."

Franks agreed.

"You're right Oswald. But the safety of the prisoner is my absolute priority."

"So the Fallschirmjaeger are unfortunately expendable," reasoned Oswald quietly. "Why is he so important?"

They watched the antics of the translator and Sergeant Herrick as they tried to hydrate the POW. Oswald placed his hand on Franks' soldier. Franks began to pull away but stopped and shrugged. Their old dispute did not seem to matter any longer.

"That whore in Spain gave me the same shit, Franks," offered Oswald. "I sure as fuck didn't give it to her."

"I figured as much."

"I'm good to go now," smiled Oswald.

"As I am," grinned Franks.

Oswald was clearly building up to the purpose for his visit. He held out his hand.

"We've made it this far without managing to get ourselves killed; perhaps we should let it go, eh?"

Franks shook Oswald's outstretched hand. Their feud was suppressed by their joint struggle to evade the Russians. Oswald looked around and settled on the translator. Prisoner 1 was drinking greedily from the canteen she offered to his lips.

"What's the whore's name?"

"No idea," replied Franks. "She may have said Natasha."

"Well, since we are comrades again would you mind if I offered Natasha a taste of some solid Krupp steel?

Oswald backed away in mock fear, intimating his request was made in jest. Prisoner 1 coughed again, shaking his head vigorously. For a moment, he faced Oswald and Franks. His face was discernible in the early light.

"What the fuck?" uttered Oswald. "Is that fucking Stalin?"

Franks stood and grabbed Oswald by the front of his flight suit.

"Shut up, Oswald!"

Oswald raised his right arm skyward, indicating a willingness to comply.

"Well, now the abandonment of the rail station makes sense." Oswald slumped to the ground and watched Sergeant Herrick manhandle the POW into submission. "Well you have quite the prize. You won't be able to stand with the amount of medals they will pin on your tunic."

"We are not even sure who the fuck he is. The whore says he's Stalin but her life depends on him being somebody we need a translator for."

Oswald stared at the back of Prisoner 1. He was uncharacteristically silent. Clearly, he was mulling over this new development.

"Look Franks, we both know what this could mean not only to the war effort but to you individually."

Franks shook his head vigorously in the negative.

"I wanted to stay with my men. Following General Student's order was the hardest thing I've done in my life." Franks pointed to his eye patch. "Leaving my command was far worse than my Me-109 accident in Spain that cost me my eye and flying career."

"There's nothing else you could have done or should have done. Your actions were completely by the book."

Hans Oswald leaned in to Franks and made his offer.

"I will not be useless to you, Johanns. I will help as much as I can. I will follow your orders."

"Thank you, Hans. As you can see, we are desperately short on everything."

"It would be welcomed if you would mention my assistance in your report."

"No problem, Hans," replied Franks. "If we are successful, there will be plenty of commendations to go around."

Oswald beamed, pleased with the arrangement. He was jolted back to the difficulty of their situation by a flight of Russian fighters overhead; barely visible thought the leafy canopy.

He lowered his head and concluded his conversation with Franks.

"I'm going to need some Pervitin."

52

August 18, 1940   **Berlin**

James Reilly waited outside Captain Scheller's office at Abwehr headquarters. The blonde secretary made a production of stuffing papers into a file. Clutching a bundle of similar sized folders, she rose and smiled at Reilly. She stepped away from the desk and walked to a row of filing cabinets.

James lit a Lucky and decided to enjoy the show. He was not sure of her name and as far as he could determine she did not speak English. He did speak some German, but it was not his best language for flirting. Despite the language barrier, he remained attentive. Scheller's secretary did have wonderful legs.

She arrived at the selected filing cabinet and bent at the waist to open the lowest drawer. Reilly could not help himself. He coughed lightly to gain her attention.

She turned and giggled. Reilly pointed at his chest and said, "James Reilly."

"Ja, Herr Reilly." She pointed at her amble bosom. "Gabby."

Gabby resumed her important work for the Third Reich while Reilly admired her efforts. He wasn't that he needed female companionship. Scheller had made arrangements so that he was never alone in the evenings. Reilly just enjoyed the thrill of the chase.

Reilly considered taking it a little further but concluded it was clearly not a wise move. Scheller had treated him fairly and did everything he promised. Reilly was now billeted in a decent hotel near the warehouse where the captured KV and T-34 tanks were hidden. He was monitored constantly either by the men that walked virtually next to him by day or by Gertrude, the dedicated female agent who was actually named Francine who served as his whore by night.

Scheller abruptly entered the waiting area from his adjacent office, solving Reilly's dilemma.

"James, how are you this glorious morning?"

Reilly stood and shook Scheller's outstretched hand.

"Karl, things in Berlin are spectacular." He pointed to busy Gabby's hindquarters. "And the views are breathtaking."

Captain Scheller laughed and motioned Reilly into his office. Shutting the door, he pointed to the chair across from his desk. Properly seated he began with the usual inquiries.

"You will never change James. Gabby is off limits." Scheller frowned. "Has Gertrude not performed adequately? She was highly recommended."

"Yes, Karl, Gertrude is quite satisfactory. And I have plenty of beer, whiskey and American cigarettes."

"And your accommodations are suitable, yes?"

"Again, yes."

Scheller reached into a small silver case and withdrew a Lucky for himself.

"It is going well in Russia. It appears the Bolshevik defenses are collapsing."

"If the newspapers and radio are even half right, I'd say the Wehrmacht has exceeded all reasonable expectations."

"I'll say," agreed Scheller. "The Fuhrer really knew what he was doing."

"I am having a hard time understanding why the Russian tanks are performing so poorly."

"Frankly, the OKW attributes the failure of the Bolshevik armored forces to two primary reasons. Confused leadership and tactics combined with substandard workmanship in the manufacture of the tanks."

Reilly nodded. Both explanations were likely sound, but he could not get past the sheer quantity of the Russian tanks. When combined with the size of the newer tanks, it seemed the German success was almost unbelievable.

"But not the capabilities of the Russian tanks?" pointed out Reilly. "I am sure Ferry Porsche has updated you on our progress?"

"Of course, he is pleased with your knowledge. He suggested that you must have paid attention at this Lehigh University."

"I mostly drank beer," offered Reilly.

"James, Moscow will fall before September. As you say in America… it's the bottom of the ninth, two outs, nobody on."

Reilly pondered Scheller's rather accurate baseball analogy. It was not surprising, considering the German officer had lived in Milwaukee years before the war.

"Karl, such a result would be incredible. Guderian is simply a genius."

"Do you care if your old employer loses?"

"Not at all," retorted Reilly. "I did what they paid me to do and they fucked it up. I am done with the Soviet Union."

"Well I would expect you to say nothing else. You are sitting at Abwehr headquarters in Berlin."

Reilly wanted to respond aggressively but he checked himself. Scheller was right. Even if he could leave the Reich, he had nowhere to go.

"So what is next?"

"Finish your work with the Ferry Porsche. Then we shall see. I may even get a promotion out of this." Scheller waved his hand expansively.

Reilly sighed and turned to the window. He may not be in a cell but he was a prisoner.

"What about me?"

Scheller grinned, "I have something special planned for you next week."

"What could that possibly be, Karl? You reward me with a visit from my mother or perhaps the American Ambassador?"

"James, nothing will benefit America more than defeat of the Bolsheviks. The British will sue for peace when Moscow falls. Nothing has happened with them other than the loss of a few ships. They are only going through the motions."

"Karl, the British are tough fuckers. Churchill is hard as nails. I don't see them giving up."

"You will see James. All three countries will be friends sooner than later," concluded Scheller.

53

August 18, 1940   North of Mtankov, Russia

Lieutenant Ericksen placed his binoculars into the case and slid back down into the hastily prepared trench. He handed the case to Lieutenant Murz.

"I am not sure what is going on, Murz," said Ericksen. "Take a look, it is a complete mess."

Murz scrambled to the top of the trench, dry dirt coating the front of his tunic. He scanned southward for more than 5 minutes. Small arms fire chattered from the village of Mtankov. Smoke rose from burning vehicles west of the village. The majority of the vehicles were civilian.

"Clearly, they are not interested in us," concluded Murz. "They are fighting each other."

Ericksen wiped sweat from his forehead. Although it was still morning, the sun was baking the earth. Mtankov was 3 kilometers south, visible over the empty fields.

"I agree. As far as I can determine, the Russians from the east captured Mtankov yesterday afternoon and stopped their advance. They did not try to pursue us north. The question is why?"

Murz nodded and added to Ericksen's narrative.

"It can only be because we were not their primary target."

"Again, why? An invading army is air dropped behind their capital and its destruction is not the main mission? How is that possible?"

Murz said the obvious.

"They have a different objective. Keeping their own forces from leaving Moscow."

"Exactly correct. The Red Army reinforcements, which we know are from another part of the Soviet Union, are being deployed against the government in Moscow."

Ericksen took a drink from his canteen. The water was warm and tasted foul. He had no choice. They desperately needed to find water. He looked at his watch. It was only 10:30 am.

Svein held up his hand, indicating to Murz he was trying to sort out the situation. Murz did not possess a critical piece of the puzzle. He did not know of Prisoner 1.

"Murz, my friend, I believe we are witnessing something historic."

Murz grinned, not entirely sure what Ericksen meant.

"I'm listening," replied Murz.

Ericksen smiled broadly. He put out his hand to shake Murz's, who instinctively reached out and grasped Ericksen's outstretched hand.

"We've won! Oh there's still more fighting and unfortunately dying left to be done but we have won the fucking war."

Murz pointed at their shallow trench and filthy uniforms. He looked back at Ericksen.

"I don't see how you reached this conclusion."

"Don't you see Murz? The Soviet government has collapsed. They are fleeing Moscow. Those troops were sent here to take over and restore control."

"I don't feel like we've won anything. It feels more like we were pummeled in Mtankov and had to retreat."

Ericksen stood up and clapped Murz on the back.

"Oh we have won Murz. You shall see what happens. It will be just like 1917. The Russians will give us everything the Fuhrer demands."

Ericksen laughed and leaned back, face warmed by the sun. After a few content moments, he shifted gears to their current situation.

"How many men do we have?"

"Maybe 100 fit men and about an equal number of wounded. We have very little ammunition. No food or medicine and very little water."

Ericksen considered Murz's information.

"We should send out a small patrol to find water and anything else of use. Otherwise, we wait here for the 7th Panzer and enjoy the show."

54

August 29, 1940   Paris

The waiter lingered, bottle at the ready, eyes focused on a familiar figure, two afternoons each week with the identical creature. He recognized her, visits to the sidewalk café including time spent with a stern looking German, his tastes limited to lager with a nauseous odor.

"Etienne." Lisle was in a strapped dress, silk fluttering in the breeze along the sleeves, fabric molded to her enticing parts, the waiter eying her with desire, her date staring into traffic as it sped by their table. Etienne awoke, tapping his glass, white wine poured and lapping around the edges. The waiter remained, a wish for a stronger breeze. His wait was brief, Lisle smiling, a light dismissal, but a dismissal nonetheless.

With her admirer gone, Lisle slid her hand across the table and brushed Etienne's. "You are in Russia," she said.

He blinked. "Russia?" Etienne reached for his glass, swirling the wine while eyeing Lisle. "An appointment," he murmured. "I do not wish to see them."

"They are visiting?"

A nod, the glass returned to the table.

"A surrender?" Lisle brushed his hand again.

Etienne closed his eyes. He knew the Germans too well. Pleading for mercy would produce only the opposite. "The German?"

Lisle's other "companion" was the German military adjutant working at the embassy. "He asks about you."

"Does he know Stalin's location?" It was a question buzzing about Europe as Moscow collapsed.

Lisle tilted her head, mouth curling down as if she were about to reveal a secret. "He speaks of Stalin."

Etienne remained patient. Pressing Lisle would earn him only sly obfuscation and his time was limited.

"He is confident."

Confidence had become an irritating Nazi trait, deepened by their successful march east. Ethnic superiority, military superiority all reflected in the cold stares jabbing him during his only meeting with the adjutant.

"I believe they captured him."

There were rumors, swiftly denied by the Germans and the Russians, so swiftly they exacerbated Etienne's suspicions.

"You would tell me if you know." Her eyes, demanding then pleading, Etienne unable to resist the combination.

"Yes," he blurted.

A pat on his hand, her shoe discarded beneath the table, toes brushing the pleat of his slacks then dropping to massage his calf. Etienne closed his eyes. It would not be this afternoon, his lunch shorter, a mere ninety minutes. The Russians demanded a morning meeting, only to be sloughed off to the afternoon, supplicants forced to take the time offered. European peace would bow to Etienne's digestion, a meeting with the hard faced communists always curdling his appetite.

He rose, bowing to kiss Lisle's hand then brushing her cheek. A nod at Lisle, who nodded in return, her discretion vaunted though it hardly mattered to a French official, a mistress a Secret de Polichinelle, one so widely known it was never discussed.

Etienne was whisked back to the foreign ministry, his Croat driver dashing through traffic with an abandon that would make a Parisian taxi driver cringe. His passenger paid little attention, his mind lost in memories of the past weeks. The French press had followed the German assault on Moscow with the renewal of the offensive. It reported the splitting of the Red Army defenses, the march around the capital and the closing of the iron ring upon its hapless populace. French correspondents were trapped within the city, their reports escaping the ring and describing a city on the verge of insanity with the government fighting the Germans on the outside and its citizens within. The last report had been received six days earlier, an interruption that meant the death of a single Frenchman or an entire city.

Then came the contact from the Russian embassy. Etienne reported to Laval, who dashed to the countryside to avoid the communists. His instructions were to offer nothing to either side beyond Etienne's expertise as a messenger. Some might have taken the instructions as an insult to their diplomatic skills, Etienne experienced only relief.

The same could not be said of Francois. Etienne's assistant eagerly greeted each morning. He relayed the latest German advance to Moscow as described by the morning newspapers and occasional cable from the new French embassy in Kuibyshev. He imagined his superior negotiating an end to the grand battle. Francois breathlessly reported the Russian request, but was downcast when Etienne delayed the meeting to the afternoon. With fewer than ten minutes before the planned Russian arrival. Disappointment was replaced by a giddiness, unbecoming a diplomat. Raised on his toes as Etienne entered his office, he gushed at his superior. "The embassy has called. The ambassador is approaching."

His eagerness was so intense Francois had tamed his hair, smoothed his slacks and for the first time, appeared the diplomat, except for his mud caked shoes.

"Gardening?" Etienne glanced toward the floor then doffed his hat and wiggled into his chair, focused on the window and the traffic outside. Francois noticed his shoes for the first time and went in search of a brush.

The Russians would have to wait while Etienne's assistant settled his wardrobe. He paid no attention, replaying Laval's instructions in his mind. When Francois returned, he bumped the door, hands twisting before moving to his tie. "Yes?"

"The Russians," he murmured.

"I will be with them."

"There are five of them."

"Five?" Etienne conjured the image of the NKVD guards that accompanied the ambassador.

"It is generals."

"Generals?"

A hurried nod.

"Ten minutes."

Francois scurried off, Etienne watching him and shaking his head, a smile improving his mood. A general. It seemed unlikely a Russian general had escaped the chaos of a disintegrating Russia to talk peace in Paris. Etienne ran through his script one final time then he sucked in air, gathered his nerves for another meeting with the Russians.

They were waiting, Francois' count accurate, his knowledge of Russian military ranks less precise. Etienne recognized the stone faced NKVD agents, three of them watching the two military men, a tube pressed beneath the arm of the younger of the pair. The Frenchman nodded, waiting for the Russians to begin, they having sought his presence.

"Colonel Tolbukhin." The oldest of the pair introduced himself. "Major Andreyev." A nod at the boy who barely looked out of basic training. "The Russian government seeks an armistice with the German Army." A nod at the major, who popped open the cylinder, papers tumbling onto the floor. The major dropped to his knees, spreading a map, the NKVD agents pressing a foot against three of the corners.

Etienne stepped around, keeping a safe distance from the agents. It was a map of Russia, all of Russia. Etienne spotted the Black Sea to the south, the sliver of land between it and the Caspian Sea, the Urals beyond it. To the north was the Arctic Circle, Finland and Sweden, the Baltic States, the Russians thoughtfully slicing off the map before it reached Germany. "Armistice." Etienne allowed the word to roll off the tongue. The armistice ending the Great War had not went well, the very mention of the word would not place the Germans in a mood to negotiate.

"The Germans are here." A nod at the major who swept across the map with his red pencil, starting near Finland, pencil sweeping down the map to the east of Moscow and the Volga then south to the Don River where it emptied into the Sea of Azov.

Etienne tilted his head, the red line a close match to the line drawn by French military intelligence as it marked the Wehrmacht's advance east. "Armistice line," he murmured.

Colonel Tolbukhin, an excess of flesh on his neck and cheeks marking his love of French dining, waggled his hand at the map. "The Red Army will never cease resisting the Nazi hordes. It is better for them to accept an armistice." He tapped his foot, map crinkling as he touched the expanse of land between the line and the Urals. "They will never reach beyond their current positions."

Etienne was not swayed. The military had briefed him, the number of Russian casualties, over a million in and around Moscow, the Red Army hollowed out during the grand battle. He leaned over the map, finger tracing air. "The Caucasus," he noted. "You are keeping the oil fields."

The colonel joined Etienne. "We would be willing to surrender the fields at Armavir." He jabbed his finger. "Grozny and Baku will remain ours."

Etienne straightened and began to stroll around the map. "And the role of the French government in obtaining this armistice?" As he approached, the NKVD guards retreated, the map rolling up then rolling to rest at the colonel's feet.

"Present our offer to the German ambassador."

Etienne knew the answer, but had not wanted to hear it. Ambassador von Hotzendorf was difficult alone, but Etienne in the presence of the German military adjutant, his rough hands touching Lisle, made a meeting nearly impossible. A swallow, his duty demanded agreement. "We will contact the German embassy," he promised.

The major retrieved the map and held it out. Etienne motioned to the far table, Francois handled all paper work. The colonel and major hesitated until one of the guards cleared his throat, a signal that did not have to be repeated. The room cleared, Etienne sucked in a deep breath, the Russians always a difficult meeting though the military men had been more coherent than the agitated ambassador who could barely speak without the NKVD interrupting him.

Francois swept into the room with the departure of the Russians. Etienne pointed him to the map and his assistant gathered it. "This?" The paper crinkled in his hands.

"The new Russia," Etienne said as he left the room. Francois skittered after him. "Contact the German embassy. We must talk with them about peace."

Made in the USA
Columbia, SC
28 March 2021

34587296R10215